## ***POWE***

**"Good writing of a**
—*N*

Into the broad sweep of *Power and Glory* come Gold Rush homesteaders and merchant princes, Southern slave owners and Northern abolitionists, pioneer women's rights activists, Indian resistance, and the little-known San Francisco Underground Railroad that helped black slaves escape to freedom on the eve of the Civil War. That war, too, enters this deeply layered novel as we meet Jefferson Davis and Abraham Lincoln and uncover the Southern strategy to seize California for its gold and access to the Pacific Ocean.

**"Always engrossing." —*Chicago Tribune***

**"Drama in plenty." —*San Francisco Chronicle***

**"A clear narrative style and a sure sense of authenticity." —*The New Yorker***

Other *Leisure* Books by Robert Easton:
**THE SAGA OF CALIFORNIA:
    THIS PROMISED LAND**

# ☆THE SAGA OF☆
# CALIFORNIA™
## POWER AND GLORY

# Robert Easton

**LEISURE BOOKS**  　　**NEW YORK CITY**

*For the Grandfathers*

A LEISURE BOOK®

September 1996

Published by special arrangement with
Golden West Literary Agency

Dorchester Publishing Co., Inc.
276 Fifth Avenue
New York, NY 10001

For further information, contact: Donald I. Fine, Inc.,
19 West 21st Street, New York, NY 10010.

The name "Leisure Books" and the stylized "L" with design are
trademarks of Dorchester Publishing Co., Inc.

Printed in the United States of America.

# POWER AND GLORY

# Prologue:
## THE GOLDEN ISLAND &
## THE GOLDEN LAND

It was a favorite story my father used to tell of a gun hidden in a cave, an evil witch doctor, an educated Spaniard seeking a Rousseauan society of "natural men and women" here on our California coast—love, murder, martyrdom—you never heard such a tale! . . . And an old Indian woman. I mean old—ninety-four, ninety-five, who wouldn't sell a single cow to a "damn Yankee" though offered nearly its weight in gold. Her son is another matter. . . . Yes, yes! And her husband actually rode with Portolá in the Conquest of 1769. . . . You can imagine how it roused my curiosity. What *had* happened, what *was* happening, right here under our feet? Thus I began my research.

It sent me back to the beginning where I found the ancient myth of a golden island called California "at the right hand of the Indies . . . very close to the Terrestrial Paradise." The explorations of the Spaniards in the late 1700s made this myth begin to be true, but it was the discovery of gold by Americans that really gave it substance. The Gold Rush made real the myth of the Golden Island. But the land proved golden in other ways, golden with sunshine, golden with grass, golden with fertility of soil, golden with the promise of the good life.

Quickly, with the inrush of people, the question arose: Who was to possess this Golden Land? Who was to have the supreme power? The glory, if any? The newcomers? The natives? Those others already here or yet to arrive?

These were some of the things that intrigued me. And what of the land itself? Land of highest mountains, lowest desert, tallest

trees, incredible beauty—a land easily thought of as enchanted.
What was it saying?

Gradually I began to put together what follows. Some is from
the memoir of Father Michael O'Hara, O.F.M., of Mission Santa
Lucía in south central California, who interviewed the ancient
Indian woman Clara Boneu, grande dame of the Northern Chumash, widow of the conquistador aforementioned, in the early
1850s and wrote a remarkable record of their conversations. Some
comes from the diary of the young Protestant Episcopal minister
and Civil War hero David Venable, which was continued by his
wife Martha out of a desire to see her husband's life and work
recorded in full. Some comes from the personal history of the
remarkable Negro woman Mary Louise Jackson, dictated to her
granddaughter years after she played such an important role in
the establishment of California's black community. And some
comes from the recent translation into English of Wing Sing's
monumental *The Land of the Golden Mountain,* first published at
Canton in 1886, giving at first hand the experience of a Chinese
Californian during the period 1850–1883.

I have pieced out the rest from early records and newspaper
accounts, including the files of the San Francisco *Daily Alta California* and *Daily Sentinel* and the Los Angeles *Star* and *Register*
and the private papers of the Sedley family, pioneer California
business magnates, recently acquired by the California Antiquar-
ian Society.

For narrative purposes I have interpolated freely in order to
make my text more readable, hoping to capture spirit without
sacrificing substance, and have added footnotes where they
seemed appropriate.

Thus we come to a day in San Francisco in June of 1853.

# PART I

# Chapter One

How much need I disclose?'' Eliot Sedley mused as he walked
along Montgomery Street in downtown San Francisco, that June
morning in 1853, toward the office of his lawyer Leonard Ogles.

Sedley seldom had such doubts. But the prospect of acquiring
the 48,000 acres of Rancho Olomosoug was particularly dear to
his heart. He wanted no slip-ups.

He'd learned prudence among other things since leaving Harvard without a degree to enter his family's firm. A decade on the
West Coast as representative of Sedley & Company of Boston,
traders of New England manufactured goods for hides, tallow,
furs and now gold had developed his natural abilities and laid the
basis for his ample fortune, and he'd seen San Francisco changed
by the Gold Rush from the sleepy Mexican village of Yerba
Buena to a bustling modern American city in which he was prominent citizen. Sedley was no more than average height but his
high-bridged nose, steady gray eyes, coolly assured yet pleasant
manner gave him distinction, and he wore a tall brown beaver hat
and Dresden-blue double-breasted swallowtail coat characteristic
of an era less turbulent than the one which swirled around him
now.

People drawn from all corners of the earth by the rush for gold,
now in its fourth hectic year, crowded the boardwalk. Some were
actually running in their eagerness to get ahead and find riches.
He picked his way deftly among them until a barrel, tossed from
a wagon, caused the pigtailed Chinese immediately in front of
him to step quickly aside and bump a red-shirted Anglo-American

miner. With an oath and blow the miner sent the Oriental sprawling in the dusty street.

Such violence was so common few people turned their heads but Sedley with habitual curiosity stopped and watched the fallen man rise without protest, replace his black silk skullcap and hurry on. There goes a realist, he reflected with wry approval. John Chinaman knows protest would be useless. He understands power because he's got so little. It reminded Sedley of the approaching meeting with his attorney. Power would lie at the heart of it. He was much more powerful than Ogles. He need disclose no more of his plan than necessary.

Ogles' office was in the magnificent new El Dorado Bank Building, pride of the youthful metropolis. Its walls were of gleaming white limestone brought from China in Sedley's ships, its floors of costly Vermont marble transported similarly around the Horn of South America, and its gilded ceiling symbolized the aspirations of an entire community. The throng crowding its lobby seemed an audience waiting for the curtain to rise on a performance of unparalleled wonder, the drama of California; and as Sedley ascended the regally broad staircase with its brass railings, he felt himself climbing toward a box seat from which he could watch that drama unfold.

"Good morning, Eliot!" Ogles' cherubic face wore its usual deceptive look of innocence. He welcomed Sedley with easy intimacy, offering a cigar from the silver humidor on his cluttered table desk. His armless left sleeve was pinned to the front of his fashionable black broadcloth coat just below his heart. Ogles had left that arm in Mexico during the recent war which brought California into the union, first as a conquered province then as a state. Like most men of the Gold Rush he was a bachelor and young.

"Leonard, how are you?" Sedley's tone was coolly cordial.

Ogles chuckled and winked, wiping his brow with his hand and wringing his fingers as if ridding them of sweat. "Not quite sure! Your ranchero friend nearly did for me last night!" Sedley raised his eyebrows and waited. Ogles went on: "What a winner with the ladies! But what a loser at cards! I'd a dickens of a time getting him into the club when they saw the color of his skin. But when they saw the color of his gold . . . !" His voice trailed away significantly.

Sedley smiled with understanding. "So Francisco the Magnificent lived up to his name? I appreciate your help. I was a little weary of him.''

''If he's this way now, what was he when he was young?''

''Now you see why his mother has so little use for him?''

Ogles nodded. ''He says quite candidly the ranch is hers and hers alone. He makes no claim.''

''In fact he has none. But it's like him nevertheless. Gamble away a herd of cattle in a night. Offer you the shirt off his back or a ranch next morning. Here's the diseño.'' Sedley handed over the rolled document he'd been carrying. ''It's all the evidence she could find as to her ownership. Entrusting him to bring it to me was the greatest responsibility she's ever placed in him. It's crudely drawn as they usually are but will give you some idea of the property.''

As Ogles slowly unrolled the map, his eyes narrowed with interest. ''Rancho Olomosoug'' ranged from a laboriously scrawled ''High Sierra'' on the east, down through an array of ''Grassy Hills'' and ''Steep Arroyos'' to what was evidently a fertile valley opening toward the sea. A river wound through it. ''Broad Mesas'' bordered the river. Its corner landmarks were almost laughable to a legal mind like Ogles'. ''A Pile of Rocks . . . An Old Skull.'' They might be as impermanent as yesterday. But without doubt they indicated a domain breathtaking even for this expansive era. He shook his head dubiously however. ''Rancho Olomosoug? Don't sound Spanish to me!''

''It's Indian. Means 'A place of new beginnings.' After her native village which stood where her hacienda does now.''

Ogles continued dubious. ''Nothing more than this,'' tapping the diseño with one finger, ''to prove her title? The Land Commission is going to be very tough, you know!''

Sedley remained unperturbed. ''Nothing more. Except of course those friends and neighbors who'll testify she's occupied the place all her life. The rest will be up to you.''

Though valuing Sedley's patronage highly, indeed feeling obligated by it, Ogles wasn't sure he wanted to risk his considerable reputation on such flimsy evidence as a crude map and the testimony of neighbors who probably couldn't speak English, unless of course the rewards were suitably high. ''How does this differ from the Vásquez case?''

''There the ranch was left to the children and the widow. Here it's the widow alone. Will the fact she's an Indian influence the Commission?''

"It might. But under Mexican law she had her rights—red skin or white. And the Commissioners may decide to confirm them. Squatters could prove a bigger obstacle—if they swarm down there the way they've done up here!" Ogles gestured toward the hills west of the city which were dotted with tents and shacks of illegal settlers. For a moment neither spoke. All elements of the transaction had been touched upon except a crucial one. "Well," Ogles continued, "I think we can confirm her title. I'm on good terms with the Commissioners, especially Wilson. But it won't come cheap." He gave Sedley a cherubic smile. "And it will take time. We may have to go all the way to Washington City, to the Supreme Court."

"I'll explain to her."

"Can she pay?"

"I'll see to that."

Ogles gave him another smile. "Don't tell me you've turned philanthropist?" Sedley merely blinked as if he hadn't heard. Ogles colored. Motioning toward the rosewood cabinet that stood against the paneled wall behind his desk, he suggested: "Have a drink?"

Sedley shook his head. He seldom drank, feeling it interfered with his clarity of thought. Yet he did not wish to give offense, for he valued Ogles. Reaching into the inner pocket of his coat he removed the envelope. "Here's my check for seventy-five. When can we go before the Land Commission?"

"When you bring me her authorization in writing." Ogles sounded reassured as Sedley knew he would. "Can she sign her name?"

The moment had come, Sedley decided, to be confidential. "Señora Clara Boneu writes Spanish or Latin almost equally well. She was trained by the mission fathers. My own father taught her English in early days when he first traded on this coast. He was a great friend of her late husband. When he and his ship went down off the Horn, she and her people cut off all their hair and blackened their faces in mourning in the Indian way."

"The devil you say?" Ogles was intrigued.

"Yes. I've spent many a night under her roof. She's been like a mother to me."

"And she's nearly a hundred?"

"Her memory goes back to the days when there wasn't a white man in California. As a girl she watched the conquistadors and padres arrive." The distant clanging of a bell interrupted. Shouts and murmurs rose from the street below as if in answer to it. "There's the steamer signal!" Sedley picked up his hat. "I'm due to meet someone." He nudged the envelope toward Ogles. "When you've prepared the papers, let me know and I'll make the trip south and get her signature."

When he had gone, Ogles sat toying with the envelope. Wonder what he's up to now? He asked himself. He knew Sedley to be among the foremost capitalists in the new state, with tentacles reaching octopus-like into nearly every aspect of its development: ranch land, city real estate, mining, timber, manufacturing, politics, as well as trade. In fact his critics sometimes referred to him as The Octopus. "He waits quietly, apparently harmless, biding his time, and then he grabs you."

Moving with the crowd toward Long Wharf past waterfront lots he owned, Sedley reflected on his good judgment in purchasing them for as little as sixteen dollars only five years ago. Each was now worth upwards of forty thousand. They reminded him of Ogles. He'd met the one-armed veteran the day Ogles stepped off the boat without any prospects but his brains. Now Ogles was worth a great deal to him. He could rely on Ogles. And Ogles kept his mouth shut.

Sedley liked to develop people in the way he developed property: letting their natural value increase while retaining his interest in them. It was one of the many secrets of his success. And as he thought of the unknown woman he was going to meet, he decided that if she proved half as useful to him as Ogles he would have no cause for complaint.

# Chapter Two

Three hundred miles to the south Señora Clara Boneu was sitting on the verandah of her hacienda, young Father O'Hara beside her, looking out over her garden with its pink and white hollyhocks and dark red Spanish roses toward the playing field and race course at the foot of the slope and the Indian village beyond by the river. "I welcomed the North Americans at first," she was saying bitterly, "just as you did. They seemed our liberators from Mexican oppression. But now this!" She pointed to the two whitehooded wagons of the newly arrived squatters standing side by side a mile down the valley.

Her rough old voice was guttural as a man's, hardened by life, O'Hara thought, devoid of illusion, and her face always reminded him of an ancient tree trunk, expressing acceptance and resistance in equal measure. The flaming red hair, almost as profuse as in youth, a measure of her remarkable vitality, was held back from her face by a simple chaplet of seashells. She had not adopted Spanish or Mexican dress but wore the Mother Hubbard of a Christianized Indian woman. Yet her bearing said unmistakably she was the Señora, once known as Lospe, daughter of a legendary Indian chieftainess, widow of a famous conquistador.

"We must endure with vigilance." O'Hara spoke with the frankness of long friendship. "The Norte Americano squatters have also occupied my orchard, tearing down fences for firewood. And I fear that in my absence they may occupy my mission itself, so voracious are they. Yet there is a law. And on that we must rely. With God's help."

"I don't think much of a law which says I must establish my right to a place where I've lived all my life!"

"I likewise must submit a claim to the Land Commission," he rejoined with irritation matching hers, "for soil hallowed by nearly a hundred years of devotion!"

O'Hara's hair was nearly as red as Clara's. A crooked nose and broken front tooth, both damaged in schoolyard scuffles, gave ruggedness to his sensitive face. Life for him was a physical as well as spiritual adventure. Son of a general in the Spanish Army who'd sent him from Madrid to a seminary in Dublin over the tearful objections of his Castilian mother, he'd felt the call to California and come marching in the footsteps of the missionary fathers, a one-man army, strong in faith that singlehandedly by sheer zeal he could resurrect from the ruins of Mission Santa Lucía what he conceived to be the greatness of a past which included Clara. It was his special pleasure once a month to ride out the eighteen miles from town on his mule and say Mass for her and those of her people who chose to attend, for she did not coerce, neither did she discourage old Indian ways of worship, but participated in both through personal conviction and to show tolerance. Afterward the gray robed Franciscan liked to sit on the verandah and talk as now. Changing to a pleasanter subject he observed: "I never tire of looking at this scene," gesturing toward the valley below.

On the playing field, Indian youths from the village were engaged in their native ball-and-stick game resembling modern hockey. Others were clustered at cockfights or dice games. On the course nearer the river still others from the village and from her household and even visitors from town were preparing a horse race. And at the village itself, the Indianada, a cluster of adobe cabins and thatched huts beside the stream that she maintained there in the ancient way, they could see groups of women rolling dice into basketry trays and girls playing the guessing game, as she'd once played it, hiding the telltale stick behind their backs in one hand. While beyond the river, magnificent grassy hills rose steeply, speckled with grazing cattle, culminating in that high rounded one where her husband Antonio lay buried. She and he had dreamed of a scene like this. All that marred it for her and O'Hara were those white-hooded wagons down the valley. He asked: "You've talked to them?"

"Yes, and they refuse to budge. Someone has told them my title is in doubt until the Land Commission rules."

"Did you send the diseño north?"

"Francisco is such a scapegrace, I hesitated to entrust it to him. But there was no other way."

"Aren't you too hard on your son?"

"Not hard enough and therein lies the trouble," she snorted. "Old as he is, he's never grown up. Yet it is partly my fault. Out of my love for his father, out of my disappointed hopes for him, out of my sorrow for his unhappiness, I have indulged him, my one and only. And now instead of coming home and attending to business, he sends back our majordomo and vaqueros while he stays up there and squanders our money from the sale of the cattle among those Gringos who flatter him and call him Francisco El Magnífico—leaving me to deal with this!" She motioned toward the wagons. "Why, sometimes I think the only thing my poor Francisco ever did right was to produce Pacifico. See, there!"

On the race course below, two youths, one her grandson Pacifico, tall, blond, one short and dark, Benito Ferrer, son of the Jewish storekeeper in the town, were racing their horses, a gray and a bay, neck and neck, while cheers urged them on. "Pacifico favors my husband. He too was fair headed!" she continued proudly. "And on the day he rode into this valley for the first time we said he was like Kakunupmawa, the Sun!"

"And the Ferrer boy favors a ranchero's life more than minding his father's store?" O'Hara observed.

"Why not? His grandfather too was a conquistador, my husband's close friend!"

The youngsters finished in a dead heat and glanced for approval toward the verandah which served as reviewing stand for all activities below. Clara raised her right hand and waved. O'Hara did likewise. "One for the Christian, one for the Jew!" he joked. And the vision he shared with Clara composed of many diverse yet harmonious elements, gathered in this special place, poured back across his mind with renewed brightness.

At that moment the matronly figure of María Ignácia, wife of Isidro, Clara's majordomo, appeared bringing the Señora and her guest a refreshment of hot chocolate. Brown skinned as the chocolate, María emanated the placidity of the earth itself. She was of Clara's people, "the People of the Land and the Sea," O'Hara remembered, "before we named them Indians." But her three-year-old, toddling after her pestering for a taste of the mysterious liquid contained in the cups, had kinky black hair and almost ebony skin like his grandfather, Pablo the muleteer, who'd come into the land with Clara's husband. Little Tomás had inherited his grandfather's persistence and hot temper. Holding up tiny hands he demanded a sip from Clara's cup. "In a moment, my dear!" she replied gently but firmly, "when it has cooled!" But he insisted. "All right," she snapped, "burn yourself and learn!" He did, and howled.

O'Hara chuckled. Her son excepted, Clara ruled the people of her domain with a firm but loving hand, standing for no nonsense, giving none. Yes, here was a special place, this Rancho Olomosoug, as if set apart by Providence. In all California there could be nothing quite like it. O'Hara prayed silently, touching the rosary that hung from the cord at his waist, as he'd prayed aloud in the Mass under the sky in the courtyard this morning—prayed that greed, prejudice, the hatred, the violence which were defiling so much of the state would spare this peaceful scene. But his reason told him his prayer was probably too late.

A mile down the valley, old Abe Jenkins, leathery, irrepressible, stood at the prow of his white-hooded wagon like the captain of a ship, observing them through his brass spyglass. Captain Horatio Sedley, Eliot's father, had given him that glass as keepsake long years ago when they returned to Boston from China in Horatio's brig *Enterprise*. "The Papist is a-settin' there a-gabbin' to her," he announced to his numerous family at ease below. It was a long way but he could make out the tonsure on O'Hara's freshly shaven head and the earnestness of his manner. "They're a-figurin' what to do about us, I reckon. Ha!"

Clara continued quietly to O'Hara: "There must be no bloodshed. The soil of this valley is soaked in blood, Indian blood, white blood. There has been enough. That's what I told that old galoot Jenkins that day he arrived back here after all these years. It's a further reason why I rely on Eliot Sedley. He knows the law. He will help us deal with these interlopers."

# Chapter Three

The steamer was entering Golden Gate. Eighteen-year-old David Venable was holding twelve-year-old Martha Mornay's hand in comforting fashion as they stood at the rail among their fellow passengers. Bright blue bay, white bluffed islands, golden mountains beyond were shining like a promise in the sunlight of that summer morning. It was all David had expected and more.

"I wish Mother could see it," Martha murmured, gazing with him in wonder.

"She will see it!" he burst out. "Through your eyes she will!"

He felt her grip tighten. Impulse had carried him away, he realized, and glanced to see its effect on the bereaved girl; but she looked stoically straight ahead, dry eyed, grave oval face framed in dark blue bonnet, and again he admired her courage and self-control. Holding Martha's other hand, Mary St. Clair, sometimes known as Mary Louise Jackson, sometimes as plain Mary Louise, gave it a squeeze and exchanged a compassionate glance with David over the child's head. Martha's mother had been buried at sea like the others. In all, forty-four had died of fever and hemorrhages since the ship left Panama on its northward voyage.

"I'm sure your father will be waiting!" Mary Louise reassured her. Fashionably dressed in black alpaca with matching cape, Mary was gracefully slender, pale olive complexioned, thirty-one years old. Chance shipboard acquaintances, she and David had become like parents to Martha since her mother's death. David adored Mary Louise with a boyish ardor which she cheerfully dismissed as ridiculous. Bystanders glanced at the trio sympathetically.

But it was a moment for reaffirming life, not of sorrowing. All had passed through the Valley of the Shadow and come safely to their Promised Land. Somewhere in the crowd a harmonica struck up the jaunty strains of "the California song." Many voices joined in the rollicking words which expressed the prevailing mood.

> "I came from Salem City,
> With my wash bowl on my knee,
> I'm going to California
> The gold dust for to see. . . ."

And the chorus grew:

> "I'll soon reach San Francisco,
> And then I'll look around,
> And when I see the gold lumps,
> I'll pick them off the ground!"

As if in response the ship's bell clanged. Her huge side-wheels churned noisily as she turned toward shore. A long wharf protruding into the Bay like a finger seemed to beckon. Cheers went up all around the deck.

In the crowd thronging toward the wharf, Charles Mornay's heart beat faster. Three long years were coming to an end. His failure as gold miner in the Sierras, his return to San Francisco and successful venture into the produce commission business, the hard work, the destructive fires which repeatedly reduced the city and his business to ashes, the bitter struggle to survive and prevail, all faded into insignificance because his wife and daughter were arriving from their old home at New Bedford in Massachusetts to occupy the new one he'd built for them on the slope of Telegraph Hill.

Forty years old, tall, sober faced, chestnut haired, side-whiskers neatly trimmed, wearing his best black broadcloth suit with high white collar, black satin stock, black top hat, Mornay looked like a decent man who will not be trifled with. As the steamer edged against the wharf amid frenzied cheering, his eyes searched for Miriam and Martha. He felt they should be among the first to disembark. Foreboding seized him as a procession of passengers descended the gangplank without a familiar face. Then suddenly he realized that the girl waving frantically at him from the rail was Martha. Her size astonished him. She'd been a child when he left New Bedford. She seemed grown up now. She is nearly thirteen! he remembered. But where was Miriam? Foreboding seized him again. At Martha's right stood a slender elegantly dressed woman he did not recognize; at her left a stocky handsome youth, also a stranger. As all three descended solemnly toward him and Martha rushed sobbing into his arms, Mornay guessed the appalling truth. It took his breath away and turned him cold. It could not be! Yet something told him it was. Clasping his child, with agonized dread he inquired of the attractive woman with those strange large eyes and patrician yet kindly manner: "Where is my wife?"

Gently Mary Louise answered: "It was Panama fever.* We buried her at sea."

Mornay heard her words as if they were the tolling of some terrible bell. He felt Martha's arms tighten around him as if she would never let him go. Stunned, he turned with mute appeal to David.

"Everything possible was done for her," David burst out. "It was a terrible time! The captain himself died!" In his rush of sympathy for Mornay, tears appeared in his eyes. He saw similar ones in Mornay's.

Dazed by grief, the merchant was thinking of that new house on the slope of Telegraph Hill which Miriam would never see, so new he hadn't even had time to paint it.

"Papa, they've been so kind to me!" Martha's head was buried in his breast. Tears streamed down Mornay's face. Controlling himself he spoke firmly through them. "Please allow me to express my gratitude, Madam . . . ?"

"St. Clair!" For the first time she seemed familiar, or was it an illusion brought on by his disturbed state?

"I am Charles Mornay. And you, sir?"

David introduced himself.

"I'm more deeply indebted to you both than I can say," Mornay continued, disengaging himself gently from Martha, drying her eyes with his handkerchief. "Please accept the hospitality of my house!" It was then, as he took their hands warmly in his, that he noticed how the pupil of Madam St. Clair's left eye was

*yellow fever

distinctly larger than her right one, and the recollection which had been struggling to shape itself in his memory abruptly did so. He'd seen those remarkable eyes before. Yes, and those patrician features and olive skin—not such a light color then, indeed quite dark—and that desirable figure. Even the reassuring voice became familiar. He realized with a shock which made him momentarily forget his grief that Madam St. Clair was in fact his old friend Mary Louise Jackson, his colleague in the secret Underground Railroad which helped Southern slaves escape to Northern states and Canada.

Back in New Bedford, Mornay's home over his chandler's shop on the waterfront had served as a "station" where runaway slaves smuggled north by ship were hidden and clandestine meetings held. More than once he and Mary Louise acted as "conductors" accompanying fugitives on perilous overland journeys to other safe havens as far north as Boston en route to Canada and freedom. Such ventures were soul satisfying to Mornay. He came from a long line of fugitives. His devout Huguenot forebears had abandoned their prosperous chandlery at La Rochelle and fled persecution in France for a better life in the New World. By powerful tradition he intuitively aligned himself with the downtrodden and oppressed, and he was about to blurt out words of recognition when he saw a warning look in Mary Louise's eyes. A fashionably gloved forefinger lightly brushed her lips.

Mornay smiled grimly to himself. Abolitionists who actively opposed slavery were unpopular in San Francisco as in New Bedford. They were regarded as radical troublemakers and publicly abused as "nigger lovers." Yet Negroes were often mistreated in California as flagrantly as in other so-called free states. Here as elsewhere Southern slavery was generally accepted as a fact of life. A man's property, even if human, was generally considered sacred. And with these thoughts the affection and admiration he'd orginally felt for Mary Louise swept back over him.

"Please," he begged in a voice filled with unspoken meaning, "let me show my appreciation."

She smiled acknowledgment of his message. "Some other time perhaps. I must go now!" and gave him her hand with a slight added pressure which he returned. But why was she passing herself off as white? Why the rice powder and carefully straightened hair? And the strange gold earrings in the form of coiled serpents?

"If there's ever anything I can do for you, Madam St. Clair," he exclaimed, "I hope you'll let me know. I live at seven-eighteen

Montgomery Street halfway up the hill toward the Signal Tower.''

She nodded with understanding, hugged Martha who threw both arms tearfully around her neck, and begged her to visit them, shook David's hand and disappeared into the crowd.

Turning to David, struck once more by the youth's innocent good looks, Mornay implored: ''At least, sir, you will come home with me?''

David accepted readily. He'd set out for California ostensibly to ''see the elephant''*—experience all he possibly could—but secretly to fulfill the westering dream of his dead parents. And he'd been drawn toward Mornay by some instinctive affinity beside sympathy.

---

*see the sights, the elephant being the chief sight of old-time circuses

# Chapter Four

The white-hooded settlers' wagons, the handcarts and wheelbarrows, the men on horseback, the loaded mules, the walkers with packs on their backs, streamed southward down the Great Central Valley of California. They'd crossed plains, deserts, mountains. They were looking for new land, promised land. They felt God and manifest destiny were with them. "Uncle Sam is rich enough to give us all a farm!" they liked to say. Pouring west through Livermore's Pass, they found the land around San Francisco Bay all taken up and continued south through the rapidly growing town of San José, on past Gilroy's Ranch, on past the later site of Salinas, due south on the old Royal Road of the Spaniards, today's U.S. Highway 101.

"It's hidden away off down yonder—a valley like you've never seed!" old Abe Jenkins promised.

They were a final probing finger of that westering movement begun at Jamestown and Plymouth Rock, coming to an end now at the continent's edge, at an ocean where West became East. They would complete a circle begun ages and ages earlier when the first men and women migrated toward the setting sun.

Watching wagons like theirs from his window in Illinois, Abraham Lincoln wished he could go along. He'd caught the fever.

On south near the famous old hacienda of Rancho Olomosoug at the head of Santa Lucía Valley yet within reach of the sea breeze, two of the white-hooded wagons—the very tip of that probing finger—mules unhitched and turned out on picket lines to graze with the horses in the lush surrounding grass, stood side

by side forming a kind of breastworks for protection against attack, a space some ten feet wide between them. At the center of
that space a small noonday fire smoldered in a ring of stones.

A gaunt woman crouched over the fire. Her hair was prematurely gray. She was shabbily dressed in frayed gingham.

With a long-handled ladle she stirred the contents of a kettle
which hung from an iron tripod above the flame.

"Get a move on that stew, Iphy!"

Her husband's harsh voice made Iphygenia Jenkins stiffen. As
usual Buck sounded as if he blamed her for his empty belly as
for nearly everything else that displeased him. He loomed above
her, a surly giant six and a half feet tall, with legs and arms and
hands to match his huge torso.

"Rabbits don't cook quick as they run!" she answered tartly.
" 'Sides, Sally ain't back from the river yet!"

"Well, now, ain't that a shame! Sally ain't back from the river
yet!" Buck echoed mockingly. "Hear that, boys? And just who
is this here Sally we gotta wait on her—Queen of England
maybe?"

A pair of guffaws greeted this witticism. Goodly, their oldest,
nearly twenty, resembled his father on smaller scale. Elmer, sixteen, looked more like Iphy, slighter, wiry. They lounged in the
shade of the family wagon, wearing the red flannel shirts and
rough homespun trousers she'd made for them.

On the other side of the fire, Buck's brother Jake crouched by
his wagon. Buck's disparaging remark about Sally touched Jake
in a raw spot. His slow mind was groping for a response. His
daughter was almost all Jake had left in the world. Even so he
found it hard to stand up to Buck. He found it hard to do nearly
everything. Jake was a despondent man. When his wife ran off
and left him at Soda Springs Junction west of Salt Lake, with a
prosperous widower bound for Oregon, it was about what he expected. Bad things always happened to Jake. Even back in Pike
County, Missouri, this had been so. Now out of timidity he directed his feeble protest toward Goodly rather than Buck. "You
lay off Sal, Good!"

"An' you lay off Good!" Buck snapped.

A perky looking teenage girl carrying a wooden bucket in each
hand appeared at one end of the wagons. She wore a checkered
blue and white calico dress and a wide brimmed straw hat. Yellow
curls peeked out from below the hat. Her face was freckled and
sunburned, her eyes defiant. "What they after you for this time,

Iphy?'' she demanded ignoring the others as she advanced.

"Mind your tongue, Queen Victoria!" Buck raised a hand as if to slap her.

"You don't scare me one bit!" Turning her back, Sally began emptying her buckets into the barrel fastened to the side of her father's wagon.

Goodly came to Buck's support in this family squabble. "I'll declare she's past hope, Dad. Next she'll go wailin' to Grandpa how we abuse her!"

"Grandpa'll roach your tail if you don't shut up!" Sally shot back.

Abe Jenkins, patriarch and leader of this fractious clan, reclined on the grass two steps away apparently dozing in the shade of Sally's and Jake's wagon, back propped against its huge rear wheel. One hand rested benignly on his breast, the other on his brass spyglass. White hair and beard flowed down Abe's scarred and wrinkled face. Under the beard he carried in a tiny leather pouch slung from a cord around his neck the asafetida on which he relied for good health. He wore fringed deerskin shirt and trousers of the plains-and-mountain man he was. After deserting Lewis and Clark at the mouth of the Columbia half a century before, he'd made his way southward in an epic journey involving captivity by Indians, illness, painful wanderings, hunger. Blown by winds of chance, Abe was one of those unchronicled discoverers. Thus he'd become the first American to reach California overland.

"Tell us about it, Gramp!" Sally would urge as they sat around campfires and Abe retold with relish the saga of his great adventure. Arrived in this valley where he reclined now, he thought he'd discovered paradise. "They was all living in a dream, a mighty pleasant dream. But when they seed me march out of the mountains all clawed up after my scrap with that grizzly, my clothes in tatters after my years of wandering, my feet nigh bare, their faces fell. They'd never seed nobody like me before. Guess they figured nothing would ever disturb their good times!"

"So they kicked you out?"

"Sent me home with Cap'n Sedley by way of China, 'cause there was a law agin furriners stayin' in the country. But I told 'em I'd be back!"

"How'd they treat you before you left?" Sally was recognized interlocutor in these narrations.

"The mother and father was right nice. That's why I say go

easy on her now. Her boy, he laughed at me.''

"Wonder what's happened to that boy?" Buck put in suspiciously.

"You heard. He's up north havin' a good time spendin' money, raisin' hell in the process, rich off American dollars.''

" 'Tain't right!''

"She called you Squatter when she come here to see us the other day, Gramp!'' Sally resumed.

"An' I called her Grandee!''

"It was right spunky of her to come alone, though. Why'd she do that, Gramp?''

"Like me she don't want no violence. She's had enough violence. If she'd brought her people, there'd likely been a violence.''

"She sounded pretty violent herself, telling you to get off her land!''

"I sounded pretty violent telling her maybe it wasn't her land anymore, now, didn't I?''

"Yeap, Gramp, you did. She looks old as the hills, Gramp. She's the oldest person I ever saw ride a horse!''

"Indians makes the best riders in the world, Granddaughter. And they live to be a hundred. See her teeth? White as yours! I never met a Indian with bum teeth.''

"And her hair, Gramp, so bright red!''

"Dunno what to say about her hair," Abe conceded. "Never seed Indian hair like that.''

"She said she could sweep you away like a puff of dust!''

"An' I said we don't sweep easy. Oh, she knows, she knows!''

"Sure she knows," Buck rejoined emphatically. "Losers weepers, Dad. Greasers know who whipped 'em and took their country.''

Abe corrected: "She's Injun, not Greaser!''

"Same difference!''

"No, 'tain't!'' Abe spoke firmly, remembering that kindly Shoshone woman Sacajawea who, favoring an eager youth, taught him the Indian tongues and the universal sign language of plains and mountains which stood him in good stead later. And then he remembered Domínguez, runaway Spanish soldier, who gave him shelter for a year in his home in a hollow sequoia in the high Sierra. "Buck, if you'd shared a blanket with 'em same as me, you'd know.''

Buck laughed. He suspected his father of senility. Soldiering in Mexico had opened Buck's eyes to what he considered profoundest truth. Person or nation you took what you could and didn't let scruples stand in your way.

"Here comes one now, anyhow you want to label him!" Iphy put in.

They fell silent watching the horseman riding toward them along the road that bordered the valley's hills, clothes and saddle gleaming in the sun, an imposing sight.

"A Grandee, sure enough!" Jake muttered gloomily. "Look at that saddle and bridle. Silver mounted. Must of cost a thousand, two thousand!"

" 'Tain't American, such luxury!" Buck grumbled. "He's a damned Papist too, I'll bet. That's what we went to war against, ain't it, all of that?" Buck gestured angrily toward the hacienda. "There they live like lords, while we camp here like peasants. Ain't right! Who won the war? Whose country is this?"

"Gonna be trouble!" Jake predicted, feeling himself on solid ground this time.

The horseman hesitated, staring in their direction, then disappeared into a grove of oaks at the foot of the hillside a quarter mile distant.

"He'll be sneakin' up on us through the trees!" Jake warned.

Buck rose. Keeping an eye on the oak grove, he went to the rear of his wagon, took out a pistol and stuck it in his belt.

"Easy, Son!" Abe cautioned.

As he spoke the rider emerged from the trees and continued along the road toward the hacienda well beyond gunshot.

"See what I mean?" Buck grinned in triumph, patting his weapon with one huge hand. "Sam Colt sends 'em on their way! Stay close to Samuel Colt, that's my motto. When Zach Taylor and I took Monterrey City, I got four o' them niggers," jerking his thumb toward the horseman, "with Sam in one day!"

Abe countered sharply: "Son, no need to tell me! Old Rigor Mortis and I, we been there!" jerking his thumb toward the ancient Kentucky rifle standing upright against the wagon near him. "But times is a-changing. Law and order is on our side. You know what they told us. Title to every one of these ranchos is in question until that Land Commission decides. Till then our claims' as good as the next fellow's. Now just don't crowd matters." He spit for emphasis. "Let things take their course while we put roots down, plant our trees, put our cabins up." He pointed to the clearing in the grass where the first logs were rising one upon another, axes resting quietly beside them. "So if you and Jake and the boys go to cut wood after dinner you keep out of trouble, you hear? Iphy, that meat cookin' or just dyin' of old age?"

"It's waitin' for you men to quit arguin' and I reckon that'll be forever!" Iphy retorted wearily.

"You tell 'em, Iph!" Sally threw in. Like her grandfather she possessed a secret sympathy for the people of this new land, especially the handsome young horseman she'd noticed that morning observing her from a distance. Her face grew warm with the recollection. She had no ambition to spend her life in a log cabin, not in California.

# Chapter Five

Sedley was looking for her on the crowded wharf. "I'll wear a black coal scuttle bonnet, black alpaca dress and black gloves," she'd written. "I stand five feet six inches tall and am quite slim."

With Fixx, an insurance man, and Lancaster, a doctor, fellow bachelors who by invitation and to provide him company shared his house on Washington Street, Sedley had advertised for a cook. Cooks were a rare commodity in the predominantly male city. Gold could not buy them where they did not exist.

"Why not try New Orleans?" Fixx had suggested. "They've got the best food in the country down there."

"She might turn out to be black!" Lancaster objected facetiously.

Sedley shrugged. "Don't matter to me as long as she can cook."

Lancaster summed up their predicament with a witty ditty:

"We may live without poetry, music and art,
We may live without conscience, we may live without heart;
We may live without friends, we may live without books;
But civilized man cannot live without cooks!"

So they placed an advertisement in the *New Orleans Picayune*. When Mary Louise read it, it seemed heaven sent. She had compelling reasons for wanting to go to San Francisco immediately and five hundred dollars a month seemed very good wages indeed, though under her circumstances it was the protective cover—the cloak of legitimacy as cook for three evidently well-to-do bachelors—which interested her even more.

Sedley spotted her just moments after she said goodbye to Mornay, Martha and David. He was struck with astonishment by her glamor. Already she was surrounded by a crowd of admiring males, because passengers had spread the rumor she was an excellent cook traveling in answer to an inviting advertisement and, besides, women were in such short supply in this masculine city that the mere sight of one was something of an event. As he approached, in the Dresden-blue coat and high brown beaver he'd promised to wear, a big florid fellow with sidewhiskers and checkered waistcoat was bawling: "I'll pay you six hundred a month!"

"Madam St. Clair?" Sedley greeted her, forging his way through the crowd.

"Mister Sedley?"

They met with an inevitability they would recall. She saw in him the person on whom her future depended. As he looked for the first time into those strange bold gray-green eyes, so different from each other and from any others he'd experienced, it was as if he were seeing two persons: one similar to himself in ruthless purpose, the other a fascinating stranger. He noted the golden earrings but did not know they were the mark of her avocation as Voodoo Queen, for in New Orleans she'd been a disciple of the famous Mary Laveaux who dominated blacks and whites of that city with her extraordinary powers.

"You had a comfortable voyage, I hope?" Her hand in his felt like a man's, equalling his own in firmness.

She was already fencing for an opening. "On the contrary, most harrowing!"

Mary Louise could play many roles. Now she chose one she shrewdly guessed a businessman would respect. She wanted to establish her independence at once—while those male voices she was quite glad to hear continued to make her handsome offers. "I'll give you seven hundred!" one of them was saying. The florid fellow with sidewhiskers declared: "By God, I'll marry you!" Turning back to Sedley she inquired gaily: "Is this customary in San Francisco?"

"Everything is customary in San Francisco," he responded in matching tone. Her sophisticated manner and aristocratic features suggested the manor house; her dusky skin the tropics. Who was she really? When they were seated side by side in the hack he'd ordered, she decided to clarify their relationship at once. Smoothing a wrinkle in her skirt, she observed in businesslike fashion: "You heard those offers I received. Suppose we consider seven hundred rather than five my proper wage?"

"But we agreed on five!" he protested with grave amusement.

"That was before I knew what my services might be worth. Surely, sir, you aren't trying to take advantage of my ignorance? Especially after all I've been through to get here!" She told of the lethal Panama fever, of the many dead on shipboard. "One poor woman left her only child in my care." He found her not only persuasive but provocative, her words saying one thing, her manner another, insinuating intimate pleasures which appealed to his sensuality. Sedley liked to possess women among other things. His affairs were invariably businesslike and discreet. At the first sign of cloying sentiment he broke them off. Most recently it had been a dancer, an enterprising soubrette, with a visiting troupe from Paris. He'd felt relieved to be rid of her. Still: "I might go to six hundred," he heard himself saying.

"And no dishes to wash?"

He chuckled with admiration. "No dishes? My, you drive a hard bargain!" Privately he felt sure Fixx and Lancaster would agree to this fascinating creature supervising their household at almost any price. "We'll be entertaining a good deal," he explained easily as the hack edged its way through Portsmouth Plaza at the crowded heart of the city. "But you'll have all the help you need, dishwashers, maids. We want you free to prepare those delightful meals for which New Orleans is famous."

"There should be no difficulty if your fish and shellfish are abundant as I hear they are. But I must have good vegetables."

"The best vegetable dealer in town happens to be a tenant of mine. Just go to his stall at the Great Pacific Market and select what you like. Charles Mornay is his name."

Rigorous self-control developed by long habit kept Mary Louise from starting at this mention of Mornay. It seemed powerful indication fate was moving her toward her secret goals. It would give her an excuse to make contact with her old friend on a regular basis, and this might suit her purposes exactly. And at thought of those purposes a change came into her face, a fleeting shadow, which Sedley noticed but dismissed as one more of her fascinating moods.

Mornay—afoot in the crowd with Martha and David, followed by two Negro porters each bearing a trunk—looked up at that

moment and glimpsed her passing in the hack with Sedley, and
the sight filled him with amazement and anger because for Mornay Sedley represented the rich and powerful who had oppressed
him and his kind and Mary Louise and her kind for centuries.
What on earth could she be doing riding with Sedley?

As the carriage drew up in front of the fashionable portico on
Washington Street, a whole new strategy was fixing itself in Mary
Louise's mind. In it Eliot Sedley was central. She sensed their
common affinities: love of money, property, hard bargaining,
ruthlessness in achieving purpose, his weakness for secret sensual
pleasure and the potential power over him it might give her.

# Chapter Six

In the parlor of the hacienda at Rancho Olomosoug Clara Boneu was demanding of her grandson Pacifico, who stood before her hat in hand: "What are the Gringo squatters up to this morning?"

Pacifico, an engaging youth of seventeen, replied dutifully: "Mamá Grande, they are cutting trees along the river and laying logs for a cabin."

She snorted. "May the wrath of God destroy them! What else?"

"That was all I saw." Pacifico wasn't quite candid. The graceful figure of a girl drawing water from the river had attracted his attention but he thought best not to mention it.

"You're a good boy. You remind me of your mother, God rest her soul. Your father never appreciated her."

Pacifico squirmed inwardly under his grandmother's gaze. Her adoration oppressed him. Indeed the heavy dark furniture, the dim light from small windows like slits in a fortress wall, the thought that this formidable old woman had shot and killed her own brother here in this very room, made the parlor a place of latent horror. He could hardly imagine such grim old days. And she was sitting in the same straight-backed chair by the fireplace from which she'd fired that fatal shot. Sometimes he imagined he saw bloodstains on the earthen floor which she resolutely refused to have boarded over in the modern fashion. True, the house was being attacked by Indians under her brother's leadership. Still Pacifico wished for a new day with happier events.

As if sensing his thought, she went on reassuringly: "There's been enough violence, as I told O'Hara. But we'll get rid of them somehow. That's why I rely on Uncle Eliot Sedley. And I shall rely on you too! Certainly your father will be no help!''

Recollection of his father's irresponsibility roused Pacifico's passive nature. He couldn't remember his mother who'd died as he was born. But his father's neglect, even outright antipathy toward him, were vivid pain. ''In that I share your feelings, Mamá Grande!''

''You're a great comfort to me,'' she sighed fondly. ''You remind me of your grandfather. He too was tall and blond and had blue eyes.''

While they were talking Francisco was riding up the valley toward them, his short compact Indian-like body still youthful and erect. He fully intended to shrug off his mother's usual criticism of his conduct. Long ago he'd resolved to go his own way in order to survive her power. As the only son of that widely celebrated marriage between Indian princess and conquistador, he knew he was regarded as a symbol of a union between two races, two widely differing ways of life. But as he grew older he found he had no desire to be a symbol but only himself, whatever that was. He could not recapture the magic of his mother's Indian village life. The Spanish conquest had swept it away—the present Indianada by the river was a pale replica. Nevertheless as a youth he'd felt drawn to his mother's brother, the famous resistance leader Asuskwa whom she was later to kill. Yet when he traveled deep into the wilderness to the secret Indian capital to see the great figure for himself, he'd felt blocked by his white blood from joining Asuskwa's outlaw band—and taking up arms against himself as it were. Then he'd tried to find himself in love. The mestizo blood of Juanita spoke to his own mixed strain. But Juanita died swiftly and tragically. Afterward, in a moment of anguished reaction, he'd married his parents' favorite, Constanza Estenega, daughter of their neighboring rancher, and embraced the conventional life.

One result was Pacifico toward whom he held mixed feelings of love and hate. The boy was a constant reminder of his own unhappy fate as he lived from day to day, taking pleasure where he found it, among Californios, among Yankees, among Indians, a true eclectic, a stylish dilettante, brilliant eccentric or feckless wastrel depending on your view. And all this was one reason why cards, women, chances, new possibilities fascinated Francisco. He became a seeker after what might happen, because it might bring what he desired most and yet never had found—identity and peace.

He was wearing the clothing of a wealthy ranchero: flat-crowned, broad-brimmed black hat, green velvet vest with gold filigree buttons, gold-trimmed trousers and leggings. But at his waist—instead of the usual red sash—was a broad leather belt clasped by that ancient silver buckle his mother had given his father as a love token the day they met. The buckle sparkled in the sunlight, as did the mountings of his magnificent saddle and bridle and the hide of his chestnut stallion. It was at this moment that Iphy Jenkins detected his approach and Jake gave his gloomy warning. Francisco had already noted with astonishment the white-hooded wagons side by side near the river. He'd overtaken many like them as he traveled down from San Francisco. He knew they carried a kind of American quite different from his friends Sedley and Ogles. The people in them greeted him sometimes courteously, sometimes rudely, but unmistakably as an adversary. His impulse now was to ride over and investigate but his keen eye caught a glimpse of Buck's pistol and on further consideration he decided to continue to the hacienda and learn there what remarkable things were happening.

As he entered the oak grove not far from the house, his attention was attracted by the familiar tree, which thrust out of the ground like a huge wrist from which five fingers, each as large as ordinary trees, spread in different directions. It was so big, so old, so draped with moss, gnarled, that some of its giant limbs had come down like weary arms to rest on the earth, and he remembered his mother telling him how as a girl she'd played in this tree before the white men came into the valley. A new feeling, roused in part by his resentment at sight of the wagons, stirred in Francisco as he remembered the great oak had belonged to his Indian ancestors. They held exclusive rights to its acorns. Every fall they gathered them ceremoniously and ground them into meal, leaching the acid from the meal by pouring fresh water over it, giving thanks afterward to Earth with solemn ceremonies. Recalling, bitterness toward the new intruders rose keenly in him, the more so when he saw a fresh stake he recognized as a land-claim marker including the sacred grove; so that when he reached the hacienda and entered the courtyard he dismounted without a word, tossed his reins to the first boy who came running and strode angrily into the parlor where his mother and Pacifico were talking.

After dutifully kissing her hand he burst out: "What are those wagons doing on our property?"

"Waiting for you to come home and meet your responsibilities!" she retorted. "And where is the money from the sale of our cattle?"

"Alas, Mamacita, I hear you. It is unfortunate but . . .," he faltered in the old way, his resolution fading.

"You brought back nothing?" she shouted. "How can that be? Six hundred animals and you bring back nothing?"

"My expenses were very high, and . . ."

"Expenses! All you've ever been to me is expense! And now you add this! I know where my money went! Whores and cards! *Whores and cards!*"

"Mamacita, you forget yourself! In front of your grandson!"

"The truth cannot hurt. And the map? The diseño map?"

"I gave it to Eliot to give to the lawyer."

"And the money to pay the lawyer?" she demanded furiously. "And to pay the taxes? And the debts you forever incur?"

"The money is all around us, Mamacita. It has hides and horns. It is innumerable. Remember, up in Sacramento City they paid five hundred for a single animal?"

"Faugh," she scoffed, "that was in '49 when the rush for gold began. Today, it's a different story. They drive herds here from Texas, as you well know, and our profits decline. You are like so many Californios who dream of endless wealth from cattle, while dressing like kings and queens and carpeting their floors with costly rugs!" And heightening her attack: "Look at yourself in your fine clothes! Francisco El Magnífico, the clever Gringos call you! As they laugh behind your back while they take your money and squat on our land!"

Roused to fury by her whiplash words Francisco retorted: "I am what I am. But I'm also what you made me. You and my father wanted me to embody this promised land of yours. Well, for you maybe it was promised! For me it was all used up—by you! Now let us have done! I am what I am. You are what you are. Let's begin anew!"

But she was not ready for reconciliation. "You speak like this in front of your only son? Have you no shame?"

But Francisco was beside himself with rage and frustration. "He's more your son than mine. His mother was your choice, not mine! Here. . . ." With a furious gesture he ripped off the ancestral belt with the silver buckle which his father had given him the day he came of age and flung it at her feet.

She did not flinch. Turning to Pacifico who'd listened aghast to this noisy wrangle with its painful revelations, wishing himself free from all of it, she commanded: "Pick up the belt and put it on!" As he did so, she ordered further: "Wear it proudly as your grandfather did! You are my true son and his! Henceforward, you are the man of this household!"

At that moment María Ignácia's husband Isidro, their major-domo, rushed into the room excitedly, and cried: "They are cutting the oaks of the Sacred Grove!"

"Who is?" demanded Clara.

"The North Americans!"

# Chapter Seven

San Francisco, like Rome, a city it was to resemble in its nearly imperial power over a vast region, would be built upon seven hills but as yet only three were in use: Signal or Telegraph Hill on the north, Ricon on the south beyond newly created Market Street, and the California Street Hill on the west—later called Nob Hill—up which settlement was beginning to climb. Most of the life of the city was concentrated in a narrow space along the waterfront and there the bustle and din were extraordinary. Horsemen dashed pellmell through crowded streets, heedless of life or limb. From saloons and gambling halls came the sounds of music and wild merriment that went on day and night. A man led a grizzly bear by a chain around its neck as if it were no more than a dog. On every side, street vendors shouted their wares and steam engines hammered out sounds of progress. The entire atmosphere was charged with exuberant vitality and an air of unlicensed freedom.

David and Martha were too preoccupied by their new surroundings to notice the momentary dismay of Mornay as Mary Louise and Sedley passed in the hack, but a moment later they came to a sight so unusual that David called out: "Who's that?"

A brawny giant, coat off, sleeves rolled up, stood on a whiskey barrel in front of a saloon. His voice rang up and down the street as if he commanded an army. His powerful hands and arms flailed the air. His great jaw thrust out like a promontory. He was preaching a temperance sermon and his bizarre pulpit and fearless eloquence were attracting a curious crowd.

"That's Reverend Bill Taylor," Mornay muttered approvingly. "Doesn't stay inside his church and wait for people to come to him. Goes to them. I must say I admire him for it."

As he spoke a young woman, her face heavily rouged, daringly dressed in bright red trousers and a blue cloth cap, emerged from the saloon in front of Taylor. A gang of drunken toughs followed her, jeering at her sensational garb, then at Taylor. Despite his own amazement at the trousers and cap David's indignation flared. Impulsively he called out: "Why don't you let her alone? She's got a right to wear what she likes!"

The hoodlum nearest him snarled back: "Who do you think you are, Shorty Ass?"

Though the fellow was a good four inches taller than he, David stepped forward and gave him a straight left to the mouth which sent him staggering. A free-for-all followed in which David might have been severely injured had not Reverend Taylor emitted a giant shout, jumped down from his barrel and waded into the fray, fists flying, loudly excoriating his adversaries as seeds of the Devil, while the crowd cheered him and David. The bullies soon went scampering.

After giving David a crushing handclasp and a pat on the back that nearly took his breath away, Taylor remounted his barrel and declared loudly: "Stick up for what's right fellows, and the Lord'll stick up for you! That's the moral of that little fracas you just witnessed! And remember the next time you meet Scoundrel Drink, he's a coward at heart! Face him and he'll take to his heels like those rascals did!"

Mornay and Martha were torn between admiration and relief when David rejoined them, out of breath, face and knuckles bleeding. Martha wiped away the blood with her handkerchief. Her father gripped David's shoulder affectionately. "My boy, your courage is admirable but I wonder about your judgment. This is a very rough town. If you wish to survive in one piece, I suggest you be careful not to let your heart get ahead of your head!"

The Sydney Ducks, as Mornay called them, because many were criminals from Australia, had terrorized the city. "Honest citizens finally rose up, organized a Committee of Vigilance in which I served, and drove them out." Now they were skulking back. "You'll have to be on your guard. They may try to retaliate."

Moving on up the slope of Telegraph Hill, the three came to the unpainted house made of a bright reddish wood such as David had never seen before. Wing Sing opened the door before Mornay could knock. Evidencing no surprise at sight of bruised-faced David instead of the Miriam Mornay he was expecting, with age-old composure Wing bowed and smiled a discreet greeting, both hands clasped in front of his blue cotton jacket. At the side of his neck all but hidden by his collar he had a bruise of his own, received that morning from the fist of the miner who'd struck him down in front of Sedley: "All velly velcome!" he exclaimed cheerfully. "But Missy Mornay?"

As Mornay explained tersely, tears welled up in Wing's eyes. Those tears in those eyes from another continent, another race, eyes dependent on him, touched Mornay profoundly. During his homeward walk he'd decided to accept the loss of his wife as God's will. Henceforward his life would be devoted more fully than ever to people like Wing. His house was known as a safe haven for the persecuted of whatever race or creed. It was a central station on San Francisco's Underground Railroad which helped runaway Negro slaves escape to hideaways in the city or by ship to Canada. Wing had arrived there one night seeking refuge after Indians beat, robbed and ejected him from his gold claim in the Sierra foothills, and the Chinese labor contractor who'd brought him across the Pacific from Canton at good profit had sent knife-wielding runners to extort money he could not pay. Mornay had accepted him without question.

David and Martha were startled by the appearance of this first Chinese they'd ever seen, with a pigtail hanging down nearly to his heels from under his black skullcap. Yet he was so friendly, so appealing. "Wing's a member of the family," Mornay concluded as he introduced them.

Delicious odors of cookery emanated from the interior of the house and Wing bowed himself away toward them while Mornay showed Martha and David their new home. "Wish I'd had time to paint the outside!" he apologized but David felt this no drawback because the interior like the outside was finished in that beautiful ruddy-colored wood. "It's called redwood," Mornay explained. "Grows in the coastal mountains north and south of here. A single tree can yield enough lumber for a house like this and it has the inestimable value of being impervious to decay as well as attack by insects." This sounded incredible to David, one more aspect of his amazing new surroundings.

Mornay's bedroom occupied one rear corner of the main floor, Martha's the other. Mornay's most pressing concern now was for his daughter's happiness and he watched anxiously as she entered her new room. It was larger and lighter than her old one in New Bedford yet contained her own little bed with its carved pine cones capping each corner post, which with other furniture had been shipped around the Horn. Martha was a bit dismayed by the didactic nature of the wallpaper which depicted Biblical scenes including infant Moses discovered in the bulrushes by Pharaoh's daughter, and the infant Jesus discovered in the manger at Bethlehem by the wise men; but she concealed her feeling and exclaimed: "Oh, Daddy, it's just perfect! And look at the view!"

The vast harbor lay before them with its forest of masts like a fairy-tale haven hidden at the end of the world. Beyond the water rose the golden Contra Costa Mountains, a glorious promise. David had seen much during his travels but nothing like this. It seemed truly a promised land full of extraordinary people like Reverend Bill Taylor and Charles Mornay, the young woman in the red trousers, the ferocious Ducks, Wing Sing, giant trees, magnificent vistas. "Come!" and Mornay led the way to the cozy attic room which would be his. It had no wallpaper which pleased him because he preferred the natural redwood, yet a dormer window provided that inspiring view. "Wing's got a similar cubbyhole in the basement," Mornay explained, "and a back door where he comes and goes privately. You may use it whenever you like. I want you to feel at home for as long as you care to stay."

At the supper table the hospitable merchant bowed his head and with simple affection took Martha's hand in one of his and David's in the other. "Bless this food to our use, O Lord, and make us mindful of Thy goodness to us!" It was more eloquent than if he'd preached a sermon, David thought, while for Mornay it was the deep-felt resumption of a ritual interrupted by three years of spiritual solitude. Then he lifted his head and exclaimed heartily: "We're having a genuine San Francisco feast in honor of your arrival. Let's see what miracles Wing hath wrought!" And Wing appeared, beaming, bearing bowls of clear beef broth into which an egg had been lightly beaten leaving golden fragments, "flowers," Mornay called them, floating on its surface. "It clears the palate and prepares the way for the next course." Then followed baked rock cod and delicious roast duck with almond sauce and then succulent pieces of deep-fried pork with sweet and sour tomato sauce.

"I can't eat all this!" Martha protested.

"It's not necessary to eat all of it," Mornay assured her. "But custom requires we take a helping. Then Wing's feelings won't be hurt." And though he himself had little appetite, thinking of the loved one missing from this feast, he forced himself to fulfill what he considered his obligation to Wing.

"Where do you come from and what brings you here?" he asked David.

"Princeton in New Jersey, most recently. I'm a college student there."

"Ah, a college man." Mornay looked at his guest with new eyes, for he himself was largely self-educated. "What course of study are you following?"

"A rather strenuous one. Classes beginning at six, some recitations as late as four in the afternoon. I'm taking the standard curriculum: Greek, Latin, Mathematics, English Composition and Literature, Geography, Ancient History, Mythology, Natural Science."

"And what will you do when you graduate?"

"I'm not sure. That's one reason I'm here—to try and find out."

"And another reason for you to remain under our roof," Mornay added warmly. "Let's have a good talk later. You might even decide to continue your education in California. They'll be opening a college across the bay in Oakland* soon."

Afterward in the parlor he read aloud to them from the Bible, as customary in many households of the time, ending with his favorite passage from the Book of Job. "Naked came I out of my mother's womb, and naked shall I return thither: the Lord gave and the Lord taketh away; blessed be the name of the Lord." It expressed his vision of life in simplest terms and seemed to give divine sanction to the mixture of sorrow, joy, and acceptance he felt now.

In the privacy of his basement room where he was keeping a journal of his experiences in "The Land of the Golden Mountain" as California was called by his people, Wing's entry for that evening included an account of Miriam Mornay's death and Martha's arrival with David. "A very well meaning young man of much promise and deep spirit but many pitfalls in store," Wing ended.

The glass-domed clock on the mantel was striking eight. Mar-

*named for the magnificent oak groves which originally grew there tha's eyes were looking heavy. "Isn't it time for bed after such a long day?" her father suggested. A few minutes later when he went to her room to hear her prayers, Mornay held his emotions in tight grip. Lying there, grave oval face framed by dark brown hair, she seemed the image of his lost wife, and the passing and renewing of all life seemed tragically and beautifully embodied in their child. He felt his throat choking.

"Did your mother leave any last word for me?"

"She said I was to love you and care for you."

"And you will!" He bent and kissed her forehead, then took from his pocket the gift he'd placed there to give Miriam. It was a small plain gold cross suspended from a thin gold chain. As he held it up it gleamed spectacularly in the candlelight and Martha cried: "Daddy, what is it?"

"It's all the gold I took from the earth of this land during my first misguided days here, when I thought to find an easy fortune. I had it made into a symbol of the true wealth. Your mother's initials are inscribed on its back." Turning the back into the light, he showed her the delicate letters, M. M. "Would you like it? They are your initials too."

"I'd love it! It's beautiful!"

"Then I shall give it to you as I would have given it to your mother and hope you will cherish it as long as you live." And he placed it around her neck.

She flung her arms around his and kissed him and as he felt the touch of her soft warm flesh all his sorrow and pain disappeared and he whispered as he held her tightly: "We have each other, don't we?"

# Chapter Eight

Sally and Iphy had finished but the men were still hungrily scraping their tin plates. "That rabbit sure did run right through that stew pot," Buck commented disgustedly.

"With you fellows after him how could you blame him?" Iphy retorted.

Ignoring her, Buck set his plate aside. "Let's get out of here! You too, Sal! You bring a sack for the chips!"

Sally was about to flare out a refusal but a glance from her grandfather stopped her. She knew it was Abe who held the family together. Sometimes she had to help. So when Buck and Jake and the two boys picked up axes, pistols and rifles and started for the oak grove to cut firewood, she followed reluctantly, trailing her tow sack over the grass.

"Remember, no trouble!" Abe called after them.

"No trouble!" muttered Buck under his breath. "How does he think we got this country in the first place?"

"No trouble now is what he means," Jake responded gloomily.

"You taking sides?" Buck snapped. "If the Greasers ever get the upper hand of us we're done. That oak grove's ours. We got to claim it and no mistake."

"I'm just a-sayin'."

"And I'm just a-tellin'. The old man's into his dotage. We've got to realize that, you and me, and act 'cordingly."

When they reached the grove Buck selected a giant tree which seemed to present itself as a natural target. Several of its huge limbs came down and rested on the ground at convenient height.

"Let's each of us take one," he instructed.

Jake objected: "It's green wood. It won't burn."

"I know that, dummy, but it'll stake our claim. A pile'll show who owns this land. Who's done work here. There's plenty of dry stuff lying around," Buck indicated a fallen tree nearby, "to take home after we show who's boss. So get busy now. You too, Sal! After that kindling!"

Four huge limbs were soon being neatly amputated while Sally sullenly gathered twigs and bark into her sack. Life seemed to her very nearly intolerable at that moment. She resented Buck's bullying of her father. She deplored Jake's weakness yet loved him. Goodly and Elmer were despicable oafs who tormented her at every turn. She detested her woman's subservient position in the family. And all of this was partly why her heart pounded with anticipation when she heard hoofbeats approaching and Francisco, Pacifico and Isidro dashed up at a gallop.

At sight of the mutilated limbs Francisco's thoughts went back to his recent communion with them and all they represented. Overpowering rage rose in him. "What are you doing to my tree?"

Buck leaned carelessly on his axe handle. "Mister, what you mean, *your* tree?"

Francisco snapped: "Get off my land!"

Next moment he was looking into the muzzle of Buck's revolver. "You damned Greaser, git off our land and stop your sass. This here's the United States now, not Mexico!"

Francisco sat frozen in disbelief. He'd heard of this happening elsewhere. That it was happening here and to him seemed impossible. It was the raw guts of the American conquest. Its naked meaning spoke from the muzzle of Buck's pistol, while his and Pacifico's and Isidro's only weapons were the reatas coiled at their saddlehorns.

Goodly interposed. "Got a idea, Dad. There's wood to cut. Why not let the Greasers help?"

His suggestion struck Buck as hugely entertaining. With a sarcastic chuckle he addressed Francisco: "Grandee, I bet you and work ain't very well acquainted. Reckon all you have to do is clap your hands and some Indian comes runnin' to pick up your socks." Buck warmed to his subject with relish. "Yeah, I bet you ain't never made love to a axe handle during your entire existence. Well, here's your opportunity!"

He motioned with his pistol for Francisco to dismount. But

Francisco sat stupefied. Pacifico too was astounded by this incredible effrontery, as out of the corner of his eye he watched
Sally and she watched him.

"Down to the ground!" Buck pointed with the barrel of his
Colt.

Slowly, uncompromisingly, Francisco shook his head. There
was a deafening explosion. Francisco felt something brush his
forehead. His hat flew off. But when he reined his frightened
horse back to a standstill facing Buck, his courage remained undiminished. Buck's eyes gleamed with murder. "To the ground,"
he commanded motioning, "if you want to live!"

For a moment Francisco resolved to die rather than suffer such
indignity. Then a new idea, one that would never leave him as
long as he lived, took possession of him and he saw a way to go
where he had never been before. The prospect delighted him with
wild and furious joy. Smiling he dismounted.

Buck's pistol moved to Isidro. "You, too, nigger!" Slowly,
with dignity, the majordomo followed Francisco's example.

"Junior!" The pistol indicated Pacifico now. "I reckon we can
use your lily white hands too!"

Elmer chimed in: "Yeah, he can help Sally pick up bark!"

"Great idea, Elm. Sal, give him your sack."

"I won't!" Sally retorted.

"Aw let him swing an axe, Dad!" Goodly interposed. "Be
good for him!"

"Son, you're right again! Wouldn't do to slight the younger
generation! We owe it to these folks to see 'em grow up manly-
like, don't we? *Get busy!*" He tossed his axe toward Francisco.

Under the muzzle of Buck's six-shooter the three gingerly took
up the double bladed axes. Jake did not approve these violent
doings but felt powerless to intervene. Sally had other ideas.
"Buck," she warned, " 'member what Grandpa said!"

"Shut up!" he retorted.

Pacifico did not understand what lay behind her words but felt
grateful for them and struck at the oak limb before him as if it
were Buck.

After watching his victims' awkward efforts a few minutes
Buck jeered: "Stop! The sight of you clumsy fools makes me
tired!" As they paused, Goodly strolled over to Pacifico with a
friendly smile. Goodly was larger and stronger though they were
nearly the same age. His tone was disarming. "Amigo, that's a
funny looking old belt buckle you got there. How does it work?"

Unsuspecting, Pacifico showed him.

Snatching the unbuckled belt, Goodly thrust a foot behind Pacifico's heel and shoved him backward, ripping the belt from his waist.

Next moment Goodly himself was sent sprawling on his face as result of an attack from an unexpected quarter. Sally stood over him, cheeks flaming with indignation. "You damn bully! He weren't doing nothing to you!" She snatched the belt from his astonished hands and gave it back to Pacifico.

Buck and Elmer guffawed while Goodly picked himself up ruefully. "That's one on you, Good! You gonna let a girl treat you like that?" they derided. Goodly, shamefaced, tight lipped, made for Pacifico. But Buck intervened. "Let him keep his belt. We don't take what don't belong to us!"

Pacifico stood watching and listening in silent admiration. Never in his life had he seen a woman do such a thing as Sally had done. Jake too was secretly delighted.

"All right," Buck announced grimly, turning once more upon the Californians, "fun's over!" He motioned with his gun in the direction of the hacienda. "Vamoose! Get off our land! And don't set foot on it again if you want to stay healthy, understand?"

Francisco laughed in his face. "Our vengeance will come. May you live to receive it! Follow me," he said calmly to his two companions, "let us leave this mad bull to his bellowing. He shall feel our ropes one day!"

With dignity he led the way toward the house, on foot since their horses had run off. Isidro's face was dark with anger. Pacifico, buckling on his belt, still glowed inwardly at thought of Sally's extraordinary intervention on his behalf. But Francisco was feeling transformed. Out of this humiliation, the most painful of his life, he saw grimly how he could rise to triumph, saw that new way he could follow, a way which might lead him at last to his true self.

Waiting in the courtyard, Clara greeted them scornfully: "You left on horseback! You return on foot?"

"We were following your admonition to avoid trouble, Mamacita. You see the consequence."

"I heard a shot. What was that?"

"That was my hat flying off." He showed her the hole in the crown.

She glanced at it, at him, keenly, apprehensively. "Do not speak in riddles. What happened?"

As Francisco told her she grew grave with indignation, then respectful with approval, for his bearing in this matter impressed her favorably. It was that of a man, not of a capricious boy. For the first time in years she spoke to him as an equal. "What do you mean to do now?"

"I don't know. But I have thoughts. And I kept my promise, Mamacita. I was guilty of no violence. Not yet!"

Suddenly a feeling of compassionate yearning swept over her and she wished to embrace him, ask forgiveness, take his hand and his heart in hers, begin a new life as mother and son.

But he was already moving away.

# Chapter Nine

I had two purposes in coming to California,'' Mary Louise told
Mornay later, "to free my daughter from slavery and to establish
myself and Hattie in this golden state from where I shall continue
to aid my people." Though she could pass as white, Mary considered herself black.

Operating in disguise in New Orleans as agent for the Underground she'd discovered that the Stanhope family was leaving for
California for an extended visit taking Hattie as maid. Thus when
she read Sedley's advertisement she leaped at the chance to make
the westward step. In a free state it surely would be easier to free
her daughter than in New Orleans. "And I saw how I might gain
access to the wealth and power of a new land, while striking a
blow at George Stanhope and all his kind."

She too had been his slave. "Fifteen when he raped me, filling
me with the seeds of undying hatred but also with Hattie." She
resolved to run away or kill Stanhope or both. "But soon there
was the child. Still he used me—shamelessly, regardless of his
wife or any outward appearance—threatening to sell me at the
slave market on Chartres Street and the baby too unless I received
him." It was then she decided on flight so that she might return
some day and free her child. Guided only by the North Star and
her fierce determination she made her way north in the clothes of
a boy house-slave, dodging the patrollers, traveling mostly at
night, knocking on the right doors by what seemed divine intervention, by pure luck encountering that heroine of the Underground, Rachel Philpot, herself an escaped slave returning south

"to free our brothers and sisters."

With Philpot's party Mary Louise reached Philadelphia and then, by ship of a friendly Quaker captain, New Bedford. Mornay knew the rest. A widowed milliner, also a Quaker, took her as apprentice and taught her to read and write. Her exceptional intelligence and strength of character quickly evidenced themselves. Soon she was serving customers and keeping the accounts at her mistress's little shop. There a friend of Mornay's, James Jackson, white, a prosperous shipowner and Abolitionist, buying sundries for his sisters, met and fell in love with her. They were soon happily married. Jackson's death left Mary Louise with the money she needed to carry out what would become her life's obsessions: freeing her daughter, freeing her people.

Now as she walked down Washington Street toward Mornay's produce stall, market basket hanging from the crook of her arm, her first thought was to learn where the Stanhopes and Hattie were staying. Then she would decide what steps to take.

In the increasing number of people around her, she heard a remarkable mixture of languages: French and Spanish with which she was familiar from her New Orleans experiences; Portuguese, Italian, German, Hawaiian, Chinese, which were strange. What struck her powerfully was that here like New Orleans was a multiracial city where she might prosper. Like New Orleans it was a gateway to the world. Its busy waterfront reminded her of the levee crowded with river boats and foreign shipping. Yet this was still so new, so young. She noticed occasional places of business operated by Negroes: a barber shop, a pawnshop, even a dry goods store. Here was solid evidence of what awaited her people and herself.

Thoughts of the evening before gave her pleasant feelings too. Albert Lancaster and Tom Fixx, Sedley's companions, welcomed her with that same easy tolerance Sedley exhibited. She perceived instantly they were all men of the world who preferred to live comfortably but not ostentatiously, and she liked the new house with its bay windows and southern exposure, two floors, the lower for parlor, dining room, billiard room, kitchen, pantry and her bedroom; the upper, for their bedrooms. Sedley explained that because of the shortage of lumber in the early years of the Rush he'd had the house shipped around the Horn from Boston in prefabricated sections. "Like you, I imported it!" he teased. She knew it was simply a matter of time before they shared a greater intimacy. But she preferred to use her charms unhurriedly.

As she reached the busy intersection of Washington and Montgomery these musings were interrupted by sight of the man she hated most. It stopped her in her tracks and made her breath come short. It was beyond her wildest hopes. Coming toward her through the crowd, massive nose preceding him like a ship's prow, was Colonel George Stanhope. Tall, imperious, he wore a Southern gentleman's flared top hat and tan frockcoat over fawn trousers and carried the Malacca cane with which she was painfully familiar. She still bore its marks on her back placed there when she refused his advances. Quickly she turned aside and gazed into a shop window. After he passed she turned and raised one gloved forefinger in his direction. Casually so as not to attract notice, she made the sign of the undying curse, the Voodoo Cross, in the air on Stanhope's retreating figure.

And at that moment, as if he instinctively felt something, he looked around, but there was little danger of his recognizing her among so many others, disguised as a well dressed white woman, bonnet partially hiding her face; and she felt fierce satisfaction that her magic had apparently taken such instantaneous effect. Adjusting her pace to his she followed him. When he reached the plaza, crossed it and entered the California House, a fashionable hotel, she turned aside to watch from a safe distance, feeling sure she'd found where the family and Hattie were staying. From her observation point across the square not far from the spot where Reverend Taylor had preached from his whiskey barrel and David engaged in the scuffle with The Ducks, she waited, hoping to catch a glimpse of her daughter.

Slipping down through the Underground with its white and black "stationmasters," for even in the deepest South there were white sympathizers, she'd repeatedly tried to abduct Hattie but the Stanhopes, moving regularly every winter from their plantation at Stanhope's Bend on the Mississippi below Vicksburg to their house on New Orleans's exclusive St. Charles Street, were keeping a close watch on the child, rearing her as companion and servant to their own Victoria, and Mary Louise was unable to catch more than a glimpse of her flesh and blood.

A hunchbacked Mexican American organ grinder carrying a sign: "I Am Blind!" and a monkey on his shoulder stopped and began serenading her. She quickly dropped a coin into his cup to hurry him along. Once at an upstairs window she saw the outline of a figure she thought was sixteen-year-old Hattie, though it might have been seventeen-year-old Victoria Stanhope. All of

Mary's painfully brutalized, thwarted, yet fortunate life seemed to rush up and stand breathless at the edge of her being, ready for this decisive next step. Resolutely she put it all back down. She must not let herself be carried away by emotion. Unlike David who saw life as essentially benign despite the blows it dealt him, Mary saw it as essentially evil. Goodness, justice were exceptions. Stanhope not Mornay was typical. People who rose to the top were those who worked and schemed unscrupulously to gain power and wealth at the expense of others, not those who tried to live exemplary lives. She revered Mornay as she revered a noble day. But he was an exception. The rule was Stanhope. The rule was Sedley. The rule was herself, obliged to deal face to face with the unpleasant realities of an existence where lust and greed prevailed and generosity and compassion were incidental. Therefore she was prepared to use every means at her disposal, whatever they might be, to free Hattie.

After watching the hotel some time she continued toward the market, intending to return later and resume her vigil.

# Chapter Ten

After saying good-night to Martha, Mornay returned to the parlor where David was sitting by the fire. The cold fog that makes San Francisco in June feel like Alaska had come in swiftly at dusk through Golden Gate and Mornay had lighted the coals in the grate for warmth as well as cheer. David was reading *The Daily Sentinel,* which informed him that President Franklin Pierce was striving to maintain a balance between antislavery and pro-slavery factions that threatened to disrupt the nation. Secretary of War Jefferson Davis, formerly Senator from Mississippi, was advocating the purchase of Cuba from Spain. But Northern members of Congress saw it as an attempt to expand Southern influence.

"So you met Madam St. Clair over a book?" Mornay resumed, taking up a subject David had let drop earlier.

"Yes, Mrs. Stowe's new novel. It's making a sensation back East. One day on deck I noticed her reading it. We fell into conversation."

"What's it called?"

*"Uncle Tom's Cabin."*

"What's it about?" Mornay demanded although he knew perfectly well.

"Slavery."

Mornay decided to test his young friend. After poking the coals, he sat down in the rocker opposite. "You aren't one of those radical Abolitionists, are you," he asked suspiciously, "always stirring up trouble?"

But David did not back off. "I despise slavery."

Mornay began to see in this likable forthright youngster an ally in what he regarded as the coming struggle for supremacy in state and nation. He probed further. "And how did Madam St. Clair feel about it?"

"As I did. I even wondered," David continued with more of that engaging directness, "if she might have colored blood, her skin's so dusky. Of course I didn't ask. Don't misunderstand me, please. She's about the kindest person I ever met. I watched her with your wife and Martha."

"Did you happen to overhear what they said?"

"They were talking about you. Once I heard them say that there was work to be done. I didn't know what they meant."

Mornay did. "Work" meant a "passenger" would soon be coming along the Underground Railroad. He wondered who the passenger was, and his heart leaped to think his wife and Mary Louise had been secretly in touch in the old way, for Miriam had been his partner in Abolition as in everything else. It also heightened his desire to see Mary again and unravel the mystery of her presence in California and association with Sedley. "There is indeed work to be done here, my boy," he continued gravely. "They were right. And now tell me more about yourself."

"I was born in Iowa Territory in what is now Davis County, in the tier of counties next the Missouri line—about seventy-five miles west of Keokuk."

"On the frontier?"

"Yes, we lived in a claim cabin made of logs. Father farmed with a yoke of oxen, Bright and Berry. One of my earliest memories is following him while his plow overturned that rich prairie soil. Once I picked up a handful and tried to eat it, it looked so good!"

Mornay chuckled. "My people too tilled the soil. I know what you mean!"

"Mother did all our cooking over the open fireplace. She taught me to read with the help of our only books, the Bible and *Pilgrim's Progress*. She was from the mountains of western Virginia. Father was from upstate New York. They met at a little town on the Ohio River when his rafting party put ashore for supplies. I guess it's an old story."

"Yes, an American one," Mornay encouraged. "Go on."

When David was seven cholera swept away father, mother and younger brother and he went to live with relatives on a homestead in the Illinois woods. "When they no longer wished to keep me they sent me with an identification tag attached to a string around my neck, as if I were a freight parcel, to Cousin Benedict in New York State. There I was bound out to a neighboring farmer.''

"You were knocked around a bit!" Mornay sympathized.

"But it gave me self-reliance and I dreamed of becoming important. When I ran away a kindly dry goods merchant, Mr. Robinson, at Lowville, took me in and sent me to school. My teacher was a fine man. He taught me to study. Taught *ab libitim,* from the lips.'' An inner radiance seemed to imbue David's words with grace so that Mornay was attracted more strongly than ever. "I left in the spring of 1850 though I had an offer to teach. Finally I reached Providence in Rhode Island where my forebears arrived from England two centuries ago seeking religious freedom.''

"Much as mine did!"

"I lived for a while with my great uncle, a Congregationalist minister. He tried to persuade me to enter the ministry. But I still wanted to see the elephant. From Providence I went to New York City to clerk in Cousin Newell's big store. He offered to loan me two hundred and fifty dollars a year for four years if I'd go to the College of New Jersey at Princeton where he'd attended. He'd become a devout Presbyterian. After a year there I caught California Fever and asked President Carnahan for a furlough. Here I am." David told of his feelings as his ship entered Golden Gate that morning.

Mornay agreed he'd had similar ones. "Yes, David, this is promised land. By God's grace it can be the New Jerusalem!* Are you ready to help?"

"Yes, of course!"

David felt a bit oppressed by Mornay's seriousness but was carried away by his powerful conviction and his own enthusiasm.

"It won't be easy. Our adversaries are the power but we can be the glory. California's a free state, but we are ruled by Southerners or Northerners with Southern sympathy, men of wealth and influence who secretly or overtly favor the Slaveocracy. We call them The Chivalry. They call us The Shovelry. The State Legislature serves their purposes, while judges interpret the law in their favor. As last resort they turn to intimidation and murder. But the day will come, David, when we, the people, will overturn this monstrous tyranny!" Mornay's voice took on apocalyptic tone, then subsided to hospitable informality. "Meanwhile I hope

*an ideal community.

you'll stay and keep Martha and me company until you find a position worthy of your talents or other lodging you may prefer.''

David accepted at once. Mornay already seemed like a father to him. "I can't imagine a place I'd like better. But I must pay my way."

"Very well. Have you money?"

"A little."

"I'll make you a proposition. The outside of this house needs painting, as you saw. You paint it for me—at the going rate of twelve dollars a day—yes," he reiterated with amusement as he saw David's jaw drop, "twelve dollars a day—that's how dear labor is. If you'll paint it for me for twelve dollars a day, less three for room and board, we'll call it even."

"But I'll grow rich at that rate!"

"Wait till you try to buy something. This is probably the most expensive city on earth, as well as the most exciting. It has everything, David, everything from highest to lowest. But beware its temptations."

The mantelpiece clock was striking ten. "I shall rise at 3:00 as usual," Mornay continued, "to be at my place of business when the growers arrive. I am a produce merchant. But I shall return later in the day and then I'll show you what is to be done. Do you know how to make paint?"

"Yes, I've done it more than once."

"Good. All the ingredients are ready in my cellar. Meantime, Wing and Martha will make you welcome. Now you must be ready to rest after your long travels!"

And he clasped David's hand affectionately before accompanying him to his room, feeling with thankfulness that perhaps he had indeed found a son.

# Chapter Eleven

That night Francisco was unable to sleep. The new path he'd determined to follow did not appear easy. But he resolved to pursue it with all the stubbornness of his obstinate nature. His mother's repudiation of him followed by his humiliation at the hands of Buck Jenkins had changed something in him irrevocably. Beneath his rage and shame, a nearly dead ember from his youth had begun to glow: that desire to be united with a cause larger than himself, something great and worthwhile such as he'd once dreamed of and sought.

As first step he decided to go in search of old Tilhini, the aged Indian wise man, friend and counselor of his youth, set aside and neglected all these years. Lighting his bedside candle he rose and went to his clothes cabinet. Rummaging through it he found the garments and equipment he'd used as a young man. Here was the ancient waistnet of milkweed fiber for carrying personal articles. Here were the moccasins beautifully beaded by his mother's hand. Here also was the bow of polished juniper reinforced with deer sinew which old Tilhini with his parents' encouragement—they wanting their son to embody both white and Indian ways—had taught him to use.

Putting on waistnet and moccasins, tying his coarse dark hair into a knot at the top of his head and thrusting the bone-handled flint knife through it, Francisco picked up his bow and took down the quiver made of a mountain lion's tail which hung on the wall with the red-shafted arrows in it, and was about to leave the room when he remembered something.

Rummaging again in the cabinet he came across a bowl containing powdered red ochre. Carrying the bowl to his dressing table he moistened the ochre with water from the pitcher, mixing in tallow fat from the candle. Then using his fingers he smeared his body with red paint to protect it from sunburn.

Glancing scornfully at the costly silk shirt, fashionable velvet jacket and trousers, and the fancy shoes and tasseled leggings he'd discarded onto a chair the night before, he suddenly changed his mind and bent and stuffed them into his waistnet. Then taking up bow and quiver again he slipped quietly out of the dark house and made his way under the stars to the Indianada, that collection of huts by the river his parents had established decades ago as an alternative to mission Indian life. There old ways had been practiced all these years.

Finding Tilhini's hut empty, Francisco thought his friend might be in the sweathouse nearby at the edge of the stream, its mounded surface clearly visible in the starlight, where men sometimes spent the night. Descending into the interior of the mound by its pole ladder, he scented smoke, glimpsed coals, heard a quavery voice he recognized as coming from Ramón, the crippled caretaker, who though bent nearly double from rheumatism brought wood for the daily fires and kept the sweathouse clean so that others might enjoy meditation and conversation there.

"He is not here. He has gone into the hills!" Ramón explained, staring in silent astonishment at Francisco's garb, and instantly Francisco remembered this was the time of the summer solstice and that Tilhini had very likely gone into the back country to worship at a special shrine. This rejoiced him because it seemed exactly in keeping with his new determination.

"Give me a handful of food, Old Man, for I travel a long trail!" Without a word Ramón took a handful of seed meal from his pouch and handed it to him.

Leaving the sweathouse Francisco proceeded into the wild back country, moving at a steady jog along the familiar river trail, the water singing beside him, the night air exhilarating. Soon he was among steep-sided mountains where dense chaparral came down with its fragrant odors and the loneliness and embracing silence opened his mind to thoughts almost forgotten since youth.

He recalled setting out along this path to find his uncle Asuskwa, his mother's brother, the famous leader of resistance against the invading white men—remembered finding Asuskwa in his hideaway deep in the fastness of the interior, and how their

meeting ended for Francisco in bitter disillusion when he decided
against embracing a cause which seemed doomed however admirable. Am I then out of my mind now? he asked himself. For
word had reached him of the terrible slaughters of Indians of the
interior mountains and valleys by white settlers and soldiers. He
was taking his life in his hands as he journeyed in that direction
with what he had in mind, yet his thoughts encouraged him too.
Because the killing had not been one sided. The hinterland was
a center of valiant resistance. White men's blood had stained Indian arrows, knives and bullets. A struggle was taking place
which had begun in the time of his father the conquistador, in
those days of first contact between native Californians and white-
skinned invaders, and continued to this moment.

At midday he stopped in the shade of a giant sycamore by a
deep pool and took a refreshing dip, ate a handful of Ramón's
seed meal and jogged on, feeling more at peace with himself than
for many years. With night came weariness and he scooped a
hollow for his body in a dry sandbar, covered himself with the
sun-warmed sand, and the earth seemed to envelop him like a
blessing as he fell asleep.

Toward mid-afternoon next day he recognized familiar landmarks, looked up and saw the outcropping of brown-gray rock
which contained the Cave of the Condors, the shrine to which
Tilhini had once conducted him and where he guessed the old
man might now have retired. As he climbed the steep path
amongst fragrant sage and prickly yucca, he saw the short
paunchy figure standing at the mouth of the huge scallop-shaped
opening. Instead of the coarse gray woolen shirt and trousers of
a ranch hand which he usually wore, Tilhini was naked and
painted red like himself and wore the sacred ceremonial skirt of
long dark condor feathers and the headdress of tall upright owl
and magpie plumes surrounded at the base by sacred white down
signifying clouds and sky power. Tilhini was painting the rock.
His brush of badger-tail hairs moved steadily from the tiny pigment containers at his belt to the wall of the cave and back.

Francisco remembered that the time honored solstice activities
of astrologer-priests like Tilhini were directed at placating supernatural forces, particularly those of the Sun, the Great Ruler, and
the Moon, the other great eye which watches the earth, and thus
were aimed at keeping the universe in balance and enabling human life to continue despite drought and pestilence and flood.
Ordinary people were not supposed to approach at these times

but Francisco relied on his special relationship with his former
mentor and advanced slowly in respectful silence.

He was surprised to see that Tilhini was painting not a sun disc
or moon crescent or a sacred condor, but a long black line of
settlers' wagons like those of the Jenkins family with white hoods
drawn by black mules following one another over a cliff into
oblivion.

Tilhini was painting to exorcise the white invader and Francisco's excitement rose because it made his arrival at this moment
seem especially propitious. The old man turned as if expecting
him and said simply: "You have come!"

Francisco was filled with joy by the intimacy and affection of
this welcome and burst out: "Old Father, I have come back! I
wish to be admitted again into the Indian way! I wish to receive
again from you my Indian name, Helek the Hawk, which you
gave me in my infancy and which I'd almost forgotten!" He was
surprised how true and strong these words sounded, coming from
deep down, like the gush of water from a spring.

"Very well, my son. I paint to preserve that way from those
who would obliterate it." He pointed to his work. "The rock
speaks my meaning. The Sky People may hear. But I have prepared myself for this moment over long hours, over long years,
so that I am sure of what I say. What about you? Are you sure?
I see you have brought your clothes with you."

"For special reasons, Old Father, that I may not disclose even
to you. Yes, I am sure. Look at me. Do you not see someone
new? I wish to take once more and for the rest of my life the
Indian way."

Tilhini smiled with pleasure but also with thoughtfulness. "My
son, I celebrate this moment. But let me speak truth. One does
not easily reenter the ancient path. First you must prepare yourself. Are you ready for the vision in which you may see the dream
helper who will guide you into the future? It is after that vision
that I may name you again and start you on your new course."

"I am ready!"

But Tilhini was not to be hurried.

"Have you lain with a woman during the past three days?"

"No!" Francisco declared, since indeed it had been four since
he'd stopped in San Luis at the home of a certain young widow.

"Have you recently eaten meat or greasy or salted foods? Such
things are hostile to the blood of the dream seeker!"

"Old Father, my hunger lies elsewhere! Except for a handful

of meal from Ramón, I've not eaten for two days!''

Still Tilhini would not be hurried. ''Suppose you spend the
night in contemplation of the stars who are the immortal First
People and are also the Great Ones from among our own ancestors? Ask them for guidance while your eyes remain open like
theirs. And tomorrow if you still are sure, I will prepare the dance.
Afterward you may have your dream.''

# Chapter Twelve

After stopping at his barber's for a shave Sedley reached his office on Portsmouth Square shortly before 8:00. Like nearly everyone in town he worked early and late, six days a week, often returning to his desk after supper, sometimes spending the night there. Yet such was the exhilaration of those heady days that he seldom felt tired. Forbes, his manager, handed him the calling card. It read: "COLONEL GEORGE STANHOPE."

"Good. We've been expecting him, haven't we? What's he like?"

Forbes, a sandy Scot, described the Colonel as impressive. "He's staying at the California House with his family. Says your fathers and grandfathers were friends."

"Yes—they did a little business in black ivory." Sedley winked, recalling silently how his grandfather Joshua Sedley established the family fortune by carrying rum to West Africa in exchange for slaves who were sold to Southern planters including George Stanhope's father and grandfather, then based in Georgia. Stanhope's recent letter recalled this old association and stated his intention of viewing California with an eye to business investment, a matter in which he deemed Sedley well informed. "I'll call on him this afternoon!" Pocketing the card Sedley moved on into his inner sanctum.

During his early years on the coast, when he acted as supercargo in his family's vessels, this old adobe, now his office, had been his northern headquarters. Along with a few others and a few ramshackle board buildings it constituted the sleepy Mexican village of Yerba Buena and looked out upon a "plaza" where loose horses wandered, cows were penned and brown-skinned children played in the sandy dust. Aside from its bleakness, fleas and perennially blowing sand Sedley liked the site because he saw its possibilities. He perceived that not far off was the day when Yerba Buena with its magnificent bay would be America's great Pacific port and its real estate and commerce of inestimable value.

Yet he still occupied the old adobe roofed with mossy red tiles, white-wash flaking from its walls. "Sedley's Hacienda," people jokingly called it; and quaintly odd it was, an anachronism amid new four-story hotels and elegant gambling houses. But he took pride in it. It evidenced his old Californianess, his long-established status, deliberate avoidance of ostentation. Its interior was divided by an earthen partition two and a half feet thick. The front room, occupied by Forbes and two clerks, was still called the trade room. In early days Sedley had slept regularly on its counter. From the back room, once a storeroom, he now directed his business empire.

Papers were waiting on his desk. A hundred things were demanding his attention yet he found himself thinking of his new cook. Why, he couldn't quite say. Partly it was the way she moved with quick gliding steps that roused his expectations. Partly it was his instant recognition—that moment they met—that here was a kindred spirit: quietly calculating, unsentimental, unafraid. What other kind would answer an advertisement from a stranger and travel two thousand miles alone to a new land? Yet he sensed something more: her unrevealed purposes. They fascinated him more than all the rest. What were they? How might he discover and possess them? "Am I getting softheaded?" he asked himself, suddenly exasperated. "Mooning like a schoolboy?"

At that moment he saw The Rat. Old friend, old annoyance, The Rat poked its long gray head through the crack in the floorboards near the opposite wall and eyed him impudently. Sedley drew a small black Deringer from the righthand pocket of his frock coat. Aiming carefully, he put a .41 caliber bullet through the rat's head. Then he calmly replaced the pistol and resumed studying the legal papers Ogles had prepared for him to take south for Clara to sign. Forbes opened the door in alarm.

"Are you all right, sir?"

Sedley replied casually: "Just The Rat, Forbes. I decided his time had come. There he is," indicating. "You may wish to give him decent burial."

Forbes examined the bloody remains. "You got him right through the noggin, sir!"

"Did my best," Sedley replied mildly. "Who knows when we'll be called to the field of honor these days? Thirty-five duels in the city already this year, they tell me. So we must keep our hand in, eh Forbes?" Sedley's cool gray eyes remained unblinking as usual. Sensing his mood, Forbes went out gravely carrying the rat by its long tail.

Rather wondering at his mood himself Sedley resumed his reading. He'd asked Ogles to prepare a power of attorney as well as authorization to represent Clara before the Land Commission. Both seemed necessary precautions in a battle which might be very long drawn out. Yet already he saw the possibility of having to postpone his southern trip because of Stanhope's arrival. While also on his desk lay word—in the form of his manifest, come by fast steamer mail via the Isthmus of Panama, only twenty-nine days from Boston—of the approach of Sedley & Company's newest clipper ship which might delay him further. Nevertheless he took pleasure at thought of the great vessel under full sail racing at this moment down the Atlantic toward the Horn. The *New Enterprise* was the largest and swiftest of her kind, designed by that master architect Donald McKay and built in McKay's yards at East Boston. She was 334 feet long, 53 feet broad, and carried 5,000 tons of freight. No other vessel had such an enormous sail area, her main yard alone being 120 feet long. And besides her three square-rigged masts she boasted a spanker mast with two gaff sails, Sedley remembered. Almost certainly she would cut the traditional six months' voyage to less than a hundred days, perhaps less than ninety, and thanks to her huge size she would more than pay for herself, $150,000, in one round trip. It was the kind of thought that made Sedley glow to the core.

Her manifest, more than twenty feet long as he unrolled it, listed almost everything needed to nourish the empire he was building: plows, printing presses, shovels, fresh New England pond ice packed in sawdust, fresh oysters, lobsters, apples, and cradles, coffins, house frames, furniture, dictionaries, clocks, clothing for men, women, children, even contraceptive devices. And as he imagined his beautiful new clipper bearing her burden so gracefully she reminded him of Mary Louise who so gracefully transformed his house into a home so that he looked forward to returning there this evening.

He called Forbes and they went over the manifest item by item, discussing current and future supply and demand, planning, calculating. Each day made a difference. They might have to reach an agreement with friendly merchants such as Coleman and Howard and with them corner the market on some items, warehouse others until prices were right. Nothing would be certain till the signal tower on Telegraph Hill wigwagged the news that the *New Enterprise* was entering Golden Gate. And even then there would be those last minute gambles Sedley loved.

# Chapter Thirteen

All night Francisco lay watching the stars. They seemed closer in the clear back country air. Some moved while he watched. Some were fixed in their wisdom. And when he prayed to the unwavering North Star, or Sky Coyote, benefactor of mankind, for steady guidance into the future, it was the first heartfelt prayer he had uttered in longer than he could remember.

Suddenly he felt transformed, renewed. And at that moment he heard the call of an actual coyote from the dark mountain side above—wild, uncanny, as if in answer to his prayer. His heart raced. He could hardly believe what was occurring. Old Tilhini on his bed of soft earth at the mouth of the cave stirred as if he sensed it too. When day came Francisco told him what had happened.

Still Tilhini sounded skeptical. "Remember, Coyote is a crafty rascal who takes many forms—trickster, prankster, adversary as well as friend."

"I have remembered that."

"Then you are sure you wish to embrace the Indian way?"

"I am."

"Very well." Tilhini took from his waistnet his magical cocoon rattle. "Sit here beside me on the Earth Mother. Close your eyes. Listen while I prepare the path."

Moving slowly around him in a circle, lifting and pressing each naked foot deliberately against the earth, Tilhini began shaking his rattle rhythmically. It was made of the dried cocoons of spirit moths. Each contained a pebble that rasped against the inner surface of its cocoon with a peculiar penetrating sound. Gradually the rhythmic insistence of this sound enveloped Francisco's consciousness, as he sat with eyes closed, until it seemed to represent all reality. He heard Tilhini asking: "Are you ready for your vision?"

"I welcome it!" Francisco opened his eyes dreamily as the rattling ceased. He watched Tilhini take six tiny white wafer-like seeds of the Jimson weed from the medicine bundle at his waist, place them in a small bowl of green serpentine rock, steep them in water from his gourd, mash them with the charmstone which hung by a thong from his neck. After tasting the mixture, Tilhini carefully added three drops of water, nodded gravely, handed the bowl to Francisco. "This is Momoy, Mother Truth. She enables us to see past, present and future clearly. But she is also death and must be treated with utmost respect. Drink, my son. Drink, then stretch yourself on the earth. And remember carefully everything you see in your dream vision."

At first Francisco saw nothing but those luminous shapes of many colors you sometimes see when you shut your eyes tightly. Then gradually he seemed to rise and float through the air. Then he was descending a long dark tunnel which was very dangerous though he could not quite tell why. After what seemed an interminable journey he emerged into a sunlit world which appeared strangely familiar, and he realized it was that long lost world of his youth and of his heroic uncle Asuskwa. Once again he'd arrived at the secret stronghold deep in the labyrinthine heart of the interior where Indians came from all over the land for refuge and trade and exchange of news and plans of resistance; and there he saw the stocky brown figure of his uncle, like his own, conferring earnestly with a group of chieftains, exhorting them to forget their differences, to unite and resist the invading white men. But one by one the chieftains' eyes glazed with inattention and soon they drifted away toward places where trade was in progress or games were being played or food eaten, until Francisco alone remained. He stepped forward and his uncle embraced him joyfully. "At last you have come! The quail have scattered, as you saw!" Asuskwa indicated the departing chieftains. "Soon we shall know if you are indeed Helek the Hawk, as you say!"

But Francisco had said nothing. Because suddenly he felt damned by his white blood. And as he endeavored to explain this important point he saw his uncle's smiling figure begin to fade into nothingness till he himself was left alone in the midst of a vast emptiness. All the great camp vanished. All the chieftains gone. He alone remaining. Until by a desperate effort he managed to shout into the emptiness: "Yes, I am Helek the Hawk!" And as if by magic he saw the figure of Asuskwa reappear and move toward him joyfully, accompanied overhead by a great dark bird.

When he waked he felt dizzy and nauseated. It seemed he'd been unconscious only a moment. Actually all day and all night had passed and dawn was breaking. Tilhini, seated crosslegged nearby, was bending toward him solicitously. "Gently, my son. One returns slowly from a long journey."

Francisco smelled the smoke of a campfire. He sat up and shook his head to clear it. "Drink this!" Tilhini held out a steaming bowl. As he sipped the broth, Francisco felt normalcy return. Yet he remained strangely elated, wonderfully transformed.

"Tell me of your vision!" Tilhini's voice was gently insistent. The old man seemed larger than life, enhanced by supernatural power.

Francisco told all that had happened in his dream. "What does it mean? I was once named for a hawk but that bird was too big for a hawk."

Tilhini nodded sagely as if a guess had been confirmed. "It means you are the true follower of your uncle. It means the blood that flowed in him flows in you, the spirit which guided him guides you!" Tilhini's voice rose with conviction. "The dark bird is Condor, your family's dream helper. Like your uncle in the days of his greatness, you too will lead your people!"

Francisco's thoughts raced wildly. Could this be believed? Could he actually reincarnate the spirit of the legendary hero who led the long bloody struggle against the white men, rallied the wayward tribes, planned the massive uprising which threatened to drive the invaders into the sea? But before he could think further, Tilhini's voice was saying: "The Sun our Father is rising. Let us proceed!"

Francisco straightened himself, the sun's rays full upon him. The seer was taking from his medicine bundle a white cord made of down from the breasts of condors and eagles.

First holding it gravely up to the sunrise, Tilhini lowered it and placed it in a circle on the earth surrounding Francisco. "My son," he pronounced solemnly, "again you are Helek the Hawk, the far flyer, the peerless hunter," and Tilhini added in a different voice, one charged with powerful intensity, "the leader your people have awaited so long!"

Francisco was appalled by the enormity of what Tilhini said. In apprehension he gasped out: "Show me the way, O wise old man!"

Tilhini smiled enigmatically. "He who holds the secret of the world holds the power of becoming. And so, my son, I leave you to find your own path."

"But where am I to go? What am I to do?" Francisco cried, still bewildered.

But like the figure in his dream vision Tilhini seemed to be receding. "That is up to you. I can go no farther."

And even as he spoke, Francisco's eyes rested with astonishment on a faint trail, imperceptible before, which led on up the mountain above them.

# Chapter Fourteen

Holding his lantern high in the early morning darkness, Mornay stretched out his other hand and felt the heads of lettuce stacked high at the back of the wagon. They were crisp and firm. "Garibaldi, they'll bring top price!"

Tony Petrini's face shone like a ruddy moon from under a battered straw hat. Tony went by the nickname of Garibaldi because of his vociferous support of that great patriot's efforts to bring freedom to his native Italy. "How the market, Mist' Mornay?"

"I'll take all you've brought." Mornay could count on Tony's lettuce, the tenderness of his celery and green peas, the rich red ripeness of his tomatoes. Today he'd even brought some early sweet corn. "Reuben will help you unload."

Since long before dawn Mornay and Reuben Stapp, his assistant, a full-blooded Negro, had been at their stall at the Great Pacific Market receiving produce brought by growers from the surrounding countryside. Next in the line of carts was Otto Eckhard's. Otto would probably be difficult. His produce was like well-disciplined children: of uniform quality, but slightly lacking in flavor. "Dees potato bring sixty cent!" He stubbornly insisted.

"Potatoes aren't likely to bring more than fifty today, Otto. If I get more, you get more. If I get less, you get less."

"But dees de vinest! Look!" holding up one which weighed at least four pounds.

Mornay shrugged. It was their usual ritual. "Take them somewhere else if you like. You might do better."

"No, you de bess!"

Next came bandy-legged Pedro, a Spanish Californian rooted like his plants for many decades in native soil. Aided by a tribe of family and relatives, Pedro painstakingly raised the finest onions, garlic, green and red peppers as well as delicious peaches, plums and cherries in his plot on the southern outskirts near old Mission Dolores. Yet his produce was distinguished by a natural grace and flavor as if left alone to flourish in sweet idleness. And though it was always of top quality, Mornay as usual put on a doleful face as he inspected it and shook his head. "*Este no vale nada*, Pedro! Pedro, this stuff is no good!" And as usual Pedro appeared crestfallen, then brightened as he realized Mornay was merely teasing. French, Irish, Chinese as well as Anglo-American growers followed, so that all together they brought Mornay not only the products of their toil and skill but a cross section of humanity. Like him many had been unsuccessful gold miners, then found their true vocation in a quite different product of the soil.

This motley group was the human melting pot from which he felt himself derived, people close to the earth who made their livings by the sweat of their brows, who would some day, he hoped, inherit the earth in the Biblical sense and thus prevail in that ongoing struggle for its rulership which so dearly concerned him.

Although Eliot Sedley owned the market and the land on which they stood—literally owned the roof over their heads and the ground under their feet—during these early morning encounters Mornay felt himself the true proprietor of his surroundings, alive in every nerve, keenly enjoying each moment, the possessor of life itself.

"All right, fellows," he cajoled, "let's not be all day!" as some stopped to gossip, impeding others. Amid renewed confusion of voices, squeals of animals, cracks of whips and creaks of wheels, he and Reuben supervised the unloading of the wagons, barrows, donkeys, mules, horses and human backs on which the produce had been transported. Before dawn the motley caravan was gone. He and Reuben arranged their merchandise for sale, while quiet momentarily reigned.

Soon after daylight buyers began appearing from hotels and restaurants, vessels in the harbor, from steamship companies like Caleb Wright's Inter-Ocean Line and the Inland Rivers Line and from private kitchens. The lean, brown-eyed, affirmative-mannered merchant was popular with these clients too, for they knew that from him they received their money's worth. And also sustaining him this morning was the thought of Martha and David and the prospect of seeing them when he got home. By eleven there was a lull, and after attending to his accounts and correspondence and engaging in conversation with fellow merchants, Mornay prepared to leave for the noon hour.

"Can you handle things a while?" he asked Reuben. "Reduce those strawberries five cents if they don't move."

Reuben nodded. He understood the business nearly as well as Mornay. Their bond ran deep. A year ago Reuben had helped Mornay defend his newly purchased Montgomery Street lot from claim jumpers by standing guard all night with loaded shotguns, one watching while the other slept. By law no Negro could give evidence in court for or against a white man, but the opposite was not true and when The Ducks attempted to intimidate Reuben forcibly, Mornay haled them before Judge Parker on assault charges.

Reuben slept in the back of the produce stall. It saved him money. Mornay paid him fifteen dollars a day and a cash bonus at the end of each month which varied with the rise and fall of profits. When questioned by the incredulous about this unique sharing, Mornay replied it was not only good ethics but good business. "You get more out of a fellow when he knows he's working for himself, too." Reuben was saving to buy a lot and build his own house.

"I'll be back soon after dinner," Mornay concluded. "We'll clear everything out by the end of the day as usual."

And leaving the market he made his way through that surging night-and-day throng which crowded Montgomery Street like blood rushing through the heart of the city, pumped and re-pumped down all its side streets too by driving ambition, and gold, and so began to climb the slope of Telegraph Hill toward his home.

# Chapter Fifteen

Clara slept restlessly after her quarrel with Francisco and the mutilation of the sacred oak by the squatters. Thought of that terrible moment which had seen her disown her son, and he her, brought her wide awake staring into empty darkness again and again. It overshadowed the violence of Buck Jenkins, threatening though that was. Had she been too hasty, too severe? And Francisco likewise? Was all her love and hope for him, all his potential to do something worthwhile in life, wasted?

Yet she remembered his new bearing when he returned from his ordeal at the grove. What did it mean? Had the shock of that experience brought him to his senses at last?

The thought gave her renewed hope. Perhaps it was not too late. She regretted rejecting in her anger his offer of reconciliation and resolved to make one of her own with calm affection that would express her inexhaustible love for him. There was too much at stake. Their future and that of the ranch and all its people hung in the balance. Surely it was a time to forget differences and face difficulties together.

Day was breaking when she woke. The tap at the door would be María Ignácia bringing hot chocolate. Clara called out cheerfully: "Enter, with God!"

María's ample figure filled the doorway. "May this day find you in good health, Señora!" Sitting on the end of the bed while her mistress sipped the chocolate, she confided the news. "Señor Francisco has disappeared!"

Clara looked up and put her chocolate down. "What do you mean?"

"He has taken the trail into the back country, naked in the oldtime Indian way except for waistnet and moccasins. Ramón saw him go."

"This must be one more of his charades!" Clara snorted, setting cup and saucer aside with determination and getting out of bed. "Come, let us see for ourselves!"

They found the door of his room wide open, things strewn about, bow and arrows gone from the wall, red ochre powder in the bowl on the table by the guttered out candle, and at sight of that candle Clara's anger rose again, for it seemed to represent Francisco and all the hope for him which had flamed in her as recently as last night. "He'll be back when the novelty wears off!" she scoffed. "He'll not live like a wild one for long. How like him to run away just when he's needed most!"

"Shall I tidy the room?"

"No, leave all as it is. We're done picking up after him!" Glancing out the window toward the dawn she added: "And ring the bell. It's time for prayer!"

There were obligations more compelling than personal woe. Whatever might befall, she was still mistress of Rancho Olomosoug. And when the people of her household and those who came as usual from the Indianada were assembled in the courtyard, more than a hundred in all, there in the coolness of first light, she knelt with them and led them in prayer:

> "Here comes the dawn,
> Making way for the day,
> Let us all say, 'Hail, Mary!' "

And then for the benefit of her secret self and of many there who felt likewise, she uttered the ancient Indian prayer her mother Koyo, the chieftainess, had taught her:

> "Great dawn, Breath of the Sun,
> You bring light to the world!
> You bring light to the world!
> May we prove worthy!"

Having thus addressed herself to her respective sources of faith, Clara went to breakfast feeling much better. Afterward with María she inspected the many functions of her enormous household. Ranged around the courtyard and in buildings adjacent was a maze of workrooms. First they visited the weavery where wool from her sheep was carded and patiently woven into cloth. Spinning wheel and shuttle were moving busily under the skilled hands of two Indian women, María Santísima and María Theresa, with whom Clara exchanged professional words. And next she visited the sewing room where garments were made and repaired by María Carolina and María Ana. Next it was the candlemaking room where tallow from her cattle was converted into candles by women and girls filling iron molds with warm kidney fat and allowing it to cool there around wicks. Then she went to the tannery presided over by Abelardo where she made sure that the fresh hides were being properly fleshed and the lime adequately slaked for removing the hair.

Outside the door of the harness and saddle shop she greeted old Miguel who rose from his stool and doffed his hat. He was patiently braiding a reata from long strips of rawhide coiled in a tub, while inside a dozen other skilled hands fashioned finely cured leather into harnesses, saddles, bridles, belts, and other useful items.

Still accompanied by María Ignácia, to whom from time to time she gave instructions to be carried out later, she visited the butcher shop where meat from two freshly killed bullocks was being prepared. Then it was the butter and cheese room where milk from forty cows was processed and then to the grist mill where wheat was being ground into flour by youthful Arturo, who drove a blindfolded donkey in a circle, yoked to a beam that rotated one huge round stone upon another, and then the carpenter shop and blacksmith shop and washing and ironing room, and the shop of Vicente the shoemaker, and the winery and the bakery and finally the kitchen hung with pots and pans, strings of red pepper and smoked tongues and hams where Rafaela presided among savory aromas of garlic and onions and marvelous simmering stews.

With each visitation, Clara felt herself grow stronger, reconnected to life again after the shock of Francisco's disappearance, while her people watched to see how the news was affecting her, much as they looked toward the mountains for daily weather signs. But she held herself proudly and gave no indication of distress.

After visiting the vegetable garden, where Jesús and Juan and their boy helpers tended a vast bounty, including the melons which made it famous, she went to the orchard where apricots were being picked, and then the vineyard where grapes were still green. Finally she returned to the house and entered the school-room where Bernardina Ferrer, daughter of her friend Santiago who owned the store in town, taught the children of her people to read and write in Spanish and English. Bernardina was a spinster more interested in ideas than in men. She was standing holding *McGuffey's New Eclectic Reader* in one hand, speaking in loud clear tones, her pupils repeating after her: "He was not a big boy. If he had been a big boy, he would have been wiser. But he was a little boy."

Clara greeted her formally: "Good morning, Señorita!" And then continued intimately: "And how is *this* little boy doing?" placing her arm around the shoulders of diminutive Alejandro, son of a seamstress.

"Alejandro is bright, but he doesn't work hard enough," Bernardina replied earnestly.

"Then box his ears, or I will," Clara retorted, tweaking one of them. "You hear me, Alejandro, you rascal? One more report like this and I'll hitch you in place of the donkey that turns the millstone. That's the place for donkeys." The child reddened as his classmates laughed, and Alejandro resolved not to be singled out again by the Señora.

When she had inspected these operations which made her hacienda such a living organism and she herself so vital to it, she went to her bedroom to dress for that part of the day she loved best, which she had shared for so many precious years with her husband. Today it would be with Pacifico and Isidro. They were waiting, hats in hands, as she stepped back into the courtyard wearing her divided leather skirt so that she could ride astride like a man. Pacifico held the reins of her bay mare while she mounted, noting with approval that he wore the silver-buckled belt she'd bequeathed him. Without mentioning his father's disappearance, she reminded: "You are head of this house now. See that you behave accordingly. While obeying your grandmother's wishes!"

He answered dutifully: "Yes, Mamá Grande!"

"Isidro, are the colts ready to be broken?"

"As you may desire, Señora. We can see." Isidro, wonderfully knowledgeable about horses and cattle, was a gentle giant, amiable as sunlight until roused to anger, his color between black and brown—the color of an acorn that has lain long upon damp earth.

"Then let us go!"

Mounting, the two men departed after her at a gallop, as they rode first to view the ripening wheat which reached nearly to their saddles as it turned to a mellow gold. In lieu of a fence, a ditch four feet wide, four feet deep, protected the crop but somehow three Jenkins mules had gotten into it. "Come, we'll teach them a lesson!" Clara cried. And at a run, whacking fleeing rumps with the ends of their reatas, they sent the mules flying. And her spirits rose still higher as they galloped on into the Hills of the Long Grass, where her livestock congregated most and thrived best, open hills rising like waves against the dark wall of chaparral mountains, holding in their hollows many fine living places for cattle and horses. These were the hills where as a girl she'd come with her mother and other women to gather seeds, beating them into baskets with woven fans, gathering herbs and flowers too, singing as they worked, the great days perfect upon them in unbroken harmony of time, so it seemed now. For nine thousand years her people and their predecessors had gathered food upon these hills, and something of this continuity welled up in Clara as a kind of tribal knowledge or gene memory, rooting her in joy and strength to the earth around her and under her mare's flying feet.

Old harmonies might pass. She was dedicated to creating new ones. Yes, that was her still unbroken purpose. Fiercely she reaffirmed it with a shout of gladness. Pacifico and Isidro exchanged glances. Her eccentric ways were familiar to them and famous throughout the valley. People said Francisco inherited his idiosyncratic behavior from her—that very thing which galled her so—for she was at heart a rebel, too.

They galloped on. "That *mañada* there!" she pointed to a band of horses which came running with neighs to inspect them. "It must be brought in, Isidro! I see the colts need riding!" And a little later: "Pacifico, there's a swollen jaw. Catch him!" pointing to a steer with head held low, infected by foxtail burr or snakebite, and the two men lassoed him and Isidro lanced the pus-filled head with his knife while she observed unflinching, for this also was part of the day's work; and then the three passed from the hills down into the river's sudden gorge where they found cattle congregated lazily in the shade of huge cottonwoods by the cool water and every blade of grass eaten. "Out, lazybones, and find food elsewhere!" she exclaimed but did not enforce the order now in the heat of the day lest it strip away precious fat from animals destined for the new herd she must send to San Francisco, but commanded it be done later by Isidro and his vaqueros so that the range be not overgrazed at this point.

Thought of the new herd reminded her of Francisco who must have passed here the night before on his way into the back country, and riding a little apart from where the cattle had made tracks she saw his footprints in the trail going eastward. They reopened her sorrow, and her anger, and a further thought: back there, somewhere, she knew, the wild ones lived, keeping up a fierce if doomed resistance to the white man's way, that way she had embraced. Since her brother's death all those years ago they had never attacked her, though she'd continually expected them. Yet while they raided other outlying ranches, killing, maiming, setting buidings afire, driving off horses and butchering cattle, they let her alone. Perhaps it is because of my Indianada, she thought, and my middle way which is open to both worlds, and to which wild ones have come. Or perhaps it was their grim recollection of their terrible losses that night when her husband and brother received fatal wounds. Sometimes she admired the broncos—the wild ones—for their unwavering devotion to a purpose, at others deplored their blindness in not following her example.

And then they galloped northward into a strange region intermediate between fertility and barrenness, where peaks that were neither hills nor mountains rose, and growth that was neither tree nor bush but comprised both prevailed. This was fine grazing country earlier in the year when the grass exposed to sunlight on heights free from frost sprang up, but was almost deserted now except for a few half-wild cows with unbranded calves. Sight of the calves prompted her to announce: "We must make rodeo here soon and mark these and others before they grow too old!"

Descending again they came to the strange North Fork, neither creek nor river but flowing intermittently, sometimes with sweet water, sometimes with foul, sometimes containing dark asphaltum which seeped from the earth at one special place on its bank to which her people had come to collect tar for waterproofing baskets and jugs and for fastening spear and arrow points to shafts. Near this spot her father had been bitten by a rattlesnake and died, and to pay respect she rode apart again to the red stone marker beside the stream, its paint weathered and flaking. There, when she was still a girl, they had burned his body on a funeral pyre. From there his spirit had flown westward to the Land of the Dead. "And this they would take away from me?" she demanded aloud, of the sky, of the universe, thinking of that distant world of commissions, lawyers, documents. "No one shall, ever!" And she resolved to do battle to the last breath in her body because of all that was entrusted to her and all she represented.

Beyond the tar spring, a finger of true wilderness came down, a forest of dense green oaks descending like the freshet of a flood from the hinterland, pouring on up the backs of those noble hills which faced the ranch house. In this mysterious place where voracious bears and lions lurked in perpetual shadow, she felt herself at the fingerpoint of the wild, her humanity challenged by it; and as the three moved quietly across its floor of fallen leaves, a huge ruddy colored grizzly feeding upon the cow it had just killed, reared itself on hindlegs, snout and claws bloody, to see what had disturbed its feast. Six, seven, eight feet it rose. "Let's get him!" she cried with fierce delight. All three flew at him, reatas whirling.

He gave a roar as Pacifico's reata encircled one forefoot. But his breath was soon choked off as Isidro's loop closed over his neck. Then Clara deftly snatched both hind feet with hers. Within a trice, the fearsome beast lay stretched and helpless, slowly throttled, then with a mighty convulsion which jerked all three horses nearly to their knees, dead.

Dismounting and loosening their nooses, Pacifico cut off its five-inch-long claws to carry home as trophies, handing Clara a pair connected by a strip of hide which she draped across her saddlehorn. Skinners and muleteers would come for the pelt and the carcass, from which steaks and magic medicines would be made. Suddenly she was very weary but made herself go on.

At a gallop they surged upward with the trees and burst out upon grassy hilltops overlooking ranch and valley. Somberly she led the way to the nearby summit. There under a solitary oak her husband Antonio lay buried. There she had had her girlhood's dream vision of his coming. There she often paid homage but never, it seemed, more so than at this moment.

Dismounting she stood silent beside the pile of stones, the others keeping a distance. Never had she felt herself so beset yet in a fundamental way so joyous. Life had her in its grip. It was as if she once again felt the fierce embrace of Antonio's love, using her for a purpose.

Inspired, she looked with clear eyes out over the valley. Below, spreading like a fan toward the sea, it lay dotted with the wagons and cabins of its new American settlers. Hazy in the distance, clustered about the mission tower, were the ancient adobes and newly erected frame buildings of the town. Beyond them she saw the magnificent white line of sand dunes and blue curve of bay, the great bay of Portolá, so named by her husband for his mentor, the conquistador leader. And as she looked, the vision she'd shared with Antonio, of a place open to all, shared by all, glowed more brightly than ever.

Faith renewed, grizzly claws dangling from her saddlehorn, she rode down toward her valley and the rising cabin of the Jenkins family, around which figures were working, axes flashing in the sun.

# Chapter Sixteen

When he woke after his first night in Mornay's house and looked out the window, David thought it was going to rain; but a few minutes later when he walked into the kitchen, Wing Sing assured him that the low clouds were merely fog and would soon disappear. David was eager to start painting the house as agreed with Mornay. Martha urged him to wait until her father returned. "Don't rush ahead," she counseled precociously. "You might get into trouble as you did yesterday!" reminding him of his scuffle with The Ducks.

"And waste half a day?" David protested. "Your father wouldn't like that!"

"How do you know he wouldn't?" she retorted. David looked down with amusement at this pigtailed twelve-year-old. Her restraint was the opposite of his impetuosity, as Wing's eye was quick to perceive. Thus each moment they were together was apt to produce a reaction. "You two velly compatible!" Wing commented smiling broadly.

"We get along, eh Marty?" David meant it as a joke but Martha considered it thoughtfully.

"Sometimes we do, sometimes we don't!" she concluded with such solemnity that he burst out laughing and Wing smiled even more broadly.

After breakfast Wing showed him the cellar workroom containing ladder, brushes, kegs of white lead, oil and other ingredients which Mornay had accumulated in preparation for the painting. "Velly spensif!" Wing explained. "Evelyting San Flancisco velly spensif. One blush, five dolla!''

"Then I won't blush, Wing!" David teased. Wing grinned but secretly wondered if David was going to join the ranks of those who denigrated John Chinaman. Wing's neck still ached from the miner's blow.

Beginning at the front of the house, David threw himself into the painting with usual ardor. Soon the fog began to lift and he was humming happily to himself in bright sunlight, high on his ladder, brush moving back and forth as Mornay's house assumed a white coat like those New England ones dear to Mornay's heart. Martha came out to appraise his performance. She carried the sketch pad which had been her constant companion on shipboard until packed in her trunk for disembarking. Her penciled likenesses of him and Mary Louise had been quite strikingly good, often with a humorous touch, and she prepared to do another now, looking up at him as he perched against the front of the house. "How do you know it's the right shade of white?" she demanded skeptically.

"It's just the primer coat. We can lighten or darken the next one. What's the dif? You're not doing a watercolor, are you?"

"No, just a portrait of Mr. Know It All perching for a fall!" she retorted, pencil moving swiftly across her pad. Ignoring her, David worked on, humming to himself. A bluff voice surprised him.

"When you've finished, young man, what then?"

Glancing down, he saw peering up at him a barrel-chested, walrus-mustached, hearty-looking man wearing the gold-braided cap of a sea captain but dressed in civilian broadcloth.

"What then? Then I'll look for work elsewhere!" he replied frankly, noting Martha had disappeared, probably just around the corner of the house and still within hearing.

"I like a man who sings while he works!" the bluff stranger declared. "Where you hail from?"

"New York City."

"So do I. What did you do there?"

"Worked as a clerk at Newell's Store."

"Ah, Newell! I know Newell! Member of my church! I'm Captain Caleb Wright. I head the Inter-Ocean Steamship Company here. How would you like to clerk for me?"

David was taken aback by this sudden offer but replied tactfully: "I suppose that would depend on the pay."

Wright grinned. "Cagey fellow, aren't you! What about twenty dollars a day?"

David was nearly overcome at mention of such a princely sum but his first impulse was to decline out of loyalty to Mornay. Then he remembered the merchant's invitation to live with him was conditional on his finding better employment. Surely Mornay would not fault him for improving his lot. Still he hesitated.

"Come, young man. I'm offering you the chance of a lifetime: a position with the largest firm on the Pacific Coast. We run ships from New York to Panama, from Panama to San Francisco. How did you get here?"

"On the *Pacific Queen*."

"That's my ship. I brought you here. You're as good as part of my organization already!" asserted the emphatic Captain. "What do you say?"

David was favorably impressed. Wright seemed to embody the robust confident spirit of this new frontier. "I accept!"

"Good. But before we shake on it let me ask one question!" The Captain became suddenly serious. "Do you indulge in strong drink?"

"A nip now and then."

"Do you realize it's a passport to hell?"

"I never thought of it that way."

Wright's voice hardened. "Young man, I'm not joking. I employ only those who touch no liquor. I touch none myself. Drink leads to the three 'Ds'—dishonesty, debauchery, damnation. Are you willing to work for me under those conditions?"

For a moment David didn't know whether to take this extraordinary statement at face value, then decided he would. "For twenty dollars a day I'd work for you under any conditions!"

Wright beamed. "Come down from that ladder and shake hands. I pride myself on being a judge of character. I see great promise in you, my boy!" David felt a grip that evidently meant business. "What does that bruise under your eye mean?"

David told of his fight with The Ducks.

"I like a fighter. When can you begin work?"

"When I finish this job. Day after tomorrow?"

"Tomorrow!" Wright broke out emphatically. "Oh, I know Mornay. He drives a hard bargain. But I drive a harder. Tomorrow or nothing!"

David hesitated, again remembering his agreement with Mornay, but an innate desire to please coupled with the vision of twenty daily dollars and the Captain's powerful insistence overcame lingering doubts. "Tomorrow!"

Wright's smile widened. "You won't regret this! Seven-and-a-half o'clock. Corner of Merchant and Montgomery!"

And the redoubtable Captain strode off down the hill as if the city below were his, which indeed much of it was.

Martha's head poked around the corner of the house. Her face wore a look of disapproval. "You shouldn't have done that! I said you were perching for a fall!"

"It's none of your business, Nosey!" David replied good humoredly. "Now, scat!" shaking his brush at her, thinking how much twenty dollars might buy him in this dazzling new city of San Francisco.

# Chapter Seventeen

As Francisco climbed higher he noticed for the first time how the boughs of pines and firs around him seemed to be reaching like human hands for light, and when he heard the song of the spotted breasted fox sparrow, the finest singer in all the mountains, it seemed to be directed expressly at him. Glancing down he noticed a solitary black beetle laboring up the slope like himself. Everything around him seemed alive and full of meaning, joined to him and he to it as never before.

The day was still young when he reached the summit. With wonder he saw the seven ranges perceptible from nowhere else, and realized he was standing on the crest of Iwihinmu, the Sacred Mountain, at the heart of his mother's people's world, "from which everything is visible," the ancient Indian world which he had never truly entered before. As he looked he felt his spirit enlarge. Northward lay the Sierra Nevadas like a line of snow-capped islands floating in sky above the Central Valley's summer haze. Southward the Channel Islands made a dark line floating in water. Eastward the deserts stretched beyond imagination in their desolation. Westward lay those fertile coastal lowlands he knew so well, fostering all manner of life and beauty and now a newly arrived menace in the form of the squatters. Beyond the fringes of these horizons, he was aware, lay an entire state, an entire continent, which had once belonged to his mother's people and those like them and by heritage to himself and other native Americans. And now it was being usurped by the invading whites, and that mighty rage which rose in him when he saw what Buck had done to the sacred tree began to rise again.

Breathing a long forgotten prayer to Kakunupmawa the Sun, Francisco took the remaining seed meal from his pouch and scattered it as offering and proceeded along the new path Tilhini had shown him.

He was almost expecting the village when he came suddenly upon it, concealed in a shoulder of the mountain among giant pines and boulders. A spring gushed into a meadow where children played and horses grazed. Various types of native houses were grouped around the meadow, some the circular thatched huts of the lowlands, some conical frameworks of poles with skins stretched over them, some made of rocks and slabs of bark like those of mountain dwellers. As if still in his dream vision Francisco saw people moving among the houses in a way that seemed strangely unreal: men at work chipping stone arrowheads or fashioning bows or crafting wooden bowls with stone knives or cleaning modern rifles; while at the base of the giant boulders women ground seeds with stone pestles in bedrock mortars, and seated in doorways others wove baskets or sewed garments.

Though on later occasions he would be stopped by sentinels before he reached it, this time he went straight to the heart of the village unheralded as if still in his magic state of the night before, and people came to greet him warmly as if expecting him. Had they known? While he slept had Tilhini somehow sent them word?

Some of the men were as naked as he. Some were clothed. Many of the women's upper bodies were bare too in the traditional way. Some wore white women's garments. Some of both he recognized by their distinctive body painting as his mother's people and his. Others were clearly strangers. It was a varied collection. Yet all their faces seemed marked by stern experience. And he noticed how the men kept weapons handy despite the atmosphere of tranquility. Clearly here was a village of refugees and resisters. He had guessed its existence. The reality was more compelling. It seemed a fulfillment of his vision.

Filled with power, he stood among them with a glad heart, as the young chief, stocky and naked like himself, bade him welcome and asked his identity.

"I am a fugitive. I come seeking refuge."

"All who seek refuge are welcome here."

But the astrologer-priestess, the wild counterpart of Tilhini, interjected suspiciously: "Perhaps he is a spy. Let us hear him say why he has come." Nipamu's upper body and bare breasts were striped with glaring red and black paint and below she wore a red-dyed skirt of deerskin. She was neither young nor old but Francisco felt her to be jealous and remorseless.

He told of his treatment at the hands of Buck Jenkins and his subsequent decision to turn against the white man's world and defy it and journey into the wilderness, but when he began to describe Tilhini painting the black wagons falling over a cliff into oblivion, Nipamu interrupted scornfully: "We do more than paint to exorcise the invader. We have closed the passes to his cattle herds. We have raided into the outskirts of his cities and put fear and trembling into his heart, and our hands have reddened with his blood. Are you prepared to do likewise?"

It was a question Francisco had asked himself and found difficult to answer. He was prepared to take Buck's life. But what about Eliot Sedley, Ogles and other friends? So he replied ambivalently: "I shall do whatever I must. I am here to be one of you."

She was not convinced. "You are a famous man. You will be recognized, perhaps bring trouble upon us." And turning to the many who by now had gathered including councilors and other leaders, she cried accusingly: "See, he even carries his clothes in his waistnet so he may become a white man again whenever he wishes!"

Francisco responded forcibly: "My clothes will permit me to mingle among whites, learn their plans, bring you invaluable information. Do not mistrust me! All we've ever needed is unity of action!" He recalled the uprising led by his uncle and that later resistance which, until overwhelmed by hordes of whites brought by the Gold Rush, threatened coastal settlements. "We are part of a continuing struggle which began with our fathers and grandfathers. United, we can continue it!"

But Winai, the young chief, objected: "We are few. How can we unite the many?"

Francisco answered: "During my life I have roamed far. I know many of our people. Given time I can visit them and persuade them to join us in concerted resistance. My dream helper tells me it is possible!"

One disillusioned veteran shook his head. "If the whites continue to multiply, they will surely overwhelm us!"

Francisco was surprised by his own words, for he had never thought of them till now, and he knew they were inspired by his dream vision. "What is the alternative? Supine surrender? So that we are dispossessed or murdered or both, or become slaves, or become like those who sit with backs against the saloon in town, the butt of jokes and blows? Resistance in itself is a virtue. It keeps the flame alight and the door open toward possibilities."

But Nipamu scoffed: "And while you travel the country talking of unity we are left to do the fighting?"

Francisco realized he must take action which would convince them of his integrity, so he told of his plan to revenge himself upon Buck Jenkins. "I have promised him he will feel my rope. Before he dies I shall humiliate him publicly, as a lesson to others."

"Well spoken," said one elder with white hair down to his shoulders who had fought Spaniards, then Mexicans, and now Americans. "This is the man of vision and courage we need. Who of my age does not remember his famous uncle who tried to unite us and, even without doing so, threatened to sever the mission chain, which yoked so many of us in bondage? He is right when he says our people are still numerous if widely scattered. Together we may yet prevail. Let him be listened to and welcomed, I say!"

There followed a spirited debate in which both men and women participated freely in a manner which astonished Francisco. At last it was agreed that raids upon ranches and travelers to provide booty and supplies be continued, while steps were taken to bring tribes and remnants of tribes into concerted action against the whites. But Nipamu insisted that nothing be done until she consulted the Sky Powers as to the propitious time and no one dared cross her in this statement of her prerogatives.

Francisco realized it was a clever ruse to place him in her power and keep others there, yet he had no choice but to accept for the present.

# Chapter Eighteen

Delayed by her vigil in front of the hotel in Portsmouth Square, Mary Louise did not reach the Great Pacific Market until nearly noon. Unaware Mornay had just left, she walked down the broad central aisle of the huge barnlike structure fragrant with aromas of fresh vegetables and fruits and fish and pungent cheeses, her eyes searching for her old friend, her mind full of Hattie.

By the provisions of the Fugitive Slave Law* a slave owner or his agent could recover a runaway slave anywhere in the United States. They could arrest an alleged fugitive and bring him or her before a magistrate, and if able to convince that magistrate of the validity of their claim, they could return the runaway to slavery. The fugitive or even someone falsely accused could offer no defense, could not testify in any way, and was allowed no trial by jury. Penalties for aiding or abetting runaways were severe: a thousand-dollar fine and six months in jail. She must move carefully. Then she remembered, with sharp self-reproach, she was thinking only of the Federal Fugitive Slave Law, that California had one of its own and she did not know its provisions. But certainly for Hattie there were the risks of beating, torture, mutilation, at least severe punishment; for herself fines, jailing, exposure—the latter perhaps worst of all. She could not afford to fail.

Next the stall of a noisy Greek fishmonger who insisted she

*part of the Compromise of 1850 which admitted California to the Union inspect a display of what he claimed were freshly caught lobsters, though they had no claws,* she noticed the modest sign: "C. Mornay, Produce." It hung above a wonderfully rich variety of vegetables and luscious looking berries and melons. But instead of her old friend she saw an impressive young black man.

"I've just landed. I'm looking for Mr. Charles Mornay?"

Reuben Stapp's close-cropped hair made his head appear sculpted in classical fashion. His large eyes shone upon her benignly. "Mr. Mornay left earlier than usual. His daughter's just landed too."

She sensed Reuben's decency and was inclined to trust him but experience made her wary. "I'm sorry to miss him. I was told to look him up." She made herself sound quite distraught.

"Perhaps I can help, Ma'am," Reuben offered. "What might you need?"

"I hear he has the best vegetables in town."

"He does. Let me show you."

As they moved from lettuce to cabbages to carrots to artichokes, Mary felt each head and bunch critically with expert fingers, astonished by their size and quality. Reuben explained: "It's the year-round growing season and the virgin soil."

"But some of these potatoes must weigh five pounds!"

"Some of our cabbages weigh fifty!"†

"My," she exclaimed laughing in amazement, "I heard California was full of wonders, but nothing like this!" And all at once she decided to probe Reuben on what was uppermost in her mind. Lowering her voice she said significantly: "They told me the railroad has reached here. I didn't know whether to believe them."

There was no railroad within a thousand miles of San Francisco. Reuben glanced at her sharply. She closed her left eye deliberately and at the same time scratched the back of her neck with her right hand in the accepted sequence. He looked around. There was no one else in the stall. In the buzz of conversation from those nearby there was little danger of them being overheard. So Reuben decided to risk a limited exposure. She was not the first who'd come to Mornay's stall for help.

"Yes, the tracks have reached here," he replied guardedly.

*California lobsters are clawless
†Mornay's records speak of fifteen-pound carrots and tomatoes twenty-six inches in circumference

"They're not in good working order yet. But the trains are running. Are you perhaps thinking of purchasing a ticket?"

Mary confided enough of her experiences with Mornay to convince Reuben of her genuiness. But she decided to say nothing of Hattie, only of her need for reliable Negro household servants.

"I can put you in touch with our colored community," he offered. "There's more than five hundred of us and we're nearly everywhere, into nearly everything."

It was just what she wanted to hear. "I'm particularly anxious to contact someone working in the California Hotel. A maid, perhaps. Would you know anyone there?"

Reuben nodded. "I can help."

And having progressed thus far toward her goal, Mary Louise purchased the vegetables and berries for the sumptuous repast she was planning that evening for Sedley and his two companions. "You'll put all this on Mr. Sedley's account? I'm his new housekeeper."

Reuben nodded, secretly a little alarmed, wondering what connections she might have with such a personage as Sedley. It didn't seem in keeping with the confidence they had just exchanged. Sensing this, she gave his arm that same reassuring yet inviting touch she'd given Mornay's and Sedley's. "I'll be shopping again soon. Please tell Mr. Mornay I was here."

As he approached his house, Mornay was astonished to see it already partially painted, David hard at work, and even more astonished when he heard what had happened. "I'm sorry I can't finish the job. I hope you'll forgive me. The Captain was very insistent."

"It's like him," Mornay muttered, trying to conceal his disappointment. "I guessed you'd get ahead. But not quite so fast. At least you can room and board here as long as you like."

At lunch Martha wasn't so charitable. "Somebody thinks he's too good for us!" treating David as if he were not in the room.

"Daughter, watch your words," Mornay reprimanded. "We can't blame him for wanting to better himself. Everyone has a right to do that."

"But he should finish the job! I told him not to start it till you came. If he'd listened to me he wouldn't have got himself into this pickle!"

David felt increasingly uncomfortable. He'd never before broken an agreement such as he'd made with Mornay, but hoped that in the newness and excitement of San Francisco such aberrations might be overlooked. Now he wasn't so sure.

"Don't worry," Mornay consoled him. "It's not the end of the world." Though disappointed he still had faith in David's goodness and idealism which had struck him so powerfully during their conversation the evening before. "I know Wright put pressure on you. That's his way. He'll take you up onto the mountaintop and show you all the kingdoms of this world, say they'll all be yours if only you'll bow down and worship him—and his dollars."

"Is he as important as he claims?"

"He is. Works hard. Thinks big. That's why the New York financiers put him in charge of Inter-Ocean here. He'll introduce you to the high and mighty. But be on your guard. There's one other thing I should tell you. He's a reformed drunkard. Wife pulled him out of the gutter. She's a grand woman. Did he ask you to take the pledge of abstinence?"

David nodded. "I didn't know whether to take him seriously."

"Oh, I'd take him seriously! He may be a bit quirky but he means every word he says and he'll hold you to yours." Mornay supplied Wright's vessels with produce under a contract which allowed little profit margin. "He's rapacious to the last penny. And that's the type he runs with. They're the rulers, David. But you'll have to get acquainted with them for yourself. I can't do it for you."

"I'm extremely grateful for your advice. And I shall follow it!" David vowed, fully intending to.

"You'll be welcome here, come what may." But secretly Mornay felt let down. He'd counted on David as an ally in that crucial struggle for human freedom in which he was engaged and in which the boy had offered his allegiance. Now he couldn't be sure of him.

Martha was more outspoken. "I think he's done us a mean trick, and he's being led astray!" She calmly displayed her bitingly penciled sketch of David perched high on a tottery ladder, clutching at empty air for support.

Wing Sing, coming and going from the kitchen on silent feet, listened and observed philosophically.

# Chapter Nineteen

As a small child Hattie became aware of her white blood. The lightness of her skin proclaimed it. But she was also similarly aware of her black blood. This gave her special distinction in her own eyes and in those of other slaves in the big house and in the fields.

As she grew older she heard rumors she was truly a member of the Stanhope family, that the Colonel was her father, her mother a slave who had run away. "But who *was* my mother?" she asked Aunt Beulah. Old Beulah shook her head and sighed. "I wish I could tell you, chile. Honest I do! It be one of God's mysteries. But you one of His children, you be sure of that!" Later Hattie learned the truth from other servants and forgave Beulah her loving deception.

Aunt Beulah and Uncle Isaiah had raised her from infancy. They were cook and butler in the Stanhope household, childless except for her. Isaiah read aloud from the Bible nightly and conducted services Sunday in a dirt-floored cabin in the slave quarters. Stanhope let him teach Hattie how to read though it was against Louisiana law, and favored her in other ways, knowing she was his own flesh and blood. And he saw in her the grace and beauty which had attracted him to Mary Louise. When she was seven, he took her into his household to be companion and maid for his adored Victoria and the two grew up together.

Except where his lusts were concerned, Stanhope treated his slaves comparatively well, aware they were valuable property. Punishments were never crippling. There was time off in the fall when cotton picking was done, parties at Christmas with gifts for everyone. He was not of the old-line planter aristocracy with hide-bound notions but a relative newcomer with that Georgia background. His father Carleton, a noted speculator, migrated westward seeking opportunities and acquired the plantation which became known as Stanhope's Bend on the river north of New Orleans. George Stanhope, titled Colonel by reason of his service in the Mexican War, enterprising like his father, was constantly on the lookout for new fields of endeavor and profit, and politically was devoutly devoted to Southern expansion. Hence the reason for his trip to California.

Hattie was the only one of the household slaves to be brought along on the trip to a state where slavery was prohibited, Stanhope wishing to avoid what he called "complications"—though slaves might travel legally with their owners in any free state, and yet he probably wouldn't have brought Hattie had not Victoria insisted, being unable to deny his daughter anything she wanted. Victoria was at this moment standing in front of the pier glass in the well-appointed upstairs bedroom of the California House she shared with Hattie, observing the effect of her new party dress in preparation for the approaching cotillion, primping her raven ringlets with one hand, smoothing her shapely blue bodice over her rising young breasts with the other. "What did you think of him, Hattie?"

"Would you sure-enough marry a California man, Miss Vicky?"

"If he was handsome and rich enough!"

"Like Mister Sedley?"

"Gracious, I only laid eyes on him when he came to call, though Daddy's right keen on him. And he's well mannered for a Yankee. And rich enough. And not bad looking. But don't you go getting ideas!" Victoria—spoiled darling, willful, ambitious, tempestuous as her father when roused—tossed her head for effect. In the looking glass the figures of the two girls, half sisters, a year apart in age, were nearly superimposed, Victoria the taller and larger, Hattie the more graceful. The difference in color of their skins was hardly noticeable.

"You never told me about the carriage ride," Hattie prompted. Sedley had taken Victoria and her father and mother on what was becoming a standard sightseeing tour, westward along the shore of the Bay past the old Spanish presidio, now an Army post, to Golden Gate and Seal Rocks, where sea lions barked and basked, then south along the broad beach where mighty combers came rolling in "all the way from China" to thrill Victoria to appropriate exclamation, and on to Lake Merced and luncheon at the Lake House. "And even after I'm married, Hattie," she continued, "whether it's Mr. Sedley or someone else, wherever we are, you'll still be mine."

"But you won't need me after you're married!"

"I will so! How could I ever dress for parties without you? Now tighten that bow at the back just a little. I'd find you a husband too."

Hattie pondered the offer. "That mighty kind of you. But supposing I don't like the man you chose for me?"

This suggestion of independence, however slight, roused Victoria. "You'd suppose no such thing, you hear?" She stamped one daintily slippered foot. "You're mine! Daddy gave you to me! You'll do as I say!"

Through the open door an older woman's voice complained tremulously from the next room: "Be quiet, you two! You're making my headache worse!"

"Mama, it's Hattie. She's getting uppity again. I swear it's this California climate!"

"What's she up to now?" Sarabelle Stanhope's tone, like her daughter's, suggested facetiously that Hattie was a habitual troublemaker. Sarabelle, once a great beauty, now thirty pounds overweight, constantly felt poorly now the Colonel's affections roamed elsewhere. Like other planters' wives she'd reluctantly accepted the fact that her husband lived surrounded not only by his legitimate wife and children but by concubines. "The young woman who waits on me and my daughter is my daughter's half sister," she wrote a Northern friend. "The young man who drives my coach is my children's half brother. It is a shameful way of life but we women are bound to it inexorably." Her chief joys were blooming Victoria and dashing twenty-year-old Beauford who so far had not shown his father's predilection "for colored flesh," as Sarabelle expressed it.

"What's she up to?" Victoria continued the dialogue. "Why, she tells me with a perfectly straight face she's going to marry somebody *she* likes, not somebody *I* like!"

"Ungrateful wretch! I declare I'll tell Papa and Beau! After all we've done for her! Taken her into our house! Taught her to read and write!" Sarabelle's complaint settled into that mixture of banter and seriousness with which she and her daughter habitually addressed each other and the world. "I told Papa not to bring her. But he insisted. He's always indulged you."

"Mama, you know it was you who wanted Hattie. It was you argued she was too young to get any wrong notions."

Mrs. Stanhope sighed audibly. "Well, I guess I was mistaken. You see how quickly spoiled-rotten some people can be! See what kindness and generosity do!"

They continued addressing each other in this way, and as Hattie listened she seemed to be hearing them for the first time. Suddenly it didn't sound right. Suddenly she was fed up with it. Perhaps it was because of the atmosphere here in this free state. She'd noticed the independence of black people. Walking the streets with Sarabelle and Victoria she'd seen free Negroes working as porters, draymen, even merchants operating their own businesses. Of course there were free Negroes back home too. But these were different. They moved in a different world. She'd talked secretly to the black maids who cleaned the hotel rooms. They urged her to run away.

It shocked her at first. Then ideas, feelings, began to stir in Hattie which had never been there before.

# Chapter Twenty

Returning from her talk with Reuben at the market Mary Louise stopped again in the crowded plaza. Watching patiently she saw her daughter appear at a second floor window of the California House and look out. Emotion choked Mary Louise despite her self-control. The girl was looking out toward her like a prisoner from jail. But there was no chance of her recognizing her mother. Hattie didn't even know of her existence, let alone her presence. As she allowed her gaze to feast on that beautiful young face, so filled with gentleness and goodness, her bitterness against life dissolved into rare tears. Fiercely she brushed them away. All the tears in the world would not free Hattie.

There was work to be done. Now she knew where. How, would be next. It was part of her gambit tonight.

She'd worked hard to make this first meal as much like a New Orleans feast as possible, in order to impress her new employers and thus achieve several aims. When all was ready in the kitchen she put on her best simple black taffeta with V-shaped tucked bodice and belt and small plain white collar and plain skirt reaching to the floor. She could not help feeling a little nervous, knowing what was at stake, but had confidence in her skill and her special reason for being there. It was not only for herself but for Hattie that she would be performing. She'd put candles on the table, flowers on the sideboard. And when she heard three male voices and footsteps on the porch, she went to the door to receive them like the lady of the house.

"Haven't eaten all day in anticipation!" Sedley declared casually, to put her at ease, concealing more intimate feelings which she nevertheless sensed.

"I hope you'll not be disappointed. It's just a little supper like we serve down home regularly."

"I'll believe that when I taste it!" Lancaster chaffed.

"Let's have at it!" Fixx proposed, rubbing both palms together. "Mrs. St. Clair has something up her sleeve, I can tell!"

To begin, she served a cocktail of cognac, sugar, absinthe and bitters; then large shrimps with watercress sauce; and next the famous New Orleans daube glacé, or finest rare beef highly seasoned and mixed with brown sauce and herbs, covered with brown gelatin and sliced thin. "Tastes like more!" Sedley assured her, the others chiming in.

So far so good, she thought as she removed their plates, letting them become aware of her proximity and rose-petal perfume. Next she gave them crawfish bisque made with a brown roux and delicate fumet, also hot peppers and fine onions from Mornay's stall, and cream. A bottle of white burgundy Pouilly accompanied it. And it was followed by crab-oyster gumbo which was followed by sole baked folded in parchment with delicious seasoning and minced vegetables, to be unfolded with an aroma that Lancaster declared a breath of heaven.

"Now you must have the *coup de milieu,* the middle draught!" she announced gaily. "It means get up and stretch a bit. It can be either Calvados or cognac whichever you prefer."

Exchanging amused looks the three stood obediently, Fixx and Lancaster sipping cognac as they walked around the candle-lit table, Sedley gallantly proposing her health in Calvados, the fine apple brandy distilled from Normandy cider. She accepted their compliments demurely. "Wait till it's all over!" she cautioned.

As they talked on, she listened, leaving the kitchen door ajar. "Bumped into Ben Davidson, the Rothschilds's representative, today," Fixx was saying. "Ben thinks there's a slump coming. Warehouses are overstocked."

"Wright disagrees," Lancaster offered. "He was in to see me about his dyspepsia. Says he's handling more gold than last year. Of course you can't believe half the old scoundrel says. But there it is."

"Stanhope feels the future's in cotton," Sedley revealed. "Wants to see if he can introduce the Southern plantation system. Thinks our large land tracts may lend themselves to it. I'm going to show him the Great Central Valley.''

Mary Louise realized how useful such information might be to her in many ways. There were twenty thousand dollars on deposit to her name at the Savings Bank of New Bedford, a bequest from her late husband. Properly invested it could provide her and Hattie—once Hattie was free—with financial security in their adopted land, while helping benefit their people here and elsewhere. And while Stanhope was away with Sedley she might strike to free Hattie. Still she must move carefully.

Now she served the roast quail stuffed with their own livers plus raisins and Madeira wine; next came sliced turkey with oyster sauce; potato soufflé light and delicious as fresh air; asparagus hollandaise; cold artichokes, their detached leaves containing mixed chopped shrimp, bread crumbs, cheese and parsley; then baked eggplant halved and its insides mixed with sausage meat, onions and garlic; along with the red beans and rice ubiquitous at every New Orleans repast—all accompanied by red Bordeaux-Médoc.

''Are you trying to founder us?'' Sedley protested, clasping his stomach with both hands.

''Why, this is nothing. You should see what we eat at Mardi Gras!''

To top off she gave them the fabulous café brûlot: long strips of orange peel studded with cloves and cinnamon, cooked in brandy with sugar and very dark coffee added.

''A feast fit for the gods!'' Lancaster, a veteran gourmet, pronounced it, as he sipped a concluding glass of Dom Pérignon champagne.

''Not a restaurant in town could equal it,'' Fixx opined.

Sedley thought it more profoundly a masterpiece in the art of exquisite pleasure giving. He'd never imagined food could be so delightful, and the extent and thoroughness of Mary Louise's creative effort astonished him so that he saw her with new eyes as an expert performer. ''Especially since you prepared it entirely by yourself and served it singlehandedly, although I promised you all the help you'd need. Why did you do it alone?''

''I wanted to impress you,'' she laughed frankly. ''I wouldn't want to try it again without help.''

They agreed she should have whatever assistance she needed. Thus she won them to her and acquired full authority to hire help of her own choosing, help who would be wholly loyal to her and thus useful in various ways as she created a base from which to free Hattie and establish them both in their new homeland.

# Chapter Twenty-one

When David walked into the office of the Inter-Ocean Steamship Company promptly at 7:30 A.M., Captain Wright greeted him with breezy gusto: "You're a man of your word, I see. Never get ahead in this world unless you keep your word!" And while David winced inwardly under this unwitting irony, thinking of his broken promise to Mornay, the Captain continued: "Meet Bekker. He'll show you what to do!" indicating a dour little man with an enormous frown who seemed the counterpart of his own cheeriness. "Bekker's our first mate. Don't be put off by his looks. He's a good fellow at heart. And this is our crew!" pointing to a dozen young men about David's age perched or about to perch on high stools in front of sloping desks or sitting or standing at the long counter where the public was received. Two older men posted at either side of the front door were conspicuously armed with clubs and pistols. "We sail a tight ship. That's our secret. Every man knows his duty and does it. Now, let's get busy!"

And Wright retired into his private office at the back of the room, while Bekker conducted David to a vacant stool at the long counter and showed him what to do. The guards had already flung open the doors. People were pouring in. It was like a bank. Gold in the form of dust, nuggets, bullion was being accepted for shipment to New York and thence to all parts of the world. It was coming like a yellow flood, David knew, down from the slopes of the Sierras, down in the pockets and leathern bags and condor quill necklaces and safe boxes of miners and mining companies, down via river steamer from the inland terminuses of Sacramento and Stockton, down by horse and mule, foot and ferry to San Francisco; and out through Golden Gate it would pour to enrich nearly every nation on earth. Under Bekker's supervision he learned how to weigh it, issue receipts, make supporting ledger entries. The guards deposited the gold in a huge vault for safe-keeping until the next steamer sailed.

David threw himself into his work with enthusiasm, Bekker at his elbow, and before long was managing confidently on his own. For two hours he worked furiously. The hectic intensity of the life of the city which he'd noticed on first arrival permeated here, he realized. Incongruously, he heard an irreverent whisper close beside him:

> "Oh, what was your name in the States?
> Was it Thompson or Johnson or Bates?
> Did you murder your wife and flee for your life?
> Oh, what was your name in the States?"*

Glancing around in surprise he saw the lanky fellow with pock-marked face and sardonic smile who sat on the next stool and now added with a wink: "Don't take it too seriously, my friend! You might burn yourself out!"

"Is it always like this?"

"No, it gets worse when a steamer's about to sail. Been in town long?"

"Three days. Yourself?"

"Three weeks."

"A regular oldtimer!"

At the noon break David learned that Virgil Gillem was from Kentucky, a Yale graduate, had wanted to be a journalist but felt obliged by filial duty to work in his father's bank in Lexington. Bored stiff, he'd walked out and bought a ticket to California.

"Why aren't you on a newspaper?"

"No openings. So when Wright convinced me I was the most promising young clerk in California, what the hell?" Gillem's light-heartedness was infectious and did not diminish even when Bekker and Wright came around to check their work, and at the end of that harrowing day of ten gruelling hours David gladly accepted Gillem's suggestion they relax together and see the sights of the city.

*meaning the other thirty

"Been to the El Dorado?"

"No."

"Come on. It's our finest gambling saloon. I'll introduce you to the Blue Blazer and the Queen of Sheba."

As they were leaving Wright suddenly confronted David and held out a shiny twenty-dollar gold piece. "A day's work, a day's pay. I keep my word, young man. I expect you to keep yours. But be careful of the company you keep!" He eyed Gillem sharply. "Good evening, young gentlemen!"

"Does he always act like that?" David asked when they were outside.

"Only on your first day. Old Bluff and Bluster's heart's in the right place. It's part of his act. Did he make you take the pledge?"

"Yes, and you?"

"And everyone else who works here. But don't take him seriously. Come on."

At the El Dorado people were standing five and six deep around gaming tables waiting a chance to turn a card or bet the wheel and ball. David saw incredible piles of gold and silver gleaming on tables under glittering chandeliers. A blaring orchestra added to the din of human voices. "A visiting ranchero from the south bet thirty thousand on the turn of a single card the other night," Gillem confided, "and lost it all. They said it was the proceeds from the sale of an entire cattle herd. He didn't bat an eye."

Shouldering his way expertly through the crowd, Gillem greeted the bartender, a portly individual with a long pointed mustache and great dignity, like an old friend. "Professor, I'd like you to meet a chum. He's new in town. Never tasted one of your Blue Blazers."

"Then he ain't lived," replied the Professor gravely.

Seeing David's hesitation, Gillem chuckled. "Don't worry. Wright'll never know." Still David felt uncomfortable. He wanted to please his new friend but also to keep his pledge to Wright. "What if he catches us?"

"He doesn't frequent saloons though there was a time when he practically lived in them. The old hypocrite, he's had his fun. Now he wants us to forego ours!"

Under Gillem's urging, David decided that what the redoubtable Captain didn't know wouldn't hurt him.

Meanwhile the Professor had ceremoniously placed two large silver mugs and a large tumbler upon the bar. Filling one of the mugs nearly full of whiskey, then adding boiling water, he ignited the liquid with a malodorous sulfur match. As blue flame shot toward the ceiling and David shrank back in awe, the Professor calmly seized the mugs and hurled the blazing mixture back and forth from one to the other several times without spilling a drop, then smothered the flame and poured the smoking contents into the tumbler, where he added sugar and a twist of lemon peel. "There, sir! Welcome to San Francisco!"

When David tasted the Blue Blazer he felt as if fire had penetrated to the root of his being.

"Like it?" Gillem inquired with amusement.

Speechless, David nodded. Gillem, his own Blazer in hand, continued: "Now let me introduce you to the Queen of Sheba!" He raised his glass to the painting of the nude young woman upon the wall behind the bar. Reclining on a sofa surrounded by pink cushions, she was looking straight at David with what seemed a shocking invitation, her only clothes a broad-brimmed hat of black straw and thigh-high black stockings. All together she revealed more of the female form than he'd ever seen before and he felt himself flush as he looked at her. Gillem eyed him with more amusement. "Like women?"

David forced a smile, hoping it would conceal his innocence. But to Gillem it all seemed a casual matter and as David thought about it in that way, helped by the Blue Blazer, it did not seem so weighty. After a second of the Professor's offerings, he confided his adventure with the girl in the red trousers and the Sydney Ducks. Gillem nodded approvingly. "That's Angie. I know where she hangs out. But first I want to show you the White Boar. Come on!"

As they emerged into the street, the foggy air felt cool on David's burning face, but his head still whirled and his anticipation rose steadily higher. The White Boar was situated in an evil looking neighborhood near the waterfront. "It's a favorite of The Ducks," Gillem warned as they approached. "So keep an eye peeled. If someone recognizes you, we'll take French leave." The atmosphere inside was so foul with the stench of unwashed bodies, liquor, spit, and tobacco smoke, it almost turned David's stomach. Depraved specimens of humanity were carousing raucously, singing, embracing, kissing, exposing their intimate parts. Crouched on hands and knees on a platform at the far end of the room a naked dark-skinned woman was about to have intercourse with a huge white boar. The boar was in the act of mounting her

posteriorly by means of a wooden ramp which supported its great
weight. Obscene cheers rose as its enormous red member thrust
repeatedly into the crouched woman. "They put a Mexican Californian under him because she's the lowest of the low, lower
than the Chinese, lower than the niggers, in the eyes of our es-
timable brethren who run things," Gillem explained sardonically.
"The whiteness of the boar may be symbolic. Behold, my son,
and take wisdom, as the Scripture sayeth. Something tells me you
need educating though you are a college man!"

David was disgusted yet at the same time gratified and thought
he was seeing the reality of life. Then he noticed a brutal-looking
ruffian with a swollen upper lip staring at him suspiciously. That
odious face was the one he'd put his fist into in front of the saloon
two days ago. As the thug started toward him, shouting: "Here
he is, boys!" David plucked Gillem's sleeve. "It's The Ducks!"

"Follow me!" Gillem darted ahead of him out of the building.
The Ducks were in full cry at their heels as they raced through a
maze of dark alleys and inky passageways which Gillem seemed
to know by heart, suddenly emerging into the lighted plaza not
far from Sedley's office. Here the crowd was dense. Gillem
wormed quickly through it and into the lobby of the California
House which was thronged with well-dressed men and women.
Some were sipping lemonade in a corner of the salon, among
them the Stanhope family, just returned from attending the opera,
and Victoria was aiming such flirtatious glances at a handsome
young man to whom she'd not been introduced that her mother
was reproving her, "Honey Pie, it ain't ladylike!" Her father and
brother joined in the teasing. Turning away with a toss of her
head, Victoria saw David and was struck by his boyish good
looks. As their eyes met his widened at her beauty. But there was
no time for more.

Gillem was striding boldly to the desk and demanding a room
for two, asking to inspect it before registering. Impressed, the
clerk summoned a Negro porter. As the porter guided them along
the hallway toward the staircase, Gillem slipped a coin into his
hand. "Show us the back door, Sam, and don't ask questions!"

Out in the darkness again, they breathed more easily and Gillem declared: "We've given them the slip for the moment. Let's
try Little China next. The Ducks hate the Celestials. They'll never
look for us there!"

\*          \*          \*

They were soon in another world. Colored paper lanterns gave the street a festive air. Shop windows displayed Chinese silks, jades, porcelains. Nearly everybody they saw, nearly every word they heard, was Chinese. Almond-eyed young females peered alluringly from doorways. "They're prostitutes kept in servitude by cruel masters," Gillem explained. He led the way into an elegant gambling hall where well-dressed Chinese and whites mingled, incense smoldered and boiling kettles gave off a fragrant aroma of tea. Discordant music emanated from an orchestra of men and women playing strange-shaped instruments such as David had never seen before. At a central table a game that was a complete mystery was being played. "Tan," Gillem called it, "short for 'fan-tan.' See that square pewter slab lying in the middle of the table with numbers on each side of it? Read them!"

David read: "1, 2, 3, 4."

"Watch now!"

From a heap of small coins beside the slab, a pigtailed croupier separated some without counting them and placed them under an overturned bowl of white porcelain. "Those are *chins* or cash," Gillem explained. "They're made of bronze and have a square hole in the center surrounded by Chinese characters. Round as the sky, square as the earth—that's their meaning!" David marveled. Gillem seemed to know everything. "Come on, let's bet!" Gillem placed a golden double eagle opposite one of the 2's inscribed on the pewter slab. "You and I make two! Let's see what happens!"

When others placed bets, the croupier lifted the porcelain bowl. With the help of chopsticks, he counted out four at a time the cash he'd placed under it. "Watch," Gillem cautioned. "The number of coins remaining on final count determines the winning number on the slab!"

Two cash remained. "That's us!" Gillem declared triumphantly, pocketing his winnings which were thrice his bet. "Now let's look for your girl in the red trousers."

"What about The Ducks?"

"Oh, fuck The Ducks!"

David felt a twinge of alarm. But there was no turning back now. As they went out into the night again Gillem was humming blithely:

> "The miners came in forty-nine,
> The whores in fifty-one,

And when they got together
They produced the native son!''

David saw her as soon as they entered the Golden Nugget. She was standing at the bar surrounded by men, her long blonde ringlets held back from her face by a red ribbon and she was wearing a skin-tight black dress which revealed her shapely form even more daringly than the red trousers.

Appearing to recognize him at once she came straight toward him. His heart began to pound. Smiling into his admiring eyes with boldly provocative ones, she put a hand gently on his arm. "Pal, didn't you take a beating because of me the other day?"

"Yes, but I asked for it!" He felt his face redden. She drew him to a nearby table and ordered champagne. All at once Gillem and everyone else in the room receded leaving just the two of them.

"What's your name, Pal?"

He told her.

"Mine's Angie. Where you from?"

"New York City."

"Me too. Old Sixth Ward!" She gave a bitter laugh. "Know that chunk of Paradise?"

He knew it was a center of poverty and degradation. So here too was a seeker after a better life! He felt a warmth of kinship rising between them, along with something else that strained at his trouser's front. By the time the second bottle of champagne was empty David decided he was desperately in love with Angie. She seemed the heady culmination of everything extraordinary that was happening to him day by day, hour by hour.

"I like you!" she announced, impulsively reaching over and patting his hand. "You sure cleaned up on those Ducks!"

"And I like you!"

"Want to kiss me?"

"Yes."

"Go ahead."

David found it delightful.

"Like to see me naked?"

David gulped. "Yes!"

"Don't gulp. Come on!"

She took him upstairs to her room, undressed and lay on the bed. "Don't be shy!" she commanded. "Pull your duds off."

He felt hot and dizzy as he sank down beside her nude body,

trembling all over with anticipation and doubt. Then something touched his throbbing hardness. It was Angie's hand. He nearly fainted. But under her expert guidance he was soon transported into regions of unbelievable delight, and as climax succeeded climax he felt himself transformed into someone completely new, rich, powerful, authoritative, a man no less. At last as they lay exhausted in each other's arms, she whispered tenderly: "You learn fast, Pal!"

"I love you!" he breathed with what seemed all his heart and soul.

But in a moment she was getting up and dressing in business-like fashion. "I have to go to work. What about again tomorrow?"

Without answering, keenly disappointed, he too began to dress.

"Are you mad at me?" she asked plaintively. "Don't you have a little memento you could give Angie before she goes?" His heart sank. He thought she meant money. But when he offered a ten-dollar gold piece she pushed it away with disapproval. "I owed you this one, Pal. Here's what I meant!" and drew him to her and kissed him with passion which inflamed his whole being. "Tomorrow night?"

"Yes!" he burst out.

Making his way back to Mornay's house through streets crowded and noisy even at this hour, he still felt himself exalted. But in the early morning quiet of his room his head cleared and as he lay thinking his conscience began to trouble him. He'd always thought of himself as good. Had this night been good? Had he sinned or merely broken barriers of shyness and prudishness? In the households from which he came, such conduct as he'd just engaged in was unspeakable. The Biblical injunction came back to him. "Now the body is not for fornication but for the Lord; and the Lord for the body." Yet his self of those days seemed far away, long ago. Here was a new, different life. And was God really watching everything he did as he'd been taught to believe? Or was there no such God as the behavior of Gillem and Angie suggested? Yet what about his broken promises to Mornay and Wright? Did they matter? Or were they inconsequential too? As for Angie, the mere thought of her filled him with a warm surge of delight and desire to explore further that new world she opened to him.

He heard someone stirring in the room below. It was Mornay getting up to go to work.

# Chapter Twenty-two

While waiting for Nipamu to consult the Sky Powers and name the propitious day for communal action against the white enemy, Francisco immersed himself wholeheartedly in the life of the village of refugees. Exulting in his new existence, he worked with the stone-chippers making arrowheads and the bow-makers re-enforcing with sinew their bows of tough juniper, and with those who crafted soft steatite stone into pipes for smoking wild tobacco, and those who practiced with rifles at a mark. And he helped make nets for catching quail and set spring-pole snares for squirrels. He hunted and fished and stood his turn as sentinel on nearby crests, and from time to time saw soaring overhead the great condors who were his dream helpers, and felt reassured by their presence. He played in games like a young man, kicking the ball the length of the field, around the post-marker and return, pounding and bruising his way among the youngsters while older men and women cheered delightedly. And as he did these things, rising in the morning with the others to pray to the sun and dip in the pool below the meadow, he felt the years shed away and his youthful joy in life return.

The faces of those he met showed their approval, all except Nipamu who continued to regard him warily yet also invitingly so that he sensed in her a mixture of animosity and desire.

Then one evening as he went to drink from the spring that gushed from the roots of a great sugar pine at the head of the meadow he met the refugee woman Ta-ahi. He'd noticed her before. With her small daughter she kept aloof like a wounded thing and went quietly about her tasks. Her face expressed a suffering which his old self might not have heeded but his new one did. She was slender as a girl yet mature as a wife and wore the long cotton skirt and blouse of a white woman, showing she like he had been touched by that other world they both now wished to avoid. Inquiring about her to young chief Winai, he learned Ta-ahi had made her way down from the north where her husband, an Indian miner, had been stabbed to death by whites who jumped their claim and smashed out the brains of their young son against a tree, while she watched hidden with her daughter in the undergrowth. The child had been stricken mute with horror at sight of what happened to her father and brother and could not speak articulately even now. Leading her by the hand, fleeing south by darkness, guided by rumor and instinct, half starved, all but exhausted, Ta-ahi had brought them to the safety of the village. "You seem sorrowful," Francisco said to her gently, knowing why but wanting to hear her own words, "what is the reason?"

She told him simply in such fashion that his heart melted, in the presence of her suffering, for all the years of his profligacy and blindness and he wished to take her hands and ask her forgiveness.

"I too have suffered," he burst out, and told of his misspent life. She listened with understanding. They talked until darkness fell. Then it seemed only natural they continue together, and taking her by the hand he led her away under the giant trees until they found a bed of soft brown pine needles where they could join their sorrow into joy.

Thereafter Francisco was happier than ever in his life. Ta-ahi satisfied him completely as he never had thought a woman could. She was considerate without being servile, loving without being demanding. And he loved her little mute Letke as if she were his own, making the child smile when he tumbled her over his shoulder, utter inarticulate sounds of delight when he got down upon all fours and let her ride on his back. He sensed the hysterical tension which caused the muteness and did his best to alleviate it by telling her stories his mother had told him, of the unhappy little girl who had no parents and was turned into a wild goose by Kakunupmawa, and flew away with the flock to the north "where she became a star that shines through darkness of the night."

Ta-ahi adored him for this. She'd already taught Letke to accompany her when gathering herbs and berries and materials for basket making and to cook and sew with intelligent fingers. But now that there was Francisco to be husband and father and help provide food, and stand up strongly for them before the world, the house he'd built of poles and skins at the edge of the meadow became for her a sanctuary of happiness and hope, which only one thing marred. "Beware of Nipamu," she warned.

"Why?"

"She fears your power will diminish hers. Besides, she's in love with you and she takes lovers as she will, since none dare refuse her because of her magic."

"Do not worry. I understand that woman."

Still Ta-ahi urged: "Act now, independently. The longer she keeps you waiting, the more she discredits you and gains power over you. I know you are eager to have your revenge on the white man who injured you and to unite the remnants of tribes into a common resistance. Act now and become the leader of your dream vision!"

But Francisco was reluctant to go against the established order. "No, I must wait."

Meeting Nipamu he asked when the time for action might come. She replied enigmatically: "When the wild geese fly."

"But that will not be till autumn!"

"Then come with me now," she suggested invitingly, "and I shall show you the Secret of Great Pleasure. It may reveal an earlier date."

He understood her meaning but replied with pretended modesty: "I am not yet worthy of such revelation, being so newly come among you. Perhaps later when I have proved myself I shall be more deserving."

She was not deceived and glared at him with the fury of one who has been rejected: "Then wait!"

When the geese came honking across the shoulder of the mountain—a benign sign because they flew from the north guided by Sky Coyote, the North Star, friend of mankind—Nipamu gave the summons and everyone gathered to hear what she would say. Many thought the occasion more momentous because the geese had come so early, and they listened with even greater awe than usual.

Nipamu's breast, shoulders and face were stained with the red of life. White and black lines symbolizing day and night radiated from the corners of her eyes, while her head was adorned with the plumage of hawks and eagles and the down of geese, and her skirt was made of the wing feathers of condors. In her right hand she carried her sacred scepter. Its shaft was of blood-red manzanita wood and the quartz crystal attached to its end radiated all colors of the rainbow as it caught the sun. An awed hush preceded her words.

"The Sky People tell me: Let the Mixed Blood say exactly how he intends to prove himself, so we may judge finally whether it is his white or his Indian self which speaks."

Smarting from her words, Francisco told how he planned to lasso Buck Jenkins and drag him through the street of the town "like a dog in the dust."

"That is not enough," Nipamu interrupted. "First you must engage in a venture which sheds white blood. That is what the geese are saying."

Then Francisco saw how cleverly she had trapped him. But he dared not express such thoughts lest he be regarded as a coward, so he said:

"When I have proven myself as the geese decree, then I shall have revenge upon my enemy exactly as I have described." And felt both strengthened and diminished as he conformed to the ways of these people he had chosen to live with. "I am ready to lead a raiding party. Let those who will accompany me step forward, and we will make our plan."

# Chapter Twenty-three

As she shopped among his vegetables, Mary Louise explained to Mornay in a low voice what she intended to do.

"Bring her to my house," he replied, also under his breath. "It'll be like the old days." When Mornay engaged in Underground work his usually grave face brightened with the light of battle in a just cause. "She'll be safe with me while we make longer-lasting arrangements. Bring her by night. Come to the back door." He began to describe the route carefully, then broke off. "Better still, take Reuben with you to show you the way." He turned to Reuben. "Will you help?" Reuben nodded. He'd already helped Mary Louise contact a maid named Jemima at the California House.

Mary Louise interjected: "First I want to prepare Hattie. She must *want* to be free of her own accord. I mustn't force her." And she described her plan for introducing Hattie to the society of free Negroes. Mornay concurred. Then he demanded sternly: "What about Sedley? What's your connection with him?" Mary Louise explained. His face brightened again. "Good. You'll be our agent behind enemy lines!"

The following Sunday as the Stanhopes were preparing for church Hattie asked if she could go to the colored people's church with her new friend Jemima.

Sarabelle and Victoria were opposed and Stanhope was ready to say no, too, but Beau bantered his father on a sensitive point.

"Dad, we've always thought we could trust Hattie. That's why we brought her with us. Why don't we trust her now?"

"And by heaven we will!" vowed Stanhope, his judgment challenged. "But I'll put the fear of God in her first!" And turning to Hattie: "There's a law in this state makes it a crime to run away. Do you understand that? So don't go getting any ideas. We'd find you wherever you hid. And we'd make you so sorry you'd never forget it, understand?" He lifted his Malacca stick.

Even so, Sarabelle continued to protest. "Papa, I can't b'lieve what I'm hearin'!" And Victoria was profoundly outraged. "These free niggers been giving her ideas!"

"She's got a right to worship same as we have," the Colonel decreed, and that was it.

The church on Pacific Street just above Stockton was a small white frame structure erected with volunteer labor and donated materials. The service had begun but the faces that turned their way seemed to welcome her cordially as she and Jemima entered, and Hattie felt at home immediately. Mary Louise who'd followed at a discreet distance took a seat not far behind them. Even with her white powder makeup and straightened hair she could pass as having black blood or as a white Abolitionist such as sometimes came to black churches to demonstrate support.

The minister reminded Hattie of Uncle Isaiah back home. He was short, strongly built, agile, with graying goatee and large bright wide-apart eyes, and he spoke in the manner Hattie imagined prophets must have used, his voice rising and falling for emphasis. In fact he was a carpenter by trade and had led in constructing the church.

He was talking about Saint Paul. "And the chief Cap'n among the Roman soldiers that taken Paul prisoner 'cause he'd spoke up for Our Lord mocked him when Paul demanded freedom. 'Why,' says the Cap'n thinking he'd put Paul down a peg, 'I had to pay a big sum for *my* freedom!' But Paul topped him: 'Man, I was born free!' So you see, brothers and sisters, even in those days there was three kinds of people: thems as was free, thems as was not, thems as *earned* their freedoms!" The pastor paused and Hattie thought he must be speaking directly to her, because what he said seemed to fit her case exactly. "Those of us as is free," he continued, "has got to stand up and demand our rights like Paul. Paul he insist his case be heard by the most powerful person on earth, Emperor Caesar; an' because he knew his rights and demanded 'em, they had to take him to Rome!''

There were approving cries. But one voice objected: "We ain't got no rights! Can't vote! Can't testify in court! Can't ride 'bus! What rights we got?''

"We got the right to demand better rights!" the speaker retorted. "And it we got to do! We're alive, ain't we? We got breath in our bodies, ain't we?" There were more cheers. His optimism was infectious. But he was out of breath. Beads of perspiration appeared on his brow. He wiped them with a large white handkerchief. Hattie felt deeply moved. She thought it the greatest sermon she'd ever heard. "Listen to one more thing, brothers and sisters!" She listened hard. "I want to tell you this from my heart. It the biggest thing I got to say. Paul he say it to that little congregation in the city of Colossae. Now that congregation weren't much bigger than we be. Didn't even have a place to meet reg'lar like we do but just gathered here and there in people's homes like we used to. But Paul he chose to tell it a mighty big thing and I want to share that thing with you. Paul he say: 'Look, some of you Gentile, some Jew, some Greek, some who-know-what. That make no difference. Bond nor free it don't make no difference. Circumcision or uncircumcision, it don't make no difference. All that make a difference is this: 'Christ in all of us!' I quote him direct. 'Christ in all of us.' That how it got to be, brothers and sisters. That how it got to be!''

Hattie was taken clear out of herself and transported to that almost unimaginably remote city of Colossae and that little band of believers with whom she identified strongly.

"Some had dark skin, some had light," the Reverend Hicks went on, his words also seeming to come from a great distance, carrying great weight. "But that don't make no difference. Didn't make no difference then. Don't make no difference now!''

Cries of "Amen!" and "All right!" greeted his conclusion. Feet stamped the floor. People stood up and waved their arms and embraced each other. Some came crowding around Hattie and Jemima, welcoming them, asking questions. Reverend Hicks was pressing Hattie's hand warmly. "I hope you'll come again?''

"I'll try!''

As she and Jemima left, Reuben Stapp stepped forward and Jemima introduced him.

"Can I accompany you ladies home?''

"Don't mind," Jemima answered. "What 'bout you, Hattie?''

Hattie accepted Reuben's offer shyly but sweetly. It thrilled her, he looked so handsome and strong. And she would be taking her first steps toward freedom under his auspices.

"You like it here?" he asked as they strolled along.

She assured him she did.

"You'd like it even better if you'd lived here a while!" They seemed to have reached a remarkable understanding. Hattie glowed with pleasure. Reuben felt impelled to explain how he'd walked all the way across the country from Philadelphia to reach San Francisco.

"Didn't your feet get sore?"

"Not to amount to anything. I just felt so good all the time nothing else mattered."

Mary Louise followed at a safe distance. A part of her had accepted the sermon and the response to it as profound truth. Another part rejected it all as wishful thinking. Yet for Hattie she wished the first part would come true. And now she was delighted that her plan for her daughter seemed to be working.

As dusk was falling, Mary Louise was attending another kind of service. It was held in a lonely clearing in the undergrowth at the outskirts of the city. A throng of Negroes surrounded a hollow where a fire was burning. Word had spread rapidly that she was an authentic Voodoo Queen, a disciple of the famed Marie Laveaux of New Orleans. She wore a simple blue cotton dress with red cord at her waist. Her golden serpent earrings, emblems of her profession, flashed in the firelight. With the aid of helpers she prepared the altar by placing two bottles of water and two jars containing magic charms next its holy cross.

Then she established the rhythm for the occasion by rattling her snakeskin rattle which was filled with small pebbles and bits of human bones. Drummers picked up the rhythm. Then she began to chant the ritual prayer to Legba, the mystical spirit who opens the secret gates to the world of gods and demons; and as she chanted she began to dance, decorously at first, then with increasingly writhing, snakelike, abandon, as her wild chant was taken up and rose around her and the flames of the fire leaped higher.

Soon others were dancing to the contagious rhythm. As it became more animated some dancers fell into a trance in which their bodies seemed no longer under their control. And as this frenzy increased, some fell to the ground and were dragged off by others and dressed in the clothing of the "spirit" which had possessed them and brought back to the circle and made to dance and testify. Women possessed by male spirits were dressed as men and spoke in male voices; men, vice versa. Mary Louise danced with each of the possessed ones, giving each a lighted candle to hold, interpreting their otherwise unintelligible babblings in a way that augmented the growing frenzy and her power.

As the orgy grew wilder, the throats of sacrificial animals—chickens, pigeons, a goat—were cut and their blood collected in a sacred bowl. Mary Louise drank from the bowl. Then she uncovered a box draped with black cloth and removed the snake it held. With the snake entwined about her she danced by the firelight. Everyone knew the snake represented eternal forces. The snake was Damballah who sits at the foot of the throne of God. Mary Louise spoke to the snake in a persuasive voice and listened to what it replied. But she did not say what she had heard. Afterward people asked her questions about their futures: would they be lucky or unlucky in love or work? She answered in a way that could be understood as the listener saw fit. Thus she extended her power further.

From time to time she accepted money for little black cloth bags she'd brought in her reticule. Everyone knew they contained secret mixtures of cemetery earth, human bones, vital red pepper. She'd brought them in her trunk all the way from New Orleans. "These will be more valuable than money in San Francisco," Marie Laveaux had told her.

Those wishing to inflict misfortune or death on someone could leave one of these black bags on the doorstep of the person they wished to harm. Finding such an unlucky charm, that person would be apt to seek out Mary Louise and purchase a charm which would counteract the unlucky one.

The dancing, singing and drumbeating continued till midnight, when the sacrificial animals were cooked and a morsel given to everyone so that magic influence might pass to the person eating that morsel. Mary Louise fashioned a doll of black clay in the form of a man, smeared it with feathers from one of the sacrificial roosters, stood it upright on the altar in front of the cross and at each side of it placed an unlit black candle. As she lit the candles she muttered a solemn curse on George Stanhope and ran a pin deep into the doll's heart. This would confirm the hex she'd already placed on him.

Then following an example being set by others, she disappeared into the undergrowth in company with a stalwart handsome young man named Samson she'd selected as her mate for the night.

She would use every weapon at her disposal in order to gain that domination she craved in both black and white worlds.

# Chapter Twenty-four

When Sally and the men returned to camp from their confrontation with Francisco in the oak grove, Abe sat in judgment while they told what happened.

"Sal made a fool of Goodly!" Elmer accused.

"He had it coming!" Iphy put in.

"Ma, she whapped me from behind!" Goodly complained.

"Sal only done what was right!" Jake defended his daughter. "Even Buck said so!"

"Gramp, they was all agin him so I stuck up for him. You'd have done the same!" Sally justified herself.

"You've all missed the point," Buck announced grandly. "The point is we showed 'em what's what!"

"And what's that," demanded Abe sourly, "if you've stirred up a hornet's nest? I warned you. We'll all maybe have to pay for this. I had her where we wanted her. Now you've gave her the upper hand. So let's git busy and git this cabin up so we'll have something to fight from if it comes to a scrap."

Obediently the men fell to work, shaping the long gray-barked logs cut from alders that grew beside the river that Clara called The Tears of the Sun, which flowed from the heart of her Indian world; while the women carried water from it, gathered firewood and prepared the evening meal. Sally fell asleep thinking of Pacifico's admiring look as she handed him back his belt.

A few days later she went off alone to explore the stream for berries and watercress and a glimpse of a young man who might take her mind off the dreary monotony of family servitude. Despite her grandfather's warning not to stray too far, she went farther than was perhaps prudent, finding ample cress edging the stream and plenty of blackberries and even some strawberries along its shady bank. Basket full, giving up hope of seeing Pacifico, she decided to return across the grassy meadowland rather than follow the winding stream, and thus she was out in the open when she heard the pounding hooves. Whirling, she saw a terrifying mass of horned cattle bearing down on her. The cattle of Rancho Olomosoug were easily dominated by a person on horseback who might ride among them at will, but were roused to curious and often furious alarm by the unusual sight of a human on foot.

Sally realized there was no use to run. And there were no trees to climb. Wits sharpened by fright, she remembered Abe recounting one of his adventures: "It's a trick old as time. When dogs attack you set down. Dogs don't know what to make of a feller a-settin' on the ground."

Would it work with cattle? She had no time to wonder. Quickly she sat down facing the oncoming herd, holding herself firmly erect, heart pounding in her throat.

The foremost animals hesitated, lowered their heads with snorts of surprise, then turned aside and circled her, and the rest of the herd, following, surrounded the diminutive figure of the girl, pawing and bellowing with puzzlement and rage. Sally thought each moment might be her last. But she remembered Abe's admonition to keep her head up.

It was thus that Pacifico found her at the center of a ring of horns. Guiding his horse skillfully through it till he reached her side, he turned and drove the cattle away, then came back to where she was standing. He was wearing white trousers and dark green bolero jacket and that belt she'd retrieved for him. Its silver buckle sparkled in the sun as did the golden yellow of his horse. He'd taken off his hat in greeting. His hair was as golden as his horse's, she thought. She'd never seen a sight so gallant or so welcome. "Thank you for saving my life!" she said frankly.

He replied in English so excellent it startled her. "Thank you for saving my belt, which in my family is as dear as life."

An awkward silence followed. Her face was burning. So was his. "I must go home now," she managed. "Will the cattle let me alone?"

"If you're on my horse they will!" Dismounting he offered her a stirrup, with a smile that invited her to take a step she knew would be a decisive one between them. Handing him her basket, she swung gaily to the saddle, guided by his firm grip, seating herself sidewise, one hand on the pommel, arranging her skirt with the other, while he swung up behind and steadied her between both arms as he held the reins.

Thus they proceeded back to camp in the manner of a young ranchero and his fiancée. Sally thought his arms the most exciting things that had ever touched her. He thought her soft sides the most delightful things he had ever touched, as their bodies swayed in rhythm with the horse's steps.

Iphy saw them first. "Well, doggone me!"

The men and boys stopped work to stare. "She's turned Grandee!" Jake blurted delightedly.

"Not while I'm around!" Buck muttered.

"You both shut up," Abe warned. "I'll handle this."

He went forward to take the basket and help Sally down. "He saved my life, Gramp!" Abe noted how bloomingly animated that life had become and stifled a smile. And when she told what had happened, he said to Pacifico: "Won't you git down and take a cup of coffee?"

Buck and the boys stayed sullenly aloof, while Abe and Jake and Iphy played host. Sipping his cup in that family circle, Pacifico apologized for the bad manners of his grandmother's cattle. Abe apologized for the manners of Buck to Pacifico and his father in the oak grove. "The point of all this," he summarized, "is that folks can git together if they want. Will you tell that to your grandmother?"

"You must come and tell her yourself!"

"One of these days I might just do that!"

Afterward Abe said to sullen Buck: "Peace is better than war if you can have it fair and square."

Buck shook his head. "Give 'em an inch and they'll take a yard."

Up at the hacienda Clara demanded: "What was all the commotion among the cattle?" And when Pacifico explained, she exploded: "I'll not have you mixing with that squatter girl, understand? You and Anita are as good as engaged!"

Pacifico nodded obediently, to placate but not necessarily to agree with her.

# Chapter Twenty-five

Sedley was showing Stanhope his domain. They'd already seen his city real estate holdings, new flour mill, new iron foundry and the fabulous cinnabar mine at New Almadén* near San José where the red mineral that Indians had once traveled hundreds of miles to possess was made into silvery mercury for the reduction of gold ore and many other valuable purposes; and now they sat side by side, golden grass up to their stirrups, at the crest of Livermore's Pass looking out over the Great Central Valley toward the snowcapped Sierras, and Stanhope exclaimed: "Why, this is an earthly paradise but will it produce crops?"

Later when he had ridden through burgeoning acres of wheat and barley and fruitful orchards, examined experimental plots of newly introduced Chilean alfalfa and hardy upland cotton, he decided it would produce almost anything that would grow. "But what's your market?"

"A rapidly increasing population, for one," Sedley replied. "For two, China, Japan, all the Far East, all being opened to progress soon. Australia too. Indeed all the world, for fast clippers like mine will carry cargo to Liverpool in less time than it once took to reach New York around the Horn."

"How will you get your crops to the clippers?"

"River boat from Stockton or Sacramento to deep-water ship at San Francisco."

*named after one in Spain famed since Roman times as among the richest in the world, cinnabar occurring elsewhere only in Serbia and China

"What's your labor supply?"

"China or Mexico, augmented by native Indians and miners down on their luck."

"Niggers?"

"Free ones only. Unless there's a change in the state's constitution. Eventually much of what you see will be irrigated," Sedley added prophetically, motioning toward the snowcapped mountains. "There's an eternal water supply up there. Continuously melting, it creates mighty rivers. Diverting that water to croplands should prove a simple matter, thus increasing productivity. And when the Pacific Railroad, in which I am interested, is built, this will become the nation's food basket."

Stanhope shook his head incredulously. "You think of everything, don't you?"

"I try to." And he invited Stanhope to join his new syndicate now in process of acquiring vast acreage in the San Joaquín and adjoining Sacramento valleys which together comprised the Great Central Valley. But during all of these proceedings Sedley made no mention of Rancho Olomosoug. If it were ever to be his, it would be his alone, the most precious jewel in his imperial crown. He would no more have thought of revealing his interest in it than he would the fact that he and Mary Louise had become lovers the night before he left town while Fixx and Lancaster were out for the evening. The tap came lightly on his door. She was holding in both hands a flat basket on which his fresh linen was neatly arranged. Her smile was demure yet ironic.

"Your laundry just arrived."

And he sensed the moment had come. "I used to send it to China," he replied easily, "in the early days of the Rush. Would you believe it? We had absolutely no services then!" And placing both hands over hers, he drew her and the basket gently inside and shut the door.

She gave herself to him deliciously, never quite yielding fully. He knew he'd never experienced such pleasure nor, spurred onward in his desire to penetrate her mystery, given so much in return. His full discovery of her dusky body did not change his feeling for her. He was by nature pragmatic in matters of race, as in others. The reciprocity of the sexual act had long seemed to Sedley life's essential business transaction: something of value given for something of value received. Now he wasn't so sure. This contained more than business. It left him feeling fully satisfied yet eager to invest more at almost any price. Hardly good business practice. But a most rewarding thought.

Similarly Stanhope was guarding his most intimate secret. He was on a confidential mission from Jefferson Davis and other Southern leaders to determine the probable status of California in the event of continued friction and even war between North and South. Davis's forward-looking group saw not only the wealth but the strategic location of California as the Pacific cornerstone of a slaveholding empire extending from ocean to ocean. Its northern boundary would be the Missouri Compromise line of 1820 separating slave territory from free at 36° 30"—extended on to the Pacific just south of the old California capital at Monterey,* but eventually including all the state if possible. The southern boundary of this vast empire would be the Gulf of Mexico and Mexican border. Additional purchase or conquest from Mexico would be a further possibility. Access to both Pacific and Atlantic Oceans would give the South power and prestige as well as territory matching the North's. And Sedley appeared to Stanhope a key figure in this scheme because of his great influence in California and because Stanhope contemplated him as a son-in-law. But the Colonel wished to move carefully. "I'm tempted to join. How does your syndicate work?"

"We're a joint-stock company. We're buying up large blocks of state-owned swamp and overflow land along major rivers for a dollar and a quarter an acre. Friends in the Legislature are lending a helping hand. It's reclaimable land and highly fertile. Adjoining or free standing tracts preempted by settlers can be picked up at close to that price. And there are various kinds of assignable scrip, as well as federal land bounty warrants issued to veterans, which can be had cheaply if you know where to look."

"Sounds sensible. I'd like to meet your associates." Part of Stanhope's secret plan was to sound out as many prominent Californians as possible while influencing their views toward his.

"You'll feel at home with them," Sedley assured him. "Many have Southern backgrounds or sympathies. True, some don't. But it's my conviction that sectional differences are best reconciled by mutual business interests."

It was just the sentiment that Stanhope was looking for.

---

*roughly bisecting the western U.S. horizontally

# Chapter Twenty-six

Roaming the city after dark, David and Gillem came to the newly extended waterfront where buildings and streets were being constructed rapidly, often carelessly, on pilings over the Bay. David was attracted by the figure of a short stoutish man in dark blue Army uniform peering down a hole in the plank pavement. "See a fish down there, Captain?"

The dumpy figure turned a discouraged face to theirs and replied with impressive simplicity: "No, I was just thinking a fellow could fall into a hole like that and never be heard of again."

Gillem responded laconically. "It's happened!"

All three peered into the dark abyss. Somewhere below water was lapping against pilings.

"Stationed here?" inquired David.

"Fort Humboldt." The Captain was waiting for a ship to take him northward along the coast to his new post at the edge of the redwood forests. After a discouraging year in Oregon Territory, Ulysses S. Grant, future commander of the Northern armies and President of the United States, was about to begin his second tour of duty in California. It would drive him to drink and to resign his commission—to try private enterprise with even worse luck. "Yet on reaching San Francisco a year ago," he was saying, "I thought it the wonder of the world, and wrote my wife that this place could be our future home, that I'd seen enough to know it to be different from any place a person in the States could imagine in their wildest dreams!" His voice rose querulously. "There is no reason why a man should not make a fortune here, every year, I told her!''

Grant, a tanner's son, had married upward, a planter's daughter from an estate near Saint Louis. Hoping to justify himself in her eyes as well as her father's and his own by making that fortune he'd imagined, he'd invested all his savings in a San Francisco general store, was in the process of losing them and now, nearly distraught, was looking down a hole such as a man might fall through and disappear forever.

Sensing something of this, David burst out impulsively: ''Come share a drink with us?''

Grant declined. Having unburdened himself in uncustomary fashion, he walked away without further word. In fact he didn't have the money to pay for a drink.

''Queer egg!'' Gillem commented.

Looking after the dumpy figure, never expecting to see the despondent Captain again, David shook his head. ''If that's what the Army does to a fellow I hope I'm never in it!''

Night after night David explored the city's seamy underside with Gillem and night after night he saw Angie, and every time he encountered Mornay or Wright he felt a little uncomfortable, but the double life he'd embarked upon seemed so mature, so sophisticated, that he hardly gave his momentary uneasiness a second thought. He continued to live with Mornay. He could not quite bring himself to break completely with the good merchant and Martha—his old self, as it were—but saw them less and less and his late night discussions with Mornay became things of the past as did his brotherly tiffs with Martha. One night returning late, he found one of her impish sketches on his bed. He was depicted on knees at prayer, hands clasped, eyes turned upward— not toward a halo or angel but an airborne dancehall girl and bottle of champagne. He decided it was beneath his dignity to respond.

Sometimes after work he went with Gillem to the newly opened Mercantile Library on the second floor of the California Exchange Building at the corner of Kearny and Clay. Its large reading room was comfortably fitted with chairs and tables. All sixteen local and many Eastern newspapers were available, also copies of latest magazines and reviews, and hundreds of books by well-known authors. Melville's recently published *Moby Dick* was Gillem's

favorite. David preferred Emerson's latest essays. Gillem derided
Emerson. "A pious fraud. Melville by contrast goes to the heart
of things. Unpleasant subjects are dealt with—prejudice, violence,
murder—topics such as your genteel Emerson would never
touch!"

"Why must one deal with unpleasant things in order to be
esteemed?" David countered. "Emerson writes on nobler level.
He deals with the universal soul, essences—the oneness of man
and nature. Evil is merely the absence of good."

"In Melville evil has good on the run!" Gillem retorted. "That
seems to me nearer the truth. Just look around you!"

When he did, David's conscience pricked him and he was unable to be sure whether he truly was part of Gillem's reality or
an apostate from his own. Thus when Wright invited him to supper at his home on Rincon Hill, he was forced to feign a plea-
surable acceptance he did not feel, at the same time wondering if
Wright might have learned of his deception, though he could see
no sign of it in the Captain's usual sharp eye and brusque tone.
When he asked Gillem what to expect, Gillem chuckled. "We've
all been through it. You're his latest prospect. He just wants to
convert you to the true faith of prohibition. Make hay while you
can. Hit him for a raise or whatever. But beware of Aunt Lucy!"

"Aunt Lucy?"

"His wife Lucinda. She's not only a temperance nut, she's a
woman's righter. Talks about attending their convention next year
at Albany, New York."

"My God! Does she wear trousers too?"

"You'll see."

Promptly at seven David knocked at the door of a mansion on
Rincon Hill overlooking the Bay south of Market Street. Its towering flat roof supported an observatory resembling a square glass
hat, surrounded by a widow's walk, from both of which Wright
could see the entire waterfront and much of the city. House and
lookout seemed symbolic of his wealth and power, metaphorically
his ship's bridge from which he could survey his vessels in the
harbor below and contemplate many less visible interests. Just
being there made David feel himself rising in the world, as he
passed between the Greco-Roman columns of the front porch. A
petite Irish maid in black uniform with white apron and cap answered the bell. He trod on rich carpet of crimson ply. From an
open doorway ahead he could hear voices of men and women
raised in polite conversation. He felt a thrill of anticipation. He

was entering the halls of the mighty.

Wright came to meet him, embraced him like a son, introduced him to a graying frail-looking little woman, the last person he would have thought a militant female, though he noticed with astonishment she wore Bloomers, loose fitting trousers gathered at her ankles under a short skirt.

Lucinda Wright declared in firm tone: "Welcome to Home Port, Mr. Venable!" At the touch of her hand David guessed she might be made of iron. He was right. As a dedicated temperance worker in New York's seamy Hell's Kitchen she'd discerned virtue in the dissolute young man who with other young blades from uptown went slumming there. Utterly sure of her perceptions and convictions, she'd attached herself to Wright then and then, indeed like a tug to a huge steam vessel, and never left him.

Now he introduced David to a regal looking woman much younger than Lucinda. She wore a stately black dress and her dark hair was parted in the center and drawn down at either side, and she had a full strong mouth and large serene eyes. "This is Mrs. Sherman and here next her is her husband—W.T. to his friends!" David's eyes rested on a red-headed, red-bearded man in rumpled clothes, nervous, intense, whom he recognized as having been in and out of Wright's office in company with leading figures of the community. Sherman, who would be the North's most famous general after Grant in the coming war, had been stationed in California during the conflict with Mexico and early years of the Gold Rush. In fact he'd collected and sent East the official shipment of gold on which President Polk based his announcement of the fabulous discovery. After being reassigned to Saint Louis, Sherman resigned his commission and came West again hoping like Grant to make a fortune. "Sherman's a banker," Wright boomed. "Stay on his good side, David. Never know when you might need him!"

"Oh, nonsense, Wright!" Sherman scoffed irritably. "Let the young fellow think for himself!"

"He does already! You don't suppose I'm going to handle upwards of eighty million in gold this year with a crew of dummies, do you?"

"You'll never handle that much!"

"Want to bet?"

With Wright's heartiness paving the way, David fell readily into the conversation. They were talking about a Pacific or Transcontinental Railway. "It's inevitable, W. T. You yourself instigated the first surveys through the Sierras when you were here as a lieutenant in '48 and '49. Why not join us now?'' And Wright confided that his principals in the Inter-Ocean Steamship Company were eager to push ahead with the railroad. ''Once Congress decides on the route, we'll provide the financing. Sedley's in on it.''

''I wouldn't put two bits into it!'' Sherman barked. ''Southerners will insist it run through slave territory. Northerners will insist it run on free soil. It'll never be built as long as each side regards it as an extension of political power. Besides it'll cost at least a hundred million. Where will you find that kind of money?''

''I'm going to London and Paris later this year to help arrange financing. When I return, you'll wish you'd signed up now!''

David was enthralled. He was not only seeing the elephant, he was hearing it. But then at supper table Lucinda turned to him abruptly: ''Where do you stand on woman's rights, Mr. Venable?''

With what seemed heaven sent inspiration, David replied: ''I got into a street fight the day I arrived here, defending a young woman for wearing trousers!'' humorously indicating the places on his face where the bruises had been while recounting what happened.

''That's the kind of support we need! I don't care if she was a saloon girl!'' Lucinda affirmed, while David blushed at her frankness and Wright and Sherman exchanged amused glances. ''We're all sisters under the skin. All oppressed by men and the laws men make. All without the right to vote!'' She became more militant with every word, simultaneously scratching her sides with both hands, an action David had engaged in more than once since arriving in San Francisco and now decided was permissible even in polite society—because of the voracious fleas which permeated even here. ''But we're progressing! Last year we passed a law permitting married women to transact business in their own names! And we're working for statewide prohibition that will get husbands and fathers out of saloons and home where they belong! Do you realize that in this city of thirty-thousand we have nine hundred bartenders? That's one for every thirty persons. I think it's disgraceful!''

''I think it means good service!'' Sherman teased.

''Have you met any nice girls, David?'' Lucinda continued, deliberately ignoring Sherman. ''There's a lovely creature just arrived from New Orleans. Don't you think he'd like Victoria Stanhope, Caleb?''

"If he's got any sense he would."

Supper was being served in style by the Irish maid, though water was the only beverage. For a passing instant David was appalled at thought he was sitting here at ease in such surroundings while downtown in the trenches, as it were, Reverend Taylor and Charles Mornay battled for a better world. But at thought of Angie all compunction left him. This was his new life. He had discovered it. He had a right to it. All his years of loneliness, poverty, obscurity were being compensated for at last. Sherman demanded: "Where you from, lad?"

"Iowa, I guess."

"Why do you guess?"

David explained the changing circumstances of his early years. Sherman's tone mollified. He'd lost his father early too, been reared in the foster household of his now father-in-law, a former Secretary of the Interior and present United States Senator from Ohio. He'd married his benefactor's daughter. "I know something of what you've been through. May make a man of you if you survive it!" And David had a peculiar inkling that Sherman found survival difficult in a very personal way, which was in fact the case. Sherman had married upward and, after an unremarkable career as soldier without battlefield experience, must now, like Grant, prove himself in his own eyes and those of his wife and father-in-law.

"David, your history reminds me of my own," Wright broke in and began an extraordinary account of his transformation from drink to abstinence. It was one of his charms, David realized, that he could be profoundly frank without sounding overly serious like Mornay. "I owe it all to Lucy," he declared beguilingly. "I was a drunkard when I met her, not much older than you are, David!" and a qualm went through David lest perhaps Wright *had* discovered the truth behind his deceptions and was giving him a special kind of treatment. Reared on a Virginia plantation, Wright had gone to New York City to enter business. "But the city turned my head, David. That's why I'm always on the lookout for young fellows like you who might fall victim as I did. Drink is our most serious national problem next to slavery."

"Don't proselytize at your own table, Wright!" Sherman barked. "I take a nip now and then. Maybe he does too!"

"Cump, don't be rude to old friends!" Mrs. Sherman admonished as though she often curbed her husband's outbursts. Her relation with Sherman seemed almost that of patient mother to unruly son.

"Yes, Lucy saved me from the gutter," Wright continued "and the gutters in this city run wide and deep!"

"Nonsense!" Lucinda declared firmly. "You saved yourself Caleb. No one can save another. Each must do it himself or her self." And she smiled so sweetly upon her mate of twenty-five years that David was struck by the realization they were still in love after all that time, still wholly devoted, and the thought placed a warm light over everything about them. Being childless they evidently enjoyed the company of young people.

"I'd like to be rescued by someone as gracious as Mrs Wright," David responded gallantly.

Lucinda smiled in acknowledgment, then looked at him so penetratingly that David saw why Wright had risen from the gutter at her command. "You've taken the pledge of abstinence, Caleb tells me. Any danger of backsliding?"

"None!" David lied cheerfully, though uncomfortable at heart

"Then I want you to meet Victoria Stanhope. There's a cotillion Saturday fortnight. You come as our guest. I'll introduce you."

Finding it impossible to say no even if he'd wanted to, David accepted with pleasure. He forgot his discomfort. Once again he was being borne along on what seemed a glorious tide. The evening seemed touched by magic. This was where he had wished to be: among the rich, the powerful.

Later when he lay in Angie's arms he wondered at the transformations a person could go through in one evening if only he dared.

# Chapter Twenty-seven

We're not boomers heading from one boomtown to another—
we're solid settlers, ain't we Gramp?''

"We is, Granddaughter.''

"Then what we got to be ashamed of?''

"Nothin'.''

"Then why don't you go see her?''

Abe smiled, spit, but would not be hurried, even by his favorite,
who evidently had a certain young man's grandmother in mind.
"I will, when the time is ripe.''

"When will that be?'' she urged.

"I'll know,'' he answered patiently. Work was bringing a rare
moment of tranquility to the fractious family. They had completed
the cabin, even to its sod roof, and were finishing its interior
accessories while also performing daily tasks. Puncheoned logs
comprised the floor by Iphy's demand. "We want to look civilized, don't we?'' She was grating corn for johnnycakes that
would cook in her tight-lidded baking kettle in the large open
fireplace-kitchen. Buck was pouring hot lead into his iron mold
to make bullets for his Colt Repeater, and for his .50 caliber
Hawken percussion rifle which brought home a good share of
their meat. Goodly and Elmer were making puncheon stools for
the puncheon table at which their father worked. Jake was whittling a large wooden stirring spoon for Iphy, while Abe sat in the
doorway fashioning the latchstring of the cabin out of deerskin.
It would hang outside the door by day, inside at night when the
door was closed and barred. And Sally had just returned with her

wooden buckets from watering the young peas, corn, beans and the young fruit trees—apples, plums, pears—they had brought, bare root, from Missouri.

Like the young plants, the family was putting down roots. Their cabin would be among the westernmost in the nation, here at the continent's edge, yet in design and purpose it was essentially the same as those first ones erected more than two centuries earlier on the opposite coast: notched logs laid one atop the other, chinked with mud, its chimney of field and river stone similarly morticed, its narrow windows of membrane-thin deerskin from which the hair had been removed. Eventually there would be a second cabin close by for Abe, Jake and Sally, a roof extending between the two to form a kind of gallery, thus making what Buck called a "Texas House," of the kind he'd observed there when passing through toward Mexico during the war.

"Better see to the stock," Abe suggested. His mind ticking like some old clock was constantly aware of time and circumstance, constantly wary, chiming out its reminders at appropriate moments. No one had looked at the grazing horses and mules for nearly an hour, likewise the chickens in their crates, and the hog in its pen. Elmer set aside his stool. "I'll go."

All were settling into new rhythms. They were putting roots into land they'd dreamed of, fought for, journeyed to, found— new land, richer land, better in every way, they deeply believed, than any they'd known previously. And for some reason none of them quite understood, it lay, must always lie, toward the West. Now they had this piece for which they felt destined. When Iphy read to them aloud from the heavy old brown-backed family Bible with its brass clasp—in which the dates of their births and marriages were recorded and their deaths would be—they identified strongly with the Children of Israel being led to a promised land, which God had reserved for them and which they deserved more than its present inhabitants. Abe spat through the open door, in deference to Iphy's freshly puncheoned floor. "Yeah, Granddaughter, when the time's ripe, I'll know. And I'll go."

She searched his old eyes and as usual found them unfathomable. Abe maintained his hegemony largely by that unforeseeableness he carried deep inside. It was more than experience, rich in that though he was, and more than wisdom. She respected and loved it more than anything else about him. It was so alive, so fresh, somehow eternal.

Iphy began sweetening the johnnycakes with sugar from what

she called "that Jew store in town." Tomorrow would be the
housewarming. "Wesley and them . . . Martin Luther and them,"
by which she meant their cousinly relatives from down the valley
and in the town, newly settled like themselves on lands to which
title was questionable, would be coming to take dinner and spend
the day, asserting a new communal unity. It would give them all
a deepfelt excitement and satisfaction. They were the new life.

From up toward the hacienda dogs began to bark. "They seed
Elmer out among the stock, I reckon," Abe giggled. "Oh, they
know we're here. They know. Even their dogs knows!"

Sally could not find it in herself to urge further. And so they
waited for time to ripen, destiny to manifest itself.

# Chapter Twenty-eight

Summer slipped deceptively toward fall. Fog no longer blanketed the city each night. Days were bright and warm. And the cotillion, twice postponed because of a cholera scare, was taking place at last. Realizing he had no proper clothes to wear to such an occasion, David confided his concern to Gillem.

"Don't worry. I know a tailor who'll do you a suit in two days."

"But I haven't the money to pay a tailor!" The more David made the more he seemed to spend.

"I'll loan you what you need."

Gillem's loans were beginning to feel burdensome but David shrugged them off with the thought he'd soon have all the money he needed and more, with one lucky turn of the wheel at the Golden Nugget; and when he saw himself resplendent in lustrous black broadcloth with black satin waistcoat, all misgiving departed and he went toward the ball with Gillem as if walking on air, confident his good fortune would continue.

"What'll we do for a drink with Wright watching us?" he asked as they approached Portsmouth Square.

For answer Gillem reached into his coat pocket and pulled out a flat brown bottle. "Here!"

David read the label: *Twinkham's Soothing Syrup.* "No kidding, what is it?"

"Mothers give it to their babies."

"No after-breath? Remember, we'll be meeting Our Maker face to face!"

"None!"

David took a swig. A marvelously sweet elixir glided down his throat and into his veins. A sense of happiness suffused him. "What is it, really?"

"I told you: mothers give it to their babies!"

"Laudanum!" David cried with sudden prescience.

"Aunt Lucy probably uses it regularly!" Gillem chuckled.

Various concoctions containing opium were in family medicine chests and could be bought from any druggist. But David had never tasted double strength tincture à la Gillem before. Yet Gillem took it so casually that here evidently was one more aspect of human behavior his inquiring spirit had investigated without tremor. "Don't confuse me with De Quincey," he continued as if sensing David's hesitancy, referring to the celebrated English author's addiction. "I have no literary ambitions!"

"Ah, but you do!" cried David, catching him out for once.

"Just journalistic!" Gillem defended. "A mere disciple of Thalia, not Calliope!"

By now they were entering the spacious lobby of the California House, where they'd given The Ducks the slip, and were proceeding into the crowded ballroom adjacent, where Lucinda preempted them immediately. "Two of Caleb's boys!" she explained, introducing them to Sarabelle Stanhope, whom David thought a sadly faded flower. "Come," Lucinda continued taking his arm, "I want you to meet Victoria!" leaving Gillem to discuss the weather with Sarabelle and Wright.

In contrast to her mother, he found Victoria the most captivating creature he'd ever set eyes on and recalled with excitement their glances meeting as he hurried through the lobby with The Ducks at his heels. There was a reckless sparkle about her which absolutely fascinated him, as did her retroussé nose and laughing eyes. Dark ringlets, carefully arranged by Hattie, were drawn back behind both ears into bunches of adorable sausage curls. In the high fashion of the times she wore no makeup, yet he felt nothing could have enhanced her beauty—or the off-the-shoulder dress with half sleeves, bodice tightly shaped to a graceful "V" above her flounced skirt. A group of admirers including Sedley and Ogles surrounded her. But she was immediately attracted by David's innocent good looks and she too remembered their eyes meeting as he passed through the lobby, also she saw a chance to make Sedley jealous. Therefore she smiled as if David were the most entrancing object she'd ever beheld. A waltz was being announced. She asked daringly: "Perhaps you'd be so kind as to dance with me, Mistah Venable?"

David had the barest notion how to waltz but was soon gliding as if by magic across the polished floor, his way soothed by Gillem's wondrous syrup. All things seemed possible, life golden, he immortal.

"Didn't I see you-all hurry through the vestibule one ny-et?"

He thought he could spend the rest of his life listening to her lilting talk. "Yes and I saw you!" Impetuously he told her why he was hurrying. Her eyes widened.

"Oh, I think that's so *romantic!* Why were they chasing you?" And when he told, those eyes widened to unbelievable dimensions. "I simply ado-ah brave may-en! Is this your first waltz in Frisco? Lucinda saise you recently arrived from the East?"

"It's one I'll never forget!" he vowed fervently.

She feigned shock. "If I took you seriously, I reckon I'd be just like those flirtatious Yankee gals. You might nevah speak to me agay-en!"

"I like the way you break words in two!" he retorted. It was as if she had bewitched him. He wanted her more than he'd ever wanted anything. Angie by contrast seemed coarse and low, his relationship with her degrading. He wanted to enter Victoria's world, that aristocratic world where everything was so entertaining, so light and easy.

"My father is thinking of buying a ray-anch." When he comprehended what she meant he burst out with beguiling candor: "I like the land too!" and told of his childhood in Iowa. "Sometimes my father let me guide the plow in the furrow. I felt like a king. And sometimes when he was away Indians came to our cabin."

Her interest was breathless. "Sure 'nuff?"

"They would wait silently outside the door, never knocking. Mother would hide us behind it, then open it suddenly and give them food or a drink of coffee. They never harmed us. But we were afraid they would."

Victoria found all this so thrilling that when the music stopped and they returned where Sedley and her father were standing she announced: "Mistah Venable's been telling me about fightin' Indians on the Iowa frontiah!"

David broke in with ingratiating embarrassment and explained the facts.

"Nothing to be ashamed of," Stanhope reassured him. "Vicky, he was only a few hundred miles above our Stanhope's Bend. If he hadn't handled those Indians the way he did, they might have come down and scalped us!'' And turning to David with a friendly chuckle which sounded like a ticket of admission to an exclusive club: ''What kind of soil have you up there?''

''Heavy dark loam.''

''Not like our sandy bottomland? Too cold for cotton?''

''I expect so. Though we've got sandy bottoms too.''

''There you have it, Dad,'' Beauford broke in warmly. David liked him as instantly as he disliked Sedley. Beneath his affable exterior, Sedley seemed coldly calculating. But Beauford wore his heart on his sleeve. ''It's not soil that matters, it's climate. I bet cotton will grow all over that property you're planning to buy in the Central Valley. What about it, Eliot?''

Sedley nodded. He wasn't sure he wanted to become Stanhope's son-in-law but he could tolerate Beau's pretentions to knowledge and found Victoria desirable and her father's wealth and influence likewise, and he knew that Southerners dominated the national government as they did California's. David seemed to him ridiculously immature. Likewise Victoria's attempts to make him jealous merely amused him. Compared to the values he perceived in Mary Louise, these two were children. So he shifted the conversation into lighter channels befitting such company, until turning to Beauford, Stanhope commanded: ''Run upstairs and see if Hattie's all right.''

''Why, why shouldn't she be?'' By natural affinity Beau was closer to Hattie than were any others of the family.

''Just take a look. Here's the key.'' That intuition which warned him of Mary Louise's presence on the street the day she put the curse on him had passed through Stanhope again. He'd noticed new independence in Hattie following her visit to church and it roused his suspicion. Justifiably so. Because a few minutes earlier Mary Louise had obtained an extra room-key from the black porter, Sam.

When the door opened and a tall graceful elegantly dressed woman she had never seen before entered with such urgent purpose, pressing a finger to her lips, Hattie put down her sewing, speechless with astonishment. ''Come, my dear, we must act quickly!'' Mary Louise drew her to the divan. ''Don't be alarmed. I'm your mother.''

Hattie gave a broken cry, raised both hands to her cheeks and stared in bewilderment and doubt, still unable to utter a word.

"I think your heart tells you I speak the truth," Mary Louise continued, "but on your right thigh is a birthmark shaped like a teardrop. I last saw it when you were a baby in my arms." And without pause she told the essentials of what had befallen her since. "I've waited for this moment for fifteen years."

Hattie flung herself into her arms with a cry of joy and for the next few moments tears and kisses did the talking. Then Mary Louise asked abruptly: "Are you ready to strike for freedom?"

Hattie hesitated. "I've thought about it. But they've treated me so well . . ."

"They treat their dogs well too. Has he made advances to you?"

Hattie flushed. In fact Stanhope had begun to fondle her in a disturbing way. Startled and reassured by her mother's intuition, she burst into tears and told of his advances and her fear of what might come next.

Mary Louise hugged her. "Thank God, he hasn't raped you. That's why I left you, baby, so I could pull myself up into a position to get you out of his power before he used you as he used me. I swore it wouldn't happen to you. Thank God I arrived in time! I can guide you to freedom. But it won't be easy. You must want to come. And you must prepare to take chances."

"Would I truly be with you?"

"If you want to. If you will trust me."

Hurriedly Hattie flung on her cape. Reuben Stapp was waiting in the darkness at the back door. Hattie's heart beat faster at sight of him. Without a word he struck out for Mornay's house. They followed at some distance. In the eyes of passers-by they were simply a fashionably dressed lady accompanied by her maid.

Beau was opening the door which Mary Louise had relocked, finding no one inside, being mystified, then secretly delighted at Hattie's daring, hoping it would succeed.

When he returned to the ballroom he whispered in his father's ear. Stanhope's face betrayed nothing as he drew Sarabelle aside and ordered her and Vicky to carry on as if nothing were amiss. Then he strolled casually out of the room with Beau.

"Where are you two off to?" Lucinda called after them.

"Men's matters!" Stanhope tweaked her.

# Chapter Twenty-nine

After the cotillion David went straight home, feeling too transported by his new found love for Victoria to go gambling with Gillem or visit Angie. He was surprised to see light behind the drawn curtains of Mornay's parlor at such a late hour. His key was to the back door. He was approaching the parlor when Mornay intercepted him. He'd never heard Mornay sound so serious. "David, can I trust you?"

"Yes, of course."

"Really trust you?" Mornay wasn't quite sure that he could but under the circumstances felt he must.

"Of course, why?"

Without another word Mornay led him into the lighted parlor, and with amazement David saw an extraordinary gathering: Martha, Wing Sing, Madam St. Clair whom he'd never expected to see again, and at either side of her a pretty Negro girl of about sixteen and a handsome young black man a few years older. "You find us in the midst of confidential proceedings," Mornay continued in that tone of deepest gravity. "Can we count on you to be one of us?"

"I give you my word."

"This is Hattie and this is Reuben." Mornay explained in general what was happening, without mentioning the Stanhopes by name or Mary Louise's relationship to Hattie, feeling such explanation to be her prerogative. Mary Louise had meanwhile decided to place full faith in David, adding it to their shipboard friendship. "Mr. Mornay said when we got off the boat if I ever needed help

I was to come to him, remember?'' David remembered, remembered too her infatuating charm which seemed more pronounced than ever. ''Hattie is my daughter. She was the Stanhope's slave. She wants to be free.''

With these astounding words to David, Hattie smiled shyly at him, asserting her trust. Impulsively his heart went out to her, to them all. All his recent activities suddenly seemed frivolous compared to this. This was for a truly noble, truly heroic, cause involving the very bodies and souls of human beings, and the relief of the oppressed.

''Of course,'' Mornay was saying gently. ''I told Mary Louise she need look no farther. Hattie has found safety for the moment. Martha will share her room with her.''

Moved by much the same feelings that were moving David, Martha took Hattie's hand in a gesture of silent companionship. Moisture came into David's eyes. Everything he'd ever witnessed seemed inconsequential compared to this.

''The risks to everyone concerned are very great,'' Mornay was continuing. ''This is the Underground Railroad about which I'm sure you've heard. California like the nation has a Fugitive Slave Law. It is a shame and a disgrace. No other free state has such a law. It is our special stigma. Under it, anyone obstructing the Stanhopes or the police in recapturing Hattie, or harboring her meanwhile, is subject to fine of not less than five hundred dollars and imprisonment of not less than two months in jail, besides civil damages of one thousand dollars for obstructing and another thousand for harboring and or concealing. I want you to know this. Of course it is nothing beside what Hattie may suffer. But you should bear it in mind.''

Mornay's caveats fell on half-deaf ears. David's head was swirling with conflicting thoughts. Hattie had been the Stanhopes' slave. He was in love with Victoria. Only a few minutes before, the Stanhopes had represented his ideal. ''You can count on me!'' he vowed with fervor but felt gripped by opposing emotions, painfully torn in opposite directions, yet unable to turn back.

''What about the National Fugitive Slave Law?'' Mary Louise was asking Mornay.

''It doesn't apply because she didn't cross any state lines in running away. Yet we must never forget that that evil measure was part of the unholy compromise which brought California into the union. We as a state, as a nation, have much to atone for!''

The plan they were discussing was to hide Hattie at Petrini's outlying vegetable farm where no one would think of looking for a runaway slave. "It may take a few days to make arrangements. I'll speak to Petrini Monday morning when he comes to the market. Meanwhile with utmost caution she should be safe here," Mornay advised. And so it was agreed.

After Martha had taken Hattie to her room and the others departed, David and Mornay talked late. It was like the old days. "My boy, it's great to have you back with us! The path ahead will not be easy, I assure you. There are hazards. But we may yet build Jerusalem in this golden land!" gripping his shoulder with a purposeful conviction as they said goodnight.

Yet as he fell asleep David's head swam again with dilemmas. He felt absolutely committed to Mornay, Hattie, Mary Louise and the cause they represented. But Sarabelle Stanhope had invited him to attend church with the family next day.

The simple interior reminded him of many he'd known back East. There wasn't time or money in early Gold Rush days to construct a more ornate one. But the outside of the church had been fireproofed with sheet iron and now the sun heating this iron made it expand and creak every few moments with a sound like a gunshot.

Over and among these gunshots the gentle voice of earnest looking Reverend Ardmore, whom Sarabelle Stanhope described as "a true man of God" but who seemed to David underfed and underpaid, though glorified in a dark preaching robe, intoned: *"The Lord is in his holy temple; let all the earth keep silence before him!"*

They were all kneeling but David was thinking less about the Lord than Victoria's adorable curls and waistline as she knelt in the pew directly in front of him.

All members of Mornay's household had gathered at breakfast that morning to discuss whether it was better for Martha to go to church with her father or stay home like Wing to keep Hattie company. "Better for her to go with me as usual," Mornay ruled. "We don't want anything to appear out of the ordinary. That's why your mother and Reuben won't be visiting today, Hattie. You'll be all right here with Wing for an hour or so, won't you?"

This was Hattie's first morning of freedom. No day had seemed so bright. "You go!" she said.

"Courageous girl, we'll be thanking God for your delivery

from bondage! Join us, David?'' Mornay added, sure he would do so, thus placing him squarely on the horns of that dilemma he'd been agonizing over much of the night. He heard his voice blurting: ''Thanks, but I've already been invited!'' Yet he could not bring himself to say by whom. He was not even sure the Stanhopes would attend church after what had happened but felt compelled to find out. He saw the disappointment in Mornay's face. Martha was scornful. ''He still thinks he's too good for us!''

''Hush,'' Mornay reproved. ''Even though we can't all be in the same church, we're all God's children. Especially on the Sabbath!''

But he felt let down from those heights he'd reached with David the night before and doubts about the boy's reliability crept back into his mind. David felt a similar letdown, while rationalizing that by learning what steps the Stanhopes were taking to recapture Hattie, he might contribute much toward protecting her.

Now he wanted to reach out and touch Victoria's dark tresses peeking from under that fetching little brown hat in front of him, with its derby-like shape and ribbon poofs and feathers. He knew she liked him. Why couldn't he instead of her mother and father be kneeling there beside her, along with Lucinda and Caleb Wright, rather than sandwiched as he was between Sedley and Beau Stanhope? He'd never attended an Episcopal Church before but heard that ''the best people'' belonged. Just being there seemed a step up from those unceremonious Calvinistic ones he was used to. *POP!* the iron walls creaked in the sun.

Walking to church with the Stanhopes and Sedley he'd reentered that world of elegance which fascinated him. At first there was no mention of Hattie as if there were nothing amiss. David admired their composure, yet loathed their slave owning. Again he felt torn. Then Victoria had touched his arm. ''The most dreadful thing—my Hattie has run away!''

He extemporized. ''Perhaps she was just overwhelmed by the idea of freedom and the temptation was too great?'' He tried to sound consoling while feeling two-faced—delighting in her, wanting to please her, but wanting to be true to Hattie too.

''Too great? After all we've done for her? Wicked girl, I just hope they find her and she gets what's comin'!''

''What is your father doing?''

''He's told the police. They're searching for her. Oh, I hope they find her! After all we've done for the ungrateful wretch!''

''Dearly beloved brethren: The Scripture moveth us, in sundry places, to acknowledge and confess our manifold sins and wickedness; and that we should not dissemble nor cloak them before the face of Almighty God our heavenly Father. . . .''

David felt as if the minister's words were directed at him, as if the frail-looking reverend and God Almighty knew of his secret life and current dilemma. During his adolescent crisis, bound out to the brutal farmer in upstate New York, he'd undergone a deeply religious experience. One scorching hot day while drudging in the hayfield at the end of a pitchfork, he felt direct connection with God. He heard an invisible voice from on high calling him to do and be something of greater worth. Thereafter he rarely felt far from a Supreme Being who made and controlled all things visible and invisible, and who spoke to mankind in words. "In the beginning was the Word." David knew his Bible thoroughly. Jesus taught in parables. Words began to have new significance for him as he realized they were an aspect of God's will. But now they filled him with uneasiness. Maybe he *had* concealed his drinking, gambling, whoring with Angie from Wright and Mornay and from bewitching Victoria and irritating Martha. But had he concealed them from God? And what about his new dilemma? Could he resolve it without God's help?

"We have followed too much the devices and desires of our own hearts." All of them were kneeling again in the general confession. "We have offended against thy holy laws. We have left undone those things which we ought to have done, and we have done those things which we ought not to have done . . ."

With awesome conviction it came to David that God *did* know about his misconduct, was aware of his every action, every thought, was speaking to him now, offering a merciful solution to his difficulties. A warm surge of hope replaced his inner anguish and he understood for the first time the miracle of forgiveness and atonement. Yet he knew he must act upon this understanding. Action would be its test.

Sedley's shoulder brushed his as they resumed their seats. Even in his newly exalted state, David could not abide the man. Not so Beauford at his other elbow. There was a gallant honesty about easy-going Beau he continued to like very much. As if in response he felt a nudge in the ribs. Beau was bored by the service and made no pretense of being otherwise as did Sedley.

"When worldliness is driving forward with such zeal all around us, every faculty strained to the utmost in the contest for material goods," Ardmore had mounted to the pulpit and was preaching with persuasiveness, "what about the goods of the spirit? Shall the followers of the Lord be slothful? When the very future of this beautiful new land, of our children and our children's children depends upon our actions, today and tomorrow?"

David felt he was witnessing a subtle adversary proceeding in which the minister by his earnestness, his appeal to their better natures, above all by his own spiritual commitment, put their materialism, their lesser natures, at challenge. It was a kind of stand-off, glory against power. Yes, that was it, glory against power! The words sank deep. David remembered Mornay using them to describe that struggle for the future of state and nation in which they were both now involved.

Time for the collection. Wright and Sedley, great pillars of the community, were passing the polished circular wooden plates. David noticed an extraordinary paucity of coins on the red velvet in the one he took from Sedley and handed along to Beau. As it came back he contributed a shiny double eagle, all the money he had in the world, just to vindicate the poor minister. He knew Sedley saw. Beau whispered: "Paying your way upstairs?"

But David remained angry, impulsive as usual when strongly moved. His true self seemed to have returned. If he ever preached, he resolved, it would be like Reverend Taylor from a barrel in the street, never inside a fashionable church like this one.

At that moment Wing looked out the parlor window and saw the stubby brown-suited figure of Constable Monaghan,* badge of office shining over his heart, stroll by the house on Telegraph Hill. Without a word Wing beckoned to Hattie and stowed her away in the secret compartment, cleverly hidden off the closet in Martha's room, which only they and Mornay knew existed.

Wright and Sedley were marching down the aisle side by side to the stately strains of "Praise God from whom all blessings flow!" while Reverend Ardmore stood patiently to receive what they brought. How much would the plates contain? How successful had he been? "All things come of Thee, O Lord, and of Thine own hath we given Thee!"

David felt glad he'd emptied his pockets. It was part of the new action he must take for the sake of glory. Indignation continued to fill him with strong resolve. He knew where he was

*police uniforms had not yet been generally adopted

going. He would work things out. Hattie would not be recaptured. He would continue to see Victoria. Somehow all could be reconciled. But now the service was ending.

People were rising to leave. The intoxicating prospect of walking Victoria back to the hotel, supporting her delicate hand on his arm, swept over David. Turning eagerly toward the aisle, he realized with consternation and embarrassment that Mornay and Martha were directly behind him in the next pew but one. They must have been there all the time. He blushed fiery red. They were the last people he'd expected to see in this fashionable church. But Mornay's presence had nothing to do with fashion. His ancestors, arriving in the New World, decided not to join the established Puritan Church of New England which had been guilty of executions and other cruelties such as they were fleeing from. His eyes met David's with extraordinary forbearance. He'd been observing him throughout the service with mixed feelings, glad to see him in church, dubious indeed of the company he was with. He'd recognized the Stanhopes from Mary Louise's description. Seeing David with them and Sedley at this crucial moment filled him with apprehension and dismay. Yet he remembered similar feelings on seeing Mary Louise in the hack with Sedley. Those had proved mistaken, these might too.

To David's stammered greeting he replied unperturbed: "Glad to see you in the Lord's House, my boy!" nodding curtly to Sedley, receiving a similar response. Lucinda greeted him warmly, for she admired his radical Abolitionism. From Wright whom he liked but haggled over pennies with he got a wink. Then they swept by him, taking David with them.

Outside on the steps they all lingered a moment, and Wright began to chaff: "Mornay, you old Shylock, you've got your nerve, coming to a Christian church!" extending a hand, finally evoking a smile from the serious minded merchant.

"Don't pay heed to Caleb!" Lucinda interceded. "Is this your daughter?"

Wearing that gold cross and chain her father had given her Martha was sulking. David knew she would give him a tongue lashing when he returned home. Suddenly an inspiration struck. After Lucinda made an affectionate fuss over her, knowing her to be motherless, he deliberately introduced her to Victoria. "This is my little gadfly," he said gravely. "She stings me when I misbehave."

With a gracious smile Victoria held out her hand. "I'm glad

to meet a gadfly. I've never met one befoah!''

Rising to the occasion Martha accepted her hand and looked her straight in the eye. With a precocity which amazed David she replied coolly: ''He's not as bad as he seems, Miss Stanhope. Just a little misguided.'' It made him proud of her despite himself. He sensed something womanly passing between the two girls which he didn't quite understand.

Sarabelle Stanhope was calling to Victoria in terms calculated to make Sedley jealous: ''Come along, you two!''

Taking Victoria tenderly by the arm, her dress rustling alluringly beside him, David guided her into the fashionable Sunday parade along Montgomery Street—Sedley and Beau, the Colonel and Sarabelle, paired in column behind them. David glowed when passersby turned and stared admiringly.

During all of this, Sedley maintained his usual outward affability, though he found much of it painfully boring, even absurd, but was prepared to wait patiently pending outcomes which might prove profitable.

At the intersection of Jackson Street the little procession was stopped by the passing of the Turnverein Band, one of many from various nationalities parading that day in native costume.

''I like their lederhosen,'' David commented. Victoria disagreed. ''Fat men's bay-ah knees have nevah appealed to me!''

After the band blared by, they proceeded—and came face to face with Angie, her cheeks garishly rouged, wearing her bright blue cap and red trousers, escorted by a villainous looking fellow in a checkered suit whom David knew instinctively must be her mac.

''Why David!'' she burst out ingenuously at sight of him and stopped to talk.

Ears burning, eyes averted, he pretended not to see her and, devoting all his attention to Victoria, passed on without acknowledging her greeting.

''Who's your attractive fraynd?'' Victoria drawled sarcastically, and she removed her fingers from his arm to register her displeasure. David heard Sedley chuckling behind him and hated him more than ever.

''I never saw her before! She must have mistaken me for someone else!'' he declared airily, and walked on, embarrassed, but also secretly a little proud and a little defiant, feeling himself a man of the world, guessing that somehow Victoria would find a way to forgive him.

Angie stood looking after them, hurt and crestfallen.

After a sumptuous dinner at the California House, Victoria and her mother and father departed for a carriage ride with Sedley, leaving Beau and David knocking balls rather aimlessly about the table in the hotel's otherwise deserted billiard room. David knew he should be home with Mornay and Martha and Hattie but the allure of the Stanhopes held him, also the possibility of learning what they intended to do about their runaway slave. "Too bad about Hattie," he offered.

Beau shrugged. "She's a good kid. I hope they never find her."

David was astounded. "You mean that?"

"Sure. What Hattie did is what any of us would want to do in her circumstances. You can't stop people from wanting to be free."

Eager to pursue this extraordinary conversation and investigate this unexpected side of Beau, David was frustrated by a party of young blades who came boisterously into the room and began play at the next table.

"Come on," he suggested. "Let's take a walk."

"Southerners don't know how to walk!" Beau protested. "Now, if you'd suggested a horseback ride . . . !"

"Walking's good for you! Keeps you fit! Old Dr. Samuel Johnson walked all over Scotland when he was more than sixty and Boswell wrote a book about it, *A Tour to the Hebrides!*" David was exaggerating to make his point. Corpulent Johnson walked very little. But Beau's reading hadn't included either Boswell or Johnson.

"Sir Walter Scott's the author everyone reads down our way. All the fellows think they're Ivanhoe in shining armor; all the girls are Lady Rowena."

"Scott's incorrigibly romantic."

"Are you suggesting we Southerners are too?"

"I didn't say that!"

They compromised by taking the horse-drawn omnibus three miles inland to the Old Mission. From there, abjuring temptations of nearby horse races and a bullfight, they started across country toward the sea and as they walked the words began to flow. "I keep telling Dad," Beau confided, "that we ought to build our

own textile mills in Louisiana. Why do we have to ship our cotton
to New England or old England to be made into cloth? The South
ought to be more self-sufficient. But people are too set in their
ways. They can't see it. Not even Dad can. He just wants cotton,
cotton, land, land, slaves, slaves. Now he's got his eye on your
Great Central Valley. That's why he's buying into Sedley's syndicate.''

"Syndicate?"

"Yeap, he and the others. They won't admit it publicly but
they envision our plantation system here with cheap Indian or
Chinese labor if not slaves. Six hundred thousand acres. They
may be right. Anyway, he's signed the papers."

David burst out: "That means you're going to settle in California?" Visions of Victoria as a California belle and someday
his wife when he was successful and rich, flashed through his
mind.

"Someday we might. Mother and Victoria have got their eye
on a house on Green Street just above Kearny. But Sedley wants
them in South Park on Rincon Hill. Says that's the fashionable
place. Of course we wouldn't spend all year here. We'd keep the
plantation and the New Orleans house and divide our time."

"Would you bring slaves here?"

"That's a touchy point. By your state law we can't—and keep
them in residence. But Dad scoffs at such fine points, says everybody's doing it."

"But what if they run away like Hattie?"

"He plans to make such an example of her that it'll never
happen again. I think he's wrong. But I can't say so."

"Why can't you? You're saying it to me?"

Directly in their path lay that gloomy body of water known as
Lake Merced. Surrounded by reeds and a few solitary trees,
haunted by cries of sea birds, it lay between them and the sand
dunes bordering the ocean, and it reminded David of one of those
mythical bodies of water where hands arise clasping gleaming
swords or spirits disappear. The isolated spot was a famous dueling ground, as he explained. But Beau expressed himself sur-
feited with the whole idea of dueling. "It's a branch of our old
mint-julep way that's got grafted onto your state. They may call
me a traitor but I'd say it must go. Like slavery must go!"

David was delighted at the new Beau he heard behind these
words and was eager for more, but just then they emerged onto
the road that ran between the lake and the sea and found it

thronged with horseback riders and carriages. From one of the carriages came a hail.

"Why, it's Dad!" cried Beau.

David looked up and, with palpitating heart, saw Victoria and with her Sedley, Stanhope, Sarabelle. Sedley was ordering the driver to halt. Stanhope was demanding: "What on earth are you two doing out here?"

"Walking!" Beau explained cheerfully as if it were the most natural thing in the world.

"You lost your mind?"

"No, Dad, this is the greatest. More fun than I've had in months!" Beau asserted. David was profoundly amused.

"Rubbish!" the Colonel snorted. "Get in. We can make room, can't we, Eliot?"

"Of course!" echoed Sedley amiably.

"Beau Boy," Sarabelle begged, picking up her skirts and sliding over, "do get in with us! There's room. And Mr. Venable can sit beside Victoria. I'm sure he won't mind that."

David, eyes on Vicky, was about to proclaim that it would be one of the best things that ever happened to him, when his astonished ears heard Beau say: "Thanks Dad, thanks Eliot, but we're on an excursion. You've heard of Dr. Johnson's *Tour of the Hebrides?* Well, this is our tour of San Francisco's outlying regions. Come on, Dave!" And before they could remonstrate he seized David's reluctant arm and dragged him off across the road through a break in the almost steady stream of carriages and down upon the sandy beach beyond, where the tide was out and the footing good. Beau was laughing. But David was astounded at his friend's temerity and disappointed at not being with Victoria. "Will your Dad stand for that?"

"Sure, he needs putting down a bit now and then!"

They walked on, David's estimation of his companion rising, and when they reached Point Lobos at the entrance to Golden Gate, they stopped to contemplate a magnificent scene. Between them and the Marin shore opposite—indeed golden at this season—a blue avenue of water opened toward the deep sea, and out there, coming toward them so swiftly they could see it grow larger by the minute was a magnificent clipper under full sail. It seemed to embody all the expectations of their new land. It was in fact Sedley's *New Enterprise* completing her record run from Boston, and the semaphore station on the headland above them was already signaling the news to the relay station atop Telegraph Hill.

From there it would be communicated to the city below. Hundreds of Sunday excursioners lined up with them along the shore watching excitedly.

"Here comes the future!" Beau announced. "And this is where it's all going to come ashore!"

"That's how I feel!" David rejoined. "I'd like to settle here the rest of my life."

"So would I!" They shook hands on it with that facetious yet serious foolishness young men will use on such occasions. "We'll form a partnership!" Beau proposed. "And outdo Sedley!"

"We'll turn the Central Valley white with cotton and strike a gold mine!"

And Beau added with a wink: "You'll marry Victoria!"

Returning homeward at sundown they stopped at the old Spanish presidio, now a United States military post. Troops were forming for the ceremony of retreat. The blue-clad ranks stood at attention. The cannon sounded. An officer raised his sword smartly in salute. The bugle notes rang out clearly, poignantly, over hillside and Bay, as the flag began to descend its pole. Beau gave an involuntary shudder.

"I hope we never have to serve in the armed forces!"

"Why should we?"

"All this loose talk about a war between South and North makes me wonder."

# Chapter Thirty

Old Clara sat in the morning sun on the portico of her courtyard. She was weaving a basket in the traditional manner of her people, using willow and juncus grass and stems of maidenhair ferns. As her fingers created its shape and designs, it reaffirmed her special identity and kept her mind off her many troubles. It was a large round bottle-necked basket such as Tilhini would use in the Snake Dance later that day to contain his rattlesnakes. It was nearly finished except for the quail plumes she was adding at intervals to its central bulge.

She recalled going with Tilhini, he a boy, she a girl, to watch his father, white-haired Quati, astrologer-priest and snakemaster, gather snakes for such a ceremony as this. It was a warm day like this. She carried a basket like the one she was making now. Tilhini carried a basketry tray. When they reached the rocky place where the snakes lived, old Quati took the tray from Tilhini and lined it with condor's down from his sorcery bag and placed it on the ground. Then he gave a low whistle and began to sing the rattlesnake song:

> "Come crawling, my deadlies,
> Come crawling, my deadlies,
>     We'll go to the dance,
>     We'll go to the dance!
> Come crawling, deadlies!

I make a soft bed for you,
I make a soft bed for you!''

As she held her breath, one by one the snakes emerged slowly
from the rocks and crawled toward the tray of soft down. Clara's
heart nearly stopped. Quati continued to sing, standing a few steps
to windward so the aroma of the balsam root, which he was chew-
ing and with which he'd smeared hands and body, would help
lull the snakes. He regarded them with deepest reverence for they
were messengers from the Lord of the Dead, Kuwaiyin, who sent
them to bring in people who had been bad. The snakes could
make you die even without biting you, or a powerful sorcerer like
Quati could take the shape of one and bite you. Clara was afraid
her beating heart might frighten them away. But when they
reached the basketry tray, they settled on the condor down and
lay still. Keeping up his song, soothing but insistent, sometimes
interspersing a low whistle, Quati slipped his hand under the largest one, moving very carefully, and put it into a bottle-necked
basket such as she was making now.

Even today she looked forward to the Snake Ceremony with
keen anticipation. Little Juana, Purísima's daughter, had already
placed a crown of wildflowers on her head, and run away laughing. Many of those coming and going about the house wore similar crowns, pale lavender farewells to spring and deep red
clarkias and white and golden mariposa lilies gathered from secluded places in the summer hills. There was that heightened ex-
pectancy about household and village which always accompanied
a festival day. From the playing field toward the Indianada she
heard shouts. It was a day to reaffirm the ancient ways of her
people, and the freedom of choice concerning them which she
had striven to maintain all these years since her Antonio's death.
The poignancy of their shared dream swept over her. "Two peo-
ples, two ways, become one." It remained her life's central meaning, though sorely battered by circumstance.

This was the second Snake Dance of the year. The first had
been held as usual in early spring when the snakes emerged from
hibernation. But since then three persons had been bitten and two
had died, a sure sign evil was afoot and must be placated. She
wondered what that evil was. She could not quite bring herself
to believe wholeheartedly in the old way, but couldn't quite not
believe.

Sedley had written he was coming soon. Meanwhile, God bless

him, he'd sent her a cattle buyer, an energetic young fellow with ruddy cheeks and foreign accent, a native of Germany. "You can trust Henry Miller, Tía Clara," Sedley wrote. "He's already our leading butcher." Miller inspected her cattle with shrewd eyes and bargained hard but fairly. At twenty dollars a head she was satisfied. Furthermore he'd brought his own drovers. It saved sending Pacifico and Isidro and their vaqueros up the bandit-infested road with another valuable herd. It also put gold in her hands to pay some of Francisco's debts and the heavy taxes on the ranch. Behind her she heard a brisk step.

Pacifico was approaching along the portico, smartly dressed, newly shaven. Intuition told her he was bound elsewhere but she pretended to be engrossed with her work.

"What are you doing, Mamá Grande?"

She displayed the quail plumes she was adding to her basket, fastening them to the interwoven grass and willow with the wiry stems of the maiden-hair fern. "You remember the legend of the conscientious quail?" She knew she'd told it him before but he would say she hadn't.

"No, tell me."

"The quail represent fair play. Once a bad snake sent the Chief of the Dead the names of good people. As result they died. But the quail told the waterskaters who passed the word to the ants, who stung the snake to death. So I've woven ants and waterska-ters into my design as well as the plumes of quail and the black diamonds of rattlesnakes. It will remind the snakes that they too must respect what is right!"

Pacifico smiled indulgently. "You really believe all that?" And Clara wondered if indeed she really did, or only wanted to and wanted him to. Her attitude toward Pacifico was ambivalent. She wanted him to marry Anita, to be accepted by the white Christian society of the ranchos which had accepted her, yet wanted him to retain the Indian spirit. "Yes," she replied soberly, "it is why I've advised you never to kill a snake. It is why I make baskets with quail plumes. I want the snakes to know someone is watch-ing them!"

"But," he teased, "I'm not an Indian. Why can't I kill one?"

She felt him escaping her—as his father had done. And now also this lad so dear to her heart? "The white man in you can. I'm speaking to the Indian!" she retorted, reaching deep for truth, at the same time striving for casualness. "And where are you off to now?"

"There's a fandango in town. I hoped you would permit me?"

"I do not approve of these public parties which everyone attends. They always end in fights. Why don't you ride over to the Los Padres and see Anita?"

"I'm sure she will be at the dance," Pacifico fibbed reassuringly. "Why don't you come too, Mamá Grande?"

Clara snorted. "And miss our Snake Ceremony? I'm surprised you don't wish to stay and see it!"

But Pacifico was bored to death at the thought of witnessing again what to him was outmoded superstition. He was far more interested in the new world of American California.

"And I suspect that a certain gringa," Clara continued caustically, driven to say what might wound him as he had wounded her, "a certain gringa may be there too and she is the true reason for your freshly shaven face and neatly braided hair; and because she is like you, you feel some mysterious affinity for her, rather than for Anita, as if color of hair has anything to do with what people truly are!"

Pacifico flushed. "Not so! I only wish to see what happens. It is to be a big affair. Everyone is going!"

"Then go!" she snapped, hurt and irascible. "Be like everyone else! Be like the gringos you seem to admire so much!"

When he would have kissed her hand she refused it. But as she watched him ride out the gate on his beautiful buckskin, his lithe young figure gleaming in the sun, there was moisture in her eyes. And the work in her hands seemed meaningless.

"Will Pacifico be there?" Anita was saying.

"How should I know?" Her father was tantalizingly noncommittal. "Shall I ask him?"

"Don't you dare!"

"Why not?" continued Don Domingo with a wink. "You two are betrothed, aren't you?"

"How can you say such a thing?" Face flaming, Anita tossed her head with a frown. "It's the last idea I'd ever have!" Whereas in fact she'd been thinking of little else.

She and Pacifico had been as good as betrothed since childhood, as Domingo well knew. He was eager to see the attachment formalized. The last meeting of the two young people had been at his spacious Los Padres hacienda. Protocol dictated the next be at Clara's. But no invitation had been forthcoming due to Pacifico's reluctance and his grandmother's many difficulties. Still, Don Domingo, as a practical man of the world, large framed, large jawed, cinnamon hair just thinning on top, was not one to let trifles interfere with results he deemed of consequence. A union of his acres with Clara's would create the largest ranch in the region, also a dynasty which accorded well with his ambitions. Domingo was a "Yankee Don," a Maine sailor who'd jumped ship and married Inés Estenega, younger sister of Pacifico's dead mother. Inés brought him proprietorship over many broad acres as well as seven daughters, of whom dark, slender, shy, fifteen-year-old Anita was eldest; and thus, also, Anita and Pacifico were cousins.

But Domingo feared lest Anita was overly sheltered for these new times. As plain Dominic Rogers he'd made his way from ship's carpenter to Grandee. From experience he believed that exposure to life's circumstances led to good outcomes. Therefore it was his suggestion that he and Anita and her mother attend the fandango at Santa Lucía. "It'll be in the new style. Plenty of Americans present."

But now his consort Doña Inés expressed disagreement. She wanted Anita reared as she herself had been: skillful at dancing and singing and sewing, playing the spinet and being discreetly charming, all in the context of an aristocratic household. "These public dances are vulgar affairs," she protested much as Clara had done, "attended by riffraff who have no manners. They're no place for a young girl!"

But her husband insisted. "We must play a part in these new times in which we find ourselves!"

Anita was persuaded to express reluctant agreement, based on the secret expectation of seeing Pacifico. And so it was decided.

Jogging his buckskin down the valley at a Spanish trot, a slow jog very becoming to horse and rider, Pacifico's eyes strayed often to the newly built cabin. He wondered if she were watching and would be going to the dance as his grandmother predicted.

Inside Sally was demanding: "Take me?" She and Goodly and Jake were seated on the new stools at the new table. Iphy was at her spinning wheel. Buck was measuring out powder he would use on a coming manhunt in the back country. Abe was reclining on his mattress of grass whittling wooden pegs in lieu of nails for the second cabin they were about to construct.

"Take yourself to the dance!" Goodly retorted.

"All right," she flared, "I will!"

Stopping her wheel, Iphygenia scolded: "You take your cousin to the dance, son, shame on you!"

"It's a Greaser dance," Buck objected. "She'd oughtn't to go! Jake, you'd oughtn't to let her!"

Jake as usual didn't quite know what to say. "It's a white man's dance, from what I heered." While he grappled with indecision, Iphy spoke up again: "It's for everybody. You all know that as well as I. Wesley and Martin are going, and Troy and them, and others from town. We can't live out here like hermits forever! I've a mind to go too!"

"Not with me you won't!" Buck declared. His hatred toward Californians of Spanish or Indian blood had intensified. Two of the family mules had disappeared. "If it ain't the Greasers it's Injuns," he'd insisted. "There's a band of hostiles back there," indicating the hills, "and they say he's gone to join 'em," meaning Francisco. "You want us to sit here idle while they eat us up?" Buck's Rangers, as they were calling themselves, composed of himself and fellow settlers, were preparing to take the law into their own hands, frontier style, and implement what they saw as necessary countermeasures. Now he turned violently on Sally. "Judgin' from all the commotion, they're havin' a pow-wow up at the Big House," jerking his thumb toward the hacienda. "If you want to go to a party, why not go there, since you're so keen on Greasers anyway?"

Before Sally could respond Iphy did. "You shut up or I'll wash your mouth out with soap!"

Abe interrupted. "Tell you what, children. Goodly and I'll escort these ladies to the ball. I reckon they've earned a night off. Goodly, you hear?"

Goodly replied surlily: "I won't dance with her!"

"I wouldn't dance with you if you was the last man on earth!" Sally turned up her nose defiantly. "Come on, Iphy. Let's get ready!"

When Pacifico reached town toward late afternoon he went directly to the house of his friend Benito Ferrer. The store at the front was closed because this was Saturday, the Jewish Sabbath, so Pacifico rode around to the back where there was a yard enclosed by a high adobe wall, containing stalls for horses, cowshed and a chicken house and vegetable garden. Ruth Ferrer's flowers too had a place there—roses and fuchsias of many shades brightening walls and trellises. Putting a little finger into each corner of his mouth, Pacifico gave a special whistle. In a moment the back door opened.

Like his conquistador grandfather for whom he was named Benito was slightly but lithely built with curly black hair, sharp black eyes, a pleasant yet wary manner which neither intruded nor held back. "Amigo!" he called. "What's up?"

"The fandango, what else?"

Benito shook his head. "I'd like to. But you know how they are!" motioning toward the house behind him. "Come in and see what you can do!"

"But it's your Sabbath!"

Benito made a face of boredom. "Not mine. Besides it's almost over!" He indicated the setting sun. "Come. We'll be eating soon. God knows I'm starving!"

His parents' orthodoxy in matters of religion, including Sabbath fasting, had not been transmitted to Benito who preferred exploring new trails as his grandfather had done, pursuing wild horses, or serenading the señoritas of the town to the life of a storekeeper's son; and in these activities it was more often he who took the lead than placid Pacifico. Though they were old friends, Pacifico seldom entered the house without feeling he was entering another world. Here there was none of the critical harshness, none of the tempestuousness of his grandmother's household. Instead he found a subtle awareness and warmth that was like an invisible blanket gently laid upon him with the touch of intimacy. And such was his feeling now as he looked into the faces of Ruth and Santiago Ferrer—Aunt Ruth, Uncle Santiago, as he'd been taught to call them—for they were old friends of Clara's and often visited the ranch. They welcomed him affectionately as did Benito's less venturesome brother Mark.

"Our Pacifico comes in his finery," Ruth teased, as she embraced him. "Let the girls beware!"

"Ah, let him beware of them!" her husband riposted in Pacifico's defense. "They're all after him, voracious creatures!" And Santiago added with a pat on the shoulder: "How goes it, my son? How's Grandmother?"

"Difficult as ever!"

"Shush, you mustn't say such things!" Ruth chided.

"And our Bernardina?" Santiago inquired further. Preoccupied with the hacienda school and neighboring Indian village life, Bernardina was less than regular in her visits home.

"She reads to Grandmother every evening from that new book by Charles Dickens, *David Copperfield.*"

"Does she really?" Ruth was genuinely amazed at this news.

"And reads it every day to her school children. But when I try to listen, it just goes over my head."

"You're a rancher," Santiago sympathized. "Books are for women, business for men. That's what I tell my boys."

This was more tact than truth, for Santiago enjoyed both books and business. Intelligence and fair dealing had won him the respect and even affection of neighboring ranchers, though few accepted him on intimate terms because of his faith and race. Yet he'd long been Clara's counselor on important matters and it was he with Father O'Hara's help who'd convinced her she must swallow her pride and comply with the law requiring them to submit claims for their land; and he had also advised her to consult Sedley in this matter, because for years he'd dealt with Sedley and his ships. Now they no longer came trading along the coast, hides and tallow being of little consequence in these new times of grand-scale commerce and high-priced beef, when Santiago needed goods for his store he went to San Francisco, bought them, chartered a schooner and brought them down to the hazardous landing at Santa Lucía. And this had engaged him during past weeks, keeping him from his periodic visit to the mistress of Rancho Olomosoug.

Ruth was spreading the table with a fresh cloth and lighting the candles that stood on it. "Join us, Pacifico. I'll soon cut the bread. And yesterday I baked a special halvah for dessert. Your favorite, remember?"

As the sun set she lighted the kitchen fire and began to warm the koshered chicken killed the day before according to that ancient ritual prescribed in the Book of Deuteronomy: "Be sure that thou eat not the blood: for the blood is life." The blood of the chickens had not been wasted, however, but had gone into the earth to strengthen the roots of Ruth's flowers.

After the meal Santiago went with young Mark to open the store. Closing all day Saturday probably cost him business which could never be fully made up, that evening or on Sunday. Nevertheless his orthodoxy remained unshaken and he worried lest Benito, now eighteen, might marry a Gentile and was thinking of sending back to Monterrey in the Mexican province of Nuevo

León for a nice Jewish girl, perhaps a relative, to come and be
his son's bride, as Ruth had come for him. But when this was
proposed to Benito he protested violently saying he had no wish
to marry, let alone some stranger selected by his parents.

"Can we trust you to behave yourselves?" Ruth was asking,
only half in jest, as Pacifico pleaded eloquently that Benito be
allowed to accompany him to the dance. Neither she nor Santiago
approved the new public dances but hesitated to forbid their ma-
turing son his freedom. Returning for a final word, Santiago admonished with a shake of his finger: "See that you stay out of
trouble!"

"We'll chaperone each other!" Benito promised lightly, kissing his mother. "Pacifico will need a protector. And as you know,
I am afraid of girls!"

And having delivered those necessary reassurances with which
young people have placated their elders for centuries, the two
departed into the summer evening and the adventure their blood
told them was waiting.

Clara watched Tilhini bury his basket filled with rattlesnakes
near the center of the dancing ground amid that cluster of huts of
adobe and thatch that constituted her Indianada. People had assembled from village and hacienda and from distant villages.
Many wore as she did crowns of flowers since this was a repli-
cation of the festival of the spring, of the second grass as distinguished from the first which followed the first rains of fall,
repeated now to deal with the evil which was abroad in the land.

She sat on her stool of rushes brought by María Ignácia and
stared at the basket of snakes, trying to put from her mind all
regret over absence of son and grandson. The fruit of her dream,
of this day, must somehow take another form. Yet the old pain
came. She'd brought Francisco into the world with such hope,
expected so much, been disappointed so often. And he'd bequeathed his waywardness to Pacifico, it seemed, and that was
almost more than she could bear. But she'd chosen her way. They
must choose theirs. Sapaqay, Tilhini's colleague in the secret society of sorcerers and snake doctors, was burying his basket a
short distance from Tilhini's, as were visiting doctors from remote
villages, while in the shade of the huge sycamore that overspread
much of the dancing ground a group of musicians made a wild
din with wooden clappers, pipes of reed and elderberry, deer bone

whistles and whirling bullroarers; and Cosme, dressed as usual
like a woman, painted and bangled, was clowning and making
bawdy jokes, presenting his penis as a snake, getting in everybody's way, making people laugh as their dread of the snakes
and of what was to come, increased. She did not much care for
Cosme but accepted him and his conduct as necessary. It too had
always been so.

Singers and dancers followed Cosme among the crowd, adding
to the general confusion and merriment, helping relieve the rising
anxiety. Some wore clothes, some were half-naked and painted
like Tilhini and the other sorcerers. Cosme, causing mock trouble
kicked the basketry tray off the top of Tilhini's buried basket.
The snakes tried to climb out. People exclaimed. Tilhini talked to
the snakes soothingly, stroking their backs with a long black condor feather, and persuaded them to remain in their downy nest
Then he turned upon Cosme and cursed and threatened him.
There was much nervous laughter. Suddenly a hush fell.

Singing softly, Tilhini was taking a huge snake out of his buried basket, out of the earth itself, it seemed, through a hole of
darkness and death with his bare hand. What power he had! Clara
felt the old tingle in her spine.

Holding his left hand under the snake's head, the front of its
body along that forearm, its middle in his right hand and the rest
of it along his right arm, Tilhini began to dance slowly, a step to
one side, a step to the other, swaying as he moved, singing softly

> "Dance with me, my deadly,
> Dance with me, my deadly!
> We make a party for you,
> We make a party for you,
> So you will be happy
> And will not bite us!"

He added words in the esoteric language of A-antap, the secret
society of sorcerers and other elite, which ordinary people could
not understand and which Clara had almost forgotten. Yet the
sound of it thrilled her to-the core, for it came from the heart of
one of those two worlds she was determined to harmonize.

People began following Tilhini hypnotically, singing, and
swaying from side to side like a snake. The snake dance. It

werful meaning entered Clara too but did not quite overcome
er. Yet she was deeply moved.

> "Dance with me, my deadly,
> Dance with me, my deadly!"

Was she then a mere spectator here? "Oh, no!" she almost
cried aloud.

The other sorcerers were removing their snakes from their baskets. Their people were following them. Four leaders, four writhing snakes, four swaying snake-like processions wound across the
dancing ground under the bright sun as the din of music from the
shade of the great sycamore rose higher and wilder.

After dancing around, the doctors put their snakes back into
their baskets, while the people gathered around them, still singing,
still dancing. Ecstatic now, one by one each came forward and
placed a bare foot over the open mouths of the baskets, placing
themselves at total risk, submitting—then when no fangs stung,
joyfully putting Indian shell money and even white man's silver
and gold money into the baskets. Thus the threatening evil was
dispelled. Thus they became immune for another year. Immune?
Clara's spirit rose in rebellion at thought of her own special im-
munity as spectator, until she felt she could tolerate such aloof-
ness no longer. When all others had taken their turns, she rose
and walked toward Tilhini's basket.

"Ah, Señora!" María Ignácia's remonstrance reminded her
that María was too far gone into civilization, into the white man's
world, to participate in such ancient rituals. Sternly, Clara held to
her purpose. Cries of approval gladdened her.

Heart pounding in the old way, excitement almost dizzying her,
she slipped off one sandal and placed her bare foot over the basket's mouth, over the dark abyss of death, almost feeling the sting
of the fangs, smelling the musky deathly odor of the snakes, almost inviting them, remembering how one had touched her father
in quite a different situation, sending him to the Land of the Dead.
Yes, she felt ready to accept whatever might befall. But the sting
did not come. Evil was in abeyance. She was alive for another
year.

Removing her foot she slipped her valuable shell-bead necklace
over her head and dropped it among the snakes. Cheers and applause rose higher.

Renewed, she returned to her seat. People were calling for

Cosme who'd been clowning all along, with his woman's re-
deerskin flaps in front and behind his bare loins, his bare breas
painted with garish stripes of red and black, hair banged in fron
like a woman's and held back by a garland of flowers, eyelid
blued, repellant yet compelling. Now it was his turn to approac
the basket, as the ritual continued, embracing them all.

Giggling, Cosme reached in and took out a huge reptile. Ther
were gasps of wonder as it coiled around his arm. Fearlessl
Cosme, the different one, the outcast unique, began to tease th
huge dark snake, death's emissary, with his forefinger. It bit hi
on the finger.

Cosme gave a little shriek of dismay which the crowd echoe
Looking comically surprised, he held the finger out toward Tilhi
like a child appealing for help. Everyone watched with bate
breath as he sank to the ground, apparently senseless.

Tilhini and the other doctors went to work on Cosme. Fir
they rubbed ashes all over him. Then they made an incision wher
the snake had bitten. Then Tilhini applied his sucking tube
hollow elderberry wood and withdrew a mouthful of blood an
poison, which he spat out for everyone to see. There were "ahs!
of awe. And then came some poisonous looking green stuff lik
mashed leaves, and then some skunk's bone and a bit of blac
hair.

Clara knew it was all spurious yet all sincere. Hair, bone, bloo
were not the evil. But they represented the evil power that wa
affecting Cosme, threatening them all, the evil Tilhini's mag
was destined to remove so long as the ancient web of things he
true.

A moment later Cosme sat up, smiled about him and wrun
his hand comically as though he'd burned his finger. Everyboc
roared. Then he shook the finger reprovingly at the basket whe
Tilhini had replaced the snake. Then Cosme stood up, pulled asi
his skirt, squatted and defecated to everyone's vast amusemer
offering his deposit to the snake by gestures.

Then the party broke up in general merriment and a licentiou
ness such as Father O'Hara would not have approved. With ga
lands around their heads, girls joined hands in a circle and beg
to dance voluptuously as on the green fields of spring, celebrati
life in the presence of death. Young men surrounded them a
also began to dance, moving in the opposite direction, teasing th
girls, joking suggestively, all moving faster and faster with i
creasing rhythm of music and feet, until the circles broke

screaming and laughing, boys seizing girls, girls boys, bystanders cheering.

Cosme came gravely to Clara to show her the fang mark on his finger. Though she suspected the poison sacs had been removed by Tilhini and the subsequent incision had obliterated their mark anyway, she nodded, duly impressed, and told María to give Cosme a silver dollar. The web must be preserved.

Many smiled at her. Yet she felt distressed that many others, especially among the young, had not participated, remained aloof, or like Pacifico poked fun at the whole affair. Still this did not suppress her grateful heart.

Unearthing his basket of snakes and money, Tilhini came smiling toward her, basket under his arm, genial as always. His vision paralleling hers back to the days when the unbroken web was strong seemed timelessly beautiful. They had not spoken in more than a week while he busied himself in preparations for the ceremony. He would pay dancers and singers as well as Cosme and himself from the proceeds. It had been a good day. They had kept the faith. Beyond that she hoped he might be bringing her word of Francisco, for she knew how news percolated down to Tilhini from the back country like water through the ground.

"Yawa!" He spoke the traditional salutation. "You've heard?" he added knowingly, beaming down upon her.

She shook her head. "What?"

"Your son has been reborn!"

Was he joking? Was this part of the general merriment? Her spirit trembled. "What do you mean?"

"Francisco. In the wilderness. He's become their leader."

She answered gruffly: "Bah, he play-acts back there! While I face realities down here! Tell me more!"

And Tilhini did.

# Chapter Thirty-one

Sedley spent all day in his office with Forbes making arrangements for disposal of the cargo of his newly arrived clipper. Her appearance was creating a sensation—as was her record time from Boston, ninety-one days, nine hours. She was the toast of the town. So was he. But he didn't let that interfere with the task at hand. Then he went home to host the dinner for the business and political leaders he'd invited to meet Stanhope. Beau and David were included at the Colonel's request. "We want our young fellows to know what's going on, don't we, Eliot?" Stanhope also requested that no mention be made of Hattie's running away. Not only was it embarrassing, it might detract from this important meeting. "The police have several houses under surveillance." He hoped she might be found quickly and the matter forgotten. "I was at fault for trusting her. But it shows how unreliable they are, no matter how much you do for them."

Sedley judiciously recalled cautioning him against keeping Hattie too long in California lest they run foul of something like this "or that provision in the State Constitution prohibiting slavery." But the provision was as much honored in the breach as in the observance, as Stanhope pointed out, Negroes being bought and sold openly in various parts of the state. And as for the Underground Railroad, the Colonel had felt himself and his property amply protected by State and National Fugitive Slave Laws, as well as the generally friendly attitude of state and local officials toward slavery and the South. In addition there was Hattie's heretofore docile attitude which seemingly did not lend itself to escapades. "But you were right, damn it," he admitted now. "Still I don't want to make a fuss over it yet."

Pearl and Roxana, Mary Louise's Negro maids, trained under her commanding eye, served the sumptuous table and its eminent guests while she remained discreetly behind doors yet within hearing of all that was said. At the back of her mind was the constant joy of Hattie's escape and the constant dread of her recapture. She scrupulously avoided visiting Mornay's house but the Black Grapevine kept her informed of the movements of the Stanhopes and Sedley, and the near presence of the Colonel now roused her desire for vengeance almost beyond control. A pinch of strychnine could put an end to him. But that time was not yet, she realized. Her curse must work its course.

David, alert in every nerve, strove to perceive and understand all that went on around him. The thought of Mary Louise nearby if invisible heightened the atmosphere of the room and gave double meaning to his presence there. He would have a great deal to tell when he got home. Even attending church with the Stanhopes might be forgiven. On the other hand he couldn't help feeling flattered at being included in this illustrious company, for these were the rulers. Their strength, their power, was almost palpable. They made him think of predatory dogs, with their easy truculent confidence: men who ruled and were accustomed to being obeyed. Top dogs.

After Sedley reported on the successful progress of the syndicate in which all were interested financially, the talk turned to politics. United States Senator William McKendree Gwin was among the first to express his views. Tall, aristocratic, prematurely white hair swept back from his lofty brow, Tennessee born Gwin had been trained as a lawyer and doctor. He owned a plantation in Mississippi, immense tracts in Texas, was not only a stockholder in Sedley's Central Valley Land Syndicate but in that fabulously profitable New Almadén Mine near San José, second only to the combined output of all the gold mines of the state in the value of its one product, quicksilver. "We must encourage immigration to California from Southern states," Gwin declared. "Bounties must be offered, people induced to move here and equalize the disproportion in population between North and South."

One of two members of the Legislature who'd come down by river steamer from the state capital at Benicia near the head of the Bay, a florid little man with bulbous nose reddened from drink, proposed the formation of three states from the existing one. "The northernmost would be called Shasta, the central California, the southern Colorado. I'm prepared to introduce legislation accordingly," he concluded pompously as if to assert his significance in the face of such company; and when asked the advantages of this proposal, he replied: "Since we control the existing state's politics we could do so in the three new ones, thus adding greatly to our power." Furthermore since the Federal Government was granting half a million acres of free land to be opened to settlement in each newly created state, the division into three would greatly enlarge the amount of land available for settlement and thus increase not only the number of rural settlers with Southern sympathies "but the possibility of large holdings of the plantation type and of course of our syndicate."

Beauford listened with apparently casual interest. But David could hardly conceal his excitement. They spoke of dividing a state as if they were cutting a pie. It was awesome. But was it what he wanted? Could he ever be like these men, predatory, ruthless?

Sitting next him was David S. Terry, tall, formidable, a Mexican War veteran and former Texas Ranger. Terry had drawn a huge Bowie knife from inside his shirt and was whetting it against the palm of his left hand absently, as he listened to the discussion, finally interjecting sharply, as he held up the shiny blade: "This can settle all questions, gentlemen!"

Most broke into chuckles. But Beau was silent and David shocked. Would they be sucked into the violence and bloodshed which seemed so acceptable to their elders? Terry advocated the creation of a Pacific Republic, independent like the recent Republic of Texas, which could establish its own institutions including slavery as it saw fit. "Our friends in Southern California are already moving in the direction I propose."

Attention turned back to Sedley whose knowledge of the entire state was second to none. Not so much advocating as informing, he reminded them that the existing movement in Southern California to separate from the north was perhaps motivated less by a desire to embrace slavery than by geographical, cultural and occupational isolation and an unfair tax burden. "Walled off by intervening mountains, sparsely but permanently settled by an old, largely Spanish-speaking society, the south owns its lands and is for the most part content to follow its pastoral ways. Our more densely populated north is inhabited by a new and more transient society, much of it miners who do not own but lease lands from the Government or merely occupy them—and thus pay no or little taxes while the burden on landholders of the South is disproportionately heavy." And when this had sunk in he continued: "I'm not sure our southern neighbors will embrace Negro slavery. De facto slavery already exists there in the form of Indian servitude, and no great additional labor force is needed at present. Although the growing of cotton and tobacco on large scale may be possible, it may not be. Therefore what inducement would Southern California have to embrace Negro slavery?"

Mary Louise, listening, realized her lover was skillfully playing a double game. Whatever its outcome Sedley stood to win. He neither associated nor disassociated himself entirely from those at his table. Whatever developed, he would remain in a position to profit by it. She resolved to be there beside him. In love or business or in counsel as now, he performed with admirable intelligence and firmness of purpose. She had no wish to be his wife. But as his partner she could be something more, something she much preferred.

Through Hattie she knew of his flirtation with Victoria but it did not bother her. Her own game must be to make herself so indispensable to Sedley that neither Victoria nor anything else could come between them, while she extended her power and secured her daughter's safety. Meanwhile she was gaining information of incalculable value. The only thing marring all this was David's association with the Stanhopes. It raised serious doubts as to his integrity.

Gwin now rejoined: "It is evident that as a United States Senator I cannot support division of California without reopening the bitterness which arose at the time of its admission to the Union, when Senators nearly came to blows and a motion to divide the state into slave and free soil would have carried had five votes changed." But Gwin could support a new division plan privately. "And in the event of a crisis," meaning Secession or war, "I believe we'll be found with the South." Furthermore now that energetic Jefferson Davis was Secretary of War, the possibility of additional military posts and resultant patronage and influence throughout California and the West were greatly increased. And since the Army like Congress and the State Legislature was dominated by Southerners, their influence in the region would increase too.

Stanhope began to see the picture as a whole. Its scope and

possibilities whetted his ambition and avarice. On Sedley's invitation he spoke next. "It is reassuring," he began tactfully, "to find myself among kindred spirits in the awareness of such important issues." He spoke of being in close touch also "with those foremost advocates of States Rights, Rhett of South Carolina, Yancey of my own Louisiana, Ruffin of Virginia. They are leading the way toward defense of our Constitutional values," meaning chiefly slavery. In fact they were Secessionist firebrands endeavoring to set the South alight. Jefferson Davis was more moderate. Stanhope's account of his relationship with the eminent Davis particularly gripped his hearers. From his plantation at Stanhope's Bend he would cross the "Father of Waters" from the Louisiana to the Mississippi side and visit Davis's plantation, "Brierfield," and there they would reminisce about Mexican War days and discuss the cultivation of cotton, and politics. Davis had strongly opposed the admission of California to the Union, predicting it would upset the balance of power between the existing fifteen Slave and fifteen Free States: But he was, publicly at least, a moderate on such matters as secession. "He wants the Union preserved. But he wants Southern territory expanded to include Cuba and portions of Mexico; and in the event of crisis, he realizes the gold of California will be invaluable."

Though Stanhope was of a more radical persuasion than his friend, they were eye to eye in their views of Southern rights and Northern infringement on same, especially by the Radical Abolitionists such as Mornay. "You've got them even here, I'm told. For nearly thirty years they've been spreading like the plague, viciously attacking our way of life, spurning all our attempts at moderation and compromise." This brought murmurs of approval. Stanhope urged continued vigilance, continued action. "I hope to remain in touch with you, possibly by part-time residence here, certainly by our joint business and political interests." There were further murmurs and he felt himself succeeding in this important aspect of his California visit.

Mary Louise saw her curse unfolding upon him in a way she'd never dreamed: delivering not only him but his fellow conspirators into her hands and Mornay's, and the forces of freedom.

David sensed a vast if subtle conspiracy in which Hattie's predicament was a small but revealing aspect. He determined to hurry home and tell Mornay what he had learned. But on the way he sought out Angie. He knew he shouldn't but could not help himself.

\*   \*   \*

"You don't really love me," she charged after they'd made love. "You really love that girl I saw you with on the street!"

"No," he lied, "that's all for show. I had to go to church with her family because they asked me. You saw what they were: fashionable empties. I love only you!" And when he felt her soft flesh enmeshed with his again, he was sure he'd spoken the truth, because in a profound way he found Angie more genuine, more deserving than any of those people he'd been with in church except Martha and Mornay. Violated first by her drunken father, then her older brother, she'd fled from horror and squalor and was trying to survive as best she could. He admired her. Yet her admiration for him was so touching it was pathetic. She considered him a grand gentlemen, a college man, moving in the highest circles of fashion. "While me, I'm just a ignoramus from the gutter!" He felt unworthy of her, yet fatefully bound to her as if God were using her to tell him something. Again his mind spun in confusion.

Sometimes he feared for Angie's sanity. He sensed in her the awfulness of nothing, an emptiness like an abyss of darkness, into which she might plunge if she did not have someone to love or to misuse her.

"Do you love me?" she asked again plaintively, like a child to its mother. The raucous sounds of the dance hall came up to them like mockery of all that was tender and beautiful.

"Yes," he reassured her.

She had such a need to believe. Illusion sustained her. He watched while she rose from the bed and moved about the shadowy room. He realized with a feeling of loathing at his callousness that he'd grown used to the mechanics of her profession, the sponge with the thread attached she inserted to prevent conception, the douche of vinegar mixed with baking soda. All this he accepted open eyed in a way he'd never thought he could. And when she caressed and kissed him, touching him all over, he accepted that too with a perversely proud thrill of submission. Whatever else it was it was life, experience unadorned. By comparison what he felt while with the Stanhopes seemed artificially genteel. But he could not put it out of his mind. His walk with Beau seemed especially important. While the dinner at Sedley's had shown him ruthless men willing and able to wield power masterfully on giant scale.

Nor could he forget Hattie and Mornay waiting like his better self for him to help them.

# Chapter Thirty-two

The dilapidated building adjacent to Mission Santa Lucía had been used as a warehouse, then abandoned until this evening. Outside its adobe-walled yard, groups of hangers-on, rough-looking characters heavily armed with pistols and knives, some with serapes over shoulders, were talking, laughing, drinking, while eyeing each newcomer to the dance. Their horses, picketed nearby, kicking and squealing at each other and passers-by, added to the confusion; for not even townspeople would have thought of walking to the fandango though it was only a few steps away.

At the entrance to the yard Pacifico and Benito paid their two reales, four bits each, to a proprietary Anglo, whose eyes shifted beadily from them to their coins; and once past him Benito muttered their private battle cry: "Onward, Compadre!" Pacifico echoed it. Something told him Sally would be there and their meeting would be part of the magic of this summer evening.

At intervals around the enclosure, temporary stalls had been constructed for the sale of spirits and were being vociferously patronized. Ahead a flight of steps ran to the lighted loft of the old warehouse, now the dancing salon. Sounds of music and revelry issuing from it made Pacifico's blood rise higher and his eyes search for a blond head like his own. Goodly Jenkins lingered in the courtyard. Dragooned into being Sally's escort, he'd stopped at a liquor stall to fortify himself in company with friends, while Sally, Iphy and Abe went ahead to the loft. Avowedly hating girls and dances, Goodly secretly desired both. Uncouth, unlovable, he'd not much hope of success with either. Emulating his father

he took refuge in a brutality resembling Buck's, and the sight of
Pacifico and Benito inflamed his latent dissatisfaction with self
and life. As they passed he jeered loudly enough for everyone
nearby to hear: "Greaser and Jew!"

Benito spun around. Pacifico grabbed his sleeve. "Use common sense!" he whispered. "There's six of 'em!"

"No, I've had enough!" Benito was pulling away when a familiar voice from behind arrested them both. It was Don Domingo
Rogers. With him were Anita and portly Doña Inés. Pacifico
flushed. He'd not expected this. But putting his best face on it,
he embraced his ostensible future father-in-law with protestations
of affection, kissing ample Inés's pudgy hand and Anita's slender
tender one. "How fortunate! Just as I hoped!" he lied gallantly
with warmth that deceived mother and father but not quite Anita.
"May I introduce my friend and companion, though I think you
already know him?"

Domingo and Inés had known Benito all his life but never till
this moment realized he had grown up. The same was true of
Anita and she could not help but feel flattered by the admiration
which shone frankly from Benito's handsome dark eyes.

"*Vamos!* Let us go inside!" Domingo proposed, to keep things
moving. "You boys lead the way!" And up the ladderlike steps
they all went. The long loft, its floor swaying to the feet of numerous dancers, was lighted by lanterns and redolent of the odors
of perspiring flesh, tobacco smoke, garlic, cologne. Californios,
Mexicans, Anglo-Americans, immigrants from various lands
who'd stopped while passing along the coastal road, halfbreeds,
outlaws, the rough, the smooth, the genteel were crammed into it
with a new democratic indifference.

Sally saw them enter but did not indicate she had, though her
jealousy flared at sight of Anita. She was sitting on a bench
against the wall between Iphy and Abe, hoping her blue calico
with white yoke and fetchy flounces was sufficiently becoming.
Pacifico's eyes went to hers unerringly and their hearts met in
that look. Doña Inés was saying: "You young people dance!"
implying that Pacifico and Anita could forego the formality of
watching her and Domingo take the floor first. Pacifico heard with
delight. It seemed part of that momentous evening, part of a future
that would be free from the constraints of the past. Music, discordant but powerful, was coming from two squeaky fiddles, two
rapidly strumming guitars, one folding and unfolding concertina.

Halfway through the first figure of the contradance he felt the tender pressure of Anita's hand. She was lovely, sweet, good. No doubt she cared for him. But when he thought of fearless independent Sally sitting so straight against the wall, Anita no longer interested him and a stubborn rebelliousness rose in Pacifico which was like his father's, and he did not respond to her pressure.

Benito was chatting easily with Domingo and Inés. Though old friends of his family, they would not have accepted him in their home were this an old-style party, conscious of class difference, and though he was aware of this it did not daunt him. Like Pacifico he sensed a new day dawning that would relegate such distinctions to the past. Gray robed Father O'Hara joined them, creating a stir and also murmurs of approval and disapproval: some seeing in him a dampener on the festivities, some a legitimizing of them. In fact there was small choice but to acquiesce in the situation as he found it if he wanted to go along with the times. Anglo settlers had appropriated the building and were using it without his consent. But his crucifix dangled from his waist cord and he was smiling tolerantly, for he did not want life to pass him by, and he wished to implement that dream of harmony in the valley he shared with Clara.

The music stopped. Pacifico brought Anita back to her parents and Benito, and with a bow, left her and, as if propelled by invisible hands, went straight to Sally. Oblivious to everything else, he looked into her shining eyes and asked: "May I have the honor?" Heart fluttering, she simply rose without a word. In fact she was too happy to speak. As the music resumed and their hands touched, all barriers fell, and they found themselves at ease. "I shouldn't be dancing with you!" he teased.

"Nor I you!" she retorted in kind.

"Because you are a gringa!"

"Because you are a Californio!"

"You're stealing my land! Will you steal my heart too?"

"I might!"

Whirling in the arms of Benito, Anita watched them. She felt her heart breaking and hated the gringa vixen with all that was left of it. Yet at the same time the admiration of Benito could not help but sustain her, it was so ardent, so unabashed.

As the two lines of couples faced each other, advanced, retreated, whirled and intertwined, the touch of Sally's fingers, the grace of her form, were bliss to Pacifico, gall to Anita. In the midst of it he felt a rough grip on his shoulder. Reenforced by whiskey, Goodly was intervening. "Let her go, Greaser!"

Pacifico struck reflexively. Goodly staggered back, blood gush-
ing from his nose. "By God, I'll kill you!" he screamed drunk-
enly. His knife flashed. Sally darted between them. Pacifico thrust
her to one side and felt a searing pain in his left shoulder as he
threw up his arm to ward off the blow. Sally pounded Goodly's
ribs with both fists. Anita shrieked. Benito rushed to his comra-
de's aid and in another instant the melee became general, mostly
Californios against American settlers. Continuing incongruously
to blare, the music was the last thing Pacifico heard as he fainted
away, blood pouring onto the floor as he fell.

Sally knelt over him, efficiently examined his wound, found it
more bloody than lethal, a long rip down the back of his shoulder.
With a daring which became much talked about she tore a strip
from her petticoat and stanched the blood, while Father O'Hara
and Don Domingo led in restoring order. Benito tenderly com-
forted Anita who'd become hysterical. Goodly was led outside
muttering dire threats. Regaining consciousness, the first thing
Pacifico saw was Sally's face bending over his. Before long they
were dancing again, his bandaged shoulder a badge of their union.

Doña Inés and Iphy exchanged wary though not unfriendly
glances as the party resumed. Old Abe, majestic in fringed buck-
skins and patriarchal beard, had not stirred during all of these
developments. Now he rose and went to find a place to spit his
tobacco juice. Father O'Hara indicated the way to the brass spit-
toon. Having relieved himself there, Abe suddenly squealed in a
high-pitched voice: "I'll call one! Wesley, git yourself a fiddle!
Britt, you bring your mouth organ?" A moment later he was
presiding over a frontier square dance, and in the mellowing
atmosphere such extraordinariness seemed quite in keeping.

"Swing yore partner!" Abe belted out. "Swing her high, swing
'er low, but don't step on her pretty little toe!" A new kind of
music, a new mood, took possession of the room. Laughter,
friendliness, became infectious. "Now leave her in the center and
leave her stan', and walk along, John, as fast as you can!" Clap-
ping hands took up the cadence with delight. "Do-si-do and the
gents don't go . . . !"

Sally led Pacifico through this new experience. Benito and Anita were caught up in its new rhythms. Perhaps most remarkable
of all was Iphy in her brightly printed calico whirling with gay
abandon opposite velvet-jacketed Don Domingo.

# Chapter Thirty-three

At the end of a day Sedley liked to stop at the Bank Exchange Saloon to hear latest news and gossip. The noted watering place occupied a ground-floor corner of the huge block-long building his friend Captain Henry Halleck was completing on the Bay side of Montgomery between Washington and Merchant. All spring and summer its four stories had been rising spectacularly, the largest structure west of the Mississippi, classical Italian in style with Roman Doric entrance columns, space for twenty-eight stores, one hundred fifty offices each with coal gas and running water—plus an interior court with potted palms and flowers. It was the newest symbol of progress, here in this new kind of frontier, this instant city.

Halleck had constructed a temporary office on its roof from where he supervised a small army of pigtailed Chinese laborers putting finishing touches on his mighty edifice and as Sedley came along the street, he could see him standing up there, massive, erect, like a commanding general giving orders. Sedley waved and Halleck waved back. At thirty-seven Old Brains Halleck, erudite in nearly everything, was not only the Army's leading West Coast engineer but the city's leading lawyer—though not, in Sedley's opinion, cleverer than Ogles. However it was through Halleck that he'd acquired his interest in the New Almadén Mine, and only five years ago they'd fished together in the Bay from the spot where Halleck's Folly, as some called it, was rising now.* Sedley didn't think it a folly. He'd invested in

*on the site of today's Transamerica Pyramid Tower

it. Halleck shared his vision of a California with unlimited possibilities.

With these thoughts he entered the deluxe saloon and proceeded across its black and white marble floor to the back room where the influential gathered. There he found himself in the middle of an argument between two of the state's most powerful figures. Senator Gwin, epitome of The Chivalry which dominated state and national politics, was confronting David Colbreth Broderick, epitome of The Shovelry, opposed to Gwin and all he stood for. Gwin was reiterating that in the event of separation of North and South over the question of slavery California would be found with the South. Broderick was retorting: "The people of this state through their Constitution have expressed their desire for their soil to be free. Congress has ratified their decision. Surely, sir, you're not attempting to reverse such a powerful mandate?" Somber-faced, steely-eyed, red-bearded Broderick was nearly as tall and even more muscular than his adversary but his speech and manner lacked Gwin's polish and grace. Broderick, once a New York City street boy, orphan son of an immigrant Irish stonecutter, had like Gwin arrived in '49 with the intention of becoming U.S. Senator from California. He was now a State Senator and San Francisco's political boss.

To avert a quarrel and possible duel between two adversaries representing such opposite views, Sedley was about to intervene as friend and confidant of both, when Edward Beale forestalled him with similar intent. "I think we ought to focus on the Indian problem," Beale, Federal Indian Commissioner for California, suggested, citing raids which had disrupted the flow of cattle herds from the great ranches of the Los Angeles area into the southern San Joaquín Valley and thence to San Francisco where they constituted much of the city's food supply. "I've just come back from the South where I met with a thousand of our Red Brethren." And the personable thirty-three-year-old Beale, the same age as Broderick but fifteen years Gwin's junior, described how after a two-day conference he'd persuaded the Indians to move onto a "reservation"* where they would be free to raise their own crops and live under direction of their own leaders, while secure from molestation by white men. "Eight of ten times it's the white who's at fault when trouble starts. Everything was going nicely last year, for example, until your Senate in Wash-

---

*both the term and the concept were Beale's invention

ington, Gwin, if I may say so, refused to ratify treaties the tribes had signed in good faith. That naturally made them mistrust us. Instead of the land and food we promised, they got nothing. How could you blame them for turning hostile? My idea of a reservation system may be new but I think it will work.''

Gwin rejoined: ''If we introduce cotton into the south of this state where the great ranchos lend themselves to it, we could import Negroes to mingle and work with your Indians, Beale, peaceably in the way they do in the South. Then we'd have a labor force to develop our natural wealth.''

Broderick intervened grimly: ''At the expense of the free working man? Never!''

Sherman, after a busy day at his bank, had dropped into the comfortable leather chair next Sedley's. They were friends from those pre-state days when Sherman first knew California as a young Army lieutenant and Sedley's adobe office on the plaza was a gathering place for Americans. Sherman, fidgeting under the discussion, was twitching his eyebrows, pulling at his sandy-red beard, as Sedley noted. But Beale continued in a quiet manner Sedley approved: ''The Indian situation is more serious than you may think. The hostiles have got a renegade halfbreed at their head. He's smart and may cause real trouble. He's being compared to those leaders of a few decades back who successfully raided just across the Bay where Oakland is now and threatened San José.''

''What's his name, Ned?'' Sedley asked.

''Francisco Boneu. He's said to be the son of a rich old ranchera of the Santa Lucía Valley. By the way, Eliot, don't you know her?''

Sedley nodded. ''She's an old friend. I doubt she has a hand in any violent upheavals.'' He deliberately kept his tone moderate in order to encourage Beale and lessen the tension between Gwin and Broderick which he perceived as potentially very explosive.

''And her son?''

Sedley shrugged noncommittally. ''I've known him for years. He was here not long ago. I can't imagine what may have happened to change him.'' The delays which prevented him from traveling south to see Clara had not troubled Sedley. In fact he rather welcomed them. It would not be a bad thing to have her expectant and thus more amenable. But now his southern trip was taking on new dimensions. He'd read accounts of the raids Beale cited and was aware of the rising apprehension caused by them.

So great was public concern that unrelated raids near San Diego and Los Angeles were being attributed to Francisco's master mind. Something like panic was sweeping the state. Newspapers editorialized that "a war of extermination must continue until the Indian race becomes extinct." Sedley saw no other solution but did not feel it wise to say so now. What effect all of this would have on Clara he could only wonder.

At his elbow Sherman, bristling, spoke up stridently: "Beg to differ with you, Gwin, about Negroes getting along with Indians. I've lived in the South. I know how they fight like cats and dogs. Some tribes even have nigger slaves. And Beale, as for your blessed Red Menace, George Stanhope tells me we've got a band of fanatical Abolitionists right here in town who're a greater threat. I just bumped into him on the street. Claims they've stolen his daughter's pet slave girl."

Halleck had come down off the roof and was asked his sage opinion. He'd declined the chair of engineering at Harvard but his *Elements of Military Art and Science* would become a classic, and though soon to resign from the Army he would rejoin it and become general-in-chief of Northern armies during the coming war. Nevertheless Old Brains disliked politics and contentious public discussion. "I believe in one nation indivisible," he growled. "Let's begin there and reconcile our differences. Lo, the Poor Indian, Beale—and Gwin, your Inevitable Sambo—will find their true places if only we behave like reasonable men. As for what Sherman says, if a slave girl's been stolen, isn't that Broderick's business? He runs this city and I'm sure one of his strikers can find her if his police can't." And like some enormous potentate with curly light brown hair and heavy jowl, Halleck settled pompously into a comfortable chair next Sherman's while a black waiter handed him his usual glass of Pisco punch.

At that moment George Stanhope burst into the room followed by Beau. "The damned Abolitionists have kidnapped my daughter's nigger maid!" he stormed unable to contain himself longer as the frustrating search for Hattie yielded nothing, while Beau stood handsomely at his shoulder as if to second him should anyone challenge his statement. As a visiting member of The Chivalry, already known to many in the room, Stanhope was immediately listened to. "By the Almighty," he continued addressing everyone as if by divine right, "they stole her out of my hotel rooms. What does that say about a man's Constitutional rights in this great state of California?"

"Ask Mr. Broderick," Gwin suggested dryly. "He contro
this city as Captain Halleck says."

Broderick, who indeed had organized the city politically alon
Tammany lines with which he was familiar from his New Yor
experience, demanded tersely: "How do you know she was sto
len?"

"She's been with us all her life, born and raised on our plar
tation as her mother was, perfectly contented until a few evening
ago. Are you suggesting, sir, she might have wanted to ru
away?" Stanhope demanded belligerently.

"Sir, I'm asking for information," Broderick continued wi
contemptuous harshness. "Although I opposed them both, ou
state and national statutes are perfectly clear. If a slave runs awa
her owner can recover her with the help of the law, and anyon
aiding her or hindering the law is subject to fine and imprison
ment." Broderick had studied law in his spare time and recentl
been admitted to the bar.

During this heated discussion Beau drifted to Sedley's side
"The Governor's really hot under the collar at last, Eliot. He'
sure it's Abolitionists. We've confirmed what you said. They'v
got a secret network here just as they have back East. A fellov
named Mornay is supposed to be at the heart of it. We're sur
Hattie's disappeared into it. Personally I'm rather glad to see he
gone if she wants her freedom."

Sedley responded cautiously: "How's Vicky taking it?"

"She's in a miff, and she's egging him on, reminding hir
Hattie was hers. That's partly why the Old Man's finally so riled
Vicky's everything to him, you know."

"Well, here comes someone who knows what's going on,'
Sedley observed as Wright entered followed by David. "Let's se
what he can tell us," and he called out banteringly: "Captain,
young black woman's run away from her owner. There's a rumo
she may be hiding at the house of that Abolitionist, Mornay
Know anything about it?"

All that day at the Inter-Ocean Steamship Company the figure
of his ledger had seemed incidental to David, as did the sardoni
presence of Gillem and the chatter of their fellow clerks. If al
went well, before dawn next morning Hattie would go back wit
Tony Petrini—hidden in his wagon after he delivered his vege
tables—to a secure hideaway at his outlying farm. This secre

illed David like knowledge of hidden treasure, as did his sense of participation in a noble cause. For the time being everything else was secondary. But toward the end of the afternoon Wright, who'd been conferring with the Rothschilds' representative in San Francisco, Benjamin Davidson, abruptly called him into his office and announced: "David, it's all settled. I'm going to London and Paris to help raise funds for a Pacific Railroad. Like to go along as my secretary? I need someone of your honesty and integrity. Someone I can depend on."

David was staggered. It seemed the culmination of his wildest dreams.

"It's the chance of a lifetime," Wright continued exuberantly. "Lord Barrington in London, Count Rothschild in Paris, have access to capital that makes Aspinwall's and Vanderbilt's look like chickenfeed, though we'll use theirs too. We'll bring Northern and Southern politicians together into a compromise and bind the nation with a steel ribbon from Atlantic to Pacific!" And with your near-monopoly of ocean and inland shipping, you'll have the country in a vise, thought David with admiration and awe. Wright was taking him up to that mountaintop Mornay had foreseen and offering him all the world. His head swam at the prospect. He saw himself mingling with princes and great financiers, shaping the nation's destiny and his own into a dazzling future. "You'll go with me? Commit yourself whole-heartedly?"

But David hesitated. Could he reconcile this with his commitment to Mornay, Hattie and the Underground? Or his love for Victoria? It seemed he could. When I return successful, he rationalized, I'll be in much better position to help the Abolitionist Cause—and Victoria and her family will admire me for my achievements, and while I'm away perhaps I'll rid myself of my addiction for poor Angie. The whole experience will be elevating, cleansing.

"Well?" Wright was asking.

"I'm honored by your confidence. I'll be delighted to be of whatever service I can!"

"Good! I knew I could count on you the first day I saw you! Here, let's shake. You've got qualities that will take you far. And now let's go along to the Bank Exchange and celebrate with a couple of lemonades!"

\*     \*     \*

"Why should I know anything about it?" Wright was snorting indignantly in response to Sedley's question. "I'm not an Abolitionist. Nor am I Mornay's keeper! What's up?"

Sedley gave further details. "Mornay supplies your ships doesn't he?"

Wright eyed Sedley sourly, then boomed out in his ship's bridge voice: "I don't know what you're talking about. But perhaps my young friend here does." And David, heart sinking, knew what was coming, as sure as fate. "David, you live at Mornay's, don't you? He got a pickaninny girl hiding there? Gentlemen, this is David Venable of my firm. He's going to London as my private secretary in a fortnight or so. David, what do you have to tell these people?"

All eyes turned on him. Conflicting emotions choked off his breath. These were the people he wanted to please, be accepted by. He wanted to go to Europe with Wright, to hold all the world in his hands. And these wants, seizing him with overpowering force, heightened by the presence of those staring eyes, made him say what he could hardly believe: "I don't know."

"Would you swear under oath and in the eyes of Almighty God there's not a black woman in Mornay's house?" Stanhope was demanding harshly.

In David's quandary an honest but wrong word slipped out. "No."

Next moment he would have given anything to take it back. But there it was, looming in the room, in the universe, in the minds of all who heard, approved by some, perceived by others as he was perceiving it: a giant mistake, a betrayal as palpable as if the whole side of a mountain had slid away. He wanted to shrink through the floor and disappear. Or cry out and retract. But it was too late. The disappointment in the eyes of Beau hurt him more than the contempt of Sedley; while Wright was blurting out brusquely, protectively: "Well, there you have it, sirs! It's the truth. Right, David? What more do you ask?" David's gratitude rose toward the indomitable Captain and the feeling began to stir in him that somehow he would make amends for his mistake.

Stanhope was exclaiming with triumphant sarcasm: "I see I was wrong! I see there are people of probity in this city after all! I salute you, my boy! Won't you join us for supper? Victoria would be delighted!"

A moment ago he would have jumped at the Colonel's invitation. Now he was scheming how to slip away and warn Hattie and Mornay before Stanhope and the police arrived at the house on Telegraph Hill. Wright rescued him by interposing: "Not tonight, George. He's coming home with me. We've got to plan our trip abroad." Stanhope persisted but Wright was firm. "Lucinda's waiting. Come along, son!" David followed thankfully. The saloon had become his private hell.

Out in the street, Wright muttered: "Glad you spoke the truth about that nigger girl. I know it was hard. But we can't have damn-fool Abolitionists like Mornay, however well intentioned, break the law and drag this nation into civil war. I freed my slaves when I left Virginia. But that don't make me an Abolitionist."

David was not cheered. The luster had gone from their coming trip. He might be making it over Hattie's enslaved body, Mary Louise's broken heart, Mornay's frustrated idealism. And yet— and yet perversely he wanted to go. Why should he agonize over the fate of others? Why shouldn't he advance his own fortune? Yet he found himself trying to excuse himself and slip away so he could warn Hattie and Mornay. Wright demanded: "What's this? Don't you want to come with me?"

Seeing he must either give in or offend his benefactor irrevocably, David rationalized: Stanhope and the authorities may not act immediately; I'll hurry away as quickly after supper as I can and give warning!

Lucinda embraced him like a son. "I'm overjoyed you're going with Caleb. He needs someone to look after him. He's not as robust as he appears, you know." She would accompany them as far as New York City and meet there with the woman's rights leaders Susan B. Anthony and Elizabeth Cady Stanton, but he was agonizing inwardly, wondering how soon he could slip away. "We've got to make the movement more militant out here. I'm hoping they'll come and speak, stir people up. You men aren't entitled to all the say-so, you know!"

"I know," sighed Wright resignedly. "Just to keep what little we've got will require a miracle. They're awfully clever, David. Try to make you believe they're the persecuted minority, whereas in fact we are."

"My dear liar," Lucinda retorted lovingly but formidably, "nobody ever persecuted you for wearing Bloomers, jeered at you in public, accused you of advocating free love and an end to marriage and the family!"

"I'll start wearing skirts and we'll see what they say!" Wright retorted.

"Don't be facetious! Men's refusal to take women seriously is at the heart of the problem!"

And they continued their affectionate dispute while David fumed, impatient to be gone. At last he hastened away into the dark and made for Mornay's house at a dead run.

When the gentle knock came at the front door it was after supper. Wing had gone to his room. Mornay and the two girls were in the parlor, he in his reading chair by the table lamp, they together on the settee knitting at either end of a shawl for Hattie. They looked up anxiously. Putting down the evening paper, Mornay called softly: "Who's there?"

A plaintive voice came back: "A fugitive, please sir!"

The possibility flashed through Mornay's mind that it was Stanhope and the police. If it were, someone had betrayed him and Hattie. Flight or concealment would be all but useless as well as unseemly. The house was probably surrounded, would be so thoroughly searched that Hattie's hiding place would be found. If it were not the police, there was no cause for alarm. Motioning to the girls to remain where they were, he rose and went to the door. As he cautiously opened it, Constable Monaghan shoved it ajar, sending him staggering backward, and burst into the parlor followed by Stanhope and Beau. "There she is!" Stanhope pointed at Hattie. "I positively identify her!" Monaghan flashed his badge at Mornay, then turned to Hattie who'd recoiled against Martha, and demanded: "Is this your master?"

As she realized the desperate nature of her situation, strength flowed into Hattie and reenforced her resolve.

"No, the Lord is my master!"

"She's lying!" Stanhope cried.

Mornay stepped forward. "She is not lying. She is a free soul, a guest in my house. How dare you intrude here, any of you?"

"Here's a warrant for the arrest of a runaway female slave named Hattie, property of George W. Stanhope, said to be on these premises." Monaghan displayed the document. "Her owner has identified her. Under the law that's all I need. And I must warn you, sir, anyone harboring her or in any way interfering with her arrest is subject to fine or imprisonment or both!"

"She's no one's property!" Mornay retorted indignantly.

"Pay no attention to him, Constable!" the Colonel interjected. "As for her word, it's of no value in the eyes of the law!"

"But mine is," Mornay rejoined, "and I say she is not a slave. She's a free soul, a guest in my house!"

Mornay was towering in his righteous indignation. Monaghan hesitated, glancing toward Stanhope, then back to Mornay. "Well, there seems to be some difference of opinion. Young lady, suppose you come along with me now, and tomorrow we can straighten things out?"

"I warn you again," Mornay thundered. "You arrest her under peril of the law!"

"I've got the law right here!" Again Monaghan brandished his warrant. Martha addressed him defiantly: "Let me get her things!"

The constable replied roughly: "Where she's going she won't need no things. Come along, girl!"

"Go with him, Hattie," Mornay advised quietly, "but make clear it's against your will. You act under duress. You are not a slave. You are a free person under the highest law, the law of God!"

Hattie disengaged herself from Martha's protective grasp and rose serenely. As she stood alone facing her adversaries, the sight nearly overcame Mornay and he burst out: "We'll be seeing you tomorrow, Hattie! Never fear! Help is coming!"

"Just what do you mean by that?" Stanhope demanded. Beau was looking on silently—he was not at all pleased by what was happening but felt powerless to prevent it.

"You'll see soon enough, sir!" Mornay retorted.

"And I'll see you prosecuted for harboring my runaway slave!"

"I shall gladly meet you in court," Mornay replied with stern dignity, "or anywhere else."

Stanhope looked him up and down contemptuously and broke into a scornful laugh. "Or anywhere else, eh? My, you mudsills are taking on airs! You talk like you're gentlemen!" His face hardened. "I'd accept your challenge if I didn't think it beneath my notice! Come on, Beau!" They followed Monaghan and Hattie outside. As the door closed, Martha ran to her father. "Papa, what can we do?"

"A great deal. Get coat and bonnet and be ready to go with me. First I must speak to Wing."

# Chapter Thirty-four

Edward D. Baker was so irresistibly pleasing even his enemies liked him. As a boy he'd come with Quaker parents from England to Pennsylvania, moved on to Illinois where he practiced law and became a close friend of Abraham Lincoln, who named a new-born son after him. After serving with distinction in Congress and the Mexican War where he headed a regiment, Colonel Baker, as he became known, felt the call to California. And now though he had a wife and four children to support he made it a practice to take the low-paying cases of people who could not afford large legal fees. If Tony Petrini got into an argument with the tax collector, he would go to Baker for advice; or if a black merchant like Mifflin Gibbs was robbed and beaten by two men posing as customers, it was Baker he thought of as a means of obtaining redress. Baker functioned as a kind of one-man legal aid society, partly from eccentricity, partly from a moral conscience he would not have admitted to, for though noted for his eloquence in public he was a man of few words concerning himself. Like Mornay he was an Abolitionist. He often spent evenings working at his office at 90 Merchant Street and there Mornay and Martha found him.

"How long has she been in California?" he asked when Mornay informed him of Hattie's predicament.

"Nearly three months."

"Is Stanhope a resident then?"

"No, but I've learned he's in process of purchasing a house and considering settling here."

"Were you harboring her?"

"Yes, I'll gladly go to jail if necessary. I'd like to test this state's infamous Fugitive Slave Law." Mornay's indignation rose. "I think it's not only in conflict with moral law but with our State Constitution which explicitly prohibits slavery. If you bring a slave into this state, why aren't you practicing slavery here? And I think it disgraceful that California's place in the Union was bought at the price of such laws!"

Martha felt a mixture of alarm and pride as she listened to her father but kept quiet. Baker looked at them thoughtfully. "I share your sentiments. It'll be a tough fight. But I'll help you defend Hattie all the way to Washington City if necessary."

When David reached the house on Telegraph Hill the lighted window gave him a surge of hope. Perhaps he was not too late. He pounded on the front door. Pounded and pounded. With each blow his hope died. At last he heard a soft shuffle of sandals and the door opened. As soon as he saw Wing's face he knew what had happened. "Velly sad!" Wing bowed, deferring to those forces which control good as well as evil. He spoke of his own land where such things happened so frequently they were considered a matter of course. It was one reason he was not going back, he said, even though here he had no rights except to exist as best he might. "Here bettah!"

But here did not seem good to David. It seemed a torture chamber where he was being torn to pieces by events he himself had set in motion. He was preparing to hurry off in search of Mornay and Martha when he heard a step and father and daughter entered.

Rushing to them, he embraced them both. "What can I do?" he burst out in agonized fashion.

"There's nothing more anyone can do at this hour." Mornay spoke with resignation. "She's in jail. We've been to a lawyer."

"Will they give her back to Stanhope?"

"Probably."

"Will they bring charges against you?"

"Probably."

"How did it happen?"

"We don't know. Someone must have told them she was here."

David girded himself. His heart heavy but his words coming clearly, he confessed what had happened at the saloon. "It just slipped out. I should have lied. I regret it more than anything I've ever done in my life."

For a moment Mornay could not restrain himself: "You hesitated to lie in the cause of justice?" he thundered. "Why, you may have to risk your life, even to kill, in the cause of justice!" He was awesome, Jehovic. David felt minuscule. "I wish there were some way I could make amends!"

"You'll find a way if you truly want one!"

"I'll find one!" David vowed. Then feeling he must be completely frank he revealed that he'd been invited to go abroad with Wright to help arrange financing for a Pacific Railroad. "It should place me in a position where I can be of great help to the Abolitionist Cause."

Mornay replied dryly: "I'm glad for your sake. Remember, I said Wright would show you all the kingdoms of the world? David, you've deceived no one but yourself. I've seen you degenerate from an idealist who struck out at evil, as you did the day you arrived here and fought those thugs, to a shameful profligate swayed by every breeze of temptation until you reached your present depth. You are fortunate in one respect. God must love you dearly. He has given you so much to atone for!"

David felt utterly crushed and for a moment had nothing to say. Martha too remained silent. She was thinking she would never speak to him again. He sensed this, felt their disgust, felt overwhelmed by shame. They had known all along of his double life. He had fooled no one, probably not even Wright.

"I ask your forgiveness."

"You have mine," Mornay replied gravely, offering his hand. He remembered the promise of greatness in this endearing youth, the promise of a son such as he never had had. But Martha turned away.

Wing had silently withdrawn to listen from the neutral shadows of the hall. Shaking his head slightly now, he slipped off to confide the events of this memorable evening to his journal.

Mary Louise sensed her strategy was working. Little by little as their intimacy grew, Sedley began to confide in her. And during their pillow talk in the early morning hours of this night he revealed to her what had happened at the saloon the evening before.

"There's a young squirt, plays the innocent Jesus, name of Venable, a pet of Wright's. He blabbed it. She's hidden at the house where he lives—you know, Mornay, the vegetable dealer?''

Mary Louise's heart nearly stopped. But she did not lose presence of mind. ''I suppose they arrested her immediately?''

''By law they can do so without the help of an officer, but I advised them to see Justice Lacey—he has Southern sympathies—and obtain a warrant. They'll need it to gain legal entry to the house. And an officer or two could be useful if anyone resists.''

Mary Louise wanted to rush away and give warning, but felt his enveloping arms. She was caught in a trap of her own making. ''You know, I'm getting rather fond of you?'' Helplessly, she felt his grip tighten and his lips on hers.

Next morning Baker secured a writ of habeas corpus at the request of Mornay. It ordered that Hattie be brought before Superior Court Judge Parker for inquiry into the nature of her detention. Although Parker, a New Englander with known anti-slavery views, was dubious he said he would call a hearing the following day. On Sedley's advice Stanhope tried to retain Halleck, but when Halleck declined on grounds of deep involvement in land cases which were his specialty, Sedley suggested Ogles. ''He's Southern born. You'll find his views coincide with yours. You can depend on his discretion. And he's brilliant in court.''

Stanhope told Ogles: ''I want to make this a test case.''

''It seems to me open and shut,'' Ogles replied. ''Under the California Fugitive Slave Law you'll get your property back.''

''But I don't want her back under California law. I want her back under the National Fugitive Slave Law!''

''Since she crossed no state lines while running away your case will be weakened if you invoke it.''

But Stanhope, mindful that his friends Davis, Yancey, Rhett and Ruffin—indeed most Southern public opinion—might be looking over his shoulder as the case progressed, was adamant. He not only wanted Hattie back, he wanted to be recognized as a champion of Southern Rights. ''She's running away from slavery—from the South,'' he insisted, ''in particular from Louisiana, not just from my control. Don't you see there's a larger principle involved? I want the rights of Louisiana and her sister states defended and enlarged. It's my contention that since the girl owed her servitude to me in Louisiana, she is running away from Louisiana and did in fact cross state lines.''

Ogles took the case somewhat reluctantly, realizing its importance and how it might enhance his reputation as well as his pocketbook. And he was struck by the Colonel's original line of thought. ''Let me ask one question which may be crucial. How long have you and your family been in California?''

''Approximately three months.''

Ogles frowned. ''As a traveler passing through, your property is protected by many precedents. But if it is perceived that you have delayed unduly or transacted business with a view to becoming a resident or behave in ways other than a sojourner, the court may decide you have forfeited your protection under the law, since slavery is prohibited by our State Constitution.''

''Ridiculous!'' snorted the Colonel with the imperiousness of one used to having his own way. ''Why, that girl represents fifteen hundred dollars! Surely under our Federal Constitution I can take my property with me anywhere in the United States?''

''That may be true,'' rejoined Ogles, speaking firmly, knowing he must control his client in order to conduct his case properly. ''But in the eyes of the law three months may seem a long time for a traveler to spend passing through a free state while in possession of a slave. Were there no extenuating circumstances, the illness of your wife perhaps?'' Ogles knew of Sarabelle's hypochondria. In fact she'd expressed to him her distaste for San Francisco's fog, wind, dust ''and the savagery of its people,'' but to no avail ''since my husband is so strongly taken by these new surroundings as are Victoria and Beau,'' and it was on their urging she'd gone with Vicky to look at that house they might buy on Green above Kearny, ''Chivalry Center,'' where homes of many Southern families were situated, as Ogles knew. Stanhope was quick to grasp his point but reluctant to use it. ''True, my wife has been unwell. But surely I need make no excuse for our visit?''

''Of course not!'' Ogles dissembled. His client's vanity must be preserved. ''But I suggest you appear as a traveler whose visit has been prolonged by your wife's unforeseen illness. I should not, if I were you, mention the transaction of business or the intent to establish residency.''

Stanhope frowned as if all law were a personal inconvenience but acquiesced on Sedley's urging, Sedley having warned him about the very point Ogles was making.

*     *     *

Now Judge Parker's courtroom was nearly full. Many of the spectators were Negroes. Mary Louise had spread word that their future and that of all blacks in California might be at stake. Mornay, Martha, Lucinda Wright, Reuben Stapp and David sat in the front row a few steps from the witness chair. David had gone frankly to Wright, feeling high in his employer's estimation, told him about the hearing and asked permission to attend. "Of course." Wright's response was hearty. "You must be your own man in questions of conscience. Lucy will want to be there too. She's more radical than I about these matters." So now Lucinda had her feathers up, like a ruffled hen's, though it meant affronting the once sought after Stanhope family. Farther along that same row were Stanhope and Beauford, Sarabelle and Victoria escorted by Sedley. As he turned and saw his once-adored, head high and contemptuous, no room for him in her eyes, David felt a catch in his throat. Though his concept of Victoria had changed drastically during the agonizing hours of his remorse and confession, he could not quite rid himself of his original infatuation. Nevertheless he was proud to be publicly taking his stand on behalf of Hattie—and in so doing declaring that he saw the Stanhopes for what they truly were: prejudiced, arrogant—all but Beau, yes, only easy-going gallant-spirited Beau represented a loss that hurt. He remembered their long walk through the countryside as a moment of true union. But he could not imagine how he'd been so deluded by the rest of the family.

Judge Parker, prematurely bald, solemn as an owl, heard the contending arguments. Baker in his turn pleaded against the detention of Hattie in concise but eloquent terms. "Under the National Fugitive Slave Law this young woman is not a fugitive because she did not cross any state line while running away. Under the California Fugitive Slave Law, she is not a fugitive because her former master in effect freed her by bringing her into a state where slavery is, thank God, prohibited and keeping her here three months, during which time he forfeited his status as sojourner by transacting business and taking steps to establish residency."

Ogles, empty coat sleeve pinned dramatically over his heart, rebutted that since Hattie was a slave according to Louisiana law, Louisiana law should be respected in California "according to the accepted principle of comity," and therefore she was lawfully

Stanhope's property while he was a traveler—Ogles emphasized the term traveler—in a free state. "Being unforeseeably detained by the illness of his wife, he nevertheless is entitled to the protection of his property under National Constitution and Fugitive Slave Law." Ogles added a point which seemed telling to many. Since Hattie herself had not asked for a writ to obtain her freedom, she might not be interested in it. "Others widely known as troublemakers appear to be influencing this girl and acting for her," meaning Mornay and his fellow Abolitionists.

Judge Parker ordered that Hattie be placed on the witness stand. She was a moving sight, in certain eyes, her hair and dress dishevelled, face and arms scratched from defending herself against the viciously prejudiced female inmates of the filthy rat-infested jail. That sleepless night of terror and anxiety had also left hollow cheeks and sunken eyes. But when she saw Mornay and Martha and David her eyes brightened, and when they met Reuben's she flushed with happiness, and fresh strength and courage flowed into her. She wondered where Mary Louise might be. But her mother dared not appear because of the presence of the Stanhopes and Sedley. Mornay had promised to send her word of what happened through Wing Sing. Since Chinese were not welcome in courtrooms, Wing waited patiently outside. Hattie let her eyes rest briefly on the Stanhopes. She'd been genuinely fond of Victoria and Beau while loathing the Colonel and Sarabelle. Beau winked at her. The others eyed her scornfully with an antagonism which could mean only painful punishment should they ever regain custody over her, and she resolved they never would.

Judge Parker reiterated the nature of the hearing to her in kindly tone, and when he asked: "Do you wish to be free?" she spoke up boldly, her eyes on Reuben's to give her strength: "Yes, sir!"

Seeing how the wind was blowing Ogles decided to object. "Your honor, if this girl owes service to her master in another state, as I contend, she has in effect crossed that state's borders when she made her bid for freedom. Therefore the Federal Fugitive Slave Law applies. Therefore the United States Commissioner, not this court, should have jurisdiction!" Of course the Commissioner happened to be a member of The Chivalry, as Ogles knew. But wishing to move circumspectly in a delicate matter and keep his record clean, Parker decided to send the case to the Commissioner.

Baker objected strenuously. Nevertheless Hattie was remanded to jail for the time being. Wing Sing hurried to Mary Louise with the news. Mornay, Baker, David and Reuben took counsel on the corner outside City Hall. "They've put themselves on ground that may prove untenable!" Baker reassured the others.

"But the Commissioner will find in favor of Stanhope!" Mornay objected.

"Not if the facts show she ran away in California, which they will. He'll almost certainly find he has no jurisdiction, and that may leave the case in a nice limbo!"

"And Hattie in jail?" Reuben protested.

"Let's cross that bridge when we come to it," Baker responded.

The Commissioner received the case the following Monday and announced he would render his decision on Thursday. Meanwhile Hattie did remain in jail. But thanks to vigorous intervention by Mornay, Lucinda Wright, Reuben and other leaders in the city's Negro community, she received better treatment. She was becoming important. On the following Thursday, Commissioner Jarrold decided without hearing arguments that he had no jurisdiction because Hattie had crossed no state lines in her strike for freedom, and returned the case to Judge Parker. Stanhope was furious. Ogles counseled patience. Through friendly members he was in touch with the state's highest court. "I'm taking steps to bring it before them, in the event Parker finds against us." And Stanhope concurred seeing at last a chance for that national audience he hoped for. "I want this case to be a milestone!"

Following final arguments, Parker announced to Ogles and Baker and a packed courtroom that he would render his decision the following Saturday. On Saturday morning Hattie was returned to court. The room was again packed with spectators almost evenly divided in their loyalties. The community was aroused as never before—as communities throughout free states were being roused over similar cases, as fugitive slaves were apprehended by owners or professional slave catchers and summarily returned to servitude, without even such hearings as this one. Across the North there was for the first time a rising tide of indignation toward slavery.

At ten o'clock Judge Parker scratched his bald head with one forefinger, cleared his throat and declared: "This court finds no legal basis for the confinement of the person in question and orders her released." Hattie was free. David felt himself delivered from a moral bondage similar to Hattie's physical one. Reuben leaped over the rail to embrace her, as a great cheer rose from much of the crowded room. Mornay uttered a silent prayer of thanksgiving. Martha rushed forward and embraced her friend. Wing set off at top speed for the Washington Street house to tell Mary Louise. With the exception of Beau, the faces of the Stanhopes expressed bitterness and contempt. But as the victors were leading radiant Hattie out of court they were met by two officers and she was rearrested. A roar of consternation and anger rose, especially from the Negroes who till now had shown remarkable restraint. But to no avail. Ogles had communicated with his friends on the Supreme Court. An order had been issued requiring the case to be brought before that body. "I'm afraid it's valid," Baker conceded as he perused the document.

Stanhope's face, glowing with triumph, made David realize for the first time that war between North and South might be inevitable, that as Mornay said he might have to kill for the sake of justice, because at that moment he could have taken up arms for Hattie.

Through the crowd he glimpsed Beau and could see by his face that he was not in sympathy with what was occurring, and this enraged David further against the Slavocracy. A vision flashed across his mind of a world free of the Colonel and his kind, a world that contained him and Beau there at Golden Gate together looking out to sea, into the future, as on their memorable walk and talk. Meanwhile, stunned, outraged, he and Mornay, Martha and Reuben and scores of others, white and black, accompanied a crushed and bewildered Hattie back to jail, voicing their anger, clashing from time to time with white supporters of the Colonel.

"You're a wizard!" Stanhope glowed, patting Ogles on the back. "We'll show these mudsills yet!"

Baker was dejected. "We may have exhausted our legal remedies for the time being."

"While that poor girl remains in jail?" Mornay demanded.

"Till the Supreme Court rules."

"Almost certainly in Stanhope's favor!" Mornay added grimly. "Come on, David. It's time for me to see Broderick. You've been looking for a chance to redeem yourself. I'll give you one."

# Chapter Thirty-five

When they did not find the city's political boss at his usual headquarters in the Union Hotel, Mornay said: "Broderick's either studying in his hideaway room where he educates himself in law, history and literature, or he's at the fire engine house. Let's try the engine house." And as they walked along Kearny Street he explained to David: "Broderick has organized the city with fire engine companies as basic units. Our volunteer fire companies are the muscle and bone of this community. They protect us from our greatest menace and serve as social and political centers, athletic clubs too. Do you ever box for sport?"

"Not regularly. But I like to." David did indeed enjoy giving and taking blows in the manly art.

"Then you'll like Broderick. He's got a wicked left. He's captain of Empire Engine Company Number One of which I'm a member. Don't let his manner put you off. He's difficult, often imperious, but a great leader. I won't say he's perfect. He runs this city by dubious means, often for his own ends. But beyond all that he has the interests of us ordinary folk at heart. He's our champion against The Chivalry."

Broderick was leaning against the highly polished bright-red hand-drawn fire engine handsomely trimmed with brass, talking to a group of partisans. David remembered his powerful somber-faced presence at the Bank Exchange Saloon and noticed again that in contrast to the clean shaven Chivalry, Broderick and those around him wore beards. They included some of the toughest looking characters he'd ever seen. They were The Shovelry, and

Gillem had told him their beards were a badge of brotherhood.

In response to Mornay's greeting Broderick did not smile but seemed to look right into him. He depended on Mornay for the votes of produce growers and small business people who were among his chief supporters, though he had wealthy backers too. In return, when there was a banquet or picnic Mornay was asked to provide the green produce. "What's up, Charles?"

Mornay's approach was deliberately devious. "I'd like you to meet a friend of mine who wants to join our crowd."

Broderick's answer was cold. "I saw him perform at the Bank Exchange Saloon the other evening. I didn't care for his style or the company he kept."

David thought he had never experienced such a look. It felt like a blow from a fist.

"That was an aberration," Mornay explained. "He's on the right side now."

Broderick continued to regard David critically. "That remains to be seen. Like to box?"

"Yes, sir."

Broderick ordered roughly: "Then peel off!" He removed his jacket and rolled up his sleeves. David did likewise. Among the bystanders there were murmurs of anticipation and a movement to make room. David glanced at Mornay. But the merchant's face was expressionless. You're on your own, it seemed to say.

Broderick put up his fists. "Ready?"

All of a sudden, anger at such treatment flooded David with resentment and he resolved to give the best account of himself possible, though Broderick was much taller and heavier. Broderick led with a left jab. David blocked it, then, quickly advancing his right foot, delivered an unconventional right lead which caught Broderick by surprise and grazed his furry chin. Coarse shouts of glee went up from the onlookers. Broderick's eyes widened. Next moment David was on his back on the floor, his own chin tingling, his head buzzing. Broderick was looking down at him with appraisal. "Like more?"

"Sure!" David tried to scramble to his feet but found himself off balance. As his head cleared he realized Broderick was steadying him while saying to Mornay: "He'll do, Charles. Shall we sign him up?" Mornay nodded sagaciously as if foreseeing none of this.

Broderick continued in the tone of one colleague to another: "David, as I tell my genteel friends: 'You don't have to face the

knuckles and pistols of The Chivalry. But I and my boys do.'
Now you know what I mean. Come along in.'' And he led the
way to his office where they devised the strategy that was to prove
decisive for Hattie's future. Broderick saw in it a chance to em-
barrass The Chivalry and Gwin, just as Mornay guessed he would.
''I'm one hundred percent with you,'' he asserted. Broderick's
support meant that all the resources of San Francisco's Tammany
Hall plus Broderick's great influence in the Legislature as Senate
Leader would be backing Hattie. ''And my boys will be there
when you need them. That includes you now, David.'' And he
held out his hand.

That night there was a meeting at Mornay's house. ''We could
steal her out,'' Reuben proposed. ''I know Seymour who brings
the jailer his whiskey at the back door after dark. We might work
through Seymour.''

Mornay shook his head. ''I doubt it. Even if we did, they'd
put the screws on Seymour. He might squeal.'' He told of the
plan he and David had devised with Broderick.

''But that means waiting till the High Court rules!'' Mary Louise objected. Her fierce determination to free Hattie was still the
driving force behind them all.

''What we need for the plan to work is a legitimate excuse for
Hattie to be outside the jailhouse,'' Baker offered, ''if it's only
to be conducted to a courtroom. I'll try getting a habeas corpus
writ from Judge Stevens. That might do it.'' Then Baker digressed
to financial matters. He was running out of money, could no
longer devote time to the case without fee. ''The tent's coming
due.'' Though he had prosperous clients who in effect helped
support his legal charity, he'd reached the end of his resources—
and there was also his natural impecuniousness and the fact that
he was not above a card game now and then. Reverend Hicks of
the Church of God in Christ, him of the V-shaped goatee whose
sermon had so moved Hattie and contributed so much to her determination to be free, spoke up. ''I think I can promise two
hundred dollars from the Negro community.'' Mary Louise said
she would match that amount, whatever it was. Mornay declared
he would mortgage his home if necessary. ''Don't worry, Ned.
We'll see you through.'' Reuben and David also pledged support.
Baker thanked them gracefully. ''I know of no group of people

I'd rather be associated with and I've lived from one side of this continent to the other!''

Rapidly as they moved, Stanhope and Ogles moved faster. Two days later when Baker, accompanied by Mornay, Reuben and David, appeared at the jail with his habeas corpus writ, he was told by the jailer that Hattie was no longer there. ''Her owner came for her an hour ago. I reckon by now she'll be getting what's coming to her!''

Without advance warning the High Court had ordered Hattie released to Stanhope's custody. The question now was to find her. ''This writ is still valid!'' Baker declared, brandishing it furiously. But when the four friends arrived with Constables Monaghan and Grayson at the California House, there was no sign of the Colonel or Hattie.

Despite the closest possible surveillance by the Black Grapevine, Stanhope had contrived, with Sedley's help, to spirit her away. Nor was Beau anywhere to be seen. Sarabelle and Victoria defied the intruders. ''Nigger lover!'' Victoria spat at David, as she turned away. ''Slaveocrat!'' he wanted to spit back but didn't.

It was Mary Louise who discovered that Beau on behalf of his father was booking passage for Panama on the *Western Star* sailing the following Wednesday. Many of the vessel's stewards were black. Some were members of her Grapevine. David confirmed this startling information when he returned to work that afternoon. ''Sure, Beau was in,'' Gillem told him. ''Took passage for the Isthmus on behalf of his Old Man. Claims the old bastard has to go home on business. What's up, Galahad? Still after the Holy Grail?'' Wright was continuing to give David time off at Lucinda's insistence. Gillem and other clerks were curious and a little jealous. But David was irked by Gillem's sarcasm.

''You're the eternal bystander, aren't you? Always observing, analyzing, never committing yourself!''

''If it were left to zealots like you, the truth would never be known—such as who's going to Panama.''

''That's just an excuse for inaction,'' David retorted as he prepared to scour the waterfront for Hattie. He took Gillem back into his confidence. ''Think she's been hidden on the steamer at the dock?''

''How should I know? It's none of my business.''

Suddenly Gillem's casualness became exasperating. ''I believe you'd stand by 'objectively' while this city burned to the ground, trying to analyze how it happened, while the rest of us risked our lives to save what we could from the flames!''

"Blessings on thee anyway!" was Gillem's parting comment. But a search of the *Western Star* by officers revealed nothing. Wing Sing produced the crucial news. Hattie had been taken to deserted Angel Island in the Bay and was being held there until *Western Star* was on its way out Golden Gate, at which time she would be brought aboard.

"How do you know this?" Baker demanded.

"I saw in the tea leaves!" Wing Sing caused everyone to break into smiles such as they'd not worn for days. In fact Wing's fisherman cousin Fatt, operating his junk* to all nooks and crannies of the Bay, supplying the hideaways on the island, had learned of Hattie's whereabouts. "In the Flowely Kingdom," meaning China, "nothing happen but somebody see it!" Wing explained.

When Mornay passed the news to Broderick, Broderick declared: "We'll hang The Chivalry yet!" But it was Lucinda Wright who finally showed them the way they could go, still using Baker's habeas corpus writ, one of the oldest defenses of human rights, as their chief weapon.

As the *Western Star* prepared to cast off from the Commercial Street Wharf on Wednesday at noon, Constables Monaghan and Grayson with Baker and David were among the partisan crowds that milled about the ship, some in favor, some against Hattie. Rumor had gotten out that she was aboard. Her trials, plus the High Court's arbitrary action in releasing her to Stanhope, were making her case more celebrated than ever. Passengers, too, were taking sides. In the confusion the officers in plain clothes and their companions slipped aboard unnoticed. As the *Star* moved toward Golden Gate they observed the surrounding water carefully. When a handsomely dressed gentleman at the starboard rail drew a handkerchief from his pocket and waved it in the direction of Angel Island, they saw someone in a rowboat near the island stand up and make a similar signal. And as the rowboat drew near the steamer, David made out three men. One was Stanhope. The Colonel was planning to take Hattie to Panama and wait there for his family to follow on the next steamer. But not till the rowboat was almost under the ship's rail did David and Baker discover Hattie. She was crouching low between its gunwales, almost hidden by the two men rowing. The dinghy's prow was touching the

*Fatt had sailed the junk from Canton to San Francisco

ship's side, and Stanhope was about to hoist her aboard when
sympathetic passengers warned him officers were present. Too
late.

Monaghan was jumping into the rowboat, flashing his badge,
shouldering the Colonel aside, seizing Hattie. "Habeas corpus,
sir! Sorry!" And Stanhope was bellowing: "What is this outrage?" And some of the passengers were voicing strong support
for the Colonel: "Let him keep his property!" Others for Hattie:
"She's being kidnapped!"

The ship's captain and officers had quietly been alerted by
Wright, at Lucinda's insistence, and helped set the trap.

After a harrowing five days in a shack on the island guarded
by an Indian woman and two Sandwich Islanders who spoke no
English, dreading what might be in store for her, Hattie was now
nearly paralyzed by fear and bewilderment. And her back, where
some of the cuts were still raw, ached and burned from the caning
Stanhope had given her. But when she saw David with finger to
his lips she understood and took heart. Monaghan and Grayson
rowed them ashore in a police dinghy which had been unobtru-
sively tied to the *Star* before it sailed. David's hands helped hold
Hattie steady against the Bay's chop, as did Baker's. Their hands
helped her forget her pain.

A huge crowd of mixed whites and blacks including a number
of newspaper reporters was waiting at the wharf. When Hattie
recognized Reuben, Mary Louise, Mornay and Lucinda her hopes
soared. Even Wright was there, arguing militantly with a Chival-
ric supporter of Stanhope, a man with a gold-headed cane which
he brandished under Wright's nose. Hattie was heartened further
by such public demonstration of support.

A few moments later the vast crowd, boiling as it moved, was
surging along Kearny Street toward City Hall, Hattie at its center,
when it was met by two produce wagons which had been proceeding in opposite directions and somehow locked wheels, bringing all traffic to a halt as their drivers berated each other in loud
voices. "Damn Dago, why don't you watch where you're going!" Otto Eckhard was shouting, shaking his fist, while Tony
Petrini shouted back: "Damn Dutchman, why don't you!"

The crowd surged around them, completely blocking street and
sidewalks. Arguing and scuffling broke out. Prominent were
Broderick's henchmen Spider Kelly, Liverpool Jack, Scarface
Charlie, a notorious gunman and bully, and Jake McGlynn, head
of the teamster's union, and Will Lewis and Bill Carr of the boat-

men. But many were from the ranks of the ordinary Shovelry, dockmen, laborers, mechanics. The result was turmoil.

Broderick and Mornay looked on with satisfaction as a full-scale riot developed, inextricably involving even the officers around Hattie. Jostled by arms and shoulders, pulled, shoved, at last shaken free, she was simply engulfed by those who'd come to save her. But it was David and Reuben, shielded by a wall of bodies, who saw her safely stowed in the back of Petrini's wagon under that canvas he used to cover his vegetables.

And as the deadlock broke up almost as quickly as it had formed, Petrini drove off, turning and still berating Eckhard, Eckhard replying likewise, still shaking his fist, Mornay and Broderick watching with silent approval, while David and Reuben fell to arguing and scuffling convincingly with each other and with other whites and blacks; and the frustrated law officers and raging Stanhope, who'd followed them, shouted and stormed and searched in vain for their escaped prisoner.

That was how Hattie came to join the family of Tony and Angelina Petrini in their shanty in the wild country beyond Lake Merced at the foot of the mountains by the edge of the sea, on a tiny shelf of soil nobody else wanted but whose natural fertility Tony perceived at first glance. "Good, she can help take care of the bambini!" Angelina exclaimed now, as Tony and his wagon arrived home at dusk and she came from the house to greet him, one baby in her arms, two more toddling after.

David, who'd shadowed the cart to its destination, returned and reported its safe arrival to Mornay, Mary Louise, Reuben and Baker. Flushed with success and comradeship, he felt he'd begun to compensate for his betrayal of Hattie, felt himself a blooded member of the Underground, fully committed to its great purpose which had inflamed his imagination and gripped his spirit, only to be lost in myriad missteps. But now regained for good, he told himself with triumphant satisfaction, as the others praised what he had done.

# Chapter Thirty-six

Albert Lancaster mingled in San Francisco society as an English American rather than as a Jew. His surname dated to those days when Jews took names of the localities in which they lived, either by order of their Gentile rulers or for better acceptance as they emerged into Gentile dominated societies. Even in appearance he was Anglo-Saxon: brown haired, blue eyed, with a genial manner which wore well as he went about his practice of medicine; so that after three years he was accepted as one of the city's leading physicians and a prominent supporter of its cultural life, especially music and the theater of which he was very fond.

Being Sedley's housemate and doctor gave him further standing though he received remarkably little in the way of professional fees from Sedley, as he liked to joke, for aside from an occasional attack of asthma which Lancaster treated with an opiate which relaxed lungs and throat, Sedley enjoyed remarkably good health.

He also enjoyed an ongoing rivalry with the doctor over the chessboard in the parlor, their skills so nearly matched that a game might continue from evening to evening and finally end in a draw. Mary Louise soon learned that the board with its pieces in place was a sacred object never to be touched under any circumstances by her or her maids.

For these and other reasons Lancaster was not entirely surprised when Caleb Wright abruptly put his head in the door of his office on Pine Street just off Montgomery on the day after Hattie's escape and complained loudly: "Bert, can't sleep! Head aches! I know it's nothing. But Lucinda insists you have a look.''

Lancaster replied with cheerful directness: "Well, come on in and let's have it!''

"I think it's all this hullabaloo over that slave girl,'' Wright grumbled as he entered. "It's got me riled up.''

"You and a lot of other people. How you been feeling otherwise?''

"Lack of steam generally.''

"Doesn't sound like you.''

"It's *not* like me! And I want to warn you, Bert, I haven't time to be sick. I'm leaving for London in a few days.''

Wright's pulse at 95 was rapid but so was his nature. His overly bright eye looked more significant as Lancaster moved his fingers to the forehead. "Bit of fever here. Had it long?''

"Comes and goes,'' Wright growled.

"Evening and morning?''

Wright nodded.

"Like to take your shirt off?''

"A rash appeared this morning,'' Wright admitted ruefully. "That's really why I came.'' He bared his huge torso and reseated himself in the examination chair.

Lancaster's fingers moved to the small round pink splotches on the lower abdomen. As he touched them they disappeared. "Tell me if this hurts.'' He sank his fingers deep into the groin on the left side. The Captain winced as Lancaster guessed he would. Wright was evidently in the early stages of typhoid fever but Lancaster wanted to be sure. Taking his stethoscope he placed its bell-shaped contact piece over Wright's lungs. The breath was beginning to be labored. Then he listened to the gurgling in the intestines.

"Well, what is it? Out with it!'' Wright demanded.

"My friend, I suggest you go home and go to bed. You're in the first stages of typhoid, or intermittent fever if you prefer to call it that. Stay quiet, take cool baths or sponge offs to keep that temperature down, and you'll feel a lot better. I'm going to give you some tincture of mercury which may reduce that inflammation of the bowels.''

"I didn't say I had inflammation of the bowels!''

"But you do, don't you?''

Wright's face clouded. "I haven't time for this nonsense!'' he stormed.

"I'm afraid you'd better take time!"

"Sorry! Can't do it!" Wright put on his shirt in a fit of temper. "Thanks anyway, Bert. Send the bill, eh?"

Lancaster offered his hand. "Call me if you need me!"

The call came two days later in the form of a handwritten note from Lucinda carried by her petite Irish maid. "Caleb is in bed feverish. Please come, Bert. I'm afraid he's seriously ill and won't do anything about it!"

When Lancaster entered the bedroom, Wright snapped: "You were right, confound you! But I still don't think it's typhoid!"

"It's what you get for drinking nothing but water!" Lancaster winked at Lucy. "Why not try whiskey?"

He found the symptoms well advanced. The pink splotches were more numerous and among them, around thighs and abdomen, were small bluish ones which seemed to reflect the morbid turbulence inside.

"They come and go like the fever," Lucinda volunteered.

"Any diarrhea?"

"Plenty!"

The feverishness at this morning hour was sure to increase toward evening. Lancaster again advised cool baths to keep the fever down and regular use of the mercury tincture.

"Is that all?" Lucy Wright's face was distraught as she saw him to the door."

"How's his appetite?"

"Won't eat a thing. Dozes most of the time."

"Rouse him and feed him every two hours. A thin soup is good, also warm milk. We must keep his strength up. I'll drop in again tomorrow."

She pressed his hand. "We're so grateful, Bert!"

Lancaster patted her shoulder. He was genuinely fond of them both and respected their outspokenness on issues that mattered to them. The one that secretly mattered most to him, intolerance toward himself and other Jews, had yet to arise. Perhaps in the free and easy democracy of the frontier it never would. But Lancaster couldn't be sure. "What's the latest on the runaway slave girl? I read of your involvement."

"They're looking high and low but can't find her, thank God!"

"Good!" And with another reassuring pat on Lucy's frail looking but iron shoulder, he left.

*     *     *

In the second week Lucy, on Lancaster's order, shaved off all Wright's hair, so that his headaches could be mitigated by cold compresses. Still the fever continued to rage, as did the Captain when roused from his torpor, confronting his disease as if it were an adverse wind and he once again on his ship's bridge. Lucy gave him iced baths and turpentine enemas. She applied mustard plasters to his lethargic arms, legs and neck to rouse him. Lancaster inserted a catheter to drain his bladder. To no avail. The once mighty Captain became a feverish mass of protoplasm, his great dreams broadcast to the world in delirious ravings. David came to see him regularly and was increasingly distressed.

"He counts on your visits!" Lucy assured him. She was worn down to nearly nothing by constant exertion and vigil. And it was true that Wright seemed to improve whenever David was beside him. In lucid moments he spoke glowingly of their forthcoming trip. "I've reserved a cabin on the *Golden State!*" Then lapsing into delirium he raved about his transcontinental railway: "A steel ribbon banding mountains and deserts, locomotives pouring forth their smoke of progress into skies where heretofore only the smoke signals of savages have been seen!"

Afterward David walked the streets lost in troubled thought. His precious trip to Europe seemed threatened. But he realized he loved the crusty old Captain for his own sake and felt guiltier than ever for having deceived him so callously with his broken pledge of abstinence. He'd not touched a drop since the night of Hattie's arrest. What had given him keenest pleasure just a short time ago now filled him with revulsion.

Having broken with the Stanhopes he now in similar disgust broke with Angie in a painful scene in which she threatened to throw herself into the Bay if he left her. He thought she was acting, tried to explain. She did not understand, kept repeating tearfully: "You don't love me!" Again the ceaseless cacophony of the saloon below rose to mock them. David finally became so irritated that he blurted out: "True, I don't love you! Now let's have done with it!" He saw her face go suddenly mute and dead as though he had struck her, knew he had spoken cruelly, felt her teetering on the brink even as he spoke, but nevertheless felt compelled by some perverse impulse, which seemed to indicate his destined way, to sever the cord. The mere thought of her was a reproach, as he tried to embark on his new life. Still he cared for her, cared deeply, even feared for her, when he thought of that dark abyss somewhere inside her.

\*          \*          \*

Two days later he read the notice in *The Sentinel* that her body
had been found in the Bay. Stricken with horror and remorse, he
tried to imagine her floating to her death in glorious tranquility
like Ophelia in *Hamlet,* but she had been found among the pilings
under the Pacific Street Wharf like a drowned rat. Perhaps she
had slipped into one of those dark holes such as he and Gillem
had seen Captain Grant peering down. Thus Angie became in
actuality a bit of flotsam and he felt responsible almost beyond
forgiveness. He felt cursed by God, unable to extricate himself
from darkness and wrongdoing, while Hattie's precarious concealment dragged on, officers and would-be slave catchers comb-
ing city and environs in hopes of the thousand dollar reward
Stanhope had offered, and he felt more than ever responsible for
all she had suffered, more than ever helpless to extricate her. He
visited Wright every day though Lancaster ordered that his patient
be isolated lest others be infected.

Mornay was arrested for harboring a fugitive slave but released
on bail pending trial.


At the end of the third week Wright lay for hours with eyes
open and unseeing. Lancaster knew the end was near and, feeling
it his obligation, told Lucinda so. She nodded, dry eyed. "What
can we do?"

"Keep him comfortable."

She summoned David. "Whenever his mind is clear he asks
for you."

David went to the bedside of the dying man. From that upstairs
room he could look out over the Bay at Wright's ships at their
docks, the real stuff of his dreams, and the great hills and mountains rolling inland so majestically beyond them, that setting
against which the Captain had hoped to perform so mightily, had
indeed performed.

One emaciated hand reached for his. The large brown eyes
were again bright and authoritative. "My boy, it was a glorious
dream we shared. I want you to carry it on. Will you?"

"I will!" David thought he meant the railroad.

"I mean the service of God which underlies all our earthly
endeavors." David started but the hand closed on his. "You are
a great person, David. Never forget that. *Never, never forget it!*
Always be true to that higher self!" Wright paused for breath.

"There is no way a young man can serve himself and mankind better than through the ministry. On this my death bed I ask you to embrace the ministry of your choice. In my will I have provided the money necessary for you to complete your college and theological studies. I had no child of my own. God sent you to me. I've seen in you the son of my flesh such as I never had. I shared you with Mornay. Be good to Lucinda..." The feeble grasp relaxed. Wright's eyes glazed as he sank back into coma; David's, tear clouded, looked out upon the shining Bay and mountains beyond, resolved as never before.

At last it had happened. He had been torn up by the roots and turned over. Some terrible thing in him had been exorcised by grief, shame, humiliation, burned away in pain as the fever had burned Wright away. And now the dark night of his soul had passed. Looking out, he saw a new day appearing.

Just as he thought the Captain dead, there came a last flash of that shrewd business acumen: "Promise me you won't delay, that you'll accept my offer, act on it at once?" Wright's eyes were fixed on him, bright and hard.

"I promise!"

Mornay was dumbfounded when David told him his decision to enter the ministry and explained how Wright had brought it about. "How grievously I misjudged the man! I shall ask his forgiveness. What wonderful news! Where will you study?"

"Southern Seminary in Virginia. After I finish college."

Mornay was puzzled by the choice of a seminary in a slave state. "Why there?"

"It was Caleb's native state. I feel it will bring me closer to him, would please him. Lucinda agrees."

Anxiety filled Mornay lest he be losing this person in whom he had invested so much and held so dear. "But will you ever come back?"

"I fully intend to. I feel this is my place."

Mornay brightened. "And we can resume our work together, do those things we've talked about?"

David became eloquent as he did when moved. "There is so much to be done! We must abolish slavery, we must give women the right to vote—make them equal in the eyes of men as they are in the eyes of God—must establish the eight-hour working day and assure the laborer a fair share of the proceeds of his toil.

And we must curb capitalists like Sedley who dominate our commercial and political systems and our personal lives with impunity!'' His eyes were shining. He seemed to emerge and stand clear, fully realized, a kind of radiance about him capable of inspiring extraordinary devotion and faith. Mornay felt awe and wonder, plus deep paternal pride. ''But first I must keep my promise to Caleb.''

''You will. You've been through your ordeal. You know where you're going.''

''What about you?'' David asked with sudden concern. Beside criminal charges, Stanhope was instigating a civil suit for damages against Mornay.

''Ned Baker will defend me. I'll be all right.''

''Shouldn't I stay by your side? What about Martha?''

''I've spoken to Lucinda. She'll care for Martha, if worse comes to worst. No, go—go when life calls you.''

''What about Hattie?''

''The same holds true for her. You've begun to make amends. We'll do the rest. Go now—and the sooner you can return and we can take up the cudgels together!''


''So you're going to become a Christer?'' was Gillem's smilingly caustic comment when David told him of his decision. ''Well, it's always good to have God on your side, I suppose.''

David controlled his irritation, resolved to turn the other cheek. ''It's not a matter of having God on your side but of him having you on his.''

Gillem shrugged. ''Personally, I never could see it. But if it's what you want to do, that's another matter.''

''I've felt it coming a long time. That final moment with Wright brought it to a head. It closed all those escape hatches I'd been leaving open.''

''Well, good luck. I'm departing too, you know.'' And Gillem casually revealed he'd found a reporting job on *The Sentinel*. ''So we'll both be following new directions.''

David congratulated him wholeheartedly. ''You'll be a success! You have a nose for news and a fine sense of impartiality!''

''That's not what you said the last time we discussed the subject. You said impartiality was an excuse for inaction!''

''I said it can be!'' David was amused that his comment had struck home. ''You're morally concerned, though you don't admit it. You know this city down to its lowest rat hole. You'll be outstanding.''

"There you go with your hyperbole again!'' Then Gillem stopped joking. "If I catch one rat, I'll be satisfied.''

David remembered Gillem never exaggerated, never raised expectations unduly, never apologized for his actions, even for his deception of Wright. Everything Gillem did, everything he saw done around him, he accepted as part of life. Was he as he claimed agnostic, amoral? Or admirably tolerant and non-judgmental? David could not be sure. But he knew he would miss Gillem. At least he would be parting from him debt free. After a lucky night at the El Dorado, he'd paid Gillem what he owed him, then quit gambling. "Let's keep in touch, what say?—as you penetrate the seamy truth of this city, and I probe the realms of theology?''

Gillem shrugged, grinned, "Why not?''

That was all, no sentimental farewells, not even a handshake, just that casual indifference which was his way. Yet David sensed Gillem cared, was truly fond of him, but could not, would not, or just plain did not, say so. On sudden impulse he grabbed him and embraced him. "Goodbye, you wonderful deluded wise man,'' and had the satisfaction of seeing something like a flustered blush come to Gillem's cheeks.

"Goodbye, Sir Galahad!'' That dry voice would echo long in David's ears. "If you get a glimpse of the Holy Grail, let me know!''

"Promise you'll come back to us?'' Mornay said a few days later when with Martha he saw David aboard the *Golden State*.

"I promise!'' They embraced as father and son.

Turning to Martha, shyly but tenderly, David put his arms around her and was reassured by feeling hers return his pressure. "Goodbye, Gadfly! Try not to forget me!'' They had celebrated her thirteenth birthday the week before.

She smiled at him through tears, her face and figure suddenly mature. "Please write to us!''

"Why, you're crying!'' he teased. "I didn't know you could!'' At that moment he realized how much she cared.

Lucinda's embrace was motherly. She'd decided not to go East to the woman's rights convention in Albany but would "remain here with Caleb. This is his place and mine.'' Then, momentarily forgetting her bereavement, she waxed militant. "Some day California will show the East the way! Hurry back, my dear!"

Reuben extended his hand in silent comradeship. David felt enriched beyond deserving by all their supporting love. In his trunk were the "fortune cookies" Wing Sing had baked. "Good luck, she smile now!" Wing assured him.

The "all ashore" call came. The ship's gun sounded. It was pulling away from the dock, its huge sidewheels churning with mighty power. Standing at the rail waving, David noticed a solitary figure in the crowd watching but not waving. It was Mary Louise. She'd had difficulty forgiving David his betrayal of Hattie. Why had she come? What did she owe him compared to what he owed her? He thought of Hattie. He had wanted to see her to say farewell. But it did not seem wise to risk a visit to the hideaway. His intimacy with Hattie and Mornay had been publicized. He was a marked man, in many ways.

Sailing over the water of the Bay which had promised him so much the first day he saw it, the Bay that had contained poor Angie's body, sailing in Wright's ship, bearing Mornay's blessing, he began his new life.

# PART II

PART II

# Chapter Thirty-seven

Sedley went south by coastal steamer, a quicker and safer way than riding horseback down the in places nearly nonexistent road, often little more than a trail, nearly everywhere infested by bandits. At supper in the dining salon a florid-faced fellow with a loose tongue tried to strike up an acquaintance. "Going down to the cow counties, are you, sir?" And when Sedley admitted he was the stranger waxed eloquent: "It's another world. I'm from Los Angeles myself. Finest climate on earth. Only thirty-five hundred people counting niggers and dogs. Glad the Gold Rush missed us. Sunshine's our gold! Sunshine and cheap land! We like the idea of dividing the state in two. Just give us the bottom half! Will you have a cigar, sir?"

As a rule Sedley made it a point to be agreeable with strangers, finding they usually told him things he could use. But tonight he preferred to be alone with his thoughts, so excused himself and went to his cabin. It was pleasant to think of Mornay in jail for two months for harboring a fugitive slave and obligated to pay Stanhope a thousand dollars damages. The Colonel's visit had not been altogether unproductive. Despite the loss of Hattie, his interest in the Golden State remained keen, augmented by his investments plus public and private concerns for its political future. Sedley had seen the family off for New Orleans with the understanding they would return. Though nothing conclusive had passed between him and Victoria, he sensed that something eventually would. Like many of his ventures, this one would mature with time. And continued association with Stanhope would keep him in touch with the dominant leadership in the South and in Washington.

Toward morning the tossing of the ship wakened him. We're probably rounding Point Conception, he thought, remembering his first view of that fingerlike landmark as he approached the coast a decade earlier—bearing in from the west aboard Sedley & Company's brig *Discovery,* following the customary course of vessels to California in those days—up the Pacific a thousand miles or more from land to take advantage of the northeast trades, then a sharp swing eastward with the westerlies behind them to Point Concepción and the Santa Bárbara Channel. Before he went on deck the sea calmed and the balmy air told him he'd entered another world. The Los Angeles booster was right, at least to that extent.

Shortly after noon the steamer deposited him at Santa Bárbara. Arriving again at the charming old Spanish town at the foot of steep mountains was like a homecoming, for he'd stopped here many times when supercargo for the *Discovery,* then ridden ahead horseback to negotiate with ranchers such as Clara for hides and tallow to be picked up by the brig later.

Those days, actually only a few short years away, seemed another lifetime, momentarily a desirable one.

The lazy atmosphere, so unlike the hurly-burly of San Francisco, tempted him to linger. This was old Spanish California, still almost unchanged by Mexican sovereignty or American conquest. Somewhere a guitar strummed faintly. Somewhere honeysuckle was in bloom. A burro with a barefoot child on its back came ambling toward him down the unpaved main street. A pair of pigeons were courting on a tiled rooftop. Everyone else seemed asleep. And when he heard the mission bell sounding from the hill above the town, Sedley could believe time had stood still and there had been no Gold Rush.

At the massive Estenega adobe, its two wings extending toward him like welcoming arms, he found Don Lázaro asleep in a hammock in the shade of the verandah, newspaper over his face to keep off the flies, and would not have wakened him had not the incorrigible green parrot in its cage nearby screeched: "Here comes Eliot Sedley!" The old don sat up with a start.

"Drat that bird!" exclaimed Sedley laughing. "Doesn't he ever forget anybody?"

"Nobody," replied Lázaro. "That's why I keep him handy. My memory's not what it used to be. But his gets better with time.'' Lázaro was shrunken and wrinkled as an old nut yet surprisingly spry for his eighty-four years. He extricated himself nimbly from his hammock, stood up and embraced Sedley. ''How are you, my dear friend? What good fortune brings you back to us?''

''I've come to see Aunt Clara.''

Lázaro shook his head sadly. ''Alas, you may be too late. Poor Clara—what's happened to Francisco has nearly broken her heart!'' He spoke with a Castilian lisp, for Don Lázaro represented the old aristocracy, features aquiline, skin old ivory white. He'd come to California as a youthful fortune seeker and feathered his nest well. Lázaro now owned upwards of 300,000 acres consisting of various ranches which were looked after by his five sons.

''And what's happened to Francisco?'' Before leaving, Sedley had read the black headline: PROMINENT RANCHERO LEADS HOSTILE INDIAN BAND.

''He's turned renegade, much as I hate to say it. He is my son-in-law, you know! His wife was my beloved Constanza, Holy Mary rest her soul!'' Tears came to the old man's eyes as he crossed himself. ''She was like her mother, so beautiful, so gentle! I should never have consented to the wedding!''

Sedley discounted both tears and piety. In fact Don Lázaro had been eager for the union of his daughter with the only son of an Indian princess and famous conquistador. It linked him to personages of greater status than his own, to a domain larger than he then possessed. Now he could afford to look back with different eyes.

''My profound sympathy, Don Lázaro! And how, truly, is she bearing up?''

''Through God's mercy Clara has our grandson to comfort her. Pacifico is a fine youngster, not at all like his father.''

''And where is his father?''

''He's joined the hostiles in the mountains, those devils we've been fighting all these years—who steal our cattle and horses and kill us whenever they can!''

''Has anyone seen him?''

Lázaro shook his head bitterly. ''Not yet. But when they do, may they exterminate him and good riddance! The fellow's a born troublemaker! But, forgive me! I keep you standing talking when you have need of rest, food, drink!'' Lifting his voice the old man called: ''Margarita, *aguardiente!*''

A comely Indian girl of such curvatures that Sedley thought she might be consoling the old don in his declining years, appeared with a bottle of brandy and two small glasses on a tray.

An afternoon spent with Lázaro and his family brought Sedley abreast of other developments. The notorious bandit Joaquín Murieta had recently attended a dance nearby despite the price placed on his head by the Governor. "Audacious scoundrel!" Don Lázaro opined. "He knows he's safe among our *paisanos*. He's the common people's hero. They'll never turn him in! But he's a menace to Americans, Eliot. As are the brigands who infest our roads. Let me send my men with you in the morning!"

When Sedley firmly declined this offer, Don Lázaro insisted he take one of his best horses. Knowing such generosity to be traditional, Sedley accepted and the talk turned to the ever present subject of the Land Commission before which Lázaro like Clara and their fellow ranchers must establish his titles.

At supper the entire family including the don's five sons and their wives and children who occupied separate quarters in the great house gathered in the huge tile-floored dining room, and when Sedley saw the sons towering above Lázaro, standing fully six feet and weighing nearly two hundred pounds, he remembered what a handsome race the Californios were—larger and more robust than their fathers—as if specially nourished by the soil of this remarkable land; and much the same was true of their good-looking and vivacious women, whose beauty and grace were almost uniformly exceptional. Fathers, mothers and older children sat at the long table, nurses and younger children on low benches or the floor. Out in the kitchen a crowd of poor waited for leftovers, Sedley knew, while immense dishes were brought in, among them a steer's head still wearing its horns and an entire roast lamb, both of which he found delicious, likewise the rich red wine. When he praised it, Lázaro explained: "It comes from Don Domingo Rogers's new vineyard. Domingo's begun to produce it commercially, you know."

"I didn't. Perhaps I shall have more of it tomorrow when I visit him."

After supper friends and neighbors came to meet or renew acquaintance with Sedley, and during this time he found opportunity to ask Lázaro and others their feelings about dividing the state in two, or three.

"We're for it."

"Where would you draw the line?"

"Just north of San Luis Obispo where the mountains run east to west and the valleys follow the sun into the sea. A new region begins there, free from North American commercialism and gold." They spoke to Sedley with the candor of old friends. "Our gold is in our land, our grass, our cattle, our horses, our life's way."

Moved but not surprised by their appeal he asked: "Would you permit slavery in your new state?"

Raising his eyebrows, Don Lázaro replied tactfully: "If one is to be candid, one must admit we have much in common with our fellow gentlemen of the South." Meaning, thought Sedley, that you own enormous tracts of land and have Indians in virtual servitude to work them and serve you in your mansions. But he did not press the issue, merely nodded to show he understood without passing judgment.

On his bedside table stood the traditional bowl of coins from which a traveler was expected to help himself if need be. A clean shirt was laid out on his bed. A feeling that was almost like remorse went through him. He was part of all that was sweeping away such hospitality, such generous trust. The thought brought him back to the documents he carried. What had happened to the rancheros of the north—the Peraltas of Oakland, the Berryessas farther north—all ruined or about to be by unscrupulous Yankee sharpers must inevitably happen here, so reason told him. He did not want it to happen to Clara nor to Don Lázaro, pious old rascal though he was. Yet he did not see how the riptides of manifest destiny could be avoided any other way than the one he had in mind.

By mid-morning he was climbing the pass behind the city on the back of the dappled gray Lázaro provided. He'd put from his mind the don's dire warnings. Many times with no other weapon than a pocketknife, he had traveled this trail, encountering only courtesy and hospitality, and he wished it might be so again, as part of this venture backward in time, for a purpose he must admit was fantastic. For over an hour he met no one, while Lázaro's warning receded even farther. Far below, the tiny town became a cluster of toy houses beside the water. Across the channel the blue islands rose like foreign lands. Around him the silent chap-

arral gave off its pungent odors. It was indeed like old times when
he'd traveled this route in perfect tranquility from one idyllic
destination to another. His horse stopped abruptly.

An almost naked Indian, short, stocky, face and body painted
red, stood barring his way. His black hair was drawn to a knot at
the top of his head. A wood handled flint knife was thrust through
the knot. This stern faced figure held a vicious looking bow and
a flint pointed arrow in one hand. In the skin quiver slung across
his shoulder were other arrows, red shafts ending in clusters of
feathers. His feet were bare. He held up his free hand and com
manded quietly in excellent English: "Raise your arms above
your head, sir, and do not resist! We are many!"

As he raised his arms Sedley sensed other figures emerging
silently from the chaparral and surrounding him. The one before
him spoke in a guttural tone and the figures stopped. Sedley's
heart nearly stopped too. Sweat had broken out on his forehead
The Deringer in his pocket was as good as useless. Don Lázaro's
warning swept back over him with powerful conviction. Then
strangely, fear began to leave him. Very strangely indeed he fel
he knew this painted figure before him.

"Now if you'll dismount, Eliot, perhaps we can talk?"

"Francisco!" The words burst incredulously from Sedley as
he stepped down from his saddle. "What on earth . . . ?"

"Yes, what on earth!" Francisco replied, advancing and em
bracing him. "What on earth brings you here?" And Sedley felt
the sun warmed flesh of his old friend between his arms and
looked once more into Francisco's dark intelligent eyes, observed
a new calmness there and smelled the wild aroma of his body
which was like that of the chaparral itself.

"Why, your mother brings me, Francisco!"

With a shake of his head though still smiling, the other released
him and stepped back. "No more Francisco, Eliot. I'm Helek the
Hawk, now. Francisco El Magnifico—the magnificent halfbreed
the magnificent spendthrift dupe of the Yankees, half white, half
Indian, that fool you knew, Eliot, is no more. I have taken back
my ancient name. I am Helek the Indian." Before a bewildered
Sedley could ask, Francisco explained. "One seeks only one's
true self while in this world. At last I have found what I sought
I side with my mother's people, though she does not side with
me. We fight for our land and our rights in our own way. But
you—what brings one of the most prominent men of San Fran
cisco to this wild place, riding alone?"

Sedley told of the papers he carried, explained the problem of
establishing Clara's title to Rancho Olomosoug. Francisco's face
darkened. "How ridiculous! It's hers, it's mine, it's ours!" He
gestured toward his shadowy men. "Here are the true title holders! How dare they thrust this indignity upon her, upon us? Just
as there can be no question about the title to this entire state if
only we could find the court to hear it!"

A warning whistle sounded from the edge of the chaparral.
Francisco fell silent. Up the trail from below them came the sound
of voices. Travelers were approaching. Francisco suggested quietly: "I think it is time for you to ride on, Eliot. But first let me
drive home my point. You spent last night at the house of my
father-in-law. On whose back were you sleeping, really? The Indians'. Who prepared your meal? Who served it? Who washed
and laid out your clean shirt? Indians. All the land that rascally
old scoundrel owns is in reality ours. And he could not operate
his vast domains for one day without our help. Do you see why
we take up arms?" Sedley nodded. He saw as never before. "And
now there is one last matter between us." Francisco took the flint
knife from his topknot. "I have sworn to shed white blood. But
I have not said how much." His smiling eyes locked onto Sedley's. "Are you game, Eliot?"

Sedley managed to steady his voice, and his nerves. "I am
game!"

"Then roll up your sleeve and hold out your right arm." Francisco's tone was playful yet formidable. Sedley did as directed.
Midway in the underside of his forearm, just deep enough to draw
blood, Francisco carved an incision in the form of an X, and
looked up smiling still. "Now my word has been kept. Thank
you for your help, Eliot." The approaching travelers were close
at hand. Francisco looked around implicitly to his men, then back
to Sedley. "Ride on quickly. Give my love to my mother. Tell
her the struggle takes many forms."

The sun was setting as Sedley rode up to the gracious hacienda
of his old friend Don Domingo Rogers, feeling glad to be alive.

The modern two-story whitewashed adobe with its balconies
and tiled verandahs, of the new style called "Monterey," stood
on a slight eminence overlooking vast pastures in which cattle
and horses grazed. Nearer the house were the orchard, vineyards,
grain fields which helped make Domingo one of the most pros-

perous of Yankee dons. Sedley noted how the vineyards had in
creased since his last visit as Lázaro had said, and the figures o
Indians toiling in them as Francisco had said, and he heard h
arrival being heralded by barking dogs, excited cries of children
the neighing of horses greeting his, as he saw the familiar broad
shouldered figure of Domingo and the lesser but still substantial
one of Doña Inés emerge onto the front steps to greet him, ac
companied by their younger children.

Domingo was more than a friend. Domingo was his othe
self—a reminder of what he might have been had he embrace
the California way fully on first arrival as Domingo did. Sedle
had been tempted to do so more than once in those intoxicatin
first days when the sweet ambience of an idyllic land envelope
him. It swept back over him now. Here was an old dream en
bodied.

"Welcome, Prodigal Son!" Domingo shouted, as an Indian la
in coarse woolen trousers and tunic came running to take hi
horse. And as he embraced Domingo's broad shoulders clad i
costly green velvet, Sedley thought of the naked ones of anothe
friend embraced earlier that day but decided to say nothing abot
them at the moment.

Doña Inés gave him a spontaneous hug and kiss. After bearin
seven children in fourteen years she was nearly as broad of bear
as her husband but this did not decrease the natural beauty of he
features or the generosity of her spirit. "How is my Eliot? Wh
are you wandering about our countryside at this time of evening
Why have you stayed away so long? We hear all sorts of thing
about you. You're just in time for supper. You look tired, poo
boy. Food, drink are what you need!"

Her graciousness made Sedley recall those days when he'd con
sidered becoming her brother-in-law; for her sisters, the Carrill
girls, were as charmingly beautiful as Doña Inés had once beer
Taking from his pocket the hard round candies placed there fo
this purpose, he handed them to the younger children and inquire
after Anita.

"Anita, Anita, querida, where are you?" Doña Inés called
summoning the girl who was lingering shyly just inside the door
"Come and see your Uncle Eliot! Foolish child, he won't bit
you!"

The enticing figure that emerged onto the terrace made Sedle
draw breath. Tonight Anita was gorgeous, her skin milky white
her hair jet black. The knowledge that Benito Ferrer adored he

nhanced her charm, though it did not quite compensate for the
aithlessness of Pacifico. Yet she gave Sedley her little hand as
f afraid he might not give it back. "She's going to marry Paci-
co, old Clara's grandson!" her mother declared in affectionate
mpatience with such diffidence. "So she thinks she's being un-
rue if she looks at another man. Are you betrothed, Eliot?"

"Mother!" Anita protested, flushing.

"Not yet!" Sedley confessed, pressing Anita's hand, while he
hought what a delightful armful she would make. He remem-
ered Pacifico as a backward youth quite undeserving of such
ewards.

"Speaking of the Boneus, how is Aunt Clara? And how are
hings at Rancho Olomosoug?"

"Ah, Tía Clara!" Inés threw up her hands and rolled her eyes
kyward. "She is immortal. But so full of contradictions! The
Virgin save us! First she urges us to support the American conquest, because her beloved husband favored the Americanos long
go. Next, when she realized what was happening as result of it,
he decided we should all oppose it. Now she's devoting herself
o her Indian people. And wants us to do the same. And all the
ime she advocates that old fairy tale she shared with Antonio—
ow beautiful it was!—that all of us regardless of ancestry should
ive in peace and harmony in this beautiful land! She often speaks
f you, Eliot!" Inés' words seemed to mock the secret purpose
f his visit, seemed to make him a scoundrel. "Of course," she
vent on, "what's happened to Francisco has nearly broken her
eart. He's always been such a sorrow to her. And now . . ." She
urned to Domingo for confirmation of the deplorable conduct of
Francisco. It was then that Sedley decided to reveal what had
appened to him in the pass that morning. As she listened, Doña
nés clapped a hand to her mouth and her eyes grew large when
he saw the wound on his forearm. Anita too expressed amaze-
nent with a gasp. But Domingo commented quietly: "Lucky he
idn't kill you. His band has blocked cattle herds from passing
nto the San Joaquín from the south. But I didn't think they would
venture so close to the coast, to civilization."

"He spoke like a man with a serious purpose."

"Yes, he's serious. After all those years of frivolity he's serious
t last!" Domingo's sarcasm was bitter.

After supper when the women and children left them at table
vith their wine and cigars, they discussed the subject further.
"When he was in San Francisco with me a few months ago,"

Sedley resumed, "he seemed his old self. What changed him?"

Domingo told of Francisco's humiliation at the hands of th Jenkinses. "That did it."

"Has he troubled you—or his mother?"

"No, but there's no predicting what a madcap like that will d next." Domingo had ordered his men to drive the horses into th corral near the house and be on the lookout during the night. " always do this when barefoot Indians are about. We've been a tacked a dozen times in the past twenty years—though not b him."

"Does he operate from horseback as well as on foot?"

"I've heard so—often disguising himself as a ranchero, whi his men masquerade as harmless vaqueros until he's ready t strike."

Then Sedley explained the ostensible purpose of his trip. " want to help her all I can. You must be going through the sam thing with the Land Commission?"

Domingo nodded. "I'm using Halleck. That's about the onl difference. We may have to divide this state, Eliot. Things a becoming intolerable."

"Would you go with the South—I mean the political South?"

"The Slaveocracy? I'd think seriously of it if they'd leave ou land titles alone."

Before retiring to bed, Doña Inés asked a little fearfully: "Do mingo, do you think Francisco will attack us tonight?"

"It's not likely. He'll know we're expecting him, after wha he's done to Eliot." But to be on the safe side Domingo took hi new Colt Navy revolver from the drawer of his bedside table an placed a fresh cap firmly on each nipple of its six loaded cham bers.

# Chapter Thirty-eight

ext day Sedley rode on. Like Don Lázaro, Domingo had pro-
ded him one of his finest horses, a strawberry roan with reddish
ane and tail and a pacing gait as gentle as a rocking chair. It
ade miles slip behind them through hills and valleys mellowed
th golden grass and dappled with dark green oaks. Toward
dday he reached the pass overlooking the Valley of Santa Lucía
d drew rein. He seemed to be looking down into paradise.

To his left white dunes outlined the blue crescent of the bay.
aching down to it like mighty arms came the grassy hills that
rmed the valley. They embraced a ribbon of river edged by
een growth through which he'd often made his way to water
s horse or drink himself or pluck stems of aromatic arrowweed
chew. And back toward those dark mountains from which river
d hills descended was Rancho Olomosoug. Sedley had a feeling
coming home. Again his brig lay in the bay while a long line
oxcarts, piled high with folded cattle hides, "California bank
tes," worth two dollars each, came creaking down the valley
companied by bantering shouts of drivers and escort of mounted
queros, he among them as one of them, Francisco beside him,
metimes Tía Clara too come to see the ship and the excitement
loading the hides through the surf to the waiting boats. As a
y listening to his sea-captain father in the tall brick house on
acon Hill, Boston, he'd heard Horatio Sedley tell of a marvel-
sly beautiful valley in a wondrous faraway land called Califor-
a. "Some day you may go there and see it!" He had gone, he
d seen. And like his father he had cherished and coveted. Some

day, some year beyond the turmoil of present moments he mig
retire here in peace and quiet with a Mary Louise or a Victor
Meanwhile it would feed the springs of his imagination.

In this mood he descended toward the crumbling mission a
surrounding adobes and the raw new wood buildings and glari
white tents and hooded wagons of American settlers which co
stituted the settlement of Santa Lucía. The dusty trail became t
town's main street, and soon he was approaching Santiago F
rer's general store where he stopped for a visit with his old frien
Santiago and Mark were serving customers but Santiago bro
off to greet him affectionately and a few moments later was e
plaining what Sedley wished to learn. "Clara has many problem
But her health is good. She's counting on your help." They
emerged under the awning which shaded the front of the sto
when a drunken clamor from up the street drew their attentio
Santiago shook his head. "It's the new saloon." He never to
erated such conduct on his premises, indeed had little need to, f
the Californios were abstemious in their drinking and he refus
to sell liquor to Indians, knowing its disastrous effect on the
Sedley shook his head in agreement. Declining Santiago's inv
tation to dinner, he added: "I'll see more of you later. Give n
respects to Ruth. I want to say hello to Father O'Hara befo
going to the ranch."

As he was passing the new saloon, a pair of fresh deer hor
nailed above its doorway, its hitching rail crowded with tether
animals, its interior similarly crowded judging from the din, 
noted loafers of various nationalities hanging about outside, s
or eight Indians especially deplorable in ragged clothes a
drunken stupors as they sat with backs against the side of t
building. A burly white was berating them to the huge enjoyme
of tipsy companions. "Lazy good-for-nothings! Damn Diggers!

Buck was enjoying a pastime common in many parts of t
state, Indians being often lumped under the derisive label "Di
gers" because they dug roots and herbs for food. Sedley wou
ordinarily have passed such a scene without much thought b
remembering his recent experience with Francisco, he paused 
see if these Indians would resist abuse. However the poor spin
less creatures merely hunched under their blankets or stared st
pidly at their swaggering abuser, and after a moment Sedle
continued toward the old mission drowsing in ruined grandeur 
a slight elevation at the end of the street.

Mission Santa Lucía spoke of past glory, enormous efforts,

driving purpose, all of which Sedley could appreciate. They were in keeping with his vision of a new California. But the huge octagonal stone fountain in its foreyard under the giant pepper tree was dry. No Indian converts washed clothes at the stone *lavandería* nearby—a huge trough three feet deep, five feet wide, thirty yards long, flanked by stone pavement—where scores, even hundreds, once busied themselves. Many of them rested, he knew, in the graveyard on the shady north side of the church. Disease, despair—who knew what else beside time?—had prevailed. The hitching rail in front of the crumbling portico was vacant. A solitary gray cat strolling under the arches seemed the only occupant of the premises. Since it was the noon hour Sedley thought Father O'Hara might be taking his fiesta, and not wishing to disturb him he tied his horse to the rail and strolled into the church whose doors stood open to congregations which no longer existed—under a belfry without a bell which looked down upon him like a vacant eye.

It was like stepping back into time, cavernous time. For a moment in the obscurity he could hardly make out his surroundings. Then his eyes focused on the red light of the candle burning inside its tinted glass on the altar at the far end of the church. Since first lit by the missionary fathers nearly a century before, that flame had never gone out—not during fire or flood, earthquake or Indian attack, not even when for a time the mission was almost totally abandoned except for one faithful old convert and used as a warehouse for storing hides. Sedley had no religion but he found all this highly picturesque.

The church was devoid of seats of any kind, as originally. Its irregularly laid floor tiles, stained red with ox blood, were worn smooth by those who had stood or knelt or sat upon them. As he approached the altar he made out dimly on the wall behind it the remarkable painting done by native artists under direction of the padres. At the center of what appeared to be an enormous white cloud, probably representing heaven, a bright golden triangle, standing for the Holy Trinity, enclosed a single huge eye, the eye of God, no doubt, looking directly at him. Sedley could imagine the effect it must have had on the simple minds of Indian neophytes.

He heard a step behind him. Father O'Hara's youthful voice vibrated with affection and welcome. "I thought I heard someone ride up. I was at my writing desk. There's so much to be recorded, I can scarcely find time to get it all down. How are you, my dear friend? You've come at last! But what are you doing here?'' They embraced.

The robust red-haired priest looked more like an adventurer in a gray robe. His tonsure seemed part of a costume adopted for the role O'Hara played with overflowing energy and enthusiasm—useful characteristics, Sedley reflected, when one is attempting to rebuild a decaying church and faith. Last of the old, first of the new, son of that Irish soldier of fortune who fought in the Peninsular Campaign of Wellington against Napoleon's forces and afterward became a general in the Spanish army, O'Hara had turned his back on quiet ways and come with missionary zeal to the new state of California where there were no longer any missions, only ruins. Expropriation in late Mexican times stripped the padres of their lands, dispersed their Indian converts, left their churches in decay. In what remained of Mission Santa Lucía, Michael O'Hara would seek his fortune in devastation and chaos, for those terms accurately described what was left of the dreams of his forerunners. He was eager for every bit of information he could discover about them, and devoted long hours to researching their archives and interviewing those who'd known them, like old Clara.

"What am I doing here?" Sedley replied matter of factly. "I was looking into the eye of God, if that is indeed his eye observing me," indicating the painting.

"You and me and all of us, yes! As my innocent hearted Indians say: we are watched by one Great Eye by day, the Sun; another by night, the Moon!" O'Hara crossed himself and genuflected toward the painting. "Let me call your attention to the fact that we are standing on the bones of one of his uncanonized saints."

On the slab at their feet Sedley read:

FRAY NICOLÁS RUBIO
BORN ON THE ISLAND OF MAJORCA A.D. 1729
DEPARTED THIS LIFE A.D. 1784 IN THE VALLEY OF SANTA LUCÍA
IN THE BLOOD OF MARTYRS IS THE SEED OF THE CHURCH

"This mission was Rubio's creation as you know," O'Hara continued with fervor. "He lighted the flame. It symbolized his dream that Spaniard and Indian, white men and red, could together create a harmonious relationship in this valley. Clara embodies his dream. He died at the hands of those he tried to help.

She lives on. She speaks of you often, Eliot. She'll be so glad you've come!''

"How is she?''

"Sore beset, sore beset!'' O'Hara smiled as if that were a fortunate state. "Step into the garden with me and I'll tell you more.'' He indicated the small side door through which he had entered, letting a swathe of sunlight into the dark interior of the church behind them. "We won't be disturbed there!'' As if in all this solitude crowds might be gathering, Sedley thought dryly, noting the solitary cat which had wandered into the church after him—as if those rowdy patrons of the saloon might come thronging to repent or those drunken derelicts of Indians awake from their stupors and come once more to their catechism. O'Hara was an incorrigible visionary, totally unrealistic, but he liked him. The priest was part of a scene which meant a great deal to Sedley.

They sat on a small stone bench in the cloister garden shaded by an olive tree surrounded by tall pink and white hollyhocks and climbing white roses. Bees hummed in the warm sunlight. A gentle breeze came from the sea as if there were no trouble anywhere. O'Hara resumed: "Yes, sore beset. Squatters camped on her land. Francisco disappeared. They say he's joined a hostile Indian band. Poor madcap. I feel sorry for him. He's never found himself in his own eyes, let alone that eye of God!'' The situation in the valley between settlers and Californios was one of hair-trigger delicacy. The slightest touch might set off bloody strife. "But all this presents us with a golden opportunity, Eliot. See that pomegranate there?'' pointing to one which hung like a huge round nut from its low tree. "Do you know what it symbolizes? Open it and you find its homely exterior contains ruby red seeds that shine like jewels, that are sweeter than wine, Eliot. The ancients considered pomegranates symbols of fertility. But to me they represent that oneness of all things, that diversity within unity. Our existence, in sum.''

Sedley had always found pomegranates messy and disappointingly bitter but thought best not to say so and O'Hara continued enthusiastically: "If we can bring together Indian, Spaniard and Anglo-American we shall have set an example this troubled state can follow.'' His face grew radiant with inspiration. "We shall have realized Rubio's dream! Clara's too! And mine! And, I think, yours!''

Sedley decided to bring the priest down to earth. "She hasn't tried to eject the squatters?''

"No, that might mean bloodshed, her dream shattered. She's resolved to accept matters, at least until she talks to you."

Sedley nodded as if that were a sensible course. "And you—don't they encroach on you too? How do you survive?"

"Yes, they press me hard. They've occupied my orchard, even my vegetable garden. They call me papist. But some day they will enter my church, I predict, and pray with me. Meanwhile I try to turn the other cheek. Like Santiago I mind my own business and they let me alone."

"But what do you do for food?"

O'Hara pointed to a newly planted plot in the far corner of the garden. "I have withdrawn within my walls. An old Indian helps me. I repay him with blessings and potatoes. Then we repair holes in the roof." His eyes twinkled. "On Sunday three or four townspeople come to worship with us, and five or six from ranchos roundabout. I've a growing flock, Eliot! Remember, Fray Rubio began with only one!"

They heard angry shouts in the distance. Then a pistol shot, then more loud cries, then the sound of a horse approaching at a gallop.

"Come, this may be our opportunity!" O'Hara led the way as they hurried out onto the portico, the gray cat following at leisure.

"Damn Diggers!" Buck's baiting of the supine and unresisting Indians seated with backs against the side of the saloon had reached a climax, to the amusement of bystanders. "Get off your ass and go to work like the rest of us!" He was about to reenforce this admonition with the toe of his boot when a magnificently dressed ranchero on a chestnut sorrel swept around the corner of the building with lasso whirling. As Buck turned in surprise, Francisco called out: "Ah, Señor, we meet again under different circumstances!"

Buck was reaching for his pistol when the reata coiled around him, fastening his arms to his sides, leaving his fingers clutching air.

Francisco's laugh was ironic. "Perhaps you would care to follow me, Señor?" Without slacking speed he continued up the street, dragging Buck stumbling and cursing after him.

In the dust and confusion they left behind, the supine Indians sprang to their feet and began milling about excitedly, getting in the way, adding to the melee of rearing horses and shouting men, so that it was almost impossible to aim or fire with accuracy. Buck's cousin Britt got off a shot but it went wild and his second cousin Lamar yelled: "Quit it, Britt, you might hit Buck!" Jumping on horses or setting out afoot at a run, they all joined in pursuit.

Francisco reached the crest of the rise in front of the mission as O'Hara and Sedley emerged onto the portico. Glimpsing their presence, he acknowledged it with a flash of smile and turned to face Buck, who'd fallen, been dragged like a log, struggled to his feet, dusty, bruised, bleeding. "I trust you enjoyed your California sleigh ride, Señor?" Francisco inquired politely. "Next time you are tempted to cut sacred trees, or abuse Indians, remember what happened today!"

"Damn you, I'll have your blood!" Buck bawled.

Francisco whirled his horse and sank spurs. Buck was jerked to the ground on his face. "I've brought you a convert, Father!" Francisco called gaily. "If you'll loosen my rope, you can keep him!"

O'Hara ran to the side of the fallen man, Sedley with him. As they knelt together over the writhing Buck, Sedley heard the shot and saw the bright red droplets splatter onto his right hand. The priest slumped against his shoulder and fell forward over the struggling figure in front of them, as blood the deep ruby red of pomegranate seeds poured from the side of his face. Sedley recoiled in horror. Francisco cried out in dismay. There came a similar cry from down the street.

Sedley knelt over O'Hara. Bullets whined above him as he saw that the entire right side of O'Hara's face was a mass of blood. Turning to Francisco he shouted: "Ride! There's nothing to be done here!" And as the sorrel wheeled and disappeared over the crest, the pursuers rushed by Sedley, yelling and firing in fury, sweeping Buck along with them, two or three pausing a moment to stare at O'Hara's body.

A hand fell gently on Sedley's shoulder. It was Santiago Ferrer's. "Am I too late?" Santiago reached for O'Hara's pulse. Sedley shook his head. "I'm afraid you are." O'Hara's blood was pouring into the dust.

But Ferrer's probing fingers had caught the beat of life. "Wait! He lives!"

# Chapter Thirty-nine

Francisco eased his sorrel into a steady lope along the coastal road northward. Truly he would be an outlaw now. The hunts for him and his that had taken place would be as nothing compared to those to come. Yet through rage and remorse—for he had loved O'Hara and almost wished the bullet had found him and not the priest—his exaltation rose; for he'd had his vengeance on Buck. His thoughts turned to Sedley. Like an addict upon a drug he and his mother had become dependent upon Sedley. Now at last he was free from that too. The man even bears my brand, he thought, remembering the incisions in Sedley's arm. But he would be grateful as long as he lived for Sedley's crucial cry of warning as they stared at O'Hara's body. *I spared him. He may have saved me.*

Ahead, fingers of fog were reaching in from the sea with the afternoon breeze. Once hidden in them he would be almost impossible to find. He doubted his pursuers rode animals that could overtake his, for the blood of the horses of the conquistadors ran in Babieca. Turning, he saw them crossing the river below the mission, sunlight flashing on the spray thrown up by their horses' feet. His plan was simple: establish a trail in the wrong direction, circle inland and swing southward to the mountain village—to Ta-ahi and little Letke waiting for him in the house by the meadow, to Nipamu and the elders who would almost certainly approve what he had done. As for the future, a new strategy must be devised. He would be blamed for O'Hara's death. The consequence would be unremitting warfare between him and his people and the valley settlers.

Well before dark he left the fog shrouded road and turned eastward into the hills, following trails he knew from long experience led deep into wild country. By the light of stars and then a late rising moon he made his way at a steady jog. At dawn he stopped in a meadow by a creek, unsaddled, watered his horse, drank himself, then turned Babieca out to graze at the end of his reata, its other end tied to his forearm while he lay prone on the warm earth and dozed.

Remounting after an hour, he rode on, bearing gradually southward toward the mountain wilderness. Lush coastal live oak and feathery green sage gave way to thorny chaparral and daggersharp yucca. The air became warm and dry. Toward late afternoon he entered the vast empty Plain of the Carrizo Grass, a boundary land between the People of the Land and the Sea, his mother's people now his, and their interior neighbors—always regarded in a special way, this place, as belonging to all and none. Ahead he saw the famous Painted Rock rise like a castle—a horeshoe-shaped outcropping into which a man might ride and see emblazoned on its walls such paintings as existed nowhere else; for at this lonely spot the foremost native artists had conspired to perform their supreme work in many colors and designs, celebrating a place dedicated to religious worship and trade and peaceful commingling. Some of this spirit hovered upon the great plain. Yet he remembered there had been warfare here too.

As he neared the rock Francisco saw a solitary horseman approaching. His initial alarm gave way to reassurance. He probably had little to fear from a stranger in these remote surroundings—perhaps a vaquero on a journey between two ranches or a fugitive like himself. As they drew closer he saw that the man wore a high-crowned Mexican-style sombrero, rode a fine black horse with a white blaze on its nose, carried knife and pistol at his belt and a rifle in a saddle scabbard. He was young, wiry, with proud bearing, curly black mustachios, and was smiling jauntily so that Francisco felt drawn to call out in a friendly fashion: "Señor, you travel a lonely trail!"

"Señor, I could say the same for you!" Though this response was merry Francisco felt himself being scrutinized with deadly wariness, and though anxious to be on his way, felt it wiser to feign leisure, unarmed as he was. Therefore he gestured in cordial fashion toward a clump of willows near the Painted Rock. "I had thought to rest at the spring. Perhaps you will join me?''

"Gladly!"

As the sun went down they unsaddled and staked out their horses, made a fire and the young man boiled coffee and offered some to Francisco, who in return offered the seed meal mixed with pine nuts Ta-ahi had prepared and placed in his saddlebags.

The stranger smiled with amusement. ''You dress like a ranchero. Yet you eat Indian food. I have decided you are not what you seem.''

"I might say the same of you who travel such a lonely road so heavily armed.''

Something intimate passed between them while the special quality of the place began to work its magic. "Before you tell me your story," said the young man in quite different tone, "let me tell you mine. I am Joaquín. I have been to a dance in Santa Bárbara.''

"That is a long way to travel for a dance!"

"Not if you like dancing!'' Soon Joaquín was relating how, filled with high hopes, he'd come to California from Mexico with his young bride to search for gold in the Sierra foothills. "One day I returned to camp with the gold I'd found and was showing it to Rosita when four Yankees burst upon us with drawn guns. They bound me to a tree while they raped her before my eyes, then slit her throat so that she died while I watched. Then they took my gold and beat me nearly senseless and spit on me and called me Greaser before releasing me, as they said, to bear witness to what happened to Mexicans who came to American gold mines. . . . I bore witness, all right! I resolved to wreak vengeance upon Gringos wherever I found them. And I may say it is well with you, Señor, that you are not one, for I kill them whenever I can. Thus I have taken justice into my own hands. And you?''

Francisco told the story of his own remarkable transformation and when he finished Joaquín exclaimed: "You must be Francisco Boneu! All the countryside speaks of your recent exploits!''

"Yes," replied Francisco. "I am he. And you must be the famous outlaw Joaquín Murieta!''

Reaching across the fire Joaquín held out his hand. "Let me touch a kindred spirit!''

In the vast plain empty of other human life, the two talked late that night. Murieta was riding to a rendezvous with members of his band in the San Joaquín Valley. Francisco, moved to confide, told of his secret home at the mountain meadow. Murieta said softly: "Never let them take it from you! Shed your heart's blood if you must."

"And you—Governor Bigler has placed a price of a thousand dollars on your head. Armed bands are hunting you to kill you yet you travel alone?"

"It is best, my friend. It is thus we find those few spirits in this world that can mate with ours."

In the morning before they parted Francisco said: "Let us go into the Painted Rock." As the sun rose they stood in its incredible semicircle while the first rays illumined its paintings, and as the murals of its walls became radiant with color, he said: "This is the work of my people. This is their sacred place. Here I pledge allegiance, Joaquín, to you and yours. Why don't we unite in action against the common enemy?"

"Why not?" Murieta's face shone like one of the paintings on the wall. And again their hands met. "While we go our ways for the time being, let us remember our essential brotherhood and plan to meet again."

As they rode off in opposite directions Francisco felt exhilarated and enlarged. His new strategy might include not only Indians but Mexicans and Negroes and Chinese such as he'd seen downtrodden and scorned on the streets of Los Angeles and San Francisco. If they could all unite against the Gringo invader, might they not defeat him or at least bring him to deal justly with all their kind?

Looking up he saw a condor circling overhead. He and the bird were the only living things visible in all the world of that morning. And Francisco remembered how the condor had been the dream helper and guiding spirit of his famous uncle Asuskwa. And from far back down the years the Song of the Condor which Asuskwa had confided came back powerfully:

> "Out of the sun I come,
> With whistling wings I sing,
> Flying where no one knows,
> Flying where no one knows!"

At that moment the condor passed between him and the sun, shading him as if with a signal of recognition, and he could have sworn he heard the wind singing through its pinions.

Years ago he had passed this way in search of his uncle and a true vision of himself. Now he had found that vision. And his meeting with Joaquín had given it even greater dimension.

Again the shadow passed over. He looked up. The condor was gliding southward as if leading him on his way.

Sedley had decided he must break the news to Clara gently. "I stopped at the mission," he continued. "Father O'Hara tells me he talks with you regularly about old times?"

It roused her indignation, never far from the surface. "Yes, a fine young man. But he does not realize that the padres, though often with best of intent, destroyed my people, broke the web of their ancient way of existence, brought diseases among them which proved fatal, farmed them out to work for Spanish settlers or soldiers at a few cents a day plus a basket of corn once a week, the money going to the mission common fund. So I have been educating him on these and other matters. . . . True, I loved Father Rubio and hated those who killed him, though they were of my blood. Yet I have small sympathy for most Spaniards—Californios, as they now style themselves, as if they were the true and original inhabitants of this great land."

"Come, come, Tía Clara, don't you paint a rather dark picture?"

"Probably not dark enough if the truth be known. Not dark enough to disturb the siestas of these fancily dressed gentlemen and ladies in their luxuriously furnished haciendas—riding on their expensively caparisoned horses—who till recently included my son!"

"Francisco is no longer with you?"

"You have not heard?"

"I've heard rumors and have had an experience which I shall tell you. But first, Tía Clara, prepare yourself. I bring bad news."

"I live daily with bad news, as I told you!" She indicated the Jenkins cabins. "I'm in constant fear lest something terrible happen."

"That something is what I must tell you." And he told what had happened in front of the mission. She gazed at him unwaveringly without a word until he finished; then answered softly: "He told me there is no salvation without the shedding of blood. But he did not say it would be his own. He's dead?"

"He lingers between life and death. Santiago and Ruth have him. They'll pull him through if anyone can."

She nodded. "And Francisco will be blamed, of course?"

"Of course."

"But beyond that, what?" She was all business—all sentiment aside. He admired her discipline, her focus.

"More trouble, I'm afraid."

She continued her steady tone. "More blood will be shed. And now—now what is this?"

Horses hoofs and rough voices sounded in the courtyard. She rose and led the way out of the parlor. As Francisco guessed, when his pursuers lost him in the fog, they divided, half led by Buck's cousin Britt continuing the search northward, half led by Buck swinging back to the ranch in hopes of intercepting him there. "Come," said Clara sternly over her shoulder, "the moment is already at hand."

A moment more and she was in front of Buck, demanding: "What do you want here?" Sitting his saddle he towered over her, still dusty, bruised and bloody from his California sleigh ride. "I want your son." His tone was menacing.

"Who are you to want my son?"

"That's none of your business, lady. We'll just take a look around, if you don't mind."

Sedley stepped forward and intervened coolly. "Before you do anything as ill-advised as that, listen to me. My name is Eliot Sedley. I am a San Francisco businessman, an old and dear friend of this lady and of these premises. As some of you will recognize, I was a witness to the shooting of Father O'Hara. I am tempted to bring charges against every one of you for attempted murder. But for the present let me ask on behalf of Señora Boneu that you leave her property without delay." And such was the authority of Sedley's presence that Buck for the moment found nothing to reply, while his band subsided into muttering silence. Still it might have gone otherwise had not an incongruous figure appeared and a high-pitched voice called out: "Hold on, fellers!"

Old Abe was riding a black mule. When he got down, he handed his reins to Buck. Doffing his battered leather hat, he greeted Clara with grave courtesy. "Begging your pardon, Ma'am, but can I join these here proceedings?"

She sensed an ally. "Please do!" And Sedley, recognizing him from her description by the livid furrows in his right cheek, the mark of the grizzly claws which had also torn off the lobe of Abe's right ear, swiftly intervened: "Aren't you Abraham Jenkins?"

"Some of the time, yessir."

"I'm Captain Horatio Sedley's son."

Abe's eyes widened with incredulity. "Not by tarnation—not my old friend's boy?"

"Yes, he often spoke of you. You voyaged with him from here to China, did you not, and then Boston?"

"Sure as heck! An' lived to tell of it! But how be you, lad? What brings you here?"

While Sedley explained his presence, the restless fidgeting of Buck and his fellows grew more pronounced. Noting this, Sedley did not shorten his explanation nor Abe his responses until Buck finally broke out impatiently: "Dad, lay off! We're after that damn halfbreed who lassoed me and caused the priest's death!"

Abe responded mildly: "Why don't you leave this neck of the woods to me, Son? If that fellow's hiding behind his mother's skirts, I'll find him. But he don't sound like the kind of wily customer who'd do a thing like that. Meantime why don't you-all take a look elsewhere," he suggested gently, "and we'll not keep this lady and gentleman a-standing here in the hot sun?"

"Buck, come on," an uneasy voice urged. "He wouldn't likely be here!"

Before backing away, Buck warned defiantly: "He can run. But he can't hide. Not from us. We'll find that bloodthirsty killer wherever he is!" Sullenly releasing the mule's reins to his father, he galloped off with his men. Clara's gratitude to Abe was heartfelt. "Thank you, Mr. Jenkins!"

"Nothing but what's right, Ma'am." And when Sedley added his thanks, Abe continued: "Your dad was kind to me. So was this lady's husband. Good turns deserve others!" With a sweeping bow to Clara that would have done a courtier credit, Abe observed laconically: "I'll haul my freight, now, if you folks don't mind!" and took his departure.

Clara shook her head. "I never would have believed it!"

Later Sedley showed her the documents he'd brought, and without hesitation, as he knew she would, she signed the authorization for Ogles to represent her before the Land Commission and Sedley to be her attorney-in-fact. "I must depend more than ever on you, Eliot. I have nowhere else to turn." And when he assured her she could depend on him, he asked at last: "Has Francisco been here?"

"Not since he left months ago."

"I encountered him yesterday in the pass above Santa Bár-bara." Her eyes widened as he bared his right arm and showed the wound made by Francisco's knife. "He asked me to give you a message."

Clara was a little breathless. "Yes?"

"He says he loves you and that you each fight on in your own way."

"The madcap!" she exclaimed, face bright with pride. "Who can predict what such a fellow will do?" Then with concern: "You've shed your blood for us, Eliot, you fight with us too!"

"Of course."

"One thing worries me terribly, though."

"What is it?"

"How shall I ever find the money to pay the lawyer?"

"Don't worry. I'll take care of that."

"But I can't be beholden to you!"

"You won't be!" he reassured her. "Just promise me one thing, Aunt Clara—you'll beware of unscrupulous lawyers and moneylenders who will try to take advantage of you?"

"I promise."

# Chapter Forty

When Francisco reached the hidden village and rode in among the pines he was welcomed as a hero. He heard the trilling songs of women raised in approval and knew the joy of acceptance as never before. Others of his band had returned before him bringing booty in the form of horses, guns, ammunition and other valuables and news of his public humiliation of Buck and the shooting of O'Hara. Some had been those deceptively supine Indians sitting against the saloon wall as bait for Buck, then melted away and could not be found when the irate pursuers returned to take vengeance.

"You have proven yourself truly one of us!" Winai said and the elders nodded agreement with these words of the young chieftain. "Worthy in every respect!" they echoed as they reached out to touch Francisco and he felt power flow into him from those touches. Even jealous Nipamu granted grudging approval by her presence, while imperiously announcing that all he'd done had been accomplished under the auspices of her wisdom. "Since I named the propitious time!" And she added bitingly: "He spared his friend, which I never would have done!" meaning Sedley.

"A powerful friend who may help us one day!" Francisco retorted, determined not to let this pass, aware of his vulnerability on such a point. "I drew his blood. I left our mark on him."

All this time his eyes were searching for Ta-ahi and little Letke and when he saw Ta-ahi's serene figure, head erect, face radiant, approaching holding her child by the hand, he knew the meaning of love. But then came the most extraordinary development of all. At sight of him, little muted Letke gave an inarticulate cry of recognition and rushed toward him, saying his name. Stepping down from his saddle in amazement, he hugged the poor maimed child and kissed her again and again. "She speaks!" he cried with compassionate wonder.

Ta-ahi was overwhelmed with joy. "Yes, for the first time—because of you!" eyes brimming with tears and rapture as they met his over her daughter's head while all present except Nipamu exclaimed with wonder and admiration at this miracle, clear evidence of Francisco's new power.

The celebration had been delayed until his return. Now fat young puppies were killed, dressed in fragrant herbs, wrapped in broad leaves of the spice bush and roasted over hot coals, while acorn and seed meal and nuts were set forth, and drinks flavored with manzanita and lemonade berry prepared. Afterward those who had been with Francisco on the raid danced in the old way naked by the fire brandishing their weapons, declaring: "We shall always see the light of the Sun!" But Nipamu, deprecating Francisco, gave a fiery exhortation urging that blood, rather than humiliation, be extracted from their enemies. "We must kill, kill, kill!" she urged. But her vehemence was little heeded in the general feeling of exultation.

At last when he and Ta-ahi were alone in their house by the spring that ran from the roots of the giant pine, the Indian summer night engulfing them with its protective darkness as they lay together, she whispered something which made Francisco clasp her with even greater tenderness, full of grave wonder, touching her lips, her eyes, the tips of her breasts with his lips. Then he asked teasingly: "Will it be a boy or a girl?"

"A boy!" Her voice was exultant as she rejoiced in his love and her womanhood. "And he shall lead his people like his father!"

"A girl!" he answered in kind, rejoicing in her love and his manhood, "and she shall be beautiful beyond all understanding, like her mother!"

"But you already have a daughter!" She motioned toward Letke sleeping on her mat nearby.

"All right—a son be it, then!"

In the completeness of their happiness they slept little that night.

\*       \*       \*

In the days that followed Buck and his companions searched the wilderness but never came near the hidden village. "We are protected by Sacred Condor, my dream helper," Francisco declared, and told how, riding homeward from the plain, he had followed the great bird. Nipamu scoffed jealously and urged that Buck and his band be attacked and destroyed. But Francisco retorted: "We must lie low until the hue and cry subsides, then decide what course to pursue. Meanwhile," he urged, "let me, now I have proved myself, scout the state for the possibilities of an organized resistance against the white invaders; for we cannot hope to prevail alone against so many!"

He told of his meeting with Joaquín, of their vision of a united counteraction. And such was his prestige at the moment that approval for his exploratory journey was given. Only one thing worried him.

"I hesitate to leave lest Nipamu harm you in my absence," he told Ta-ahi. Little Letke had regained full power of speech and was chattering like a happy magpie and he hated to leave her too.

"Don't fret," Ta-ahi assured him. "I am not afraid of Nipamu. Only those who fear her are pervious to her spells."

So Francisco rode south to Los Angeles, in his guise of ranchero, and entered the little town of adobes and ramshackle frame buildings along its unpaved main street, Calle Principal, and stopped at the chief hotel, his old favorite, the Bella Union, opposite the present site of city hall. He did not think anyone would recognize him. He'd let his beard grow. They would, anyway, be thinking of him as renegade Indian off in the wilds. Pulling his hat low over his eyes, he stepped to the crowded bar, a gathering place for leading citizens, ordered brandy, and listened for talk of resistance to American rule. But instead he heard one prominent rancher say to another: "I think I'll buy me some Indians on Monday to work in my vineyard."

Francisco pricked up his ears. He'd noted the extensive new vineyards surrounding the town, which in fact was becoming known as the "City of Vineyards" because of these vast new plantings intended to supply the burgeoning wine market of San Francisco, and he'd seen many Indians laboring in them as in Don Domingo Rogers's. Now he boldly asked where he might buy some himself. The rancher looked astonished that anyone should not know.

"Why, sir, go to the mayor's court on Monday morning and make your bid!"

On Monday Francisco went to the court and watched the sheriff "auction off" dozens of unfortunates of Indian blood who'd been arrested for drunkenness and disorderly conduct over the weekend. Their fines of one to three dollars were paid by landowners in return for a week's work. So that is how you buy Indians! he thought with angry disgust.

On Tuesday, disguised in ragged woolen trousers and tunic and old red bandanna around his head, Francisco labored beside them among the grapevines from dawn till dark and again next day and next, till their misery entered his bones too, and fueled his mounting rage; so that on Saturday night he pretended to get drunk with them and to stagger and argue, fight and copulate up and down Calle Principal as they tried to forget the horror of their lives. On Sunday he was thrown in jail with the rest and on Monday auctioned off as the process began anew. Yet when he spoke to these poor benighted creatures of resistance, they looked stupidly at him as though he were mad, their debauched minds and spirits uncomprehending; and he realized that for them the web had been irrevocably broken and there was no hope. In the slave markets of the South they sell a man once, he told himself bitterly, but here the clever Gringos sell the same one every week!

Resuming his guise of ranchero he went to the Calle de Los Negros just off the plaza near his hotel, the Street of the Black Ones, known among Americans as Nigger Alley,* gathering place for thieves, cutthroats and the lowly and oppressed of many lands, male and female, scene of twenty or thirty murders a month, hoping to find here the savage spirit of resistance he sought—but instead he found in its dives and gambling hells only a sordid search for pleasure or gain or self-forgetfulness, and no one interested in revolt.

Discouraged he rode north to investigate conditions there. It seemed that the mighty land, so beautiful, so bountiful, must somewhere hold the justice he sought. As he neared the booming town of Stockton on the broad San Joaquín River, chief terminus of supplies brought by boat for the gold mines of the southern Sierras, he met an Anglo-American teamster driving a wagon loaded high with sacks of grain, who greeted him cheerily: "Gonna see the head, are ye?"

*where the Hollywood Freeway Downtown-Los Angeles Old Plaza off-ramp is now

"The head? What head?"

"Why, the head of the famous bandit, Joaquín Murieta. Ain't you heard?"

When Francisco said with deep dismay that he had not heard, the other told how Murieta and his band had been surprised and several including Joaquín killed. "You can see his head yourself. Right down yonder at the Stockton House! Costs fifty cents but it's worth it." And the man pointed with his whip.

A repulsively obese, bald-headed creature with a droopy yellowish mustache was standing at the doorway of a room just off the lobby taking money from the stream of the morbidly curious. "It's the sight of a century, folks!" he was huckstering in a loud voice. "Yessir, the noggin of the murderin' bandit hisself! Don't miss it!"

Floating in alcohol inside a huge glass bowl, features distorted by hatred, dark hair streaming out around it, the head of Joaquín looked, to raging and anguishing Francisco, like some sort of horrible crustacean. With murderous disgust, he heard the voices around him: "The Governor give a thousand for it yet they say it ain't really him! . . . Well, it's a Greaser, anyway, and good riddance!"

Francisco turned away, more than ever determined to resist and wreak vengeance on a people who perpetrated this and similar outrages, swearing by the memory of their meeting that evening by the Painted Rock that Joaquín's spirit would live in his. But when he met intimately, now and elsewhere, as he traveled on, with Spanish speaking people like Joaquín, he found none willing to act in concert against their American oppressors but only individual resentments; and he began wondering if resistance was, as Joaquín had said, an isolated matter among rare spirits.

Northward he found greater horrors. Two brothers, notorious for mistreating and casually killing Indians, were in their turn killed—and in response nearly two hundred Indian men, women, and children at a nearby village were indiscriminately slaughtered by Army troops. Farther north forty-eight Indians came to a ranger camp to make peace with a band like Buck's and were shot to death while negotiations were in progress. Countless murders went unreported. But others were accurately counted as white hunters scoured the hills to claim bounties for Indian scalps offered by white settlers who put up the money. Francisco grew more and more appalled. What he was witnessing, he realized, was the extermination of an entire race.* And thinking of his personal connection with it through his father and thus his white blood, he felt even greater responsibility and indignation, and a determination to stop it. But how, how? Everywhere his efforts met with apathy or despair. "The whites are too numerous, too powerful!" Or there was resentment at a stranger suggesting what should be done. Or they remembered his failure as a young man to follow his uncle's example. Or as usual since the first Spanish conquest, there was the almost insurmountable difficulty arising from the fact that never had there been a union of Native Californians—but only a collection of fragmented groups each speaking a different language, each thinking of itself as The People, each often warring with its neighbors. Francisco finally returned southward disheartened.

United action was clearly out of the question. Was the best that could be hoped for submission? But this Francisco could not accept. He kept thinking of Murieta's head. And it seemed just possible that in his mountain hideaway a core of resistance could be kept alive like a warm coal which might someday take fire again.

Remembering it was winter solstice time and he might find Tilhini at the Cave of the Condors at this ritual season, he went that way and found the familiar figure executing a painting on the cave's scalloped wall. As before Tilhini waited for him to speak, while continuing his work, and Francisco saw that he was executing a fiery wheel representing the Sun, ruler of all earthly life.

"Father, I am perplexed!"

"Son, what is your trouble?"

They spoke as if they knew intuitively what the other had been doing and thinking in the months since they met, and there was no need to discuss it.

Francisco explained his present dilemma. For several minutes Tilhini continued to paint. Then he turned and said thoughtfully: "My son, I am thinking of the bear."

"The bear?"

"Yes, the bear. When winter comes and conditions are adverse,

---

*at the moment of first sustained contact with European invaders in 1769, Native Californians numbered probably 300,000; by 1853 this number had been reduced to about 60,000 and was rapidly declining

the bear hibernates. In the spring when conditions improve, he emerges. Meanwhile he remains a bear." And Tilhini pointed to the huge bear paw which had been incised in the rock by their ancestors ages ago and over one toe of which he had painted a corner of his fiery wheel, connecting it to the spirit of the bear, the rock, the ancient ritual traditión.

Francisco waited, sensing more to come.

"And I am thinking of the turtle," Tilhini continued, indicating a figure in the rock near his wheel drawn long ago in the simple black line of the old style. "If you go to the river and look for Turtle you do not see him. Why? He is hiding under the mud. He is invisible. But he remains a turtle. And when night comes and conditions are favorable, he emerges."

And Francisco burst out: "But what about man?"

"The bear does what is best for the bear, the turtle for the turtle."

"And man for man?"

Tilhini did not answer. He had turned back to the rock and was completing, with a stroke or two, his fiery rendition of the universe.

Confirmed in his decision, Francisco hurried toward the mountain meadow and as he climbed he saw the giant head and shoulders of the peak circled by winging condors like bits of dark cloud and knew that his guiding spirit was with him.

# Chapter Forty-one

The council meeting which followed was heated and at times bitter; for when Francisco reported what he'd found on his journey and what he had concluded from it, confirmed by his meeting with Tilhini, Nipamu objected contemptuously: "He travels all that way, is gone all that time, to bring us *this?* Has he not heard what's happened while he was absent?" Angry and frustrated after their fruitless search for Francisco, Buck and his rangers came upon a small camp of wandering Indians, killed all the men, brought back women and children for sale as slaves to white householders and even to some ranchers whom they pretended to despise. Don Domingo Rogers bought two girls as house servants for forty dollars each.* Nipamu recited the gist of this atrocity. "And he asks us to submit tamely, to hide? Will our Sky People continue to send us power then? No, they will scorn us as cowards! Are we not entrusted with preservation of The Ancient Way?" Thus she made Francisco appear to be afraid as well as to profane the sacred. "We must kill, kill, kill! And trust to my magic power to bring victory!"

Francisco retorted: "I advocate hibernation, not submission." And he cited the examples of Bear and Turtle. "If we attack now, we may be annihilated. But if we bide our time till conditions are favorable, who knows what may happen? The best method of preserving The Ancient Way, the best course to vengeance, is the

*California law encouraged de facto slavery by permitting indentured servitude, but slavery of Indians and others was practiced without benefit of law

one I suggest,'' he concluded, thinking of the bodies of the massacred and mutilated he had seen, and the hopelessness of the living. ''Let us not be tempted into rash action!'' But Nipamu continued to heap scorn upon him, backed by all the weight of her position as astrologer priestess. Over her painted chest and bare breasts were draped strands of magically enhanced shellbeads and in her right hand she carried her magic quartz-tipped scepter which sparkled in the firelight. ''The blood of this person is mixed.'' Her tongue spit out the dreadful indictment. ''So he hesitates to attack his own people. When I see him cut the heart out of a white man's body or a white woman's body and eat it, I will know who he truly is!''

Francisco cried out in disgust: ''An attack on the valley will bring not only settlers but soldiers upon us. And they will surely find us. I cannot be a party to such foolhardiness!'' This roused murmurs of approval.

''There!'' proclaimed Nipamu undaunted, glancing around at the assembly. ''What did I tell you? If he is truly one of us, will he not accompany us, even lead the way?'' It seemed she was prepared to sacrifice the very existence of the village for the sake of vengeance upon him for threatening her power and for loving Ta-ahi. Then she added the calamitous words: ''Will he dare attack his own mother?'' This brought gasps.

''What has my mother done that we should repay her with violence?'' Francisco retorted indignantly. ''She harms no one, coerces none. All at her Indianada are free to come and go. Those who stay are treated well in return for their labor. She refused to sign the infamous treaties with the white men which would have robbed us of our land. Is she not our champion and friend? Why should we attack her?''

''Because you fear to!'' Nipamu accused. ''And as long as you do, you are our weakness! Your mother is not our friend. She is our ruthless enemy. Did she not kill your famous uncle in whose steps you try to follow? Her own brother? Shot him down as he tried to lead the united uprising you are trying to lead now? Or thought you were? And does she not craftily induce many to follow the white man's way, who might otherwise join our resistance? No, if you are truly what you say, you will not let your mother stand in our way! *Let nothing stand in the way of the Sun!*'' she proclaimed, glaring at him, at them all, in a voice that sent fear and trembling into nearly every heart except Francisco's.

To gainsay her now would be widely regarded as sacrilege, he knew, yet he must.

"Those who wish may join you in self-destruction," he answered resignedly. "I shall never lift my hand against my mother."

"But what about the American settlers?" Winai interposed.

Francisco replied as before that an attack would bring soldiers as well as an army of settlers upon them. "And I have seen what happens then. As some of you know, I am not without experience of warfare. I fought years ago with the Californians against the invading Americans and at one point we defeated them soundly. I know what it is to see bloodshed and to cause it. But now we must lie low—like the bear or turtle—until a favorable time comes."

The others were silent. Winai, who'd conducted many successful raids under Nipamu's guidance but never one so ambitious as she now proposed, inquired dubiously: "Should not as usual our purpose be to damage and disrupt?"

"No," she retorted vehemently, "to kill, to exterminate, as our enemies are exterminating us. Have you not heard what he said?" again pointing scornfully at Francisco. "What he describes as happening all around us? Must we hide like turtles in the mud while such things go on? I shall lead the way myself! But first I shall dance!" she announced serenely. And before their amazed eyes, sensing this to be the moment of decision, she began her magic dance in the firelight, and for many of her watchers it called up mystical religious experience imbedded in their blood over ages of time, as her supple body swayed under the dark trees and her powerful voice, accompanied by the rhythmic shaking of her cocoon rattle, called upon the forces of Sun, of Moon, of Stars, of Earth, to come to the aid of the People of the Land and the Sea. Her effect upon those watching and listening was such that it overcame their skepticism, and their belief in the truth of what Francisco had just said, and substituted unquestioning faith for the moment in this other reality which Nipamu represented.

That night as they lay together Ta-ahi whispered to Francisco: "My beloved, I fear for you if you do not go with the warriors and I fear for you if you do." Again Letke was beside them in the cozy round of their home, sleeping happily, wholly at peace now Francisco was returned. Ta-ahi placed his hand upon her naked belly. "Feel this?" And he felt with joy the quiver of that new life he had helped create. "That is our son. I fear for him too!"

He kissed her tenderly in the white man's way he had taught her. "I also fear for him, for all of us. That is why I spoke as I did. We can, we must, stand firm."

# Chapter Forty-two

Sally was dreaming of a four-poster canopy bed, her very own chest of drawers, a China rug on the floor—all in a magnificent hacienda on a knoll overlooking a great rancho where she and Pacifico were mistress and master.

As she waked she could tell by the feel of the dark air that it was early morning. Her first drowsy thoughts were of Pacifico. They'd met again when she was gathering watercress and he had kissed her. The memory of it made her tingle all over with anticipation and pleasure.

The cabin window above her head glowed with milky moonlight. She remembered the old saying: "If you sleep in moonlight it will make you beautiful." She hoped the moon had been shining on her during her dream. Jake was snoring in his corner. Even in sleep her father was a bother to others. But Gramp who never snored, never did anything to needlessly bother himself or other people, lay soundless. Last evening he'd put a stern end to a terrible argument. Iphy, referring again to the slaughter of the defenseless Indian band, had accused Buck of murder.

"Them Diggers ain't people!" he argued back. "They're no different from hogs. They eat roots and nuts. It ain't murder to kill a hog, is it?"

"An' then to bring back them poor mothers and children and *sell* 'em!"

"I didn't sell 'em. Cousin Britt did!"

"You're traffickin' in human beings, Son, and it don't pay!" Abe pronounced with solemn finality, and that ended it.

Sally was horrified by all of it. She wanted only the moonlight, and Pacifico.

Slipping outside, now, to pee, she hiked up her nightie and squatted in open ground toward the river, where the trees made deep shadows, and imagined Pacifico making love to her on such a night as this in their four-poster bed with silk canopy, silk coverlet, and a feather mattress instead of the corn husks or grass she was used to. She heard an owl hoot. The chorus of frogs along the stream fell suddenly silent. So did the crickets. She felt a sharp pain in her left side and at the same time heard a whirring sound as the arrow passed through her flesh.

Clara was dreaming a recurring nightmare in which she relived yet again that terrible moment when her brother, naked and painted, burst into the room at the head of his raiders and drove his arrow into Antonio—as she raised her pistol and shot him dead. She'd been practicing with that pistol again lately, the antiquated muzzle loader with long barrel that Sedley's father had given her. For years it had lain untouched in the table drawer where she'd replaced it that fatal night. But of late as danger threatened—especially since the massacre of the defenseless innocents by Buck's rangers—she'd begun practicing again. "Defenselessness invites attack!" she warned Isidro and Tilhini, Pacifico too; but Pacifico, preferring other considerations, in particular a certain tender one, thought her mind gone off again into old matters—as she banged away at a newfangled tin can, set on a stump against the hillside. The sound of a shot, whether that fatal one of years ago or of her recent practice, was ringing in her ears as she waked now. Moonlight was flooding the courtyard. The dogs were barking—at the full moon or at something else? An ancient instinct warned her. She rose and, taking the pistol, slipped toward the window and saw the shadowy figures creeping into the courtyard.

Sally screamed and darted for the cabin. Nipamu had ordained that only arrows be used—"which kill silently and give no alarm while my magic quiets the dogs and deepens the sleep of our enemies!" And she declared further: "I shall kill his mother myself and carry her right hand to him as token. You," she instructed Winai, "take our vengeance on the settlers, when the owl hoots!"

As arrows whirred about her Sally stumbled and fell. Jake rushing out to help her met one with his throat and dropped with a gurgling sob of regret as life passed from his unhappy body. She saw this, knew it all, in a glimpse of anguished horror, as she clutched the ground with both hands.

Abe was crouching in the doorway, Rigor Mortis at his shoulder. She saw its long barrel gleam in the moonlight and its muzzle exploded with fire, while Buck and Goodly rushed from the doorway of their cabin opposite, pistols blazing at the shadowy figures. Sally hugged the earth and played dead, praying. Abe's bullet hit Winai in the center of his chest. As he fell his followers hesitated.

Clara had reached the window. With a chill of horror she saw Pacifico step onto the portico a few feet from her in his white night dress and stand staring in disbelief—in foolish, trusting, ineptitude, she thought with anger—while Nipamu raised her shrill cry of: "Kill! Kill! Kill!" Clara knocked out a pane of glass with her pistol barrel. The sound caused Nipamu to turn her head. Clara shot her between the eyes as Isidro and his sons burst from their quarters in the opposite wing, and at the same time she recognized with profound gratitude voices from her Indianada coming to her aid—Tilhini and his people, who had not rallied behind the attackers as Nipamu predicted.

Suddenly feeling very tired, Clara sat down amid the broken glass, her pistol beside her, her breath coming heavily.

After two more were hit by Abe's carefully aimed shots, the rest withdrew, shrieking imprecations. Buck's oaths followed them, supported by Goodly's and Elmer's. Flaming arrows fell upon the roofs of the cabins but the sod would not burn.

"Where's Sally?" Iphy shouted from her doorway.

Abe answered laconically from his: "Looks dead but I reckon she ain't."

Sally raised her head. Her father's body lay directly in front of her. "Help me, Gramp!" she cried.

They dragged Jake inside. "We're too late, Granddaughter," Abe muttered, putting his arm around her shoulder as they knelt over his son. Sally bowed her head. Sobs shook her. "He was comin' to help me, Gramp!"

"He died brave, Granddaughter. Can't beat that!"

The sun was high now. The boys laid Jake's body in the grave. Sally said: "Go ahead, Gramp!" Abe picked up a handful of fresh earth from the pile and let it fall gently upon the body. One big tear stood in each of his old eyes. "Jake, boy, you wanted to come West. You did. You done the best you knew. God rest your soul." Then Abe turned to Sally. "He loved you, Granddaughter. He wanted you to be happy. I reckon you will be, if I have anything to say about it." Sally's throat was choked but her heart was rising on Abe's words. "I found this place long time ago," he continued, his voice prophetic. "I led you people here. Now we've all fought for it. Jake he's died for it. I reckon that gives us a stake."

But as they turned away from the grave, Buck was muttering: "That Greaser renegade will pay for this," meaning Francisco, "if I have to go to hell to find him."

Some from the Indianada who died in the fight were buried in the native graveyard nearby, Tilhini saying the traditional prayers to help their spirits fly through the air to Point Conception, that lonely finger extending far into the sea, the "Western Gate" from where they would continue to the Land of the Dead. Their characteristic belongings—for women, baskets and bowls; for men, arrows and bows—were hung on red-tipped poles above their graves. The bodies of Nipamu and Winai were burned on pyres of brush in the fashion traditional for those dying far from home, and Tilhini prayed for the safe passage of their souls too. Others were given burial in the Christian plot, Father O'Hara officiating for the first time since his wounding, he reassuring his hearers: "The Lord will open to them the gates of Paradise and they will return to that homeland where there is no death but only everlasting joy!"

After the solemn Mass he sat with Clara in his favorite spot on the verandah overlooking the valley for their first full talk since his injury. The bullet had smashed through the side of his face obliterating his right eye. Ruth Ferrer had nursed him back from the brink of death. The black patch where his eye had been made him look like a pirate in a gray robe. "You said there can be no salvation without the shedding of blood, but you did not know it would be your own?" Clara was recalling.

"Yes, like Rubio's, like that of those we've just buried, mine has gone to enrich the soil of this valley. I have joined an honored company."

She shook her head sadly. "Sometimes I think we all live upon visible blood. My own hands drip with it. I have killed to save my husband. I have killed to save my grandson. Must I also kill to save my son? Yet I wish only for peace and happiness. Why are there such contradictions?''

"Some things are beyond knowledge. This may be one."

"And what can happen next except more violence and bloodshed?" she cried on. "The soldiers will come. The settlers will join them. They will go into the back country, and this time they will surely find and kill Francisco and all who remain with him." Wounded captives from among the raiders had made clear Francisco's absence, related how he strongly opposed the attack. "But who will believe them? Who will not see him as the arch villain—instigator if not participant?" She spoke with sorrow of Jake's death. Abe had come to her, bringing news of it, inquiring with grave courtesy what had happened to her and hers. And she had told him, extending sympathy to him and his. "So there is that bright spot amid all this hatred. But the others will surely blame Francisco, and the old man's son will lead in the hunt to kill my son!" she cried out in still greater anguish. "Why is that, Father? How can such things be?"

O'Hara took her hand in his. "Perhaps it will happen otherwise—if the Indian Commissioner comes with the troops. The Bishop writes that he's a man of compassion and vision, a true friend of Indians. His name is Beale. He has established a place called a reservation where they may be free from molestation." And he added to soothe her: "We must always believe in a savior—one who comes bringing new truth. If we learn anything from the Scriptures it is that. He may be difficult to recognize. That is our responsibility—to recognize him. But he is always coming."

"I hope what you say is true. I dare not allow myself to believe it. And I hate to think of my people or any like them cooped up in a reservation. Yet I hate to think of more bloodshed. I am growing old, Father. Who is to carry on after me? I hunger for peace. I hunger for good will. I hunger for someone to come who will carry on after I am gone—a child of my spirit if not of my flesh. Do you understand me?"

"I do."

"A child, a savior, who will bring peace to this land, such as I have dreamed, and not strife."

After the priest had gone, feeling urgent need of the wisdom of the earth, she climbed, not without pain in her legs, not without

shortness of breath, but with joy at the fragrant life of the grow
around her and the eternal verity under her feet, to the shrine
the summit of the high bluff above the house where Tilhini at th
solstice season led the procession and erected the red-tipped pole
with their condor plumes to signify reverence and gratitude fo
the return of the sun at the beginning of each new year.

In the distance she saw the figure of a horseman approachin;
As it drew nearer she recognized Santiago Ferrer. Could he b
the one O'Hara predicted? At least he was her loyal friend. De
scending she greeted him. "You've returned from San Fran
cisco!"

"Yes, and I bring you this!"

He handed her a letter from Sedley, carried down by him o
the schooner with a shipload of goods for his store and a bell fc
O'Hara's empty belfry sent by the Bishop. She opened and reac

> Dear Aunt Clara,
>
> The Land Commission will hear your claim on the twen-
> tieth of next month. You should be here so that you can
> testify before them in person. It would also be advisable to
> bring others who can attest to your long occupancy of the
> ranch, and you should also obtain as many written statements
> as possible to that effect from those not able to come. Your
> attorney reports conditions are not unfavorable to your ap-
> plication.
>
> Regarding the squatters, a Writ of Ejectment would, I con-
> tinue to feel, serve no useful purpose at this time. Up here,
> such documents lead only to violence and bloodshed [Clara
> winced at the words] and the streamer brings intelligence
> from Santa Bárbara of two dead and three desperately
> wounded them including the sheriff. Therefore with your de-
> sire for harmony [if he only knew what harmony we have
> here! she thought] I suggest we wait until the Commission
> rules in your favor. Then the squatters will have no ground
> to stand on.
>
>                                          Devotedly always,
>                                                   Eliot

Handing it to Santiago, she asked: "What do you think, ol
friend?"

After reading the neat bold handwriting Santiago nodded.

"I think he's right about the squatters, and probably right about the Commission. He has great insight and great influence, Clara. Everyone up there's talking about him. Some say he's the best. Some say he's the worst. But I'd say rely on him. You know what he did to help us when he was here. And after all, what other choice have we? If you appear with his backing and your own strong convictions, I feel sure you will prevail."

"But I fear what may happen while I'm away. Squatters may seize my land, even my house."

"I can see they don't, if you will trust me to do so."

"You won't go with me—to testify?"

"Either way, whichever you prefer."

# Chapter Forty-three

Francisco watched them come with grim sympathy: the leaderless remnant of the once proud raiding party straggling back to the mountain village, demoralized, bleeding. "You were right!" they told him. But he did not wish to be justified in this tragic way. "Lead us now!" they begged. He shook his head. But others joined in these entreaties, until they became unanimous. Thus leadership was thrust at him at a dire moment. Still he protested warily: "Nipamu is dead. Winai is dead. You turn to me only for lack of another."

"No, we believe in your wisdom!"

"My mother and son live. But the day may come again when you wish them dead."

"No, no," they insisted. "That day will never come! Lead us!"

"But what of my white blood—have you forgotten that?" he demanded harshly.

"It does not matter. Lead us—lead us as Helek the Hawk, the Far Flyer!"

When these sentiments were confirmed a few days later in communal council, held at the base of the great boulder under the giant pines, Francisco rose and did something sensationally unusual. He asked Ta-ahi to stand up beside him, "for what I say must concern us all equally, whether man or woman." And when she had done so he expressed the thought which had been ripening inside him: "We can no longer exist as a village. This time they must surely find us and they will come in overwhelming numbers. If we are to survive we must change our life drastically.'' And he paused to see if they were listening, and when he saw he had their total attention, continued: ''We must scatter as the quail before a hawk, each to his own, yet remain in touch as quail do. We must exist so secretly that no one else knows we are here, yet be able to assemble when need be. We must abandon all white man's things, guns, ammunition, all need of his clothing, his horses, all things which make us in any way dependent on him, and we must exist as our forefathers did on the things of the earth, which come naturally to our hands—things of wood and stone, and grass, and skin, the bow, the arrow, the spear, the snare, all of which work quietly. We must subsist entirely on herbs and nuts and fish and game. Like the turtle in the mud, we must submerge ourselves in the wilderness and wait—wait for a more favorable time—while never submitting, never abandoning this land which is our birthright!'' And seeing his hearers warming to his words, hoping to hear in them an answer to their fears and uncertainties, Francisco went on: ''Only small fires must be made and with greatest care so that their smoke disperses gradually and does not rise to reveal our presence. There must be no unnecessary sound or movement. Think of the turtle and the bear! We must use stream beds as trails, traveling in water, stepping from stone to stone, never leaving telltale footprints and no scent which dogs may follow. And we must always remember that our guiding spirits, Sacred Condor and Sky Coyote, are in the sky above us every day and every night!''

At that moment a sentry appeared and announced breathlessly: ''A swarm of our enemies is approaching, including soldiers!''

''See, it is already as I said,'' exclaimed Francisco. ''Let those who wish to fight come with me,'' he ordered tersely, ''while all others disperse and hide!'' He quickly led his fighting men to defensive positions on the mountainside facing the approaching forces. As a rule all incoming or outgoing tracks of horses were carefully obliterated by soft strokes of brushes as were all human footprints, while the almost impenetrable chaparral prevented any access except along two routes, which were carefully guarded by sentinels. But in the hasty retreat from the debacle in the valley this precaution had been overlooked, thus accelerating the speed with which Buck and his rangers and Beale and his soldiers had found what they were seeking.

At sight of their numbers Francisco was appalled. Cavalry composed the vanguard, moving warily up the trail and also through nearby openings in the brush, followed by Buck's men and other settlers. But it was the sight of the familiar figure of a small slight civilian riding with the blue-clad troopers that gave Francisco a completely new idea.

He'd first met Edward Fitzgerald Beale at the battle of San Pasqual eight years earlier. Charging horseback with the California lancers against the American invaders, Francisco, at the heart of the melee, had lanced the American commander, General Stephen Watts Kearny, through one buttock, while Beale in return nearly took Francisco's head off with a saber stroke. They'd met again this past summer at the Pacific Club during Francisco's visit to San Francisco. He knew Beale as both adversary and friend and respected him.

Now with sudden inspiration he shouted: "Ned Beale, is that you?"

At the sound of his voice the column halted and some took cover but not Beale or Lieutenant Haislip who commanded the dragoons, or Buck. After a moment the steady voice of Beale replied: "Is that you, Francisco Boneu?"

"It is. Advance any farther, Ned Beale, and men will die. This hillside is a fortress. You may take it at bloody cost. Or you may have it without bloodshed. The choice is yours." And Beale replied with continued steadiness, unperturbed as if they talked together like this every day: "If you will agree to lay down your arms and come with us to the reservation, no one shall be harmed! I speak as Indian Commissioner for the State of California, and your friend!"

It was the kind of bizarre situation in which Francisco delighted by nature, with everything to gain or lose. He motioned to his men to lie quiet. "I am ready to parley."

"Then let us meet under the lone pine that rears midway between us," suggested Beale. "I shall be unarmed."

"So shall I." Leaving bow, arrows and knife on the ground under a manzanita bush, Francisco slipped down the slope, fully aware of the risk he was taking, delighting in it. This seemed a moment for which he was made: utterly out of the ordinary, absolutely quixotic.

Standing by the reddish yellow trunk of the pine, Beale greeted him with a familiar chuckle. "Last time we met in the field, our situations were different, eh?"

"Reversed," Francisco agreed with a corresponding chuckle. "I had you where I wanted you. Hemmed in. Surrounded.* And

*after the battle of San Pasqual

if you and Carson hadn't slipped through our lines, that night, and got to San Diego to bring reinforcements, the whole story of California might be different. I was patrolling your perimeter about one in the morning," he went on, laughing at the recollection, "and heard something move in the brush. Lucky for you I thought it merely an animal."

"Whereas in fact it was Kit and me crawling on our bellies."

"If I'd found you I'd have pinned you to the ground like a couple of bugs!"

"If we hadn't blown your head off first!"

So they reminisced in cordiality, breaking the ice, feeling each other out.

"Well, Ned, this could be another personal triumph for you," Francisco resumed, seeing an opening. "Famous outlaw band surrenders. Comes to reservation of its own accord. Feather in your cap, Ned. Those who led the raid are dead, as you know, or should. Others are wounded and prisoners. I had nothing to do with it. Many like me took no part in it, even urged against it."

"So I've learned. I stopped at the hacienda, talked with your mother. Sedley advised me to." Beale explained he had accompanied the troops in hopes of achieving a peaceful solution. "We're trying to do something new, Francisco, break up this circle of violence and bloodshed, reprisal upon reprisal."

"Will you guarantee no reprisal against anyone?" Francisco was creating the situation as he talked, ad libbing his terms.

"You have my word."

Francisco suddenly changed tactics. "Why should I trust you? A couple of years ago a Commissioner like you made a similar proposal. A treaty was drawn up, signed in good faith by leaders of my mother's people and mine. It was adhered to by them but disregarded by that Great White Father in Washington." Francisco spoke sarcastically, from old sophistication, his other self, brought back for current use. "So that when my people came down from the mountains, they found no new home as promised—while unscrupulous settlers slipped in and usurped the ancestral lands they'd left. Why should we trust you now?"

"Because I am different!" Beale replied with conviction. "My predecessors, Francisco, were well-meaning. But unfortunately they did not have the power to carry out what they'd agreed to. It required approval by Washington, as you say. The Senate rejected their agreements. My actions require no such approval. I have full power."

"My mother, how is she?" Francisco asked, again changing his position, feeling his way.

"Formidable. It was she who killed the witch doctoress."

"That would be like her. You understand, Edward, that she goes her way, while I go mine?"

"I understand. I promise that while under my protection you will be safe. Under my reservation system, Indians live in their own way protected from intrusion by whites. You will have your own houses, your own lands, seed, farm implements, privacy. There will be plenty of room to hunt, fish, and forage—seventy-five thousand acres. Your leaders will consult with me on all important decisions. I foresee a system like this spreading across the nation. By giving Indians a place of their own and removing them from harassment by whites it will, I believe, do much toward reducing hostility between the two races."

Francisco did not quite believe all this but Beale's proposal was compelling and he realized he could not foreclose consideration of it by the village community as a whole. "May there be time for thought?"

"Of course. At the new moon, three weeks from now, I am inviting all tribes, all bands, to a meeting. Why don't you come with yours?"

"I will think about it. The members of my band will think about it."

"Good!" exclaimed Beale. "Here is my hand!"

"And here is mine!"

And Beale returned down the mountainside to his people, while Francisco climbed back to his.

But when Buck Jenkins heard what had been agreed he shouted uncompromisingly at Beale: "My brother is dead! My niece orphaned! And you offer this murderer pardon?" There was brutal logic in Buck's statement which had to be taken into account, Beale realized, not to mention the influence of the rapidly growing Settler's League with politicians at Sacramento and Washington, who in turn, could bring pressure on an Indian Commissioner. Nevertheless he defended his agreement by pointing out that both ringleaders in the attack were dead, others dead or wounded, that Francisco had in fact not participated and, indeed, by independent account, had done his best to prevent hostilities. "Furthermore the agreement I've made could remove the threat of Indian attack from your valley without shedding another drop of blood."

Buck growled, scuffing the ground with his boot as if Francisco were under it: "I doubt it. They don't want peace. The sneakin' murderers want our lives!"

Francisco waited until the last of the troopers and settlers had disappeared down the mountain. Then assembling his band by means of the secret quail call passed from hiding place to hiding place, he reported what had transpired. "The choice is yours. In going to the reservation there is risk. In remaining in the wilderness in the solitary way I have proposed, there is risk. But I believe Beale to be trustworthy." And to present the matter fairly in all its aspects he added: "In either case the resistance can be maintained—on the one hand passively, on the other actively."

Some who were disillusioned and weary of hiding and hardship and bloodshed cried out in favor of the reservation, which appeared the more comfortable and safer course, but others disagreed, saying: "Let us remain free at any cost!" Division ran deep. So at last they split. Some under leadership of the venerable councilor, Halashu, chose to attend the gathering at the time of the new moon and to see if they preferred a reservation way to the hazardous wild one Francisco proposed and was now resolved to follow. Thus what became known as The Great Dispersal began.

Francisco and Ta-ahi, in company with others, packed all necessary belongings in carrying baskets and nets. Slinging his bow and quiver of arrows over his shoulder and taking little Letke by the hand, Francisco led the way into that chaparral which is the California jungle, dense as a giant hedge yet filled with myriad life.

# Chapter Forty-four

You will ride as your grandfathers rode," Clara informed Pacifico and Benito, who listened grudgingly for their minds were on their girls and they had no wish to leave, "and I shall ride as I did that first time I went north with my husband to the capital at Monterey, before any such place as San Francisco existed, so that people may see how one looked in the days when this land was first ours. And I want you, Benito, to ride a dappled gray as your grandfather did, and you, Pacifico, a chestnut sorrel like your grandfather; while I take my golden palomino—which they say is the color favored by queens," she added proudly, knowing she would have to dramatize herself and her cause to be effective.

People who saw them never forgot the formidable old woman riding astride like an ancient Amazon, cape of dark blue velvet thrown over her shoulders, head bare except for that chaplet of white seashells encircling her fiery locks, proclaiming her race unashamedly for all to see; the two youths escorting her accoutered in the style of conquistadors: broad-brimmed black hats, leather jackets, blue woolen shirts, lances held upright in stirrup cups, broadswords sheathed at the left of their saddles, carbines at the other—as if time had rolled away or the vanguard of a fantastic dress parade approached; for a number of friends and neighbors accompanied them, all dressed in their finery with horses caparisoned likewise, to give evidence at the hearing as to Clara's long occupancy of her ranch. Others joined as they went along.

Their route was generally that of today's U.S. Highway 101,

once known as the King's Highway though never much more than a trail winding northward in the footsteps of those first soldiers and padres. Each night they stayed at a great ranch house where Clara had been welcomed in old days. Each day they rode on among the folded green hills in the spring sunshine, beside clear streams. From time to time she pointed out spots where the conquistadors had camped, or hungered, or withstood rain and snow in their quest for the Bay of Monterey and the glory of God, King and Country. "Though it wasn't all for glory," she explained sensibly. "They wished to forestall the avaricious Russians and English from grabbing this land as the Yankees have done. And of course they hoped to find gold, too, as the devilishly fortunate Yankees have!"

Everywhere they were welcomed and celebrated until by the time they reached the charming old Spanish capital of Monterey on the bay of that same name—where once she'd visited with Antonio and danced at the Governor's ball and seen her first tall ships—they formed a triumphal progress like a giant family on its way to a fiesta.

For Clara it was a reliving of old days, in preparation for a momentous new one. With Santiago staying at the ranch seeing that all went well in her absence, she enjoyed herself more than she had thought possible. For the boys who'd never taken such a trip it was revelation of a former mode of life and their status there by reason of inheritance of which they could be proud, and they began to enjoy what had at first seemed tedious, feeling themselves persons of distinction in a new way.

At Monterey correspondents for San Francisco newspapers were so impressed that their stories, forwarded by steamer, prepared her advent into the city in a manner Clara could not have improved had she devised it herself; while she and her entourage lingered a few pleasant days with hospitable friends in the gracious idle manner of time past. INDIAN PRINCESS COMING TO ASSERT HER RIGHTS, the *San Francisco Daily Sentinel* headlined. "Señora Boneu looks like a piece of the Rock of Ages, yet is astonishingly alert in mind and body. She gives as good as she receives in any exchange of questions and answers. Accompanied by her grandson and a large retinue of friends she is visiting this place en route to San Francisco to assert before the Land Commission her claim to one of the most magnificent domains, by all account, that exists in this Golden State."

When Sedley met her at the foot of the long avenue of poplars leading north from San José toward San Francisco, she was already a celebrity. Dismounting he welcomed her "in the manner of a vassal to a feudal lord," as Gillem, who'd been dispatched to cover the story, wrote David at the College of New Jersey, while for readers of *The Sentinel* Gillem found it "ironic that a leading representative of our new civilization should so greet a leader of our old!"

At the present site of Palo Alto, Sedley guiding her, she stopped to rest under the solitary redwood where, as Clara pointed out to Pacifico and Benito and reporters: "My husband camped with his party after discovering the Bay of San Francisco!" And when the newsmen heard this, one exclaimed: "Why, she's a bit of living history!" and another, going one better, cried: "She's Queen Calafía incarnate!" referring to the mythic queen of an island called California somewhere near the Terrestrial Paradise. This seemed a bit far fetched to Gillem's skeptical taste but the phrase caught on and the label stuck so that even he had to use it. And as she entered San Francisco it was as the mythic queen of the fabled Golden Land of California. And all this was exactly as Clara had hoped.

The exuberant young city, partial to eccentric characters and constantly looking for an excuse to have fun, turned out to greet her. At City Hall she was welcomed by Mayor Garrison* as "Queen Calafía come to reclaim her own!" Garrison was careful to treat the occasion humorously. It would not be politic to treat an Indian, even a legendary princess, seriously, since no Indian could vote or give evidence in court and since numerous Indian "wars" and massacres were at that moment in progress in various parts of the state.

Clara responded coolly to the Mayor's fulsome rhetoric. "I on my part welcome you one and all to California on behalf of my people, its original proprietors!" which brought delighted laughter and cheers though she had not smiled or meant it as a joke.

"You were superb, Tía Clara," Sedley said afterward, as he conducted her to the new five-story International Hotel where he'd reserved rooms for her and her party. "What nerve!"

"Nerve? What nerve they have to steal our land! I like the chance to give them a piece of my mind. Just wait till the hearing!"

Meanwhile he showed her the city all bustling and surging with

*Cornelius K. Garrison, mayor in the spring of 1854

that air of reckless energy and optimism, and the harbor crowded with vessels arriving or departing or at anchor until Clara found it unbelievable that so many buildings, so many people, so many ships, so much activity could be crowded together in one place. She felt oppressed, even a little alarmed, but did not say so, as Sedley showed her his new iron foundry and flour mill and the new U.S. Government Mint "where money is manufactured." Though amazed by such an incredible idea, she refused to show it. So that when they passed the offices of the newly established Magnetic Telegraph Company—whose lines ran all the way to Sacramento City, the new state capital—and he explained how the telegraph worked by an invisible current "which can be transformed into words," she replied dryly: "Much like our smoke signals which are carried by the invisible air."

As they passed along, people recognizing her called out good humoredly: "Hi, Queen!" and "Hello, Clara!" and she responded in kind, continuing to enjoy herself as she never thought she would, while Sedley declared she should run for public office. But finally when she'd seen it all including the steam engines knocking down the hills and the wagons filling up the Bay with them or spreading them to make new streets or buildings where carpenters' hammers were ringing and masons plying their trowels, she exclaimed in frank doubt: "Won't a day come where there is too much of everything crowded into this one spot? Will there be room to move? Air to breathe?"

But he laughed at such naïveté. "What you see, my dear, is progress such as never has been known anywhere on earth before, and now let me show you my house."

When Sedley brought Clara up the steps, Mary Louise was prepared. He'd confided to her the chief events of his trip south, including his meeting in the pass with Francisco, and when she saw the scar on his forearm, her eyes grew large, for though she'd heard much about the wild Indians of the West she had never seen one. "You will soon," he told her, chuckling. "But she's not wild. Or bloodthirsty." Even so Mary Louise was astonished by the reality of the old woman.

"You're a handsome thing," Clara declared, eyeing her narrowly. "Do you make him behave and hang up his clothes?"

And Mary replied smiling: "Mr. Sedley gives me very little trouble!" Clara with her intuition guessed how things were between the two, while Mary Louise, deeply admiring, remembered that the Indians of California were like her own people, cruelly oppressed, and felt an instantaneous bond. "You must come and stay with us!"

A few days later when the noise at all hours in the street below her window kept her from sleeping, Clara accepted and moved into the room Fixx had vacated by marrying a wealthy widow and establishing his own household, while the two boys and the rest of the party remained at the hotel. The cost of maintaining all of them there had become an increasing worry to her as her hearing was postponed owing to the Land Commission's backlog of claims. She'd brought gold but not enough, she realized. She hesitated from pride to mention the matter to Sedley but as the days went by and she multiplied them by dollars, she changed her mind. "Don't worry, Aunt Clara. It's my present to you!" he reassured her casually.

"But how can I ever repay you?"

"You won't need to. You are all my guests."

She felt uneasy about accepting such largesse but decided it was in keeping with the laws of hospitality under which she had received him under her roof so often, and his father before him, and decided not to worry but enjoy herself and her status as celebrity. When she appeared at the Metropolitan Theater on Sedley's arm for a performance of *Hamlet,* the *Daily Alta* reported that "The Queen of California, escorted by one of our leading capitalists, was outstanding in the sparkling crowd. With a diadem of seashells over her extraordinary red hair, her gown of muslin was noteworthy for its regal simplicity"—a euphemism for one of Clara's drab Mother Hubbards, for she had no fine clothes and wanted none. Thus the city took her to its heart in a variety of ways.

One evening when Sedley was detained at his office and Lancaster out on an emergency call, Mary said to Clara: "I want you to meet some friends of mine!" and took her a few blocks down Washington Street to the Athenaeum Saloon and Cultural Center where she introduced her to Reuben Stapp and other Negro leaders, including Mifflin Gibbs and his partner in the Boot and Shoe Emporium, Peter Lester. Like Reuben, Gibbs and Lester were from Philadelphia where like him they engaged in anti-slavery activity. "There's direct connection between Philadelphia, the birthplace of American liberty, and the San Francisco liberation movement for Negroes," Gibbs explained. Clara told of the long-standing resistance movement among her people "which my son now leads in his way, and I in mine."

She was grateful for this opportunity to meet with free Negroes. But she understood, hearing them talk of establishing a newspaper and participating in political activities, that their preoccupation with their own struggle preempted them from immediate concern with hers. "Yet we endure common injustice," Gibbs assured her. "The day may come when we can join forces for change." And she agreed. Mary Louise was tempted to tell Clara of her own daughter in exile and hiding at Petrini's farm, where she and Reuben occasionally visited Hattie under cover of darkness, but decided best not to under the circumstances, as Stanhope had posted a reward before leaving and police and others were still searching.

Meantime Pacifico and Benito, "our two young conquistadors" as the press effusively termed them, were being shown more intimate sights and experiences of the town by Ogles; while Gillem piqued the popular interest by revealing Clara to be the mother of "that notorious renegade and outlaw Francisco Boneu, leader of many successful forays against outlying ranches and settlements." And Gillem, after diligent research, was able to point out that no Indian, let alone an Indian woman, had yet successfully petitioned for so much as an acre of land "not to mention a principality such as Rancho Olomosoug."* Thus when the day of the hearing before the Commission approached, public interest had transformed the occasion into an event.

"Documents, lost, all but this one?—how lost?" Commissioner Wilson sounded dubious indeed as he held up the diseño map Sedley had brought Ogles, that day in June, and which Ogles unrolled and studied so carefully and had now submitted as evidence.

"Vicissitudes of time, sir," Ogles explained airily, beaming his cherubic smile at Wilson, while Clara's thoughts returned to that day years ago when she'd warned little Pacifico and little Benito, as she left them playing in her room, never to open the old trunk, holding up a forefinger gravely to impress the two children, and when she returned found them to her horror sitting amid the torn scraps of documents like the snowflakes they'd seen falling a few

*in Mexican times, however, several ranchos had been granted to Indians and to women

days before. And their heads were together looking at the picture-like map, all that remained.

"And why no replacements?" Wilson demanded.

"The troubled nature of those times, sir, followed by the American invasion." Ogles's tone was deferential yet firm. "I have managed to locate a confirmation of the receipt of all original documents by the Mexican Departmental Assembly—to which Governor Figueroa referred them in the usual manner of those days."

"After which they were returned to her?"

"And inadvertently destroyed, all but this map." As Ogles traced the legal status of her long possession, Clara felt exasperated by its inconsequentiality compared to what she knew in her heart. "All inhabitants of New Spain, without distinction of European, African, or Indian origin were citizens of the Spanish monarchy," Ogles declared, "with the right of all employments according to their merits and virtues without distinction of blood and this held true under the Republic of Mexico, successors to that monarchy."

She could hardly believe she was here at last, that it was actually happening, the decisive moment she'd awaited and dreaded so long. The room was so crowded she could hardly breathe and many more were standing outside. Sedley patted her hand encouragingly. "He's good, isn't he?" Yet she felt it all to be superficial, all inconsequential compared to that fundamental truth only she knew, only she could utter.

Now she was hearing herself described by Ogles's opponent, the United States Government's Law Agent, a cadaverous young man, hungry looking, as if he wanted to gobble up her land and regurgitate it for Jenkinses and others to settle—describing her as "one who as an Indian was in a condition of pupilage and perpetual dependence on Government authority under Spanish rule, and de facto so under Mexican." According to this impertinent puppy, her inability to manage her own affairs was "evidenced by the confusion into which they've fallen, raising doubts as to the validity of her claim to the property in question." He would like to see her acres added to the public domain for use by deserving settlers. "And we must also guard against fraud," he warned in sepulchral tone. "There's evidence that unscrupulous and designing persons have organized a conspiracy to forge documents or fallaciously explain their disappearance, and to suborn witnesses to obstruct justice. . . ."

She raged inwardly yet was reassured when those others who had accompanied her began to attest to her long possession of the ranch, and she thought with contempt of scoundrelly old Don Lázaro who'd excused himself "lest I do you more harm than good, since I'm known to favor division of the state." And she thought with scorn of Domingo Rogers who'd similarly excused himself "because of important business in Los Angeles." Whereas in fact both were fearful of espousing her claim lest it injure theirs, and did not want to be associated publicly, she suspected, with an Indian in a matter of such high importance. High importance? Yes it was! And she would make it so! She swelled with pride when Benito read the letter signed by his father attesting to her long and honorable possession known to Santiago and his father before him, Benito improvising boldly on his own initiative: "I personally have known of her occupancy for the past eighteen years!" an exaggeration since his memory could not possibly go back to age one but she forgave him, also for that rifling of her trunk long ago.

And now the moment had come. The Chairman was saying: "Let us hear from the claimant herself."

For inspiration she thought of her mother the chieftainess, always fearless against heavy odds. Strength filled her. She rose and advancing deliberately to the front of the room spoke from her heart, from her bones, from her blood, softly at first but with rising intensity. "Surely you won't say I don't own the land where I was born and have lived all my life? Is it alleged that my claim is imperfect because of certain details? Then let us consider details!" She permitted herself a touch of sarcasm. "Because of my Indian blood I cannot testify in a court of law, so I must testify here against the foulest crime I know, the theft of all of this beautiful land from its rightful owners, my people." She paused, then in the astonished silence continued, eye to eye with the three Commissioners: "It is not I who should plead for your consideration but you for mine. This land," she swept her hand to include the entire state, "was ours before it was yours. We were here when you arrived. I know what happened. I welcomed you with friendship and gifts. I know how you starved and begged for food and would have perished but for our hospitality. In return for which you stole our land and enslaved us and killed us." And again she paused and again there was awed silence. "To whom does my ranch belong? It belongs to me and my people. We should be conducting this hearing. We should be sitting where you are. You should be standing where I am.''

"I object!" The youthful Law Agent was on his feet protesting excitedly. "This is all irrelevant and immaterial and should be stricken from the record!" And Chairman Wilson was admonishing in paternal tone: "Madam, we're not trying to take your land. We are trying to protect your claim to it if you can demonstrate that claim in reasonable rather than emotional fashion!" But Clara had turned her back on them and was returning to her seat.

"The whole affair was a personal triumph such as is rarely seen in this city," the *Daily Alta California* reported. But it was Gillem's story in *The Sentinel* which truly caught the spirit of the occasion. "At Thursday's meeting of the Land Commission we were treated to the spectacle of the accused becoming the accuser when Señora Clara Boneu, claimant to the 48,000 acres of Rancho Olomosoug, suggested she should be sitting in judgment upon the Commission, not they upon her." And Gillem, with certain acidic comments of his own, presented Clara's words in such fashion that they gripped his readers as they had gripped her hearers, with such effect that they were reprinted and read widely throughout the state and republished by Eastern newspapers; so that for the first time some inkling of the true state of affairs with regard to California land began to permeate the national mind.

Despite her eloquence, rejection of her claim might have become inevitable due to the antipathy aroused among the Commission by her scathing outburst, had not Sedley suddenly stepped forward and interjected his long knowledge of her occupancy and possession, and likewise the knowledge of his father before him. "You were superb!" she complimented him afterward. "I'm so proud and grateful. What happens next?"

He replied with usual matter of factness. "They may certify your claim to the United States Attorney as valid, or they may find it invalid. In the former case, he will almost certain appeal to the District Court; in the latter, we will."

"And then?" she asked with rising dismay.

"And then there is the Circuit Court and the Circuit Court of Appeals. And then we may go to the Supreme Court of the United States."

"What?" she cried in horror, "all the way to Washington City? And how long will that take?" And seeing herself bankrupted in the meantime or dead, she added: "What am I to do?"

"Trust me, my dear. I'll be helping in every possible way!"

"But I can't rely so heavily on you, can't be so beholden!"

"It doesn't bother me, my dear, why should it bother you?"

In fact seventeen years were to pass before Clara's claim was adjudged—and this interval was not unusual, as Gillem foresaw in his acerbic indictment "of a process which seems designed to strip its innocent victims of their land or their money, or both."

Mornay wrote David: "A most extraordinary thing has happened. An Indian, in this case a woman, has been accorded some consideration other than as the butt of some cruel joke." While Gillem described the hearing in detail: "The Old Woman was sensational. Even my iron heart was moved!" And David, after reading their letters in his musty dormitory room at the College of New Jersey, replied: "I hope to meet Queen Clara some day, when I return from these tame pursuits and rejoin the fray beside you fellows."

# Chapter Forty-five

During those years while Clara waited for her claim to be settled there was time for a boy to become a man and a man or a woman to grow old, and for David to grow a beard. "I do it like Broderick out of protest against The Chivalry, to show I'm a member of The Shovelry," he wrote Gillem.

"Bully for you!" Gillem replied. "I'm doing likewise. We'll overcome them with hair, if nothing else."

David smiled with amusement at Gillem's new-found commitment but decided to let it go unremarked lest he dampen it. When he wrote he was homesick for the sight of a mountain and weary of the monotonous New Jersey landscape, the endless trees, the sticky heat, the insects, Gillem replied: "You're not homesick, you're lovesick. Get yourself a woman. Forget that precious New Testament. Read those lusty Old Testament authors. They knew what makes the clock tick."

But David answered: "Bewitching lips, breasts, thighs, pubic regions are no longer for me. I leave that field to you. While I make love to Plato and Xenophon and the irregular verbs of Suetonius. And contemplate my eternal soul, and yours." And the prospect of divinity school after college seemed intolerable, yet he was determined to follow the course he had set for himself and keep his promise to Wright.

In 1855 California's Fugitive Slave Law was allowed to expire, thanks to the efforts of Broderick and others in the Legislature,

# Power and Glory 273

and to changing public opinion. Safe from prosecution under it,
free also from prosecution under the National Fugitive Slave Law
which the Federal Commissioner had ruled did not apply in her
case, Hattie left the Petrinis' farm—with a motherly hug from
Angelina and a "Viva Garibaldi!" and a blessing from Tony—
and went to live with Mornay and Martha; and when parents and
teachers and the principal objected to her attending public school
with Martha, Mornay indignantly appealed to the Board of Education, and when it turned him down he withdrew both girls,
taught them himself for a while, then with Mary Louise's approval sent them to the newly opened school for Negro children
conducted by Reverend Alphaeus Hicks at the Church of God in
Christ on Jackson Street between Stockton and Powell.

The San Francisco Underground Railroad continued to aid fleeing Negroes to escape north to Victoria in Canada or concealed
them till immediate danger was past. And Mary Louise continued
to move in both white and black worlds, investing money in real
estate as Sedley advised, loaning it profitably to Negroes, conducting Voodoo ceremonies on the isolated shore of Lake Merced, attending church at Reverend Hicks's, and contributing to
the needs of the Cultural Athenaeum where she had taken Clara.
When word reached her secretly through her black lover John
Samson, who'd overheard it at Sherman's bank where he worked
as porter, that Page, Bacon & Company, the city's leading banking house, was about to fail, she passed it to Sedley. "Nonsense,"
he replied. "Page and Bacon is sound as a rock!" Yet to be on
the safe side, for he'd heard similar rumors, he withdrew his funds
and deposited them with Sherman where Mary and a number of
Negroes banked, finding integrity in Sherman's brusque manner.
The following week when Page, Bacon & Company failed, Sedley
escaped unscathed and his respect for Mary Louise's judgment
increased.

Failure of the city's leading banking house triggered a business
depression which caused unemployment and severe financial loss
throughout the state. It also gave that comeuppance Clara foresaw
to ranchers like her in-law Don Lázaro Estenega whose lavish
style of living as result of easy profits during the cattle boom
offended her sense of propriety.

Falling prices coupled with mounting debts for money borrowed to maintain life in a grand manner or defend titles to their
ranches, spelled ruin for many. Interest rates rose eventually as
high as ten percent per month. By then cattle were selling for as

little as six dollars a head, land for ten cents an acre. And when Don Lázaro, nearly as hardpressed for cash as Clara, was obliged to sell many of his quarter million acres, though not his parrot, Santiago Ferrer acquired one of his ranches, thus becoming the state's first ranchero of Jewish descent.

Ironically to his orthodox mind it was called The Hills of the Purification of the Virgin—22,000 acres for $2,200. "Would you believe it—we've bought a piece of the Holy Mary as if we were good Catholics!" he chuckled to Ruth. It was situated between Don Domingo Rogers's and Clara's and made him their neighbor and equal on new terms.

Domingo escaped disaster thanks to the success of his new vineyard, Clara by her increasing dependence on Sedley, Sedley by those diversified investments to which he was continually adding. He'd just become acquainted with W.W. Hollister, a canny fortitudinous Ohio Yankee who'd driven a herd of sheep across two thousand miles, despite many obstacles including hostile Indians, to California. It was the longest drive of a large herd of animals in U.S. history.

"Why?" he asked Hollister.

"Wool's the coming thing," Hollister replied. "And grass like you've got here will produce it like nowhere else."

"Where's your market?"

"New England, Old England, wherever mills spring up."

"What about uniforms?"

An American civil war would create a demand for wool on a scale undreamed of.

"Ah, yes, uniforms!" muttered Hollister as if he'd not thought of the profits war might bring.

Sedley purchased seed stock from Hollister, and his huge San Joaquín Valley Rancho del Río was soon teeming with hardy Merinos bearing fine silky wool, but when he proposed that Clara do likewise she threw up her hands and snorted: "Become a sheep rancher? Never! What would my beloved Antonio say? He who introduced the first cattle to this land? And what would become of our precious brand? Smothered in all that greasy wool? Besides," turning up her nose still farther, "they smell. And my cattle know it. They never mingle with my sheep!" Yet as she thought of her growing need for money she hesitated, but then she remembered Antonio and their shared dream. "No, I refuse to stink up these beautiful hills. And besides the sheep eat too closely and stamp out the roots with their pointed feet."

"Very well. The decision is yours."

"But what am I to do for money?" she cried in distress, for she was very hardpressed. "As my lawsuit goes on and the courts eat me up?"

"Don't worry," he consoled. "Leonard Ogles and I will care for everything. But if it will make you feel any better you can give me an undivided one-tenth interest in the ranch as security. So far as I'm concerned there's no difficulty. But I want your mind to be at ease."

Pacifico and Sally, Benito and Anita were married by Father O'Hara in a double ceremony such as Mission Santa Lucía had never seen. Clara balked till the last moment at thought of a Gringa daughter-in-law. "Come, now," O'Hara chided her, touching the black patch over his eye, "it is time for healing." As part of that healing process he'd been instructing Sally and Benito in the new faith they were about to embrace. "Haven't we had enough wounds?"

"But mine remain open!"

"Only if you let them. The young people must have their way sometimes. You cannot always have yours!"

Still she remained mortified. "First they seize my land! Then they marry into my house!"

But O'Hara rebuked her gently: "If God wills it, it cannot be so wrong. And hasn't your grandson something to do with it?"

"He's been very stubborn!"

"Like his grandmother? Have I not heard you declare a hundred times that you wanted harmony among the differing elements of this valley? And isn't Sally perhaps the daughter you asked for but never had?"

Meanwhile Don Domingo was fuming to his wife that Benito was a fortune seeker. But Doña Inés reminded him: "Just as you were when you married me! Santiago is putting Benito in charge of that new ranch. He and Anita will have their own home. And much of Santiago's wealth may some day be theirs." This thought quieted Domingo who remembered he was the father of three other daughters approaching marriageable age and their dowries would be considerable, whereas Santiago had asked him for none.

Santiago, meanwhile, was threatening to disinherit Benito at prospect of his oldest becoming a Catholic and marrying a Gentile. "I should read the Prayer of the Dead over him!" But Ruth argued patiently: "We cannot compel him to be like us. He is as he is. Yet he is also ours. Let us believe in him. He has always wanted to be a rancher. And Anita is a sweet good girl. We've known her all her life. Let us welcome her to our hearts."

Still Santiago grumbled: "Our son among the Goyim!"

"Aren't we all among them? We cannot be like islands. We must touch others. You carried O'Hara's bloody body here and I nursed him. We love Clara as a mother. And Domingo and Inés have been our customers and friends for years. Why should we hold aloof in this instance which touches us even more closely?"

"I hoped he would carry on our store!" However Santiago was weakening.

"We have Mark to do that."

Whereupon he capitulated to those reminders of his better self he had learned to expect from his wife.

Buck and the boys registered their objections by not attending the ceremony, though Abe in fringed buckskin and Iphy wearing a red bandanna in lieu of hat or reboso were there, fulfilling O'Hara's prediction that the settlers would one day enter his church in amity.

There was speculation among some of the guests as to the missing Francisco. Outlaw or no, renegade or no, if alive he was still Pacifico's father. More than once Clara had thought of him with pain and sorrow—mixed now with bitter defiant pride, because O'Hara had brought her this morning when she stopped at the Ferrers's to freshen up before the ceremony, the red-shafted war arrow draped with a necklace of breathtakingly beautiful seashells he'd found on the altar of the mission church. They were Francisco's presents to groom and bride—not only bizarre but representing sheer reckless bravado under the circumstances. "Say nothing of the arrow but give me the beads!" Clara muttered. O'Hara did so and Sally was wearing them over her wedding dress, under her veil, despite Pacifico's strong protest to his grandmother. "Why must he interfere even now?" he demanded. But yielded under her insistent: "Because he is your father!"

Abe gave Sally away. As they waited at the back of the crowded church, he whispered: "Be happy, Granddaughter. That's all that matters." She squeezed his weathered hand, that anchor she must now let go. The prospect of becoming heiress to 48,000 acres did not dismay her. She would fight for them as she had for Pacifico. He was waiting for her at the altar, dressed in dark blue velvet, wearing the silver-buckled belt which first became a bond between them that day in the oak grove, and would, she hoped, pass to their oldest son as symbol of their love and proprietorship of the great ranch. And as for Benito, waiting beside Pacifico, his relationship to Anita was much like her own to Pacifico. Anita needed Benito's sturdy self-assertion as Pacifico needed hers. And Anita, standing beside her, squeezing her other hand, would, she sensed, put jealousy away and become her friend because the four of them were the future.

The traditional celebration was held afterwards at Rancho Olomosoug. Music was provided by flute, guitar and violin. The dancing was on the hardpacked earth under the huge canvas that shaded the courtyard. As usual, older couples began with a stately contradance led by Clara and Abe. The younger followed with a rollicky waltz. To cheers and whistles Benito and Anita stamped out a passionate jota in a circle no more than three feet in diameter, now back to back, now face to face, anticipating their joy and desire for each other in this customary prelude. Quadrilles and round dances followed. At intervals during the night cold refreshments of poultry, ham, cakes, coffee, chocolate, champagne—the latter purchased in San Francisco and provided by Santiago—and other wines were served. The crowd dispersed when the morning sun shone above the hillside.

Still no one went to bed. There were cockfights and horse races, and a contest to see who could catch a greased pig. There was gossip and preparations for a picnic upstream by the river and then the picnic itself under the oaks, with bullocks roasted whole on spits over beds of live coals, with attendant music and courtship and feats of horsemanship and coquetry.

At discreet intervals older people retired to rest while the younger kept on, nor were the newlyweds allowed to be alone. Sally and Anita were tireless in their enjoyment of the festivities and the continuous activity they demanded. But by late afternoon of the second day, even hardy Benito felt exhausted and slipped away for a nap in the hay mow, only to find Pacifico already there. "Move over, man, and let me lie beside you! By God, I'm fagged!"

"Same here!"

"Wish you were my wife!"

"Wish you were mine!"

Informed by observing eyes, the brides and their girl friends discovered them and laughingly dragged them back to the party, where Ruth and Santiago performed a traditional Jewish wedding dance, the *broyges tanz*, in which a man and woman portray a quarrel and reconciliation. "As will happen to you!" they admonished the young couples affectionately. Next Abe and Iphy did a solo jig to uproarious laughter and loud applause.

"It was a moment of epiphany," O'Hara recorded in his account of it, "and a new reality was perceived as possible."

As the sun rose the morning of the fourth day of the celebration, the grooms had hopes of being alone with their brides at last. But a farewell breakfast intervened. Then came lingering goodbyes. Not till that night did Sally lie in Pacifico's arms in the four-poster canopy bed which had been her dream and his wedding present. Like those of its time it was short in length, because people slept semi-upright propped by pillows, but they found it long enough for their tender purposes. While in their new home at Rancho de Las Lomas de La Purificación, Anita and Benito likewise found means of reconciling their once differing faiths.

And Clara slept in happiness at thought of the young people. Then woke to think of the red war arrow and the beads. To her as to Sally they were romantic tokens of caring, however bizarre; but to Pacifico they were reminder of a grim old life best forgotten, and they roused again his resentment toward his father.

# Chapter Forty-six

What shall we name our child?'' Francisco asked as they lay together on their grass mat on the soft gray earth of the cave floor. The dawn, the breath of Kakunupmawa the Sun, who rules the world, enveloped them with its silent presence.

"If a boy, Helek, like you."

"Ta-ahi like you, if it's a girl."

Letke was already sitting up playing with the doll he'd carved for her of dark red manzanita wood. His bow and quiver full of red-shafted arrows rested against the cave wall nearby. Beside Ta-ahi lay the Y-shaped cradle carrier of fresh-cut willow she was making for their baby. Beyond the carrier in a recess in the rock stood the large storage basket containing seeds and nuts she and Letke had gathered, and at the cave's entrance was the ring of blackened stones where they made a small fire after dark when its smoke would be all but invisible in the upper air.

He'd chosen as hiding place the secret valley to which Tilhini had led him as a boy. Shaped like a giant amphitheater, it was hidden deep in the chaparral jungle and known as Masitumun-umu-u A-almiyi or The Nesting Place of the Condors. At its head rose a sheer cliff where the great birds nested. Around its sides were ledges of sandstone like giant ribs in which weather and time had scalloped caves. While the valley's floor was one vast grassy meadow where huge evergreen oaks grew thickly and through which a small stream ran.

Old Tilhini had led him here by clambering directly up the stairway-like bed of that tiny stream from the river far below, the only way it could be approached by humans, up through rushing water and tangled undergrowth until they emerged miraculously into this valley wholly hidden from view except from the air above. Tilhini whispered as if reluctant to disturb its secrecy: "This is a place of great power. Few know of its existence. But I want you to know!" And Tilhini added with impassioned eyes so that the impact on Francisco's mind was unforgettable: "Remember!"

Remembering, he had come here to live with his loved ones amongst the great birds—his guardian spirits and those of his ancestors—and when he looked up and saw them soaring overhead he felt inspired and protected by their presence.

From time to time to keep contact with his fellow resisters, he emerged stealthily from the valley, journeyed to some mountaintop or stream junction and gave the haunting two-note rallying call of the mountain quail, which might or might not bring a fellow chaparral dweller to the rendezvous for cherished moments of reunion and talk. Then, faith renewed, hiding their tracks, they would separate and slip away.

But he never went near the site of the mountain village, their former home. Buck and his rangers had found it and burned what was left of it.

Informed of the approaching wedding of his son during a secret visit to Tilhini, stealing into the lowlands invisible as air, Francisco had not been able to resist making that gesture of defiance and of caring represented by the arrow and the beads, though he knew it was a vestige of that white blood, that white pride, he wished to eradicate in himself.

So now he turned his full attention to the day's hunt. He began by rubbing himself all over with bay leaves to remove body odor. Then he donned his decoy headdress of a deer's skin, complete with ears, which covered him to below the waist. He was going to hunt deer. But really he was going in search of his Indian soul, for these days in the hidden valley were changing him profoundly. Though he had lived as an Indian before, it seemed merely a matter of externals compared to this. Because this was entirely his own doing: himself against and with and immersed in the wild nature which surrounded him. And as that surrounding, at times indifferent, at times hostile, at times sympathetic, became his companion daily—as he learned to live with and be part of it— he felt he was learning to find his place. Picking up his bow and arrow he said goodbye to wife and daughter and slipped away under the trees.

Approaching the grazing deer herd, he became like a deer in his movements, taking a few steps, lowering his head, pretending to graze, lifting his head again, thinking of himself as a deer, as he prayed to the Deer Spirit for understanding and forgiveness for what he was about to do.

The deer would give him and his family life. Its heart, its liver, its brains, its flesh would enter into him and his wife and daughter and become part of them. They would make fishhooks of its bones. They would use its antlers as flakers for making arrow and spear points. And they would use its skin to make garments to cover their skins and to create those pliable thongs and strings that tied together so many little things that went to make up their daily lives. In this way the entire deer would become part of their existence and its spirit enter theirs.

Bow held diagonally in front of him with arrow nocked, he was scarcely ten steps from a young buck with high-forked horns. The buck raised its head and looked at him for a moment as at a fellow deer. That look penetrated deep into Francisco where it touched something beautiful yet terrible, tender yet hard. And in that moment he seemed to know himself one with the universe around him, one with the deer, one with its killer.

After gazing at him curiously, the buck lowered its head to feed again. Extending his bow fully, Francisco drove the arrow behind the shoulder into the heart. The buck sank without a sound, with scarcely a quiver. And so truly was it done, so in accordance with principle, that it seemed entirely natural. The other deer did not run off. It was as if they too accepted the naturalness of what had happened.

Francisco moved forward, stood above the buck and saw its eyes were glazing dark blue with death, blue as farthest parts of the sky that covered them both.

Breathing again his prayer to the Deer Spirit, he bent and removed his arrow.

At this the others took alarm and ran off and he seemed to become a man again, rather than a disembodied spirit. Yet he knew that for a moment he had been that spirit, been united with the great invisible which surrounded him and all earthly life.

Slinging the carcass across his back he started for home.

*     *     *

Moving through the ripe grass of the meadow, which was nearly as tall as she, bent forward slightly, gathering its seeds into her shallow basket by flailing the stems with her paddle-shaped beater, little Letke sang softly to honor the Earth Mother:

> "Seed you yield to me,
> Seed you yield to me,
> Be nourishing forever!
> Be nourishing forever!"

From time to time she came upon a golden mariposa lily, springing magically out of the grass. These were the little Cups of the Sun which Kakunupmawa himself had drunk from and then scattered. Thus their oval shaped bulbs were especially nutritious and delicious and she extracted them with her forked digging stick and put them in the carrying basket slung over her back.

Though alone she did not feel lonely. The spirit of the grass, of the flowers, was aware of hers and kept her company and made her part of a greater family much larger than her actual one. Time and love were continuing to heal the wound caused by the brutal killing of her father and brother before her eyes. But it would never be forgotten or forgiven. Now she was longing for the new brother her mother promised was coming to join them soon.

Ta-ahi, sitting at the mouth of the cave, grinding acorns into meal, watched the mother and father condor exchanging responsibility for hatching the egg that would become their child. Gliding on giant wings that whistled like a flute as he passed over the amphitheater of the valley, the male bird landed on the ledge before the nest cave. After a moment the female emerged and as if in complete understanding soared away while her mate entered the cave and settled upon their egg.

And in that bird soaring off into infinity, Ta-ahi saw herself and her dreams for her daughter and unborn child, and for herself and Francisco. It was an effort for her to raise and lower the stone pestle in the mortar because she was so heavy inside, so near her time. Yet all discomfort she'd ever suffered, all bliss she had enjoyed became as nothing compared to the satisfaction she felt now, beloved and fruitful, as she recognized her kinship with all that company which creates life upon earth.

The child within stirred and gripped her. Her first impulse was to call out. But who would come? She had no mother, no aunts, no friends to conduct her to the birthing house and administer the potions and support her with their presence in traditional fashion. Nor was this a matter in which Francisco and Letke should be concerned. No, she must do it entirely alone. And she felt fiercely glad that this was so. The child would be entirely hers. And as the pangs increased she knew he was coming fast.

Taking up the two fire sticks she stepped out a little way from the cave until she was between the sky and the earth. Pressing the anvil stick upon the ground firmly with both feet, she fitted the drill rod deftly into its hollow and twirled the rod quickly between the palms of her hands, feeding the delicate fresh flame that rose from the hollow with dry grass, careful to see that it gave off little telltale smoke. And when she had thus warmed the ground beneath the fire she scooped out a hollow place and lined it with fresh grass blades and, squatting over it, breathed a prayer to Moon, helper of women in time of travail.

As if in answer the pangs seized her harshly. It is a son, she thought. I feel his strong grip. And again the grip came, forcing itself upon her and the world, and she pushed against it, with it, with it to bring it to life, to bring that strong force to life, and within a moment, almost miraculously, almost without pain, her son came into being.

Joy such as she had never know surged through Ta-ahi. After cutting the umbilical cord with the special cane knife she'd brought for the purpose, she cleaned the little body with fresh grass, thrilled by its first cries of protest and assertion, and carried it to the stream that flowed from the nesting place of the condors and bathed her son there as if he were a wild bird. He is one, she thought. He is my Helek, my young hawk!

Then misgiving followed her joy. For a moment an appalling vision of the future came to her, of this little creature she had newly brought into the world hunted and driven from place to place, in pain and sorrow, perhaps finally to torture and death; until she almost despaired. But then instead she saw him bravely in defiance of all circumstance, carrying forward to victory the name and meaning and value of her people into times to come that she could not even imagine. Tears filled her eyes.

Would he be slim like herself, she wondered, or stocky like Francisco? Would he have their dark hair or the red hair of his Grandmother Clara or the yellow of his Grandfather Antonio? And the thought that he would carry white as well as Indian blood both dismayed and elated Ta-ahi. In any case it would mark her son with distinction. "And you were born free!" she murmured softly, holding him tenderly to her. "You were born wild and free!"

She heard Francisco's shout as he came up the meadow carrying the deer on his back.

# Chapter Forty-seven

In 1856 the newly formed Republican Party which Mornay joined and urged David to, nominated a California, John C. Frémont, the famous explorer of the West, as its first Presidential candidate. The Party had been founded in 1854 as an anti-slavery response to the Kansas-Nebraska Act, passed by a Congress dominated by Democrats, permitting slavery on previously free soil; and Frémont had been U.S. Senator from California in 1850–51 and owned a huge ranch and gold mine in the Sierra foothills. Along with Frémont, the Republicans almost but not quite nominated as their first Vice Presidential candidate a relatively obscure Illinois politician named Abraham Lincoln.

With usual perspicacity Sedley contributed generously to Frémont's campaign as to that of his Democratic opponent James Buchanan; while at state level with similar pragmatism he supported both those bitter adversaries, Broderick and Gwin, both Democratic candidates for United States Senator, one a Northerner, one a Southerner. "Why not?" he retorted when Mary Louise objected to this apparent inconsistency. "Both are my friends?"

"But look what they stand for! Broderick for the North and freedom, Gwin for the South and slavery!"

"You oversimplify, my dear," he resumed, running a forefinger possessively along the enchanting curve of her nose, as she lay beside him. "Things are not always as they seem. Take you, for instance. You haven't revealed to me one quarter of yourself."

"You haven't asked."

"Neither have I asked Broderick or Gwin. Nor will I." And he foreclosed her reply with a kiss.

In fact two Senate seats were open and Broderick and Gwin might both win election* since the fledgling Republicans offered no viable candidates. "So how can we lose?" Sedley concluded. It was the first time he'd used the plural pronoun to describe their relationship and she did not miss it.

In the event, both Broderick and Gwin were elected, and thus the struggle for dominance of the state was extended to Washington City and a national stage, where the leading contenders would play increasingly prominent roles. Meanwhile Buchanan's relatively narrow victory over Frémont, 1.8 million popular votes to 1.3 million, encouraged Mornay, who'd worked hard for Frémont, and likewise David, who with other young progressives on the College of New Jersey campus at Princeton, joined in torchlight parades carrying banners bearing the stirring slogan: "Free Speech, Free Soil, Free Men, Frémont!"

"We'll win in 1860," Mornay predicted, "because we are the party of the common people and the free working man. And now we have Broderick to speak for us to the nation. He's a Republican in all but name."

Along with Mary Louise, Mornay was secretly contributing money to buy rifles and ammunition to send settlers in troubled Kansas Territory where fighting had broken out between antislavery and pro-slavery forces. Kansas's leading free-soil militant was named John Brown. National attention was focusing on Brown and Kansas to see which side would prevail in this miniature civil war.

Another who would soon receive nationwide attention was despondent Captain Grant, whom David and Gillem had talked to that gloomy night on the waterfront. Grant had concluded his California experience by taking to drink—up in the fog and rain of Fort Humboldt on the "redwood coast"—at contemplation of his many failures and bleak prospects—resigned from the Army and become an unsuccessful farmer near Saint Louis in Missouri on land belonging to his father-in-law. Working the farm with Grant were slaves owned by him and his wife. They helped him

*by the State Legislature, popular election of U.S. Senators being far in the future

cut firewood and haul it into Saint Louis where he sold it on streetcorners.

Sherman, soon to share national limelight with Grant, had become a major-general in the California militia—under unusual circumstances, which Mornay related to David. "A blackmailing editor named Casey shot and killed a rival journalist here who'd exposed his criminal record. When our corrupt law enforcement officials as usual proved reluctant to act, we outraged citizens took the law into our own hands, formed a new Committee of Vigilance, and hanged Casey. 'Damned if I'll stand for anarchy, however well intentioned,' Sherman stormed when he heard of it, and found himself at the head of a party opposing us. Sherman sympathized with our wish to rid the city of criminals who've inundated us like The Ducks of earlier day," Mornay continued, "but disagreed with our methods. But we finally had the laugh on him. When the Governor offered him a major-generalship in order to cope with the situation, he accepted but then suffered humiliation when the commandant of the federal arsenal here refused to furnish his militia with arms. Sherman's face was as red as his hair. But that's nothing new. We must all thicken our skins and forge on."

David replied that he was bored stiff studying about life "while you and Gillem and Sherman are living it so dramatically." The thought of having to attend theological school before rejoining them seemed more than ever intolerable.

Meanwhile Gillem revealed the seamy side of Broderick who'd discreetly absented himself from the city during the disorder described by Mornay, and as result of Gillem's disclosures *The Sentinel* trumpeted: "Why can masked men appear openly in our streets and garrote honest citizens? Why do heelers, thugs, sluggers and other rowdies control our ballot boxes? Only because of Broderick! Everyone knows that nobody can be elected to office without his consent. 'This job is worth $50,000 a year,' he tells the would-be candidate. 'You get half. I get half. My half goes to maintaining our organization, without which neither you nor I nor the Broderick Wing of the Democratic Party may prosper.' Thus Broderick rules this city though he may be in Sacramento or Washington prating about the rights of free working men and black slaves!"

Broderick replied by purchasing *The Evening Standard* so he could have his own journalistic voice, and Sedley continued to be among his secret backers.

Meanwhile Mornay's Committee of Vigilance, having hanged four known killers and driven many like them out of town, disbanded.

Lucinda Wright continued her temperance and woman's rights work. "The two are inseparable," she wrote David. "A drunken husband is a tyrant. The founding fathers declared all men are created equal. But they didn't mention women. We've got to change that!" And she added proudly: "Nearly half the states have anti-liquor laws. Someday there'll be a national prohibition. Meantime our Order of the Sons of Temperance has fifty branches up and down the state and we have organized flourishing unions of the Daughters of Temperance here and in Sacramento, also we're enlisting youngsters of twelve to seventeen in the Cadets of Temperance. I hope you're not succumbing to temptation?"

And succumbing herself to untypical sentiment she confessed: "I miss Caleb terribly but I stay busy. That is the best antidote for sorrow, that and the thought of the better world we are working for."

Just before Christmas 1856, Hattie and Reuben were married by Reverend Hicks in the Church of God in Christ, thus fulfilling Mary Louise's dream of freedom and security for her child. Her present to the young couple was a small house on Pacific Street which Sedley advised her to purchase at bargain price, knowing its owners were selling under duress. Mornay gave the bride away, Martha served as maid of honor. Colonel Edward Baker, the Petrinis, and others who'd helped defend and rescue Hattie attended. "Viva Garibaldi! We're all fighting for freedom, aren't we?" Petrini declared afterward as he embraced "my foster daughter," as he called Hattie.

As wedding present, Mornay took Reuben as his partner. Mornay & Stapp became the city's first interracial business enterprise.

Yet early the following year, the pendulum of power swung heavily in favor of slavery. As if an omen of things to come, the most violent earthquake in its recorded history struck California on January 9.* Trees swayed as if in a high wind. Rivers changed courses. Escarpments were thrust up along what would later be

*centered near Tejón Pass, estimated to have measured 8 on the Richter Scale

called the San Andreas Fault and the earth groaned as if in actual pain. In Los Angeles homes collapsed. In San Francisco buildings trembled and items fell from shelves. Two-and-a-half-year old Helek, seated with Ta-ahi and Letke on the cave floor, cried out in alarm as he saw his father, standing at the entrance against the rising sun, topple and fall. His mother and sister screamed as the ground shuddered. But Helek bravely scrambled toward his father to help him up. "You move boldly, my little Hawk!" Francisco murmured approvingly. He had reached hands and knees, the child beside him. His tone was grave. He'd glimpsed the face of the cliff at the head of the valley begin to crumble and the condors take to their wings in fright. When it was all over and the little stream in the valley flowing downhill again instead of up, Francisco explained, using the words of his mother's people: "The two great serpents, far larger than any rattlesnake, on which the world rests, are coiling and uncoiling themselves. We must be patient," he added as an unexpected aftershock nearly knocked them down again.

Filling his tubular soapstone pipe with wild tobacco, he blew smoke to the six directions, to placate the Sky Powers and those that move in the darkness below.

During the first week in March, the United States Supreme Court handed down a decision which was to prove earth-shaking in a different way. In the case of Dred Scott, a Negro slave, the justices declared that no Negro, slave or free, was entitled to United States citizenship and that Congress could not prohibit slavery in any territory of the United States.

Most Southerners were elated, Northerners furious, Negroes crushed or enraged. David was outraged. "Such tyranny is intolerable," he wrote Mornay. "What can we do?" And Mornay replied: "We must stand firm. Such cringing of Northern men here as I never expected to see!"

And as if to confirm Southern elation and Northern cringing, on March 7 James Buchanan—who believed the Constitution protected slavery—was inaugurated as President and Jefferson Davis, just retired as the most distinguished Secretary of War in the nation's history, resumed his seat in the U.S. Senate where he could once again be the South's recognized spokesman.

To George Stanhope this seemed an opportune moment to re-visit California and look to his business interests and those political ones, covert and overt, he'd kept alive in the secret manner of those Committees of Correspondence of Revolutionary days* he liked to cite as example. Indefatigably Stanhope had written and worked, worked and written on behalf of "Southern principles, human rights, and defense of the Constitution." Membership in the Southern Rights Clubs he assiduously promoted with the help of his firebrand colleagues Yancey, Rhett and Ruffin was spreading throughout the state as throughout the South. So was membership in the clandestine, even more radical, Knights of the Golden Circle, dedicated to opposing Abolitionism, Catholicism, and "Northern Aggression" by force if necessary.

Stanhope felt convinced that now was the time for the South, backed by the Supreme Court, to expand its territory and influence against the increasingly populous and anti-slavery North by bringing part or all of California into the Southern sphere, along with Cuba and part or all of Mexico. Yet it was pride, as much as anything, that brought him back to the scene of his former embarrassment. With head held high as befitting a member of the nation's ruling class, he would return to San Francisco "and show The Shovelry what's what," he wrote Sedley with renewed confidence, though Sedley advised him it was useless to think of recovering Hattie because of the lapse of the state's Fugitive Slave Law and rising anti-slavery sentiment.

Otherwise what he found confirmed Stanhope's view. Sedley took him on tour of their expanding empire—up the coast to the great sawmills in the redwood forests where huge logs were being floated down streams and lumber at the rate of thousands of feet a day being prepared for loading onto nimble schooners for transport to San Francisco and other Bay communities; eastward to the Sierras where their fabulous Eureka Gold Mine, like every similar mine, was using the mercury extracted from their even more fabulous quicksilver monopoly at New Almadén—where Halleck was manager and Gwin their co-owner; down again to the Central Valley and the newly acquired "overflow lands" which their syndicate was amassing "and which will definitely prove very favorable to the cultivation of good-staple cotton," Stanhope wrote Beau; thence back to San Francisco where he reported more tall buildings than in New Orleans and an equally sophisticated and cosmopolitan atmosphere. And when Stanhope

*organized by towns, counties, regions and very effective in the revolt of the colonies against England

sensed again the vital energy of the place and saw the splendid mansions of South Park on Rincon Hill where Sedley had recently purchased a residential lot, he became convinced that California was not only the future frontier for Southern power but a place to live. He wanted to be in the vanguard of that power. Like Gwin and others he would keep his existing plantations while establishing new ones here, "install King Cotton here," as he wrote Beau. He might even unite his daughter in marriage to Sedley, the rising young giant of the West, though he did not mention this in his letter. "Moreover the state appears a mighty prize in the event of Civil War—with its great wealth and strategic location. As it goes, so may the nation go."

Sedley had taken him as far south as Visalia in the southern San Joaquín, a bastion of Southern influence. There and elsewhere they met openly with Southern sympathizers and secretly with dedicated members of the Knights of the Golden Circle and found many who were prepared to help seize control of the state by force should occasion demand. Stanhope saw himself as possibly leader of a coup that would bring California into the Southern fold, creating a domain where he and his son-in-law might rule.

But when he informed his wife of his decision to establish residence on "the Coast," Sarabelle was horrified. She continued to loathe the very thought of San Francisco "with its fogs, fleas, blowing dust and nigger lovers—and that hateful Hattie and all the misery she caused us!" Vicky felt otherwise. The stream of young gallants surrounding her had begun to seem immature and frivolous compared to a man of power and substance like Sedley who commanded an empire of clipper ships and industries and mines and boundless acres. Venturesomeness stirred in Victoria as in her father. Likewise his hunger for wealth and influence. She'd not forgotten David. He still embodied something innocent, good, which would always attract her, being so opposite to herself. But now she preferred to think of the experienced steely core of Sedley and the gold around it. And when like many women of prominent position, she consulted the famous Voodoo Queen of New Orleans and fortune teller Mary Laveaux, mentor of Mary Louise, as to her love life and was told in Laveaux's magnetic words that good fortune lay toward the setting sun, Vicky made up her mind. Beau obeyed his father as usual. So did his mother.

# Chapter Forty-eight

The rising furor following the Dred Scott decision, coupled with the strife in Kansas Territory between by pro- and anti-slavery forces, made Mary Louise wish to go East, see for herself what was happening, renew acquaintances from Underground days.

With Hattie safely settled in Reuben's care, she could turn her attention increasingly to the welfare of her people, and hearing that John Brown was collecting men and arms for an invasion of the South, she resolved to seek him out and offer support.

"I'm going to visit relatives," she told Sedley. He only half believed her.

"What will I do for a cook?" he protested ruefully. As usual at decisive moments they stared into each other's eyes with absolute candor of a special kind, and each saw there what permanently attracted them. Implicit in it was the understanding that neither could infringe on the other's freedom.

"I know of an excellent China boy," she resumed. "His name is Ah Sing. He will take good care of you while I'm away. He can prepare food in any style. And you can count on his discretion."

Thus Wing's cousin, on whom she and Mornay could rely for accurate reports, came to cook for Sedley and his friends while she was gone.

She carried five hundred dollars in gold coins collected from the Negroes of San Francisco and a twenty-five hundred dollar bank draft of her own to give John Brown if she found him and his plan deserving. Mornay was prepared to send her more when she gave the word.

But Brown, by now a celebrity and recognized champion of the anti-slavery cause, was himself on the move to gain support for his struggle, and it was not for several months that she caught up with him at Chatham in Canada, a refuge for escaped slaves and Abolitionists, not far across the border from Detroit, Michigan.

There at a meeting Mary Louise listened while this spare white-bearded man with glaring eyes and military bearing expounded his views. "Slavery is a most barbarous, unprovoked, and unjustifiable war by one portion of American citizens upon another," Brown declared fervently. And he cited the prophecies of Isaiah and Jeremiah predicting God's vengeance upon Israel unless it mended its sinful ways. "Perhaps only blood will wash away our own sin of slavery!"

Brown believed slaves throughout the South were on the verge of rebellion. "At the appearance of a strong leader they will break their chains and flock toward freedom!" With a handful of trusted companions "black and white, symbolizing the united determination of this nation to redeem itself," he proposed to invade Virginia in the region of the Blue Ridge Mountains and march southward into Tennessee and Alabama. "The mountains will be our bastion while slaves from plantations rally to our standard!" Brown also believed free Negroes from Northern states and Canada would join him once his invasion was launched "and swell it to an irresistible flood! The territory we conquer will become a free state where Negroes will establish their own government, farms, workshops, churches, schools!"

Though moved by Brown's ringing words, Mary Louise believed his vision utterly impracticable. She knew that slaves were much too tightly controlled to flock to freedom. Nor could free Negroes be organized overnight into an effective fighting force. And meanwhile how could Brown's handful of guerrillas hold off United States Army troops and state militias?

"You are misguided," she informed him afterward when they met privately in his boarding house room. "But I admire your courage and determination. Here is a token of my esteem." And she gave him the money from the San Francisco Negroes and her draft for twenty-five hundred. She also told him of her experiences in the Underground Railroad in the East and in California. Brown was so favorably impressed that he proposed she be his secret agent to reconnoiter the slavery states and report back on conditions there. Though dismayed by his impetuosity which trusted her without investigation and seemed confirmation of his faulty judgment, she accepted his proposal and prepared to go South once again in disguise.

Sarabelle, Victoria, and Beau arrived in San Francisco on August 29, 1857, on the *Golden Era*. Sedley met them at the wharf. He found Vicky more desirable in her new maturity, her vivacity more winning, her recklessness less giddy. A progression of courtships had given her a poise which was impressive. A dynastic marriage uniting him with the dominant Southern power had long been among his calculations, increasingly so this past year. It came to the forefront now. It would enhance his growing grip upon the state and give him standing in the nation's highest circles in Washington.

The decisive moment occurred a mere two weeks after Vicky's arrival during which their intimacy ripened as if by mutual consent. Sedley kept a spirited Arab stallion at "Fair View," his newly acquired estate down The Peninsula—that neck of land between bay and ocean running southward from the city towards San José. He foresaw its immense popularity as a place of residence for those wishing to escape city surroundings and had acquired large tracts there. With increasing wealth and power a subtle gentrification was overtaking Sedley. As quaintness became outmoded in the face of rising sophistication, he'd sold his old adobe on Portsmouth Square for a small fortune and moved his offices to the most luxurious suite in Halleck's Montgomery Block; and while keeping his Washington Street house quietly purchased that residential lot in exclusive South Park Circle, foreseeing a day he might build there, for a wife. He'd put away his Dresden-blue swallowtail coat and now dressed in fashionable dark broadcloth. Vicky found him more to her liking in this new role, a modern man of princely power and possessions who lacked only a princess to complete his image. She'd become an accomplished horsewoman and given her Southern escorts many a scare with her daring. "I'd like to ride Barbary," she told him now as he showed her and Stanhope and Beau about the lovely woodland grounds at San Mateo where as yet the only structures were a stable and caretaker's quarters. Vicky could imagine a plantation mansion here, as she stroked the neck of the fiery gray stallion.

"Barbary's too spirited for anything so precious as yourself!"
Sedley replied gallantly.

"No horse is too spirited for me!" she insisted. Still, he firmly
refused. It was their first test of wills.

"Mind your host!" her father counseled paternally.

"Don't let her have her head, Eliot!" Beau joked.

Piqued, with a defiant toss of that head, she waited her opportunity and when Sedley's back was turned sprang to his saddle
and dashed off at a gallop.

Overtaking her after a wild chase, he sternly but admiringly
handed her down. Her face was white but her eyes shone with
triumph.

"See what you get for disobeying me?" he admonished.

She demanded provocatively: "Is that all?"

Seizing her in his arms, he covered her face and throat with
kisses, enflamed by the reckless pleasure of her laughter, yet
coolly sure where he was going.

# Chapter Forty-nine

David stepped down from the stagecoach in front of Gadsby's
Tavern in Alexandria, Virginia, just across the Potomac from
Washington City, and asked the driver the way to Southern The-
ological Seminary.

"Yonder!" The driver pointed along a tree-lined street toward
the south.

"How far?"

" 'Boot three mile!''

Taking up his carpetbag David started walking. He'd chosen
Southern Seminary for several reasons. Caleb Wright's boyhood
home was nearby. To carry out fully his deathbed pledge, he felt
he should study for the ministry near his benefactor's place of
origin. Besides he was curious about the South. Just being there
made him think of the Stanhopes. Above all Victoria. Frivolous,
prejudiced, vain, spoiled though she might be, he could not put
her out of his mind. And beyond that blue ridge of mountains
he'd glimpsed from the stage, far to his right, was his mother's
birthplace. Someday he must fathom that fact and its meaning for
him now, for he too carried Southern blood.

Some of the trees along the street showed their fall colors. The
fine white houses secluded behind them looked palatial. Negroes
seemed to be everywhere. Some looked free. Others clanked by
in chains linking them in a long file. They reminded him with a
shock where he was. He hadn't gone far beyond the outskirts of
town when he was overtaken by an open wagon drawn by two
black mules, driven by a solid middle-aged white man wearing

galluses and tattered straw hat, who hailed him in friendly tone.
"Need a lift?"

David gladly tossed his bag into the rear of the wagon among
empty wooden crates and climbed up beside the hospitable driver.

"Name of Sol Evans!" A work-hardened hand gripped his. Sol
had been to market in Washington that morning with vegetables,
chickens and rabbits and was returning home. "Where you from,
son?" When David told him he spat into the dust at the roadside
and inquired: "Tell me true, is the streets of San Francisco paved
with gold?"

David explained that many of San Francisco's streets weren't
paved at all, then asked: "Know of a family named Wright
hereabouts?"

A peculiar look crossed Evans' face. "If you mean old Ashbel
Wright of Belle Meade Plantation, he's long dead."

"Did he have a son named Caleb?"

Sol spat again before replying. "Yeah, but Caleb went North
years ago," as if when you went North you stepped out of history.

"What happened?" David prompted.

Suspicion crossed Evans' face. "You related to Caleb?"

"Just a friend. I knew him in California—before he died."

"Died rich, I hear."

"Tolerably. I wonder what made him leave home?"

Sol looked as if he were going to spit again but decided not
to. "Since you were his friend and since he's dead I reckon
there's no harm in telling. Old Ashbel his dad was whipping a
slave boy named Wall Eye. Ashbel was mighty hard on his niggers. I don't own Niggers myself. Not many of us does. But we
knows those as does. And Old Ash Wright he was one of the
worst." Sol cracked the reins over his mules. "Git 'long, you!
We ain't got all day!"

"And so?"

"And so Caleb he intervened between the old man and Wall
Eye. And so the old man whipped *him*. Caleb hit back. Ash's
head hit the corner of the stoop as he fell. Never did regain his
conscious mind. Died four days later. Some called it murder.
Some called it a accident. Nobody done nothing aboot it. That's
the story, son. I was just a kid then, younger than you. I never
seen it happen."

But it had the ring of truth. Caleb Wright was a patricide,
fleeing a past he wished to forget, perhaps intending all the rest
of his life to make amends for his mistake, as David himself was

intending. And had Wright knowingly or unknowingly passed the burden of that misdeed along to him in that final deathbed request to devote his life to the church? Wright's presence became almost palpable as they trundled along this dusty road he must have traveled many times through gently rolling countryside where woods and fertile fields intermingled. David felt confirmed in his decision to continue his quest here. "What happened to the plantation?"

"Sister has it. She's a spinster lady. It's just down the road a piece, and over toward the river. But here we are at the Semin'ry!"

They were approaching a cluster of red-brick and white-trim buildings on a low hill in a park-like setting of ancient oaks and elms. David could see young men walking under the trees. Evans insisted on driving him to the front steps of what he called "the dean's house," a comfortable two-story vine-covered structure with a large brass door knob. "I know old Swallow. I sell him my truck. He's a fine man even if he is a 'Piscopalian. You can tell him Baptist Sol Evans said that!"

"I will! Now let me pay you what I owe you."

But Evans indignantly refused. "For giving a chickadiddy preacher a lift? Up North you might. But not down here!"

A gangling, smiling, young Negro dressed like a farm boy in high pantaloons and homespun work shirt opened the door and, with a little bow, ushered David into a comfortably furnished parlor where a thin intellectual looking elderly man, narrow head covered by a few gray hairs, reclined in an ancient chaise longue, a pink coverlet across his legs. The book he'd been reading lay open on the coverlet; others were piled on a table beside him.

Dean Swallow apologized for not rising. "My rheumatism flares with the change of season. Sit down. We've been wondering where you were."

David discovered he'd arrived late due to misreading the schedule but Swallow brushed his embarrassment aside. Over steel rimmed spectacles which remained halfway down his nose, the dean declared benignly. "We have your record from Princeton. Excellent. But do you consider yourself an Easterner or a Californian? You list San Francisco as your home."

"A Californian."

"There's never been a Californian at this seminary. I welcome you on that score alone." Swallow facetiously likened David to an emissary from a foreign land. "I'm told the need for the Word is acute out there!"

David admitted California was godless in some respects "but divinely inspiring in others."

"Inspiring? Divinely?" Swallow was intrigued. David explained that in all his travels he'd never found the spirit of place so manifest. "It's so beautiful!"

"Ah, the genius loci of the Romans! And you equate that spirit with the Holy Spirit?" Swallow demanded, not so facetiously.

David's throat contracted a little under the dean's challenge but he stood firm. "I do."

Swallow raised his glasses with one hand and looked out searchingly under them. "Young man, do you realize that verges on pantheism?"

"But pantheism isn't heresy, is it?" David burst out. "Weren't our founding fathers pantheists? Didn't they find God in Nature?"

After a moment Swallow replaced his glasses and said reassuringly: "We have regular discussion meetings in which students and faculty air their views with complete freedom. Perhaps you'll defend your convictions there?"

David felt relieved. "I'd be happy to, sir."

"Then join me in a glass of barley water?" When David accepted Swallow called out in fatherly tone: "Celia, come meet our newest! And tell Sam to fix barley water!"

A young woman's voice floated back with that lyrical inflection David now regarded as the Southern song: "I'll fix it, Daddy! Sam's gone to work at the dormitory!"

David was half expecting a belle like Victoria and thus was shocked when Celia Swallow appeared with two glasses on a tray. Celia was nearly thirty, six feet tall, homely, buck-toothed, thin, stoop-shouldered, evidently resigned to being an old maid and devoting her life to her ailing father. But such loving warmth emanated from her that everything else about her seemed secondary.

"Just sit still," she insisted in motherly tone when she discovered he'd brought no towel, soap, or bedding.

Disappearing, she returned almost immediately. "Take these until you can acquire your own!" thrusting an armful of necessities upon him.

When David demurred, Swallow advised: "May as well accept. She'll have her way!"

"Daddy's supposed to be a man of God, but he never has

learned to tell the truth. And now why don't *you* tell the truth, Mr. Venable, and explain why you chose Southern Seminary?''

Moved by what seemed her intuitive sense of his purpose, David explained his relationship to Wright and his commitment to the ministry. Father and daughter were looking at him with new eyes when he finished.

''Belle Meade Plantation is not far from here, as Sol Evans told you,'' Swallow observed, ''and Elinor Wright is a friend of ours, a particular friend.''

Celia said simply: ''I think it's wonderful that you've come, in this way!''

# Chapter Fifty

Blindfolded, Buck could see nothing but darkness. The man guiding him by one firm hand on his arm knocked with the other, three times in measured fashion on what must be a closed door. From beyond the door a stern voice asked: "Who cometh?"

"A man!" Buck's guide replied in similar tone. "We found him in the hands of Despotism, bound in chains, well nigh crushed to death beneath the iron heel of the Oppressor! We have brought him hither and would fain clothe him in the white robes of Virtue, and place his feet in the straight and narrow path which leads to Truth and Wisdom!"

The first voice answered: "Brother, the purpose ye declare touching this stranger is most worthy! Let him advance to our altar by regular steps!"

Rigid with awe, Buck heard the door open, felt himself being ushered into a room. As the door closed behind him he sensed himself among a number of people. Then his blindfold was removed and he saw the most dazzling sight he'd ever beheld: a candle-lit altar shrouded by a white cloth and on it a magnificent golden cross, apex and cross-arm enclosed in a circle of similar gold. Standing beside the altar was a tall figure wearing a white-hooded gown with slits for eyes, nose and mouth. Others similarly garbed stood to right and left, and all these ghostly figures were staring straight at him. Buck had never felt so awed or so important.

He was being inducted into the Knights of the Golden Circle by its new Grand Commander for California, Colonel George W.

Stanhope. "Place your hand with mine upon this Bible!" Stanhope ordered.

Buck did so.

"Repeat after me. 'Before God and these witnesses, I vow never to reveal the signs, grips, passwords, tokens or significants of the Knights of the Golden Circle except to a fellow Knight, and then only as hereafter directed and for the lawful purpose of this Order. . . . ' " Buck's tongue was dry but he repeated: "I will never speak evil of a brother of the Knights of the Golden Circle, either before his face or behind his back. I will never dishonor the wife or daughter of a Knight, knowing them to be such, but will shield and protect the character of all my brethren, their wives, daughters and families . . . I will vote against the admission of any confirmed drunkard, professional gambler, rowdy, convict, felon, Abolitionist, Roman Catholic, Negro, Indian, idiot or foreigner to membership in this department of the Knights of the Golden Circle but will get as many good and eligible Southern-born men to join this Degree as I can."

There was more in similar vein. Buck swore to it all including a promise to reveal the names of any Abolitionists known to him and report same "likewise all Northern teachers and Roman Catholic ministers," and in the event of aggression by Abolitionists "I will muster all the force I can and go to the scene of the danger."

Despite Sarabelle's misgivings, the Stanhopes fitted easily into San Francisco society. Their Southern credentials plus intimacy with Sedley gave them immediate standing among the dominant Chivalry, and in the still largely free and easy atmosphere of the city where memories were short and people constantly coming and going, their former embarrassment was either forgotten or became a sympathetic rallying point. And after they were invited to a soiree by elegant Mrs. Hall McAllister, the city's social leader, wife of a prominent attorney of Georgia origin, they felt quite at home. Opera, cotillion, or concert of the Philharmonic Society made the days pass very pleasantly despite the necessity for scratching fleas, "a quite acceptable pastime, my dear, even in the best circles," Sarabelle wrote her mother in New Orleans, "could you believe it? Nevertheless we have chosen a house."

It was Caleb and Lucy Wright's old mansion on the crest of Rincon Hill, Lucy having put it up for sale and moved to simpler quarters over her waterfront rescue mission to be nearer—and more closely identified with—her work. She was asking sixty thousand. "Jew her down to fifty," Sedley advised. "She'll take it." Stanhope did and she did.

Sedley was rushing to completion a three-story town house for Victoria in exclusive South Park Circle nearby. And while Beau fell pleasantly into the relaxed life of club, bar, boxing match, bull and bear fights, plus an occasional excursion with his father to inspect their potential cotton land, Victoria, her engagement announced, became the cynosure of many eyes whenever she appeared in public, her dress and manner described minutely in newspaper columns—her comings, goings, plans, matters of public moment. She relished this. She frankly saw herself as someday Queen of California as the news columns dubbed her.

"We can win this state," her father wrote Yancey, Rhett and Ruffin, "either by ballot or by force of arms should the test come," and in public as in private he actively advanced the Southern Cause, particularly in the inland valleys and southern portion of the state where sympathy for the South was strong. At Sacramento, Marysville, Stockton, Visalia—where he inducted Buck—San Bernardino and Los Angeles he conducted public meetings, and secret sessions with the Knights of the Golden Circle, talked with newspaper editors, ranchers, businessmen, until a strategy came into his mind that was both sweeping and daring: the southern portion of the state and Great Central Valley stretching northward from it might serve as a salient thrust into the heart of California, separating not only north from south but east from west, isolating the Sierras and their gold from the less sympathetic coastal and Bay Area regions, so the state might be divided vertically as well as horizontally and the gold of the Mother Lode would go to the South to help finance the war he felt sure was coming. "Furthermore, the Los Angeles area may serve as base for internal uprising or for Secessionist forces advancing across New Mexico Territory from Texas," he told Sedley.

It was a grand and simple scheme, Sedley agreed, and fully in concert with long-standing Southern strategy. But when Stanhope urged him to join him publicly in fostering it he replied cogently: "I'll be of more use neutral."

Iphy was chopping wood when Buck and Goodly returned from Visalia and Buck's induction into knighthood. Buck had taken his son into his confidence. "I'll induct you when we form a 'castle' back home." Resting her axe on the ground, she surveyed them caustically. "And where have you gentlemen been?"

"None o' your business," grunted Buck, dismounting.

"Come on, you look like the cat that swallowed the canary," she persisted. "Cough up!"

And when he wouldn't cough, Iphy said, to snap him out of it: "Well, I have news for you, then. You've got a new daughter-in-law."

"What the devil do you mean?"

Elmer had taken advantage of Buck's absence to do something he knew his father wouldn't approve: marry his cousin Opal Gatlin, daughter of Homer Gatlin, the fundamentalist preacher and faith healer who with a later surge of settlers from Kansas-Missouri had moved into the lower valley. Buck loathed Homer and vice versa. Homer advocated abstinence from coffee, tea, alcoholic beverages, all fat and greasy foods and even had anti-slavery leanings. And he claimed the power of healing by laying on of hands, though some said it was just an excuse to paw young women. They said Homer was a Mormon at heart. His feud with Buck extended back to youthful days when they both courted Iphy and Buck had won. "Worse luck!" as he often flung at her. Later he raged jealously when—out of spite, as he alleged—she went to hear Homer preach. "That humbug took up with God 'cause he's lost out everywheres else!" Buck ranted, not without some truth, for Homer had failed as a farmer. Yet Homer was his second cousin, bound to him by blood good or bad, as was Homer's boy Britt.

"By God!" he exclaimed now. "And behind my back?"

"Elmer's always had your back and that's near the heart of the matter!" Iphy retorted taking up her axe as if she would strike him with it, then thinking better and setting it down.

True, Elmer, the unfavorite son, had increasingly felt left out of life by his dominant father and brother and had abruptly taken matters into his own hands, as backward people sometimes will, out of a sudden urge to rebel and survive, by secretly marrying. He'd been attracted to Opal, a retiring sort like himself, who looked at him favorably during Saturday night play-parties when taffy was pulled, and during the services her father conducted in his cabin or other people's, or in summer under an open-air brush arbor to keep off the sun—when from time to time Elmer alone among her menfolk kept Iphy company "at church."

Iphy had long ago declared herself on the side of God. "Who else's gonna lend a poor woman a hand? Look at them fee-male Judges he backed—Deborah and them? And look who stuck by Jesus at the end when all his men friends skedaddled! And who was it found out afterward he'd risen from his grave? Nobody with trousers on! Not by a long shot! They was all miles away— looking after their own skins!"

With Opal to help she would not have to care for two households, her own and Abe's. Abe raised no objections. As usual he hesitated to intervene in these balance-of-power adjustments within his clan, which he regarded as natural forces at work. "Only human nature," he replied soothingly when Buck blamed him for not preventing the marriage. "Why not say yes to it?" Opal and Elmer had appeared in the doorway of the cabin beside him. "They'll live with me. I need company now Sally's gone."

But suddenly Buck perceived an enormous objection. "Who tied the knot?"

"Homer."

"Then it ain't legal. He's no certified preacher—just a jake-leg."

"He marries and buries," Iphy thrust in belligerently. "Has for years. You know that."

"Damned if I'd have him marry or bury me!"

"Dammed if he'd want to, if he had any sense!"

Buck made a fist as if to strike her.

"You touch me and I'll lop your block off!" she threatened, raising her axe.

Grumbling, Buck subsided. He wished he could reveal to his fractious spouse what had happened in Visalia. It would take her down a peg—to know that he was now a man of significance, that they both might be people of consequence some day. But this did not seem the moment to break the news.

Goodly made no comment on the situation. Marriage was not for him. Like his father he had great plans. Meanwhile Mexican and Indian whores of San Luis were his consolation among the opposite sex.

Iphy resumed chopping her wood and Opal emerged shyly to help her, wondering if she would ever be able to stand up for herself as Iphy did.

# Chapter Fifty-one

David shared a dormitory room with a stalwart friendly student from Boston named James May. "You'll like it here once you're used to it," May assured him. "Food's not much. But the fellows are all right, though the Southerners pick on us outsiders a bit." This sounded encouraging but David was horrified when he learned that Sam, the young Negro who'd admitted him to Swallow's house and also acted as servant for the students in the dormitory—cleaning their rooms and running their errands—was actually a slave hired out by his master to work at the school.

"I don't like being waited on by a slave."

"I don't either. Some of us are doing something about it," May added, lowering his voice. "Like to join?"

David assured him he would. He'd noticed other blacks about the grounds. May told him they too were slaves hired out by masters who kept most of their meager wages. David boiled. "I think it's disgraceful!"

May grinned. "Wait till you hear them argue how the Bible justifies slavery!" David asked about the file of chained Negroes he'd seen in town. "That's a coffle. Alexandria's a center of the trade, you know! Probably headed for the slave pens where they keep them before shipping them South to the rice-and-cotton states."

The supper bell rang and they hurried down to the dining room in the basement where they found the choice seats taken by Southern boys and were obliged to sit at the far end of the table. The Southerners helped themselves first and plentifully to limited quantities of meat and potatoes and there were good-natured yet condescending jibes about a Yankee's place being below the salt. David controlled his resentment. It's the same thing here, he told himself. They think they're The Chivalry, we The Shovelry. Sam served while Mrs. Wilkins, the housekeeper, prepared food in the adjoining kitchen.

"Any more 'taters, Sam?" a fat-faced boy demanded rudely, brandishing an empty bowl at him.

Sam responded politely: "I'll see what Miz Wilkins say." Slow, awkward, he tried hard.

"Tell her I sent you. Get a move on now. Get the lead out. Hear?" This brought a scatter of chuckles and a "You tell 'em, Porky!"

David boiled over. "Is that any way to talk to a human being?"

Shocked silence. Antagonistic faces turned to him. "And who are you, sir, to tell me what to do?" Porky flared.

"If your own conscience won't, somebody ought to!"

A handsome lanky fellow opposite David drawled authoritatively: "Come off it, you two. This is supposed to be a Christian supper, not a dogfight!" He leaned over and extended his hand. "I'm John Hampden. Welcome to our madhouse."

It was a graceful gesture and David felt grateful to Hampden but it avoided the central issue which was Sam. He decided serious subjects like racial discrimination would be taboo at meals and perhaps elsewhere. Yet at the prayer meeting afterward conducted by the students in a hall next the dining room David was impressed by the zeal of the Southerners. Their earnestness alarmed him for fear he could not match it.

Nevertheless at recitations in the days that followed he found them, with the exception of Hampden and one or two others, woefully unprepared. The faculty too was for the most part unimpressive. Dean Swallow was a shining exception. His course in doctrinal theology which traced the development of Christian thought from Jesus through the New Testament writers to Saint Augustine and Thomas Aquinas down to present time was inspiring. Until his rheumatism improved, Swallow taught from the chaise longue in his parlor, Celia providing barley water and cookies afterward. Her simplicity and dignity continued to charm David and rouse his curiosity. "She's no beauty. But she could make some man very happy," he told May.

"She's a great person," May conceded. "Without her and her father this wouldn't be much of a seminary. There's a lot of backwardness among the trustees and they put him under a lot of pressure.''

When David found the library woefully lacking, Swallow loaned him volumes from his own shelves, including the *Patrologia* or lives of the church fathers, and Milman's *History of the Jews;* and he reread favorites brought with him: Emerson's *Essays,* Whitman's daring new poetry, *Leaves of Grass,* and Richard Henry Dana's *Two Years Before the Mast,* which whetted his nostalgia for his promised land.

Feeling homesick he took walks in the surrounding woods alone or with May and felt restored by the beauty of the colorful autumn foliage. From the window of their room on the seminary's hill they could see the nation's capitol across the river and he wrote Gillem: "I intend to visit the Senate Chamber and watch Broderick and Gwin perform.'' And to Mornay: "I'd like to return as soon as ordained, perhaps to your church of Saint Giles.'' And added a postscript to: "My Dear Gadfly, with a hope that her sting remains undiminished!'' The image of Martha's suddenly mature, tear stained face as they said goodbye on the wharf remained with him vividly.

Gradually he began to feel at home. After another spat Porky Carter gave no further trouble. Sam was treated with more respect, and thus when time came to participate in the forum discussion, which Swallow had challenged him to the day he arrived, he felt ready. The meeting took place in the barren prayer room in the basement furnished only with a desk-table and several rows of wooden benches. It looked to David at first glance more like a courtroom than a forum, with Swallow at the desk as judge. Swallow introduced him as "our new candidate for the West Coast which, I remind you, is our spiritual as well as territorial frontier.'' David sensed hostility among some of his audience at the prospect of being addressed by a youthful newcomer from distant parts, with Northern affiliations too, but stiffened his determination and plunged ahead. "Since God made all things he is in all things as the craftsman his handiwork and the father his children.'' And he cited the Sermon on the Mount where Jesus declares that God clothes even the grass of the field with glory. "Is not then God present in that grass?''

"But isn't that paganism?'' someone objected. "Would you worship a blade of grass? Or a tree?''

David asserted that he would reverence them as part of God's Nature.

Whereupon doddery old Professor Plum became incensed and announced disparagingly: "What you are suggesting, sir, strikes me as animism, or the attribution of a living spirit to inanimate objects. It is one of the oldest heresies on record and was practiced by idolatrous tribes such as the Canaanites of the Old Testament who worshipped a golden calf, and at the present time by our Western Indians. Possibly you yourself have observed it," he added acridly.

But David was roused rather than dismayed and retorted: "Just as no two people are the same, no two places are the same. Just as God made each of us different, each with our own personality, so he made each place on earth different, each with its personality. That is at the heart of my conviction, sir. And as the personality of each person is in the spirit of him or her, so the personality of a place is in the spirit of it; and the divine spirit in both and all."

This eloquence and originality produced silence in which John Hampden came to David's support: "Weren't Jefferson, Franklin and their colleagues believers in 'God in Nature'? Notice their Declaration of Independence speaks of 'Nature's God.' Yet surely we should not consider them heretics!"

"What nonsense!" desiccated Professor Robinson broke in. "Are you suggesting a secondary role for the Holy Trinity as compared to the Founding Fathers?"

Dean Swallow decided to intervene. "Pantheism is as old as human history. Pious Hindus practiced it before the birth of Christ. In Greece the concept of a fundamental unity behind the plurality of natural phenomena was present from very early times. Nearer our own, Spinoza finds God to be the all-pervading principle of the universe who manifests himself in an infinite number of aspects."

"Spinoza was a Jewish heretic!" Plum shouted. "How can we establish any relation between the individual and God if God be merely an amorphous presence everywhere? What then happens to the idea of 'personality' this young man mentions? To the most important personality of all? The personality of God?"

The discussion concluded without agreement. Afterward Swallow told David approvingly: "You stirred up a hornet's nest and that's good." Hampden and May also congratulated him.

He felt he was adding to his standing in the school while clarifying his own views on a subject particularly dear to him, for the golden hills of California and the blue hand of its great Bay, reaching into the continent, were constantly in his thoughts.

\*    \*    \*

Later at a coffee session in Hampden's room, David noticed that his friend liked his coffee sweet, packing his cup full of sugar first. It made David think of Beau Stanhope who had a similar preference. He wondered if he would ever see Beau again—charming, happy-go-lucky Beau, scion of a Slaveocracy he did not really believe in but could not extricate himself from. "Why did I give up the study of law," Hampden was saying, "to devote myself to the ministry? It seemed more meaningful." Still there was much that puzzled David. "Where are all your fire-eating pistol-duelling Secession-minded young dandies we hear so much about?" he asked.

"Down in the cotton states under the magnolias killing each other off. Or at West Point under Lee. Or at Virginia Military Institute under General Jackson.\* I've got friends at V.M.I. They talk about Secession and war. But I don't believe them."

"Lee's no longer superintendent at West Point," May corrected. "He's gone to Texas to fight Indians, so the Alexandria *Gazette* says. And it ought to know. It's published right here in his home town."

"My point still holds," Hampden replied. "All of us aren't preparing for war."

"If war comes, do we go with our states or with the Union?" runty pug-faced Tom Squires queried. Tom was older than any of them. He'd peddled pots and pans before entering the seminary and now lived with a wife and two small children in a ramshackle house in Alexandria where she took in boarders to make ends meet. Tom hadn't attended college and consequently was obliged to work extra hard to keep up in his studies.

"Why, I'd go with South Carolina, of course," Hampden replied without hesitation. David was startled. He'd expected Hampden, not Squires, to be the anti-slavery voice.

Squires shook his head. "North Carolina is my home. But we're a nation first. Not a collection of states. Besides slavery is wrong, John. You know that as well as I do. It's got to stop."

A heated argument followed over the justice or injustice of slavery, Hampden citing Genesis 9, and David realized here it finally was—the supposed Biblical justification for servitude: "'Cursed be Canaan, a servant of servants shall he be . . . God shall enlarge Japheth and Canaan shall be his servant.' How can

\*later nicknamed "Stonewall"

you argue against that?'' Hampden went on to cite the widely accepted belief that Negroes were descended from Ham, one of Noah's sons, while whites were descended from Noah's other sons, Japheth and Shem.

"That's Old Testament mythology!" objected Squires. "It won't wash!"

"All right," cried Hampden. "Let's go to the New Testament. Take Paul's letter to Philemon where he speaks of sending back Philemon's servant who has run away. Right there, in my opinion, is justification for our Fugitive Slave Law! If Paul returned a runaway slave, why shouldn't we?"

David fumed inwardly, having had painful experiences with Fugitive Slave Laws, but said nothing.

"Nonsense," Squires retorted bluntly. "Jesus said: 'Go ye unto the world and preach the gospel to every creature and he that believeth and is baptized shall be saved.' He makes no distinction between slave or free, black or white. Notice he says 'every creature.' And he carries more weight than Paul, doesn't he?"

So the argument raged, Hampden finally demanding: "I suppose you'd let your son marry a nigger?"

And Tom replying: "Why not? Moses married one, didn't he? Just read Numbers 12:1. There's your first interracial marriage on record! Moses and the Ethiopian woman!"

# Chapter Fifty-two

Later that fall, Gillem's banker-father died and with his inheritance he purchased *The Sentinel,* pledging it to "an unbiased presentation of the realities around us" and immediately attacked Sedley for his domination of the California scene. "Like an octopus, he spreads his tentacles stealthily in every direction, until they sense prey in the form of valuable property or persons of influence, which they seize upon relentlessly. The result is a stranglehold on our commercial and political and personal throats. It is in fact, dear reader, only by permission of Mr. Sedley that we citizens of this state may breathe at all."

And he wrote David: "The competition is fierce. Broderick has bought *The Standard* to advance his interests. Sedley subsidizes *The Tribune* to do likewise. But I intend to steer an independent course without fear or favor. And in the top drawer of my desk I keep what is known as a Desk Lawyer in the form of a six-cylinder Colt Repeater, to help moderate the views of those who may come in person to disagree with me."

James May revealed to David that he was teaching Sam how to read.

"Can I help?" David asked.

"You might be expelled. It's against Virginia law."

"I'll take my chances."

When Sam entered the room next day with mop and broom, May locked the door and explained in whispers David's wish.

Sam accepted the situation with a trust which stirred David deeply, while May extracted *McGuffey's Eclectic Reader* from under his mattress, opened it and read slowly and softly, much as Bernardina Ferrer at the ranch instructed her pupils.

Then Sam took the book and softly read aloud after him. Next time David did the teaching. It filled him with a feeling of brotherhood for Sam and pride and strength in himself.

After several sessions Sam confided he wanted to go North. "I'll help you!" David replied impulsively.

But May counseled: "We've got to wait for the right moment. If he gets caught, he'll be sold down to the rice or cotton fields or worse."

David had deliberately postponed visiting Caleb Wright's old home until he felt emotionally ready.

Walking out from school along the river road now, on this crisp Saturday afternoon, to what he expected would be a great estate, he found instead a simple white farmhouse on a knoll overlooking the Potomac.

"So you're the one Lucinda wrote me about!" Wright's spinster sister Elinor greeted him jovially from the front steps. "I wondered when you'd come. But I wasn't going to ask." Elinor's forthright manner resembled her brother's as did her energetic figure.

Driving the buggy herself, she showed David her farm. Instead of that endless expanse of cotton or tobacco he'd pictured there were small fields of snap beans, cucumbers, potatoes, sweet corn, tomatoes, a vineyard, a pen for chickens and turkeys, a modest herd of dairy cattle, all neatly tended. "Caleb used to milk the cows himself," she confided. "I still do sometimes."

Discovering Wright's earthy origins to be like his own delighted David. "He never mentioned his early life to me."

A shadow passed over Elinor's rugged face. "He wanted to forget it, I guess." She hesitated. "You heard about him and his father?"

"I heard they disagreed, and your father died as result."

"It's true. And it changed Caleb's life." She saddened, then brightened. "Otherwise he might be here like me, stuck in this same old rut!"

But it didn't seem like a rut to David nor did she sound as if she truly believed it one. As they drove on, black men and women, working in the fields, greeted them cheerfully but not obsequiously. "I share the produce with them," Elinor explained. "We have a communal arrangement."

"Isn't that unusual?"

"Yes, but practical. People work harder when they work for themselves." It seemed he heard Mornay speaking.

Elinor introduced him to a venerable gray-haired giant. "Caesar, this is Mr. Venable, a friend of my brother's."

Caesar broke into a mighty grin and clasped David's hand in a crushing grip. "Mastah Caleb was a good man. God res' his soul! He set us free!"

As they drove back to the house David asked: "Why did Caleb free his slaves? It must have represented a tremendous financial sacrifice."

"Because his conscience told him to."

"And you say there are many like him?"

"Many, many, many. And we look to Senator Douglas of Illinois, one Northerner who understands our plight, to save us from the terrible threat of Civil War that hangs over this nation because of the radical Abolitionists. Many of our slaves are better off than the wage slaves of your Massachusetts factories. Slavery can take various forms, Mr. Venable! I just wish Mr. Garrison* and other Abolitionist fire-eaters would realize it."

David's eyes were opened further to a South far different from any he'd imagined.

"I loved your brother!" he told Elinor fervently as they sat on the verandah during the warm noontime, overlooking the river, and Juno brought them slices of delicious ham with spoon bread. He explained how very deeply he was indebted to Wright. "He changed my life."

Juno reappeared and said to Elinor: "Gentleman to see you, Ma'am."

"What's his name?"

"Name of Barrows."

"Do we know him?"

Juno shook her head significantly.

"Do we want to?"

Juno rolled her eyes.

"Well," Elinor's tone sharpened, "show him here!"

Barrows, hat in hand, materialized into a stoutish little man

*William Lloyd Garrison, New England anti-slavery leader

about forty with an unctuously pious manner David found objectionable. Elinor introduced David as her nephew from California, a statement which startled him but he soon saw the reason for it.

After some pleasantries, Barrows lowered his voice and leaned forward earnestly. "I come from Philadelphia, Miz Wright." He emphasized the Philadelphia and added, "I'm connected with a certain committee there." And he emphasized the committee. "May I have the privilege of speaking to you alone a few moments?"

"No need for that, Mr. Barrows. My nephew here is privy to all my affairs. Please proceed."

Barrows glanced at David. David nodded sympathetically. Barrows decided to proceed. "Our Committee of Freedom is anxious to help in, ah, shall we say—the transportation of certain passengers along a railway line?" He glanced sharply at Elinor, then at David, and David began to be sure that Barrows was not what he seemed.

Elinor looked blank. "I don't know what you mean, Mr. Barrows. Won't you please speak plainly?"

Barrows smiled coyly. "I think you understand my meaning quite well Ma'am!"

"I do not, sir," snapped Elinor. "Please speak out or I shall have to bid you good-day."

Barrows' face suddenly darkened. "We're ready to help," he whispered somberly. "We know you have several bales of black wool waiting to be shipped."

Elinor stood up angrily. "Mr. Barrows, I have no time for such nonsense. And I don't raise sheep. Good-day, sir."

Barrows got to his feet, his manner transformed to one of ugly menace. "You don't fool me," he sneered, "or anyone else! We know what you're up to!" And turning on his heel he departed.

"Who is he?" David asked.

"A spy. They send them from time to time. Pretending they're Quakers or members of this or that committee. They even sent a black one once. I turned him over to mine. He never showed his face around here again!"

"They're aware of what's going on?" David asked without naming what was going on.

"Yes, but they can't prove it. Lucinda has told me of your work in the San Francisco Underground Railroad," she added softly. "Welcome to our station!"

# Chapter Fifty-three

Out in California, Stanhope, David S. Terry and Sedley were discussing the chances of state division. Sedley shrugged his non-committal shrug and replied enigmatically: "One never knows. Does one?"

"Oh, damn you," burst out Stanhope good humoredly. "Come out from behind the bush and let's see you!"

Sedley smiled even more enigmatically. "I remember a deer who did that. He got shot."

"There you have it," chimed in Terry, "the wisdom of success. Don't expose yourself."

"You might profit from such wisdom," observed Stanhope drolly, "if I've read the newspapers correctly," referring to Terry's numerous involvements of a personal nature with knives and fists.

Terry answered: "I follow a simple rule. I insult no man. I allow no man to insult me unchallenged."

They passed to other matters concerning division of the state. "We'll stir up Estenega in Santa Bárbara. He's been on our side from the beginning. Right, Eliot?"

"With some exceptions," thinking of Clara, "the rancheros tell me they favor division. They feel over-taxed, and under-represented in the Legislature."

"What'll we call the new state?"

"Why, South California, I suppose. Why not? Like North and South Carolina?"

"And it would be a slave state?"

"Of course. Most of its labor is already that—Indian. Darken the color a shade and they're black." This brought chuckles.

"Broderick will fight it!" Stanhope warned.

Terry put in grimly: "Leave Broderick to me."

Gillem asked the bearded, bespectacled Edwin M. Stanton when they met for an interview in the lobby of the International Hotel: "Sir, what is the reason for your visit to San Francisco?"

The pugnacious looking Stanton replied: "I'm special counsel of the United States Attorney General to investigate possibly fraudulent land claims, and thus protect the interest of the people of this country."

"Protect in what way?"

"Protect their right to settle on Government land claimed by unscrupulous and designing persons."

"There's one such you'll never touch!"

Stanton demanded belligerently: "Who's that?"

"Eliot Sedley. He's too big."

"If he's that big he ought to be able to be touched," Stanton retorted with determination.

In the ensuing months, with the same intensity and single-mindedness that would make him Lincoln's outstanding Secretary of War, Stanton pursued his goal; and having examined several hundred cases, he told Gillem: "I've uncovered a vast conspiracy to fabricate fraudulent land claims, involving collusion by Mexican officials, forged documents, counterfeit seals, perjured witnesses."

Gillem relayed this information to his growing readership. Stanton felt sure the evidence would lead to Sedley and Ogles. "But I can't prove it yet," he told Gillem privately when they met over brandies at the Empire Club. "Their method is cleverly within the law. They don't do anything illegal. They skirt the table and pick up choice crumbs that fall." He'd examined Clara's claim. "It's shaky. But I think she'll prevail."

But when Stanton investigated the fabulous New Almadén Quicksilver Mine, with an output worth a million a year, it was a different matter. "Despite testimony by Sedley, Halleck, and others I think he'll show to the eventual satisfaction of the Supreme Court," Gillem wrote David, "that the claim of those worthies and their colleague, the inestimable Gwin, is not only questionable but invalid."

The indefatigable Stanton visited the mine, crawled along its
tunnels burrowing into the mountainside near San José, inspected
the huge sheds where the rich red ore was roasted and its mercury
distilled, marveled at the history of the place running back to pre-
Spanish times when Indians came from as far as Oregon to obtain
its blood-red pigment for body and facial paint; and he obtained
an injunction against further working of the mine until its ownership could be proved.

"Thus putting the first crimp in Mr. Sedley's pocketbook of
which there is any record," Gillem sardonically informed his
readers.

To Stanton he joked: "Won't your injunction work a hardship
on syphilitics, since mercury is the major cure for syphilis?"

Taking him quite seriously, the humorless Stanton responded:
"I don't think so. Though this is our chief source, I believe there's
enough without it to tide us over. Any shortage may encourage
chastity."

Like Grant and Sherman he was an Ohioan. "Western" men
in the parlance of the times, they would serve the first "Western"
president well—in fact enable him to prevail.

Gillem wrote David: "Stanton is a bearcat, works eighteen
hours a day, fears nothing and nobody. I think he'll clip The
Octopus's tentacles if anyone can."

In a postscript Gillem added laconically: "By the way, The
Octopus got engaged the other day to an old friend of yours, Miss
Stanhope. It's to be the event of our social season. But I don't
suppose you care about such things, having your mind on higher
matters."

But David did care. He read Gillem's words with a sharp pang
of regret. Victoria back in California and married there to Sedley
of all people, seemed part of a mighty irony, God's dark humor,
bringing them all toward each other again.

In April, 1858, David went to the nation's capitol to hear Broderick speak.

A few days before, Senator James H. Hammond of South Carolina had defended black slavery by denouncing the industrial
laborers of the North as white slaves and "the mudsills of society," and Broderick was to reply. As David hurried along the
corridor outside the Senate Chamber, hoping to find a seat in the
spectators' gallery, he encountered a familiarly tall commanding

figure, white hair flowing back like a mane from his prominent forehead. It was Gwin. On impulse he reintroduced himself.

Gwin's recollection was immediate and warm. "Of course. Stanhope's young friend. I remember well—that dinner at Eliot Sedley's. Didn't recognize you behind that beard. At the seminary now? Good for you! You shall come to the ball my wife and I are giving!"

The Gwins' fancy dress ball was to be the event of the Washington season. Newspapers were full of it. Costumes were being ordered from as far away as Paris. President Buchanan would attend. Though not the kind of occasion he sought now, David realized it would provide an opportunity to view intimately those who wielded supreme power in the land. And he felt flattered by Gwin's attention. "But I'm afraid I have no costume."

"No difficulty. We members of Congress will be arrayed in what we wear to perform our daily duties. The same can hold for divinity students." He offered to write Dean Swallow asking permission for David to attend. "But now you've come to watch our proceedings? Here, let me give you a pass. The gallery may be crowded!" And Gwin scribbled a note on a scrap of paper and handed it to him. "See you a week from Monday night!"

David, exhilarated, scurried up the stairway and found a seat among a bevy of fashionably dressed ladies just as Broderick rose to speak.

Broderick's appearance hadn't changed since the day they fought at the engine house. His auburn beard was still neatly trimmed, his expression somber, his carriage erect and manly. But now at thirty-eight, one of the youngest ever elected to the Senate and the first to have been born in Washington City,* son of an immigrant stonemason who'd worked in the construction of the new capitol before moving on to New York City, he was quite famous.

Broderick wasn't a polished orator. He spoke bluntly but sincerely, using no notes or gestures. "Many Senators have complained of the Senator from South Carolina for his denunciation of the laborers of the North. Yet I am glad that the Senator has spoken thus. It may have the effect of arousing in working men that spirit which has lain dormant in them for centuries. It may also arouse the two hundred thousand men with pure white skins in South Carolina who are now degraded and despised by thirty-

*some say Broderick was born in Ireland

thousand aristocratic slaveholders.''

His words bit. Nothing like them had been heard before in the Senate Chamber. On the floor there were murmurs. In the balcony the ladies around David twittered. Broderick continued: "It is not long since I served an apprenticeship at one of the most laborious mechanical trades pursued by man,'' meaning that of mason, for as a boy he'd not only watched his father decorate the capitals of the chamber where he spoke but learned the craft himself. "I have not the admiration for the men of the class from which I sprang that might be expected,'' he continued with surprising candor. "They submit too tamely to oppression. They are too prone to neglect their rights and duties as citizens. But that class of society to whose toil I was born, under our form of government will control the destinies of this nation!'' As this prophetic remark sank in, there was audible derision from Southern members. But Broderick bore on: "If I were inclined to forget my connection with them, or to deny that I sprang from them, this chamber would not be the place where I could do either. I have only to look at the beautiful capitals adorning the pilasters that support this roof, to be reminded of my father's talent and to see his handiwork.'' Now there were sympathetic murmurs from the ladies around David and even from the floor below.

David watched Gwin. Arms folded, eyes aimed at Broderick like two pistol muzzles, he seemed imperturbable and formidable, and David remembered Mornay's dictum: "The struggle for California is the struggle between Broderick and Gwin—with Sedley the inevitable winner as he backs both." Here it was before his eyes—a struggle not only for California but for the nation, because Broderick, a Democrat, was proceeding to speak against his own ruling party and its President. His words were scathing as he denounced the "pro-slavery Constitution" which the Buchanan administration and Gwin, its floor leader, were trying to impose on the people of Kansas Territory who had overwhelmingly rejected it. "I hope," he concluded, "those writing the record of these times will ascribe this attempt of the Executive to force this constitution upon an unwilling people to the fading intellect, the petulant passion, and trembling dotage of an old man on the verge of the grave."

Though its rebellious courage thrilled David, the speech was political heresy of the first magnitude. Loud applause from the handful of Republican seats followed it, mingled with cries of scorn from the slavery Democrats. A lone duo of anti-slavery

Democrats had the courage to press forward and congratulate their fellow heretic. With them was Republican Senate Leader William Seward of New York and others of the minority party.

David sensed a momentous truth. Broderick, the native son returned to the scene of his birth, to the building where he'd played as a boy and which his father had helped erect, had spoken for the majority of the American people in a revolt against their leadership.

Out in Springfield, Illinois, Abraham Lincoln read Broderick's speech with shrewd amusement, for it embarrassed Buchanan and the slavery Democrats. Lincoln felt keen admiration for its courageous statement of principle. "Here's a man for us to watch!" he remarked to his wife. But Mary Lincoln was too occupied caring for their young son Tad, ill with chronic croup, to listen while Lincoln read. So he put down *The Register* and thought about the speech he himself would make soon if he received the Republican nomination as Senatorial candidate. It would be a short speech, he thought, and it would hit hard as Broderick's had. Words came to him that seemed just right. "A house divided against itself cannot stand. I believe this Government cannot endure, permanently half slave and half free." Broderick had encouraged him to speak out.

Lauding Broderick's outspokenness, Gillem editorialized: "Nearly since the birth of this Republic, Southern politicians have had almost complete control of it, and are now stung by the consciousness that the Northern States are at last showing a disposition to take a hand in its management. The politicians of the South have always believed that the people of the Free States are too ignorant, cowardly and selfish to have a controlling voice in the halls of our National Legislature. They have so long fostered this idea that they have finally deceived themselves into believing that all that is grovelling and degrading in human nature belongs to the North. Where all that is great and ennobling is indigenous to the South. They truly believe they have all the talent, bravery and generosity, the North all the ignorance, cowardice and selfishness. And it may be that the time will come when only a sound thrashing—or a fearless tongue lashing such as Mr. Broderick has given them—will induce them to correct these views."

*     *     *

As David approached the house it glowed like a radiant jewel in the spring dusk. Gwins' mansion at the corner of Nineteenth and I Streets just off Pennsylvania Avenue reminded him of Victoria Stanhope, Victoria Sedley to be, and the new name made him wince, for he associated her with houses like this one, and he remembered his dreams, held her in his arms, sensed again her reckless desirability. "Fatuous!" he muttered aloud. "What a fool I was!"

But as he joined the fancifully costumed company mounting the steps, his heart rose in that old way, for here once more were wealth, power, beauty, life, and he part of them. Black footmen wearing costumes of high-heeled shoes, white stockings and long purple coats of the preceding century stood at either side of the palatial doorway. As chandeliers dazzled him, a steward dressed like a courtier announced: "David Venable, Esquire!" And suddenly Gwin was introducing him to a strikingly charming woman. "Mary, here's the friend I told you about meeting the other day." Mary Gwin's appearance amazed David. She was dressed as Marie Thérèse, queen of Louis XIV of France, with towering white wig, flashing jewels, stiff moire skirt with lavish train of cherry colored satin. Yet her manner retained the directness of the tavern keeper's daughter she was, while her wit and high spirits helped make her Washington's leading hostess. Holding out a frank hand she greeted David with gusto. "A fellow Golden Stater! Welcome to Washington, Mr. Venable!" And turning to President Buchanan who stood beside her in the receiving line, she inquired playfully: "Mr. President, may I present another Californian?"

David noted the polished gallantry of Buchanan's reply: "If he's as handsome as you are, my dear, I don't see why not!"

Silver haired, portly, affable, "Old Obliquity," as opponents labeled him because of his notorious vacillation, was a gentleman farmer from Pennsylvania who'd served in House and Senate, been ambassador to Russia and negotiated the first Russo-American trade treaty. At sixty-seven the nation's only bachelor president loved parties and was thoroughly under the influence of the Southerners who dominated Washington society and Congress. He wore his usual distinctive white cravat which contrasted to the satiny blackness of his broadcloth suit. But David felt flabbiness in the hand which gripped his, as Buchanan declared with a social smile: "I'd go West too if I were twenty years younger! That's where the future lies!"

"That's where I'm bound, sir!" David answered roundly, moving on into the festive whirl as Buchanan's attention turned to those behind him.

"Like to dance?" The sparkling young woman was dressed as Byron's Maid of Athens—white satin skirt over white pantalettes, tunic and bodice of similar rich blue, boots of blue satin. She was in fact Gwin's seventeen-year-old daughter Lucy and her sharp eye had noted David's somewhat bewildered innocence. He tried to match her tone. "With you I would!"

With a delightful laugh she swept him off onto the polished floor under the glittering gas lights of the chandeliers where they mingled with Little Red Riding Hood and Friar Tuck. Lucy introduced him to handsome young Mrs. Jefferson David as Madame de Staël, speaking fluent French and broken English to play her role, and to glamorous Mrs. Senator Douglas from Illinois resplendent as Aurora. There were also milkmaids, Highland Chiefs, and the Kings of France, England and Prussia. David was fascinated, at the same time appalled. Thinking of Hattie, Mornay, and Mary Louise, and Sam and Reuben, he felt these people were frolicking on a volcano. Champagne flowed freely as if to quench that volcano. It was served by black slaves from the Gwins' Mississippi plantation.

He looked everywhere for Broderick. All Washington seemed to be here. But not its most controversial Senator.

Learning he was from San Francisco, Lucy was saying: "Why, we have a house there too!" as she led him vivaciously through the intricacies of the newly popular galop, as well as the familiar schottische and waltz, so that he penetrated to the heart of the gaiety. And when David commented what a wild party it was she replied: "It's time Washington woke up!" He was beginning to feel the old headiness, when abruptly she was carried off by a knight in pseudo armor, while David overheard Titania Queen of the Fairies snidely remark: "That's Lucy Gwin. Her father spends seventy-five thousand a year, I hear!" And old Mother Hubbard reply: "My dear, he can afford to! He owns half of California and most of Texas!"

Emblematic of such talk perhaps, and of Gwin's great fortune, the World Bank Building would one day rise from the site of his house, but tonight Gwin moved tactfully among his guests as if guiding a bill toward passage on the Senate floor. He was Buchanan's right-hand man, close to the heart of power. Taking David by the arm he propelled him to the side of a short thick square-jawed man locked in conversation with a much taller, almost gaunt, intellectual looking one. "Senator Douglas, Senator Davis, I want you to meet a friend of mine from California. He's a divinity student over at Alexandria. I want you to know we export more than gold!"

"Something far more valuable!" rejoined Davis gracefully. David was struck by his unnatural pallor, for Davis, seldom robust, was recovering from a severe illness. "You chose a Southern seminary, Mr. Venable. Was there a reason?" Davis's courtesy of address was impressive and though David had been prepared to dislike him as a leading representative of the Slaveocracy, he found himself feeling quite otherwise.

"I'm a Westerner by birth. I want to understand the South."

"Hear that, Douglas?" Davis bantered. "I wish you'd adopt that attitude!"

"But I have!" protested Douglas. "Like me here's a Westerner come East to understand the South. Isn't that 'popular sovereignty' in action?" referring to his support of local decision with regard to slavery. Douglas was a Vermonter who'd "gone West" to Illinois at the age of twenty and become known as "the Little Giant" for his achievements in law and politics. But in speaking of popular sovereignty he was on shaky ground that would betray him, for although many like Elinor Wright saw him as savior and potential President—leader of their anti-slavery wing of the Democratic Party against the increasingly dominant pro-slavery wing—many others saw Douglas as a fence-straddler whose compromise policy on slavery would eventually lead to civil strife as in Kansas.

He spoke now of the convention of Illinois Republicans which would soon nominate a candidate to run against him at the fall elections. Davis asked slyly: "Will it be that scarecrow Abraham Lincoln?" and Douglas replied candidly: "I hope not. He'd be hardest to beat."

David had never heard of Abraham Lincoln before but felt sure Lincoln stood little chance against the Little Giant and his powerful friends.

Again he was finding power while he searched for glory, glory of vision for mankind, glory of conduct, glory of spirit. Therefore while favorably impressed by Gwin and Douglas and Davis and entertained by the gala whirl around them he remained untouched at heart while Davis took up the subject of the purchase of Cuba from Spain. Davis had long advocated a Greater United States, stretching from Canada to Panama, where slavery might flourish.

Buchanan and others agreed. But Congress had not yet provided money for the purchase of Cuba. "Can you muster enough votes?" he asked Gwin, "Counting on friend Douglas, of course?"

Dawn broke as David took his leave. His thanks to the Gwins was unfeigned. He understood now how power worked through personality and social occasion, how the South reigned as well as ruled here as in San Francisco, and how this gifted charming couple who stood before him also stood at the center of a network from which they shaped national policy and secured lucrative benefits for their state and their friends. Gwin indicated he wanted him among those friends. "We'll meet again soon, I hope?"

"I hope so!"

Lucy exclaimed, coming up: "He's a peachy dancer, Dad! Let's invite him next time!"

David said he would be delighted yet didn't quite mean it. He'd overheard beak-nosed Senator Seward, soon to be Lincoln's Secretary of State, liken the ball to that famous one given by the Duchess of Richmond at Brussels the night before the Battle of Waterloo—immortalized in Thackeray's *Vanity Fair*. David had read the novel and could not get the analogy out of his mind. Tonight the fun. Tomorrow the blood.

He was in the street now. His eye rested upon the unfinished dome of the capitol at the upper end of the avenue. Illumined by the rising sun, it seemed to beckon with a shining yet somber gesture of abiding truth. Impulse propelled him toward it.

Entering the rotunda he noticed a solitary figure, back toward him, tall, broad shouldered, looking thoughtfully up at the decorative stone capitals adorning the pilasters between the arches. There was something familiar about the figure. All at once David recognized Broderick.

With a surge of emotion he was about to cry out and rush to him, but something held him back. Broderick was studying that stonework his father's hand had carved and he'd vowed to walk under as Senator some day. Here in bitter irony he stood alone, outcast by his own party, by genteel society, perhaps by fate. Evidently Broderick had come at this early hour to ponder in solitude the forces at work upon him and the nation—which focused in this building his father helped erect and he'd played in as a child.

David stole away, deeply moved.

# Chapter Fifty-four

For days beforehand the papers were full of it, even Gillem's, while *The Tribune,* regularly subsidized by Sedley, gushed: "The union of two such illustrious families, one from the North, one from the South, their ancestries stretching back to colonial times, and now happily to be united here on our West Coast, stands in striking contrast to the disunionist sentiments wracking this nation."

Sarabelle wanted an exclusive guest list. Stanhope wanted just the opposite, for he wished the marriage of his daughter to be a political as well as social event. So did Vicky. Affable as usual, Sedley said: "I don't care who comes as long as Vicky and I are there." Beau would be best man. There were arguments over the refreshments and flowers and at the last moment even the weather seemed to conspire: fog, wind, dust. Until the day itself dawned calm and clear.

From that moment everything went in accordance with expectation: the ceremony at new Saint Giles on Pine Street, the huge reception afterward at the International Hotel, the shower of rice as they left, followed by his carrying her over the threshold of their palatial new house on exclusive Rincon Park Circle, the glass of champagne before bed.

But now as he slipped in beside her Sedley found his wife surprisingly naked. What followed was unprecedented in all his wide and varied experience. He prided himself on being able to hold back for as long as forty-five minutes during which most women were elevated to ecstasy and reduced to moaning putty in his hands, became in effect his property. Nor was this Mary Louise's subtle partnership—like a companion in a dance, moving to music, in his arms yet never quite his.

Vicky came at him with proud ferocity as if challenging him to withstand her desire. She's like her father, he thought. In fact she'd gone unfulfilled far too long for her needs. Sedley had given her Barbary as engagement present. In the great stallion pulsating between her thighs—for she rode astride in the daring California fashion he approved—she'd imagined Sedley himself there. Like him she held shyness in contempt, pleasure her right. And she remained proudly unmastered by him now, herself intact, stating her demands against his. He sensed she would master him if she could. For the first time he knew her true mettle. It put him on his in a new and provocative way.

Afterward as they lay satisfied, neither one victorious or defeated, quietly talking, he reached out to light the bedside candle. As he did so she saw for the first time the purple criss-cross scar on his forearm. She pointed to it. "What's that?"

"What'll you give me if I tell?" he teased.

"A kiss."

"Is that all?" He felt his desire rising in response to her promise.

A while later, he told her of the encounter with Francisco in the pass, of Clara, of the ranch he hoped to possess some day, of his young manhood there, of his father before him there, of its beauty and majesty.

"Oh, how exciting! I want to see it!" She spoke as if it were already theirs. "I've a feeling I'm going to like Rancho Olomosoug!"

"More than Fair View?" Down the peninsula their white porticoed mansion, Southern plantation style, was rising on its eminence overlooking the Bay, the only one of its kind west of the Mississippi Valley, truly an edifice. She'd helped him plan it. It too was to be hers.

"No, I want Fair View as well. I want it all. I want to share all of it with you!"

He'd not expected this. Certainly not right away. She was challenging that wall of distance he kept between himself and others. Was he to take two women into his confidence? Never beyond a certain point! Yet the thought of playing Mary Louise against Vicky piqued his ever present curiosity. It would make sparks fly. It would be interesting.

"What'll you give me if I take you on as partner?" he bargained again, and again she gave him what was to become known between them as earnest money.

While they slept the compositors were setting next day's headlines: THE OCTOPUS WEDS . . . THE KING TAKES A QUEEN.


"Master gonna sell me down to the rice fields." Sam's eyes rolled. The hated rice fields of South Carolina were to the slaves of Virginia and Maryland what the cotton plantations of Louisiana and Mississippi were to those of Kentucky and Tennessee—death traps.

"When?" David asked, laying aside their *McGuffey Reader*.

"Next coffle." Sam's owner was being pressed by creditors. Sam was among his most valued assets. "I want to go North," Sam asserted quietly again.

David realized the time had come to risk himself more fully for what he believed. He turned to James May. "If we can get him onto the Underground Railroad it would be easier," and described Hattie's escape.

"How can we make contact with the Railroad?"

The three got down on their knees and prayed for guidance in what they thought was privacy. The door opened and Hampden came in. "Hullo, what's all this about?"

"Any law against it?" David inquired gently.

"You fellows are going to be tarred and feathered if you keep this up!" Hampden warned, and slammed the door in disgust.

Next day an invitation came in the form of a note from Elinor Wright delivered by Sol Evans when he brought his usual wagonload of truck for the school's kitchen. Elinor hoped David could come for lunch on Sunday "as there will be an old friend of yours here."

David found two strangers with her on the verandah overlooking the river, one a slim well-dressed young fellow of patrician bearing who wore dark green eyeglasses and evidently suffered from toothache because a brown linen handkerchief encircled his face and head. The other appeared to be his Negro servant, about the same age, very stalwart, coal black.

"The train arrived day before yesterday and brought me these passengers." Elinor spoke with quiet satisfaction. At sound of her code words David almost jumped out of his shoes. "This is Francis Percy of Louisiana." She indicated the young man with the green glasses. Mary Louise's disguise had served her well and continued to. David did not recognize her even when he took her hand. But when she said in her melodious voice: "Last time I saw you was from the wharf at San Francisco!" his memory began to bring her back, and when she removed her glasses and handkerchief he burst out: "Mary Louise!"

And when they'd embraced and she'd introduced Samson, "You remember—the porter at Mr. Sherman's bank?" and explained how she and Samson had been working in the South to free slaves, David suddenly felt a rush of profoundest wonder and gratitude, for here evidently was the answer to his prayer for guidance in helping Sam.

"You've come at just the right moment!" He explained Sam's predicament.

"He can join our coffle!" she answered, using the term ironically. Reconnoitering on behalf of John Brown, she and Samson had penetrated as far South as her old home at Stanhope's Bend Plantation. Disguised as a slave she went among the familiar cabins singing the coded words of that grand old spiritual Uncle Isaiah had taught her:

> "Oh, go down, Moses,
> Way down to Egypt's land!
> Tell old Pharaoh,
> Let my people go!"

In this secret message, Moses was the liberator, herself, of an oppressed people, the slaves, just as he was of the Children of Israel in the Bible. Egypt was the South. Pharaoh was Stanhope. Returning to the scene of her suffering and Hattie's filled Mary Louise with fierce satisfaction. By depriving Stanhope of his slave property she was making him pay in flesh and blood and money, while enhancing the cause of her people's freedom. She would strike at him and his kind wherever she could.

One of the house girls whispered: "Miss Vicky marry a rich man out there!"

"What's his name?"

"Dunno."

Mary Louise could guess. She was not greatly surprised. She'd anticipated Sedley's "faithlessness," knew she had no claim over him, knew he would never marry her, never even think of it, nor would she. It was his innermost self she was determined to dominate. She would share part of him no other woman would: his business heart, his power center. Smiling to herself she imagined him coping with spoiled, headstrong Victoria because Victoria could add to his power. Yet Victoria was Hattie's half sister. In marrying her he would be marrying part of Mary Louise. It was how the world worked. And she began to lay plans accordingly.

Aunt Bessie was dead but Uncle Isaiah heard her singing and rejoiced. Falling on his knees on the dirt floor of their cabin he gave thanks. She opened the door. "Come on, we're going!" But he was too old, too crippled to follow. Not so with others. She went on into the woods where Samson was waiting, and after dark those willing and able came to them.

Guided by the Pole Star she and Samson led the way north, hiding by day, traveling by night, adding to their "freedom coffle" as they went. Until at this moment there were fourteen ex-slaves temporarily hidden in the cabins of Elinor Wright's plantation. But slave catchers were on the alert and it would be difficult for Sam to join them.

"I've an idea," Elinor proposed. "When Sol brings his produce to the school tomorrow, David, you see that Sam gets hidden in his wagon and Sol will bring him here."

David agreed. "But you people can't run all the risk. What else can I do to help?"

Elinor turned to Mary Louise. Mary eyed David keenly. Could she trust him? She recalled his betrayal of Hattie but also his redemptive help afterward. "You could contact Portugee Joe."

"Who's Portugee Joe?"

Mary Louise explained that Joe captained a sloop that would carry her and her coffle and Sam to freedom. Though Washington City was a southern terminus of the East Coast's main Underground line, slavery flourished in the nation's capital. Coffles clanked past the White House. Every day newspapers carried notices of runaway slaves and rewards for their capture. Twenty thousand dollars was being offered for the capture of the notorious "Mary Louise," alias "Rachel," alias "Rebecca," and "Roxanna," said to be a former slave herself, operating periodically during the past dozen years between South and North. It was said she'd cost slave owners over two hundred thousand dollars in stolen property. "She may be disguised as a man," the notice warned. So Mary Louise wished to avoid Washington City. "Joe trades up and down the river and carries cargo to free soil

at Philadelphia in Pennsylvania. We need to get word to him to
pick us up here."

"Where will I find him?"

"At the Oyster Shell Tavern."

At dusk David stood facing the Oyster Shell Tavern on Alexandria's riverfront. The tavern reeked of spirits and resounded
with noise. Mary Louise had given him the passwords but he must
devise a way of contacting Portugee Joe. "You'll know him by
his loud voice and bow legs," she said. "Not much taller than
you. Dark hair. Long mustaches."

David's heart pounded. How was he to single out Portugee Joe
and find opportunity to speak to him privately? He closed his
eyes momentarily. Into his mind flashed the image of Reverend
Taylor preaching from the barrel outside the saloon in San Francisco. There was no barrel outside the Oyster Shell. But he had
practiced impromptu sermons on his classmates. Here was a
chance to do so in real life. Raising his voice, David began to
preach where he stood. "Jesus is like the pearl in the oyster, my
friends. When you open that humble shellfish, you never know
what a jewel you may find. Same with Jesus. He often waits in
humblest guise to surprise you if only you'll look for him."

A curious crowd began to gather. Some jeered, some paid silent
attention. When he realized that the loudest abuse came from a
fellow who looked like a pirate in baggy black trousers and red
tunic open at the throat, with bow legs and dark hair and mustache, he knew with joy that he had found Portugee Joe. At that
moment a hog-faced man wearing a soiled white apron, emerged
angrily from the tavern and roared: "Stop blocking my door—
and get the hell out of here, damned Christer!"

"Aw, let him be, Jerry," Joe intervened. "He's off his noodle.
Why, the poor fool's bringing you business! Look at this crowd!"
Jerry subsided, grumbling, and returned indoors, while David kept
on with his testimony, declaring that Jesus saves all who are willing.

"If you want to save somebody," Portugee Joe interrupted
sarcastically, "come down to my boat! I'll give you a job loading
salt fish, young feller, and you can save yourself with some honest
labor!"

This raised guffaws. Ike Gullidge, Alexandria's leading slave
catcher, remarked: "I bet he ain't got no stomach for that! He'd

rather push wind for a living.'' Gullidge's jaw thrust out truculently. His belly protruded too. A huge carbuncle marked his left brow. David hated the man on sight. But turning to Joe, he replied steadily: "I'm ready, sir. Jesus labored with his hands. So did his disciples.''

"Then come along," growled Joe, "and we'll see if the pearl is in the oyster like you say." And David felt he was being guided truly, for "the pearl is in the oyster" were the passwords Mary Louise had given him.

Gullidge called after them derisively: "That's nigger work, Joe. He won't last!''

"I don't work niggers, Ike! You know that!''

On the way to his sloop Joe muttered under his breath: "You say the pearl is in the oyster?''

David whispered: "Yes, tonight at midnight.''

"Where?''

"River Farm Plantation.''

Gullidge was calling from behind them: "Stopping at River Farm Landing, Joe?''

They paused and waited for him. "Hadn't planned to," Joe lied easily, "but can.''

"Wish you would. And keep eyes peeled between here and there.''

Joe raised his brows. "Why?" David sensed his resourceful strength. As a boy Joe had fled a harsh taskmaster in the Azores where landowners, abetted by the church, often ruled as oppressively as some in the South. But it was as stowaway on a ship captained by a devout Roman Catholic that he reached Maryland. From there he made his way to freer soil at Philadelphia. There by hard toil and careful saving he'd become owner of his own vessel—trading with it up and down Delaware and Chesapeake Bays. Joe never had anything to do with Negroes in public. When in Virginia or Maryland he openly reviled them. Thus he was an ideal captain for the Underground Railroad's sea line. "What's up, Ike?''

"Big wool dealer, Joe," Ike winked. "Mebbe twenty bales to load out. Mebbe by land, mebbe by water. Mebbe big money in this, Joe.''

"What's he look like?''

"Slim young feller. Dark green glasses. Could be a girl dressed up.''

"I'll keep my eyes peeled, Ike. Will I see you at River Farm?"
"Mebbe," said Ike knowingly. "Mebbe."

As the sloop nosed through pitch darkness toward River Farm
Landing, human shadows loomed on the dock ahead. There was
no light in the house up the slope. "Swing her in!" Joe ordered
his tillerman and the little vessel veered abruptly toward land.
Moving to the prow, David beside him, Joe called in a low voice:
"Train a-comin'!"

The soft-voiced reply came from Mary Louise: "Passengers
a-waitin'!"

With Samson she stood at the head of their coffle which included a mother and baby. The baby began to cry. Mary Louise
whipped out her bottle of paregoric and it quieted. Joe sprang to
the dock, David behind him, and they quickly made the sloop
fast. "All aboard!" Joe's tone was urgent.

Hastily the fugitives scrambled down the hatchway. David saw
Sam among them. Up the slope there was a cry. Lights appeared
in the house. He heard horses approaching at a gallop. "Gullidge!" muttered Joe. "Step lively, everyone!"

But one exhausted fugitive's nerves broke. He was unable to
take this last step toward freedom. Mary Louise drew her pistol.
"Get on with you!" she commanded. "Dead niggers don't talk!"
He got.

David cast off the lines and stood alone on the dock. "Change
your mind, lad?" Joe was offering a way out of the plan they'd
agreed to. And Mary Louise urged: "Yes, come!" But David
stubbornly remained where he was. A force greater than himself
seemed to have taken charge of him and was telling him exactly
what to do. Someone scrambled back onto the dock and seized
his arm. It was Sam. David released his arm. "Not this time,
Sam. Go, quick now! Write me when you reach Canada!"

He gave the boat a powerful shove with both hands. Joe was
raising the mainsail. The sloop was disappearing into darkness as
horsemen clattered onto the dock. David hurried to meet them.

Two muffled lanterns swung clear of coverings. Rough hands
thrust them into his face as the brutal voice of Gullidge demanded: "What we got here?" and then in surprise: "By God,
it's the little preacher!"

David was looking into a pistol muzzle. Strangely he felt no
fear, only elation. "Joe had to catch the tide. Said to tell you he'd

seen some bales of wool upstream half a mile.''

"Blow his brains out, Ike!" It was Barrows, the spy, galloping back from a dash down the shore. "They was here. We seen the boat headed down-stream."

Gullidge hesitated. "Clay, you sure it was Joe?"

"Sure, Purvis and me we both seen it."

"He claims Joe set him ashore with a message for us." Gullidge had lowered his pistol.

"Don't believe a word of it! Here, let me finish 'im." Barrows drew a big Navy Colt from his saddle holster. "He's the little son of a bitch I seen on her verandah the other day. Damned Abolitionist—I can smell 'em a mile off!"

But Gullidge snapped: "Hold on, now, Clay. We just might have the wrong fox. And he happens to be a white one."

"And he happens to be a student at Southern Seminary and his name is David Venable," David interjected quietly. "And now, gentlemen, I'll appreciate it if you let me pass." And he stalked by the confused pair and ascended the slope toward the lighted house feeling better than ever before in his life.

Three months later a letter in halting but sufficient handwriting came from Saint Catharines just across the border from Niagara Falls. It told David Sam was safe.

# Chapter Fifty-five

They've already got Ferguson,"* Gillem wrote David.

"Lured him into a duel. They'll get Broderick next."

Gillem, with his talent for uncovering unpleasant realities, had discovered what he regarded as a plot to keep control of California in the hands of The Chivalry by force and intimidation if need be. "With the President, much of Congress, and the Supreme Court behind them, they feel they can sooner or later take California into the slave camp by fair means or foul."

"It's undeclared war," Mornay agreed. "They're killing our leaders." Years ago at the beginning of his commitment he'd hoped to bring about Abolition by peaceful means. Now he doubted it could be done, yet drew back in horror from the looming prospect of disunion and violence. His growing sense of responsibility toward Martha, toward David, toward Reuben, and Hattie, all the young who must suffer most terribly from war, added to his apprehension. He wrote David: "Shall we turn the other cheek? Or shall we take up the sword against this evil?"

During that summer David worked on Elinor Wright's farm, renewing his roots in the soil and marveling at the mysterious manner by which Elinor and her free Negroes produced such fine crops. "It's the marl, chiefly," she explained, meaning the clay mixed with calcium carbonate which they spread on her fields as fertilizer. One day when a visitor rode up she summoned David

*State Senator W. L. Ferguson, political ally of Broderick

to the verandah and he met a strikingly determined man with
shoulder-length white hair named Edmund Ruffin. "Edmund is
this country's leading agronomist," Elinor declared. "His theo-
ries of soil nutrition are revolutionizing our rural economy."
Touring the farm with Elinor and Ruffin, David saw how marl
was applied as Ruffin advised, and crops were being rotated in
the manner he'd pioneered whereby corn—with peas broadcast
and plowed under to enrich the soil—was followed by wheat,
then clover mowed and grazed, followed by oats. "So that each
crop prepares the way for the one that follows," Elinor explained
and Ruffin nodded with approval. And from being an impoverished land, its virgin fertility exhausted by ignorant methods, Virginia had become a bountiful one. Then the talk turned to politics,
and Ruffin demanded abruptly of his hostess: "Are you ready to
help us take Virginia out of the Union?"

"Certainly not!" she retorted indignantly. "Edmund, you stick
to what you know, which is agriculture, and keep your nose out
of what you don't, which is the movement toward freedom in this
nation and state!"

An argument followed such as David had never heard between
man and woman. He was amazed to hear Stanhope linked with
the noted Rhett and Yancey as working closely with Ruffin toward Secession. Elinor remained unmoved and Ruffin left in considerable dudgeon.

"A strange man!" David hazarded.

"Yes, and a brilliant one, if he is misguided in certain ways."

Broderick returned to California for the summer and fall and it
was not until Congress reconvened shortly before Christmas that
David again tried to contact him. He'd thought often of Broderick's great speech to the Senate, and of that lonely figure discovered in the rotunda of the capitol the morning after Gwin's ball.

On sudden impulse he sought out Broderick in his simple quarters in a mews of small dwellings near that same capitol and
reintroduced himself.

"Certainly I remember you," Broderick replied, cordial yet
aloof. "You fooled me that day in the engine house with your
tricky right lead." And when words of praise for Broderick's
courageous speech flooded out of David, Broderick replied soberly: "I hope you are right, for we shall need clergymen fighting
beside us as well as politicians. And we shall need businessmen
like Mornay. Authors too, like this one." He touched Dickens's
recently published *Hard Times,* which lay open on the table be-

side him. "Some day our Dickens will tell the story of our working classes. And yet my own taste often runs to poetry above prose, for poetry touches the mainsprings of thought and emotion more directly." The self-educated Senator indicated a volume by Shelley. "Are you familiar with Shelley's 'Song to the Men of England'?"

David with amazement and delight responded impetuously:

> "Men of England, wherefore plow
> For the lords who lay ye low?"

And Broderick answered with a shy twinkle:

> "Wherefore feed, and clothe, and save,
> From the cradle to the grave,
> Those ungrateful drones who would
> Drink your sweat—nay, drink your blood?"

From that moment they were sealed into a special intimacy as if their own blood had mingled. "We are at the verge of a second American Revolution," Broderick confided, "that will transform this nation into a true democracy. The question of slavery is in my opinion simply an aspect of a larger issue: whether the people of these United States shall be entitled to full rights as American citizens."

David was so moved that he felt he had at last found the man of glory he sought and secretly wished to become. He talked with Broderick as he'd never talked with anyone, not even Mornay. Then suddenly overcome by the realization he was occupying much of a Senator's time and not wishing to presume, he abruptly stood up. "I must go."

Broderick halted him with a gesture. "I'm glad you sought me out in order to express your views. Apathy, sloth, are the chief enemies we face." But when David said, as a parting pleasantry: "I suppose you'll be spending Christmas with your family?" Broderick's face darkened. "I have no family." And David remembered he had no one on earth to whom he was related by blood and with sudden inspiration cried out: "Why not take Christmas dinner with us? Dean Swallow will be delighted! It's his custom to send each of us who must remain at school at Christmas season, for lack of home or relations, into the streets to find someone who may be in similar state and to ask him to our common board. I now ask you.'' And Broderick, stirred, replied: ''My friend, I accept!''

''Some more oyster stuffing, Mr. Broderick?'' Celia offered in motherly tone. ''It goes very nicely with turkey.'' Broderick's reticence at the dinner talbe did not discomfit her though it made David fidget. He even wondered why Broderick had come. But now this strange man of unpredictable mood began to thaw under Celia's warmth. ''If you'll warrant it won't spoil my appetite for these popovers, Ma'am, which I believe you're also responsible for?''

Swallow, Tom Squires and his wife Maxine made up the rest of the party. Tom and his family had been invited by Swallow who knew their larder was often bare. Five-year-old Tommy Junior sat between his parents, elevated upon a dictionary, feet dangling several inches above the floor. Baby Iris slept in Swallow's chaise longue in the parlor. Broderick helped himself to Celia's oyster stuffing.

''As we were saying,'' Swallow continued, ''this has been a momentous year.''

''Not so dire as the one to come,'' Broderick predicted gloomily.

''You mustn't be so gloomy!'' chided Celia.

''I must be honest, Ma'am. What I foresee is gloomy: no leadership in the White House, in Congress only faction.''

''What about the working man?'' Tom Squires, who'd been one, inquired.

''In the long run prosperity; in the short, such terrible hardship as he's recently been through. Thousands in our cities are still unemployed. These vicious cycles of boom and bust must be controlled by laws which protect the laborer and mechanic from the greedy manipulations of the lords of commerce and finance.''

Celia listened with rapt attention. ''How do you propose to do this, Mr. Broderick?''

''By wresting power from the Slavocracy which rules this country. Until then we are a house divided—as Mr. Lincoln of Illinois so aptly terms us. Defeated though he was, he sees the situation clearly.''

''You sound like a Republican,'' Swallow joked.

''Sir,'' Broderick continued seriously, ''the division I speak of is exemplified in California as in no other state. We have one

Senator, Mr. Gwin, who represents the aristocratic slave-owning class; one Senator, myself, who opposes slavery and stands for the rights of the free working man.''

Celia's eyes were shining. ''The election of a Republican President in 1860 is now well within the realm of possibility?''

''Sit up, Tommy, and eat nicely!'' Maxine Squires admonished her son. ''Don't you realize you're among gentlefolk?'' Maxine, a slatternly blonde, was painfully decked out for this occasion in faded best taffeta and costume jewelry. She often deplored in public her husband's ''crazy ambition to become a minister,'' yet toiled faithfully to support him while he did. Perceiving her situation and wishing to gloss over it, Broderick abruptly inquired: ''How old is Tommy?''

''Six come February.''

''My age when I last enjoyed Christmas in these parts.''

''Tell us about it,'' Celia urged, ''please.''

Broderick told of his immigrant parents and their humble household. ''My father worked with heart and hands. They were the true tools of his trade. He came from Ireland to this country for freedom, for a better life—for a table such as this.''

''You had no sisters or brothers?''

Celia's sympathies were strongly roused, David saw. Broderick's face darkened again. ''A brother. He too is dead. I alone am left to tell what I am saying. But it is to people like you, Miss Swallow, and to you, Mr. Squires and Mrs. Squires, and to you, Dean Swallow, and to my young friend here from California, that I confide these things, because I feel you are like me.'' And now Broderick's rough eloquence took hold, and that quality of leadership that he possessed in high degree and which so many were attracted to emanated from him and gripped his hearers. ''You, we, are the foundation upon which this great nation was erected and will grow to heights as yet undreamed of. It was not lords and ladies who came to Jamestown and Plymouth but humble folk who dissented, as I have dissented, from established ways and sought out new ones in the name of God and humanity.''

In the next room Baby Iris began to cry. Squires rose to go to her. ''Oh, let me!'' Celia interposed with a restraining hand. ''I don't want you to miss a word of this!'' In a moment she was back rocking the baby in her arms with an expression of radiant love which made David's heart ache for this woman so full of tenderness, so eager and willing to give it, who received none from a child of her own. Cradling now quiet Iris to her pathetically flat bosom, Celia urged: "Do continue. Good conversation is like prayer, isn't it? Doesn't it arise and become food for the Gods, as the ancient Athenian said?"

"Sophocles, wasn't it, Ma'am?" Broderick rejoined.

For the next few moments there ensued a remarkable dialogue between them upon the subject of Sophocles to the exclusion of everyone else. And later, when Celia sat at the piano and played the newly popular "Jingle Bells," it was Broderick's rich baritone that accompanied her with evident pleasure.

David saw a new man emerging, one who had been submerged in toil and care far too long. He felt destiny had guided him to the apartment of Broderick and brought Broderick here this day. But then remembered it was really the great speech of Broderick which had done so, and thus the man was shaping his own destiny as well as David's and the nation's.

As he prepared to leave, Broderick turned to Swallow: "This has meant more to me than you can know."

And Swallow replied, echoed by Celia: "You must come again."

And Broderick said: "I will."

# Chapter Fifty-six

The definitive meeting for the purpose of dividing California into two states was held at Santa Bárbara a few months later. Clara made an impassioned plea against the idea. "Divide a land which once belonged to all my people, and give half to those who secretly wish to perpetrate on them an even greater servitude? Never!"

But she was overborne by the majority led by Don Lázaro Estenega who blamed "the Yankees of the North" for their misfortunes—the loss of many of their ranches, their disproportionately heavy taxes, lack of attention in the Legislature, the general disdain with which they were treated as the state's "poor cousins," as one speaker put it. Racial animosity played a silent part: many of Spanish or Mexican ancestry resented the dominant Anglo rulership in Sacramento and San Francisco. Little was said, too, about slavery or the Southern Cause but both were powerful factors in the minds of many who continued to see in the way of life of the South, with its vast acreages and plantation system, a similarity to their own way; while one recent emigrant who spoke up did not hesitate to draw parallels between the right of Southern states to secede from the Union, and the right of southern Californians to separate from northern California.

The new Territory of Colorado would consist of the counties of San Luis Obispo, Santa Bárbara, Los Angeles, San Diego, San Bernardino and part of Buena Vista.* Thanks to the Dred Scott

*forerunner of Kern County

decision slavery would be permitted in it, as Gillem pointed out when he commented editorially on the growing movement. "Is this state to divide over The Peculiar Institution, as The Chivalry euphemistically term it?" he challenged his readers. "Are we to become an example for the nation? Let us hope otherwise! The Slaveocracy is using the legitimate discontent of southern Californians to extend its evil influence!"

He pointed out that the proposed boundary, just north of present-day Bakersfield, might leave the strategic passes of the southern San Joaquín in Southern hands in the event of war. "Thrusting northward through them, a hostile force might try to seize the Sierran gold fields."

Despite such opposition, the Legislature, dominated by Southern sympathizers, passed an act proposing the new territory. It was overwhelmingly approved by voters in the region in question; and, despite vociferous opposition by Broderick and other Free-Soil Democrats, and the few new Republican members, the Legislature endorsed the action of the voters and prepared to petition Congress for formation of the new territory. Mornay wrote gloomily to David: "Unless some miracle occurs, the rape of this state will be complete."

But Sedley and Stanhope were jubilant. The Colonel's Knights of the Golden Circle had worked secretly for the common success, while Sedley's influence with the Legislature was decisive. The Territory of Colorado would be the first monument to their collaboration as father- and son-in-law.

In Sedley's drawing room on Rincon Circle, they lifted their glasses of champagne to the new Southern Empire. "We'll have the laugh on that fool Lincoln, who says we cannot exist half slave and half free, eh?" Stanhope declared sarcastically. The vision was dazzling in many ways. Royal concourses. Imperial balls. Fox hunts. Power. Victoria sparkled at the prospect as did Sarabelle. Raising their glasses again, they clinked with their consorts' in an apex which seemed indeed symbolic.

"What fun to have two states to live in!" Victoria exclaimed.

"And perhaps a finca in Mexico?" Sarabelle suggested.

"Or Nicaragua!" Stanhope added.

"Congress hasn't acted yet!" reminded Sedley, always cautious in such matters. Still, it seemed only a matter of time before the new territory, including Rancho Olomosoug and thousands of other acres in which all four were interested, became a Southern state.

Beau was busy at the club with billiards—with Gillem. A deliberate happy-go-luckiness insulated him from matters such as these, which he did not like. His earlier enthusiasm for the cultivation of cotton in the San Joaquín Valley had died under his father's strong will. Stanhope wished to begin it in the Sacramento Valley where he found it already in progress. But Beau argued for the more southerly San Joaquín where climate and soil seemed to him more favorable. Then when his father proposed that he join the Knights of the Golden Circle he could not help but spoof: "Come off it, Dad. It's that old secret society stuff which's bug-a-booed we Southrons for decades. Time we outgrew it!"

"What?" stormed Stanhope. "You don't believe in the cause I'm devoting my life to? For your sake and your mother's and sister's?" Stanhope was furious, seeing in his son a hopeless frivolity, even a lack of manhood. "Have you turned your back on your heritage?"

But Beau reassured him: "I'll be there when you need me. But I won't have a costume on!"

Throughout that winter and into the spring of 1859 Broderick escaped more and more frequently from the turmoil of the capitol to the peaceful haven of the Swallow home. Though powerfully attractive to the opposite sex, Broderick never had been in love, never involved himself with a woman. Washington hostesses tried hard to include the now much discussed young Senator in their dinner parties and soirees, but he refused all invitations and thereby became more sought after.

It was the day following the unseasonal ice storm that the crucial events in the relationship between him and Celia occurred. That March Sunday dawned clear and unusually warm. Ice melting from limbs allowed new green buds to appear miraculously. Broderick had come to take his leave. Congress was about to adjourn. He would be returning to California. After the noonday meal at which he remained unusually silent, he turned bluntly to Celia: "Shall we take a walk?"

As they strolled side by side under the oaks, great branches spreading overhead like protective arms, he opened his heart to her as never before. "I shan't see you again until the Senate reconvenes next fall." It was Celia's turn to be unusually silent, while he continued: "I have a premonition. Lately it has grown more intense. I don't know why I'm telling you this. But I feel compelled. Each time victory has appeared within my grasp, fate has snatched it away.'' And he told of his impoverished struggles as a young man in New York City to mount the political ladder ''until finally I received the Democratic nomination to our National House of Representatives. But when I refused to accede to the bosses' corrupt rulership through bribery and other means, they withdrew their support and I lost. So I disposed of everything I possessed and went to California to make a fresh start. There as I stepped ashore I vowed to become a Senator some day and return to my native city of Washington in triumph. I did. But my triumph is hollow.''

With a rush of sympathy for this tortured man Celia found her voice. ''Oh, you must not allow yourself to feel that way. You must believe in God's guidance!''

''God has never helped me,'' Broderick replied harshly. ''I have always relied on myself, in a terrible uphill struggle against what seemed God's wish for me—that I was destined to be parentless, brotherless, sisterless, and trapped always in the dregs of life, that I was never to succeed, that I was never to know happiness. That seemed God's plan for me. Only by resisting that plan with all my heart and soul am I where I am. And some of the things I've had to do have not been very nice, Miss Swallow.''

''But perhaps your struggle—your successful struggle—was God's will too!''

Broderick shook his head. ''I cannot escape the conviction I am touched by the mark of Cain, cursed, doomed to strive mightily, to come close, as I have come so often—only to find myself finally rejected, my policies and person in disfavor, deprived of my rightful place and patronage—even of the love of such a person as yourself such as I now,'' he hesitated, then turned to her, ''quite wonderfully find myself desiring above all other things on earth.''

''Oh, my dearest, you must not feel so!'' With an inadvertent movement she embraced him like a mother a child and held him as tenderly as one. ''I am here to shield you from such terrible thoughts, to encourage you and inspire you with my love!'' she cried, eyes brimming with tears.

And for the first time since childhood her lips were touched by a man's and his by a woman's.

When they returned to the house Swallow and David discreetly asked no questions. The faces of the pair said all that was needed.

Afterward Celia accompanied her lover a little way under the trees to where his horse was tethered in the shade.

Broderick was returning to California to campaign for the anti-Gwin, anti-Buchanan, anti-slavery forces in what he knew would probably be the bitterest contest of his career.

"The Chivalry hate me," he confided to Celia. "There, as here, they regard me as an obstacle to their rule."

"Our thoughts, our prayers go with you!"

"Would you, my dear lady, pray for an old bachelor like me?"

"I would—oh, I would!" she exclaimed fervently.

"Then do so!" taking her hand in his and lifting it to his lips, "for I shall need it."

For a long time after he swung to the back of his black horse and was gone off down the drive under the budding oaks, she stood holding that hand in her other, her gaze fixed after him.

Watching from the front steps, Swallow plucked David by the sleeve and led him inside.

Standing alone with her thoughts of the man she had come to love and who had discovered his love for her, Celia never knew what struck her.

From inside the house, David and Swallow heard a sharp crack like a rifle shot. They both started. "What is it, sir?"

"The crack of doom?" Swallow joked.

"I'll go and look."

David found Celia quite dead. A limb of a giant oak above her, weakened by the sudden thaw, had split from its trunk and smashed her into the earth.

Broderick, beyond hearing, rode on, his thoughts set toward his coming battle.

# Chapter Fifty-seven

Searching again for John Brown in order to report on her reconnaissance into the South, Mary Louise found him at Rochester, New York, in the home of the Negro leader and former slave, Frederick Douglass, whom Mornay had known as a ship's caulker on the New Bedford waterfront. Douglass had been a member of Mornay's underground unit there.

"I see no possibility of a general uprising of slaves occurring, let alone succeeding," she told both men, as they sat in the secret basement room of Douglass's house, which was also a station on the Underground Railroad.

Douglass, broad of face and mind, a towering figure physically and spiritually, who had written his autobiography and was now publishing an anti-slavery newspaper, *The North Star,* nodded agreement. By bitter experience and clearer insight he was more knowledgeable of the South than Brown. But Brown insisted on proceeding with his grandiose plan for capturing the U.S. Arsenal at Harper's Ferry, Virginia, distributing its weapons and ammunition to "my guerrillas and the thousands who will rise to join us," and invading the Southern mountains "which will become freedom's redoubt!"

Mary Louise shook her head. "It's doomed to failure!"

"If so, it will be God's will!" Brown retorted, more fiercely determined than ever. "And perhaps it will provoke such a crisis that the sins of this nation will be washed away in blood!" Gesturing with hand held high, he seemed, with his long white beard and glaring eyes, like an Old Testament prophet.

Mary Louise thought him deluded but divinely inspired. She'd intended to give him additional financial support but decided it would be a waste of money. When she left she carried a letter of greeting to Mornay from Douglass, who had heard of Hattie's painful case and was keenly interested in Mary's account of the activities of the San Francisco Underground and the involvement of his old friend there.

When he reached San Francisco, Broderick was goaded almost to insane fury by David's letter bringing news of Celia's death, and fought against the black feeling of doom which threatened to overwhelm him.

The Chivalry's spreading menace seemed like that tree limb which had killed innocent Celia and destroyed the love of his life, the only spark of that kind which ever had arisen in his heart. Unbosoming himself to Mornay, he told of her gracious innocence in such moving terms that tears came to the merchant's eyes. "The death of innocence! Innocent suffering! How can we explain it? Sometimes I think like Job we must simply accept it!"

"Never," cried Broderick with choking voice and blazing eyes. "I shall fight it to my dying breath! I shall thwart that miserable scoundrel Gwin and his cohorts if it kills me!"

Mornay feared for his sanity as he raged up and down the state. At stake was California: its Governorship, Lieutenant Governorship, Chief Justice of its Supreme Court, a Congressional seat, the Legislature. Everyone knew this was the decisive moment. The election would confirm or deny the power of The Chivalry and division of the state.

Broderick fielded his slate of anti-slavery Democratic candidates; Gwin his pro-slavery ones; the Republicans theirs—and though neither Broderick nor Gwin was running for office, both took the stump and in effect became candidates, tearing at each other in terms so abusive that Gillem openly predicted blood must flow.

Broderick spoke without notes, bluntly, harshly, but so effectively he drew large crowds. "Doctor Gwin represents a supposedly free state. Yet of course you Californians are not free. You are in bondage to Gwin and his Chivalry—who are your masters as surely as if you were black-skinned workers on their Mississippi and Louisiana plantations."

"Broderick is a traitor to his party, a vulgarian, not a gentleman, a failure as Senator, and a liar beside!'' Gwin retorted.

Gillem heaped criticism on both: ''Each is guilty of the cor
ruption he decries in the other. Broderick, as everyone with a
memory ten years long knows, amassed a fortune by manufac
turing counterfeit money, shortly after his arrival on our fai
shores. Those currency slugs he so thoughtfully provided us, with
Mr. Sedley's backing, supposedly contained ten dollars in gold
but actually eight.'' While of a hundred and fifty officeholders in
San Francisco owing their appointments to Gwin, Gillem could
find only five Northerners. ''Yet behind these two worthies loom
a shadowy figure who stands to gain whichever loses. His name
is Sedley. Ask what he thinks of Broderick and he replies affably
'An honorable man and my good friend. He has my support.' Ask
what he thinks of Gwin and he replies with equal affability: 'An
honorable man and my good friend. He has my support.' Yet
while this Janus remains reticent his money speaks for him. From
the timberlands of our North Coast, from Sierran gold mines, from
the vast wheat fields of our Central Valley, from vessels entering
Golden Gate, from rentals of choice Montgomery Street property
it comes pouring into his pockets in a golden flood. He is the
power behind the scenes. He is the King of California. And your
vote, dear citizen, will in reality be for Eliot Sedley, no matter
for whom it is cast.''

Broderick received the backing of most of the state's newspapers. But Gwin controlled the party machinery. Party loyalties
were strong. Many hesitated to step out of line despite their preference for Broderick. Gwin won overwhelmingly. His pro-
Chivalry slate was everywhere victorious.

Broderick returned exhausted and discouraged to San
Francisco.


''The challenge came from Judge Terry of all people,'' Mornay
wrote David and David remembered the fiery Texan who'd sat
next him at Sedley's dinner that evening, drawn his Bowie knife
and, whetting it against his thumb, proclaimed it the final arbiter
in all questions of power. Terry had since risen to be a justice of
the state's highest court and become a noted brawler and duelist.
''Having befriended Terry earlier, Broderick was taken totally by
surprise,'' Mornay went on. ''It is true that during the campaign
Terry attacked his anti-slavery stand and, true too, that when
Broderick heard of it he exclaimed in the presence of others:

'Why, the miserable turncoat—I thought Terry an honest man and my friend. Now I take it all back!' Which was reported to Terry. But Terry waited three months until after the election before using Broderick's statement as pretext.'' Though dueling was illegal, Broderick felt he had no course but to accept. ''The usual preliminaries followed and the meeting was arranged for early the morning of September 13 on the lonely shore of Lake Merced,'' where David had walked with Beau Stanhope in what seemed another lifetime. He remembered that deserted spot, haunted by the cry of sea birds. ''I urged Broderick to spend the night at my house and get a good rest,'' Mornay resumed. ''But he was gripped by forces which seemed to move him inexorably along a path of their own, and his gloom was aggravated by his exhausted condition. 'Sometimes I wonder if the Evil Eye isn't upon me, and all those near and dear to me doomed to perish like my beloved Celia!' he told me. 'Look to yourself, good friend. Perhaps you better keep your distance.' But he added suddenly: 'Stay near me! I trust you!' And I promised I would.''

Over Mornay's protests, Broderick's inexperienced seconds took him to a flea-ridden country inn where he spent a sleepless night on a hard cot ''without benefit of any comfort or even a hot drink or food next morning, when we all rose in the foggy darkness and made our way to the deserted ravine that opens onto the shore of the lake, within sound and smell of the sea.'' Terry and his seconds by contrast had rested comfortably at a house not far away, enjoyed a warm breakfast and appeared in good spirits. ''Broderick became more gloomy at sight of them and looked at me appealingly, much as to say 'See how it is?' But what could I do? I too felt fate intervening. Our seconds won the choice of position and the giving of the word to fire, but lost the far more important choice of weapons.''

Terry's pistols, of which Broderick must now choose one, were Belgian made, barrels nearly a foot long, triggers refined to hairlike touch. Terry had been practicing with them. Broderick, though a practiced marksman and veteran of more than one duel, had given up practicing when he became Senator and hadn't touched a firearm for over a year. ''Unknown to him,'' Mornay continued, ''one of the pistols was so refined that a slight jar or even a sudden movement might set it off. But our armorer failed to notice this important point when making his examination. The other was of more normal pull. Terry's seconds promptly chose it though the choice should have been by lot.'' Though Broderick's seconds failed to object, he was too astute to miss this blunder. "My seconds are babes at this business, Mornay. They may trade my life away. Look! The vultures are already gathering!" pointing to the crest of the ravine above them where a crowd had assembled. It had been impossible to keep the meeting secret. Not since Aaron Burr challenged Alexander Hamilton had a duel been fought between such prominent Americans—a United States Senator and a former chief justice of a state's highest court.

Both men removed topcoats and stood in long dark frock coats. They were equally tall, Broderick broader and heavier.

Ten paces were carefully measured and white lines drawn with chalk dust where they were to stand. "Take your positions, gentlemen!" Broderick's chief second, the inexperienced Colton, directed.

The loaded pistols were handed the duelists as they faced each other, and Broderick became increasingly uneasy as he fingered his unfamiliar weapon, "trying in vain to adjust it to his hand," Mornay continued, "and while he was doing so he inadvertently strayed from the line; and when Terry's seconds remarked on this, Colton spoke to him and he resumed his position but now somewhat quartering toward Terry rather than sidewise in the best posture for presenting as small a target as possible." Colton inquired: "Gentlemen, are you ready?"

Terry, wholly calm, promptly responded: "Ready."

After several seconds during which he still seemed to be coming to grips with his weapon, Broderick nodded: "Ready."

They were holding their pistols at their sides pointed downward as Colton began in measured fashion: "Fire—one—two—" Broderick fired at "one," Terry at "two."

Broderick's bullet struck the ground midway between him and Terry on direct line with his opponent. Terry's entered Broderick's chest an inch above the right breast.

Broderick staggered backward and gradually sank on his left side until his shoulder touched the ground, while his pistol dropped from his hand and blood poured from his body. Terry commented sourly to his seconds: "The wound is not mortal. I have hit too far out."

So poorly served was Broderick that his physician panicked and Terry's doctor, with Mornay's help, tried to stop the blood.

"A mattress was brought and we took him by carriage to Leonidas Haskell's house at the edge of the city," Mornay continued. "At first we thought his wound not mortal, as Terry said.

But blood gushed from his mouth as he bravely declared to us: 'I tried in vain to stand, but blood blinded me.' In his delirium he told me and Ned Baker of his conviction he would be hunted down and killed. 'There was something wrong with my pistol. It discharged while I was in the act of raising it,' adding: 'They have killed me because I opposed a corrupt administration and the extension of slavery.' "

While Broderick clung to life Gillem demanded with indignation echoed by papers throughout city and state: "What has this man done to be hunted down like an animal and shot? What crime has he committed? Where is the court who would find him guilty of any wrongdoing?"

For two days the city seethed with anger and sank deeper into gloom as Broderick sank toward death. The wrong he had done was for the most part forgotten while the good was remembered and magnified. Sedley came to pay respects. "The Octopus couldn't keep his tentacles off something so momentous," Gillem wrote David, "and needed the pretext of seeming to be concerned. After being refused admission he sent an enormously costly display of flowers."

Broderick was shot on Tuesday morning and died Friday morning, September 16, 1859. Mornay wrote: "His next-to-last words were: 'Protect my honor.' His last was a fervent: 'Celia!' "

When his death was announced, people left their homes and places of business and gathered in groups on the streets to discuss the terrible event. Shops were voluntarily closed, mourning crepe displayed. "San Francisco never has known such a day in all its stormy history!" Mornay declared.

Broderick's body was placed in a chamber at the Union Hotel at the corner of Merchant and Kearny, his longtime headquarters, to be viewed by thousands. On Sunday it was removed to a catafalque in Portsmouth Square. There without any formal preliminaries Ned Baker, who so eloquently had defended Hattie, now recognized as the city's leading orator, spontaneously addressed thirty-thousand people gathered in somber silence.

"A Senator lies dead in our midst. We to whom his toils and cares were entrusted are about to bear him to that place appointed for all living. Near him stand the noblest of our State; while beyond, the masses he loved and for whom his life was given, gather like a thundercloud of swelling wrath. . . ."

Mornay termed it the greatest speech he ever heard. "When it was over there was hardly a dry eye or unmoved heart. Afterward his body was borne at the head of a mighty procession, many of them Negroes, to Lone Mountain Cemetery, at the western edge of the city overlooking that Golden Gate through which he entered just ten years ago—alone, impoverished, with no certain prospects but such high hopes!'' David thought of his own entrance there, his high hopes then, his resolutions since—strengthened now by Broderick's death.

Two days later Gwin boarded ship for Panama and New York to resume his seat in the Senate. The hundreds gathered at the dock watched him silently. Instead of usual exuberant farewells, there was accusatory silence. Even the newsboys and peanut vendors were quiet. A single large sign prepared at the instigation of Mornay and held aloft by Mornay and Reuben together proclaimed: ''THE WILL OF THE PEOPLE—LET THE MURDERERS OF DAVID C. BRODERICK NEVER RETURN TO CALIFORNIA!''

Below the inscription a lifelike portrait of Broderick looked out upon the crowd and Gwin. It had been done hastily but effectively in charcoal by Martha on a large canvas. Martha and Hattie with her young Charles, named after Mornay, stood nearby.

Sedley indicated the sign to Stanhope as they descended the gangplank after seeing the Senator aboard and wishing him well.

''Let the mudsills beware,'' Stanhope sneered, ''or they'll receive the same medicine Broderick did.''

But Gillem's editorial expressed the general view. ''The Chivalry has California in its grip as never before. But we predict Broderick will rise from his grave and haunt them from office!''

So moved was much of the nation that when news of Broderick's death reached New York City, the funeral solemnities were repeated there in the form of a procession two miles long following a catafalque drawn by eight gray horses caparisoned in rich black velvet; and a funeral oration in grand style similar to Baker's eulogized Broderick as a champion of freedom.

A month later John Brown and eighteen followers seized the federal arsenal at Harper's Ferry, fifty miles west of Washington City.

On orders from President Buchanan, troops under command of Brevet Colonel Robert E. Lee recaptured the arsenal and took Brown prisoner. He was found guilty of treason and hanged on December 2.

Broderick's death followed so closely by Brown's, a double martyrdom as many called it,* sent deep tremors of outrage and hostility throughout the country; while Mary Louise journeyed homeward to carry on her work and Brown's, and Broderick's.

*after Lincoln's assassination Broderick would often be referred to as "the California Lincoln"

# Chapter Fifty-eight

Clara was scolding Sally affectionately: "You'll never be pregnant at this rate. You must do as I did when I couldn't conceive."

They'd gotten on very well since their first breakfast together after the wedding when Sally refused to kiss her grandmother-in-law's hand in traditional fashion but instead pressed it warmly in hers. Outwardly offended by this breach of etiquette, Clara was secretly pleased by such independence, for it seemed just what Pacifico and the ranch needed. And in the days that followed she came to love sprightly fearless Sally as the daughter she never had had, one like herself who'd married outside her own people.

As they made the rounds of the hacienda she taught her to be the Señora of Rancho Olomosoug, which she would indeed be someday, God willing. Clara taught her in the Spanish that was the lingua franca of household and Indianada and much of the surrounding countryside where English was still like a foreign language. Thus the chair was the *silla*, the table the *mesa*, the herbs used in cooking were the *salvia* or sage, and *yerba buena*, and when some member of the household became ill and remedies must be administered, there was the *yerba santa* or sacred herb for colds, sore throats, or rheumatism, and *yerba mansa* for skin diseases, cuts or bruises; and for stimulant of the heart the *boca de león* or foxglove and for the suppression of Sally's own excessive menstrual bleeding the *manzanilla* or camomile; and so for a host of useful native plants borrowed from Clara's people by the conquering Spaniards, now transmitted to yet a third race in the form of Sally. Sally learned readily in her new tongue,

liked its melodious tones and romantic connotations, and before
long was exclaiming *Válgame Dios!*—God save me!—as if born
to it.

She learned the operation of weaving and sewing, candlemaking and cheesemaking, and of the tannery and leather shops, and
how the thick bed mattresses must be taken in hand regularly
with María Ignácia's help and their wool thoroughly washed and
dried in the sun and made fluffy by much pulling. And in the
center of the courtyard near the fountain Clara showed her the
circular Wisdom Stone, hollow at its center, which had marked
the heart of the Indian village, her native village, which stood
where the hacienda did now. Chieftains and chieftainesses, sitting
on the stone, had passed judgment. Her brother Asuskwa, intrud-
ing stealthily by night, had left the red arrow of resistance on it
before he attacked and was killed after mortally wounding Antonio. And in order that Sally might clearly understand and become part of the continuity of the life of this place, Clara taught
her to weave baskets from willow and grass stems and to fashion
soft doeskin slippers for Pacifico, so that the Indian way would
continue in her too. Occasionally they enjoyed together a cigarette
made of a carrizo grass stem stuffed with wild tobacco, which
was Clara's pleasure at relaxed moments. And Sally was capti-
vated by all this and the vistas it opened toward the future. She
helped Bernardina in the hacienda school, and she rode the hills
with Clara, Pacifico and Isidro, and the wonder and beauty of the
marvelous land passed into her with possessive pride but also with
calculating ambition, for she foresaw the day when her son might
inherit all this. Yet no son came.

"You must pray!" Clara told her. And she did pray, nightly
after supper when everyone gathered in the parlor to recite the
Rosary; and later in the solitary darkness lying awake beside Pacifico, she prayed while in his arms surrounded by his love, his
seeds warm inside her; and at the solemn Mass of the Annunci-
ation, on March 25, nine months before Christmas, she listened
and tried to comprehend when Father O'Hara told of the Annun-
ciation which came to all women, each in her own way, as it had
to Mary. "Almighty Father of our Lord Jesus Christ, you have
revealed the beauty of your power by exalting the lowly virgin
of Nazareth and making her the mother of our Savior." And as
Sally listened she felt he was speaking to her also.

Still her menstrual flow continued and she began to despair,
while Clara grew impatient, repeating bluntly: "You must do as

I did. Go to the birthing hut!'' And when Sally agreed she added:
''I shall make arrangements. As you know, Eliot and his new
wife will be down soon. Evidently she's not pregnant either,'' she
said with callousness which hurt but was unintentional, as when
Clara mentioned enviously Anita's and Benito's son and daughter.

Over Pacifico's objections—he deriding it as foolish superstition—Sally went to the birthing hut, at the Indianada, and there,
when she'd stripped naked, two old crones under Clara's watchful
eye wafted purifying smoke from smoldering fresh *romero** over
her naked body, and then they ceremoniously handed her a small
gray cup of soft feminine soapstone shaped like a womb and
incised at four opposite points on its rim with four sharp grooves
representing penetrating masculinity. In the cup were fragments
of a green substance Sally did not recognize. Next they handed
her a hard phallic pestle stone and told her to grind the substance,
which was actually serpentine rock, into powder.

Still following their instructions she swallowed a pinch of the
powder, then inserted a pinch into her vagina. Then they trans-
ferred the remainder to a larger bowl, added water, and painted
her entire body green like the fertile earth in springtime and,
wafting sage smoke over her once more, uttered their time-
honored incantation:

> ''Mother Earth, Mother Earth, Mother Earth,
> Open your daughter to seed,
> Open your daughter to seed,
> As you open yourself!''

Sally could not quite believe in the efficacy of what was happening to her but felt she ought to. Incongruously she felt,
too, that all of this was so that Clara might be able to tell Sedley
when he came that she was pregnant, and it seemed vain and
foolish on the part of the old woman; but in Clara's nearly
hundred-year-old heart was the conviction that the flesh like
the earth—the ongoing flesh—might somehow prevail, that somehow flesh, somehow spirit would prevail over business, over lit-
igation, over what she dreaded; for her increasing financial
indebtedness to Sedley was troubling her deeply. Francisco
seemed lost and Pacifico ineffective and she needed reassurance
that life was with her.

*coastal sage

While she was thinking these things, Francisco was journeying warily to what had become the accepted rendezvous place at the junction of the two streams. There he gave the haunting two-note call of the mountain quail. But there was no answer and no one came, and he knew himself alone in his resistance. Earlier, word had filtered back with time into the wilderness that the members of his band who'd gone to the reservation were faring well; but Francisco felt in his bones that this would not last, that they would return and would again, one day, in their unhappiness, ask him to be their leader. Now he wondered. Had those who'd fled like him to the chaparral gone to join them on the reservation or were they dead? And when later he came again and gave the call, and still there was no answer, he still could not be sure, though the feeling in his bones continued.

# Chapter Fifty-nine

In the spring of 1860 having thriftily saved sufficient money to do so—and having reached a settlement with his creditors—Wing Sing became a partner with his cousin Yee in The American-Chinese Laundry on Dupont Street in what was being called Chinatown, while continuing to labor at his monumental account of his California experiences titled *The Land of the Golden Mountain.* To survive, he and Yee made regular extortion payments to the all-powerful Six Companies, that association of merchants which dominated Chinese life in The City and California, and thereby escaped the visitations of their hatchetmen; and The American-Chinese Laundry prospered wonderfully thanks to hard work and good service at low prices. Its customers included Mornay and Martha, Mary Louise and Gillem. Wing's departure from the household meant that Martha took over his duties in addition to teaching at Reverend Hicks's Negro School and helping Lucinda Wright at her Temperance Rescue Mission on the water-front.

Martha had developed into a gravely beautiful eighteen, her sting hidden beneath an angelic exterior. Thus when her father appeared before the Board of Education to protest continued exclusion of Negro children from the city's schools, pointing out that many Negroes were taxpayers as well as free citizens of the community, and to urge a socially integrated system such as recently adopted in Massachusetts, she insisted on appearing with him—much to the astonishment of the board and his own deep pride—and expressing her views in no uncertain terms based on personal experience.

"It was the first time a female member of our community has been known to appear in such fashion," Gillem editorialized approvingly, "and sets an example others of the fair sex may wish to follow if this State is to lead in social as well as material progress."

And when David learned of it he wrote: "Dear Gadfly, I'm glad others beside myself have felt your bite!" But he omitted the terms of endearment she wished to hear. Would he ever take her seriously? She wished she could be of help to him in some fundamental way that would make his life better. At the Rescue Mission she went about her work among drunkards, deadbeats, unfortunates of various kinds, with a quiet serenity which brooked no familiarity while rousing admiration. Wearing her prim brown muslin with that gold cross her father had given her at her throat, she administered soup, bread, clothing, a sympathetic ear—in a manner some of them regarded as that of a beneficent angel. "She's a regular Florence Nightingale!"* one hardened panhandler averred, and the label was picked up by *The Sentinel* and other papers, so that Martha became famous as "the Florence Nightingale of the San Francisco waterfront."

"It happens at the right time for me," Lucinda confessed to Mornay. "My vim's not what it used to be. And we have more to do every day. They keep pouring in. With the Seaman's Home and the French, German, Swiss, Jewish and even Chinese hospitals and all the other eleemosynary institutions in this city, you'd think the unfortunates would be taken care of. Not so. I think they come to see Martha."

Martha wrote David: "The alleviation of human suffering inspires me in a way I suppose your dedication to the ministry does you." She felt herself treading on ground they might someday share, and wondered if she were being too forward. But when he read he was moved by her gentle hesitancy and the apparent innocence of her motives. Later it seemed this was the moment he began to love her.

"We'll go East for David's ordination," Mornay promised, knowing how much it would mean to her as well as himself.

"If it comes it will be the War of Northern Aggression!" Hampden was telling David angrily. "Why are Southern Rights

*English nurse in the Crimean War, 1854–56, regarded as the founder of modern nursing

Clubs springing up all over the South? To offset your militant
Abolitionists! And now comes your John Brown leading an actual
attack on our soil!''

As Brown's plans were revealed, rumors of other Abolitionist
invasions and of slave uprisings threw the South into a turmoil.
''Brown is typical of your Black Republicans committed to the
destruction of our Southern Way of Life,'' Hampden declared
indignantly. ''Hasn't that baboon Lincoln proclaimed that this
nation cannot endure half slave and half free? Isn't he of the same
party as Senator Seward who's asserted that North and South are
locked in an irrepressible conflict? Who's attacking whom? Do
we Southerners have any choice but to protect our homes and
families either by seceding from the Union or taking up arms, or
both?''

It was difficult for David to find any answer but the one he
secretly felt was coming, the one Brown prophesied: war—war
to purge the nation with blood.

When Congress reconvened in December a few days after
Brown's death, many members carried concealed knives and pistols as did their supporters in the galleries; and as the new year
wore on, the deliberations of the lawmakers degenerated into a
bitter comedy of brandished weapons and threatened duels.

''If Lincoln is nominated by the Republicans in June it will be
the next to last straw,'' Hampden predicted. ''And if the Republicans win the White House this fall, that will be the last!''


During Easter holidays David went on a pilgrimage to his
mother's birthplace westward beyond the Blue Ridge Mountains
to the log cabin on Willow Run where she'd been born. It stood
on a rocky hillside above the stream on a patch of soil laboriously
cleared by hand. His aged Uncle Lemuel and Lemuel's aged wife
Bea occupied it. Their son and wife and children lived nearby.
They showed him the graves of his grandfather and grandmother,
spoke of his mother. ''She allus was a little fay,'' Lemuel declared through snaggled teeth, meaning she'd been a little strange,
a little enchanted; and enchanted indeed she had been, David
remembered, full of rhymes and sayings and tales upon tales in
which her fancy took flight and carried him along. Those who
remained behind here were the unenchanted. He saw it in their
faces, heard it in their words. He spoke to them of California.
''It's the coming place, the Promised Land!'' They said they

wanted to go. But he guessed they never would.

Standing there among them, looking West he felt himself flow-ing West like Willow Run, flowing into the Ohio, West as his mother and father had gone, West as the American people were moving. Feeling he understood his origins as never before, he felt ready to take the next step, to graduate and enter the mainstream of life as that little branch did the great Ohio.

Early in May he and James May went to the small parish church at Sharon not far from the seminary where there was no regular pastor and students often went to practice their skills. He noticed two well dressed gentlemen sitting at the back of the room as he preached. Afterward they approached and introduced them-selves as from Philadelphia, and point-blank asked if he'd like to become rector of their historic Church of Saint Matthew "after your graduation and ordination next month."

He was incredulous and burst out: "I'm tremendously honored. I hardly feel worthy of such an offer!"

"Tut, tut, sir, no false modesty!" Lippincott, the stouter one, chided paternally. "We now know with our own ears what a gifted speaker you are, Mr. Venable. And Dr. Swallow has rec-ommended you highly on that and other ground. We can offer you a starting salary of twelve hundred dollars annually."

Astounded by such a princely sum, David answered: "This takes me by surprise, gentlemen. May I have a few days to think it over?"

"No hurry!" Lippincott's companion Stroud, assured him. Da-vid agreed to let them know within a fortnight.

May joked on their way home: "Your fame is spreading. A big rich Philadelphia parish! I'd snap it up!"

But David wasn't so sure. He'd wanted to go straight back to San Francisco and still hoped to, though Mornay wrote there was no opening at Saint Giles' where Reverend Ardmore still endured. A pulpit, however rich and prominent, in a staid old city like Philadelphia seemed a backward step by comparison to anything in California.

He discussed it all with Swallow. Since Celia's death they'd drawn closer than ever. Though cruelly wounded by the loss of his daughter, the aging pedagogue's spirit still radiated warmth and light. "You'll have problems wherever you go. Your pred-ecessor was an old fogey who didn't know when to quit. That's one reason they want somebody young. As for wealth, fashion, power—Jesus didn't let them hinder him. Why should you?"

"But these are challenging times. Wouldn't I be playing it safe in a comfortable position like that?"

"Don't worry. The times will find you out wherever you are!"

At their convention in Chicago, with a huge portrait of Broderick, framed in black crepe, looking down from the wall, the Republicans nominated a dark horse, Abraham Lincoln, over the highly favored Senator Seward. "Why shouldn't Broderick have been watching?" Gillem asked his readers. "His spirit lives. And he was a Republican in all but name." And Gillem added sardonically: "For the first and probably last time a dead Democrat was a driving force in a live Republican convention."

A few weeks later in Sacramento Mornay met with Leland Stanford, a wholesale grocer, the Crocker brothers, Charles and Edwin, dry goods merchants, and other leaders of the new Republican Party to try and win California for Lincoln. "I'm still lukewarm about the Railsplitter," Mornay wrote David. "His attitude toward slavery is too moderate. He says he'll permit it in states where it exists. That's dodging the issue." But Mornay was favorably impressed by his Sacramento colleagues. "They're strongly anti-slavery. We're going to organize a statewide network of Wide Awake Marching Clubs such as are being formed all over the nation. Every member will pledge to vote the party ticket, drill, march in all parades, carry a torch of freedom, wear a uniform consisting of a glazed cap and cape." And he concluded: "We must win California. If we can defeat The Chivalry here, we can defeat them anywhere!"

At the National Democratic Convention at Charleston, South Carolina, hotbed of Secession, the party's split was formalized when pro-slavery delegates nominated John C. Breckinridge of Kentucky—already Vice President under Buchanan—as their Presidential candidate. Whereupon anti-slavery delegates walked out and later nominated Senator Douglas of Illinois as theirs. David recalled his conversation with the "Little Giant" at Gwin's ball.

"He'd beat Lincoln if he had a united party behind him," he told Gillem, "just as he beat him for the Senate."

"But he doesn't have a united party," Gillem replied and predicted Lincoln's victory on mathematical grounds. "He has four candidates against him: Breckinridge and the Secessionists, Douglas and the Regulars, Bell of the Constitutional Union Party who won't hurt him much but will the other two; and for good measure General Sam Houston of Texas, the independent candidate, who won't hurt anybody." Lincoln wouldn't get a majority of the popular vote but would carry enough states to win in the Electoral College, Gillem predicted. "Still, I don't see how he can carry California, or Oregon, and they may make a crucial difference in many ways if secession or war follow, as you may be sure they will!"

Then Gillem digressed into one of his humorous asides. "I was out among the literati the other evening, at the home of the Frémonts no less, Mrs. F. being quite a patroness of the art, one more of those strong-minded women married to, in this case anyway, a less than impressive husband." Jessie Benton Frémont had praised his article on "The New Politics" in the current issue of *The Golden Era,* "our West Coast *Atlantic Monthly* as she enthusiastically terms it. Young Harte who works for me and has literary ambitions* was present too, basking in her charming encouragement," wrote Gillem. "But her spouse is another matter. I find him ungenerous, weak and vain and wonder how he ever found his way through Western wilds to become our famous Pathfinder. I suspect it was Carson who led him, rather than vice versa, and thank God he didn't find his way to the White House. He'd have bungled the job frightfully, I fear. Even such eminence as he enjoys now seems to go to his head. . . . By contrast Emperor Norton† came into my office yesterday and demanded his usual tribute without any fanfare. His uniform and epaulettes have faded a bit since you saw them. Nevertheless I gave him a cigar and a gold piece. Then he spoke of his plans to make me Governor of the Sierra Nevadas. I accepted gratefully. Crazy as he is, I think I'd rather have him ruling us than either Chivalry or Shovelry. At least he's harmless. And his graft is honest."

On the day after commencement, July 1, David was ordained by the Right Reverend William Meade, Bishop of Virginia. Mornay and Martha were not present nor was Lucinda Wright. Mornay wrote disappointedly that Lucy's health had deteriorated so rapidly, despite all Bert Lancaster could do, that Martha was

---

*Bret Harte became a noted author
†a deranged eccentric, generally beloved

obliged to assume virtual management of the Rescue Mission. "I'm tempted to come on alone but am in the thick of the fray to elect Lincoln and hesitate to leave the battlefront at this crucial moment. Consequently my thoughts and Martha's must speak for us. Bless you and keep you. Remember: this is your place eventually!" And having shed tears privately, Martha added a cheerful postscript: "Dear Reverend: I hope this finds you well. We're so proud of you. But remember not to become too pompous!"

Lucinda wrote deploring her lack of strength but offering congratulations "on your triumphal progress toward that shining goal you and dear Caleb envisioned. I'm sure he would be as happy as I. You are the son we always wanted." And she added how proud she was too of "the brave Pony Express lads who will carry this to you. They've taken an oath not to use profane language or drink intoxicating liquor. Isn't that wonderful? And they have reduced the time this will take to reach you to a mere thirteen days. What can we expect next?"

David felt it perhaps best that he should be taking this decisive step by himself. With ordination his financial dependence on Lucinda—and his emotional reliance on Mornay—must end. "My debt to you and Caleb," he wrote her, "continues. I consider you my parents in a life to which I've newly been born."

A week later he began his ministry. He found the venerable red-brick Church of Saint Matthew at the corner of York and Elm in the historic heart of Philadelphia in deplorable condition. Few people attended. The roof leaked. Half the pews were unrented. Since most of the church's revenues came from pew rent, expenses exceeded income. There was a debt of $8,000. Repayment would depend largely on his ability to attract new members. On the positive side, the favored form of worship was the simple one he preferred—"low church"—no cross or candlesticks on altar, no choir wearing vestments. Lippincott, Stroud and other vestry members were supportive, but David saw his work was cut out for him from the moment of that first meeting.

He chose as subject for his maiden sermon the following Sunday that powerful passage from Psalms 118:24: "This is the day which the Lord hath made. Let us rejoice and be glad in it." And as if the Lord were listening the day was a perfect summer one, a refreshing breeze blowing in the open door under the ancient white-trunked plane trees from the nearby Delaware River, and the church nearly full. Abandoning his laboriously prepared text, setting aside also his fears and apprehensions and soaring ambitions, he spoke on impulse from the heart, letting the words flow as they might. "This is the first day of our lives together, of our new beginning in the name of Him who made that first day, this day, and all days to come." As he saw their animated faces turned up to his, he realized in a flash of grace it was not he but the power speaking through him that was affecting them. And afterward he could tell by the warmth of their greetings that he'd done well, and felt relieved and grateful and more than ever determined to follow the course he had set for himself.

# Chapter Sixty

On April 10, 1860, Clara was a hundred years old but she'd insisted there be no celebration. "Why celebrate? What is so unusual about the fact that we grow older the longer we live?"

Instead she rose before dawn and, leaving María Ignácia to rouse the household for morning prayer in the courtyard, went alone across the river to the hollow in the gently rounded green hills where her mother had been gathering brodeia bulbs that morning when she'd been born a century ago. Standing there on that same ground—among those same yellow violets and white milkmaids and lavender cyclamen and blue brodeias—she felt the strength of the earth flow into her.

Looking back through time she saw the long vanished village of her childhood which stood where the hacienda did now—saw the unbroken web of life existing then, so perfect in its completeness, its unity with its surroundings. Remembered the coming of the conquistadors and padres, her Antonio among them, to be welcomed as gods and brothers. Saw again the promise of that moment of first contact with all its glorious possibilities. Saw all fade into suspicion, hatred, violence, bloodshed, oppression, until she alone remained, it seemed, to carry on. She felt like crying out with a great voice of anguish and protest at recollection of the fatal diseases which destroyed her people, the broken treaties, the continual betrayals, the destruction, the death. And now what? Francisco lost to her or dead or an adversary? Pacifico impotent? Sally barren? Herself hopelessly in debt to Sedley? And must she live another hundred years before that person O'Hara predicted should come and be the true heir of her spirit if not her flesh?

Facing eastward as her mother had taught her, raising arms high and wide she thrust her fingers up into the sky to grasp all possible light, while as their people had done for immemorial time she prayed aloud:

> "Great Dawn, Breath of the Sun,
> You bring light to the World,
> You bring light to the World,
> You bring light to the World,
> May we prove worthy!"

Later it seemed that moment was when she heard the music, though how long actually passed while she stood in exaltation she could not be sure. Turning, looking back across the river, she saw the gay processions coming up the valley, or winding in across the hills, on horseback, in oxcarts, violins and guitars playing as in olden times when rancheros visited one another in the spring; for despite her wishes invitations had gone out secretly from Pacifico and Sally, and friends and neighbors were coming from far and near.

Feeling quite overwhelmed by good fortune, ashamed of her dark thoughts, she began to move toward the music, slowly, deliberately relishing each step as she proceeded among the flowers—*the same as were here when I was born, she thought, yet not the same, and so it will be forever long after I am gone.*

She came to the river, to the very pool where she'd bathed daily with her companions as a girl, and there she undressed as if directed and immersed herself once more in the water which was more than a river—which was the Tears of the Sun shed for the benefit of mankind, flowing from the Heart of the World, where the side of the Sacred Mountain had been riven by a mighty lightning bolt ages ago.

As she stood naked in the sun on the sandy bank, feeling purified and renewed, she thought tenderly of Antonio making love to her their first time on such a bank as this by this same stream, and their first complete joy in each other, sacred and everlasting. She thought of him as alive and watching her from his resting place under the oak, atop the high rounded hill above their river.

Putting on her Mother Hubbard she ascended the path as she'd done so often; and the people of the Indianada, her people, all that was left of them, old Tilhini at their head, came to greet her

murmuring a low chant of welcome and happiness. True they
were a motley crowd, some in white man's clothes, some half
naked. But they were the Ancient Web, all that was left of it. She
heard the almost forgotten music of a sacred deerbone flute. While
she and Tilhini were alive that web might hold. "Señora!" or
"Tía Clara!" they greeted her. And a pang of regret went through
her that no one again, as long as she lived, except perhaps Tilhini,
would ever remember her as the girl Lospe, the flower, slim
daughter of the People of the Land and the Sea. His knowing
look seemed to say he understood.

He was wearing his traditional feathered skirt and headdress as
astrologer-priest. There were seven strands of shellbeads around
his neck. His upper body was painted with the red and white
stripes of their long vanished village, and in his right hand he
carried a sprig of feathery green sage and in the left his hollow-
reed cane, his staff of office, with its tuft of feathers representing
Sky Power, and its little bag made from a deer's scrotum containing his magic charms. He handed her the life-enhancing sage.
Others placed garlands around her neck, decked her hair with blue
fiesta flowers, presented traditional gifts of sweetcakes made of
seeds and wild berries and honeydew. And as she passed on
through them, her heart full, they closed behind her, continuing
their chant of jubilation, following her up the slope toward the
house.

Waiting on the verandah among the others, watching her come
slowly up the hill at the head of her people, O'Hara marveled at
her radiant vitality. And as the two groups met and merged—she
the element between, red hair decked with blue flowers gleaming
in the sunlight—she assumed in his mind her true significance.

Victoria exclaimed: "How picturesque! How romantic!" She
and Sedley were standing with Pacifico and Sally, Benito and
Anita, and the other guests. Clara thought her beautiful—beautiful
and hard and over-effusive. Sedley too seemed different than she
had expected, more remote. But all of them were part of that New
Web she and Antonio had helped create. Yes, and they were
waiting joyously for her in the house he and she had built. And
she felt grateful for all this too. Yet with her new clarity of per-
ception saw what would follow—beyond the loving greetings and
the music and the laughter and food and drink—as if it had already happened.

After the festivities were over and O'Hara given her his blessing and she hers to Pacifico and Sally, and to the others including Abe and Iphy, there came that moment when she must be alone with Sedley and his proud new wife. "You two are the greatest surprise of all!" She embraced them again with the traditional words: "My house is your house!"

Struck by the irony of her statement, wondering if she suspected his hidden purpose, Sedley released her hand and lowered his voice. "Any word of Francisco?"

"None."

Vicky gushed: "Oh, but I think it's so *romantic*—the way he marked Eliot's arm with his stone knife! It's like something out of a story book!"

To change an unpleasant subject and silence this silly haughty girl, so effusively possessive, and because she could not anyway resist the inclination to do so, Clara asked Sedley the status of her claim to the ranch.

"We're taking it to the Circuit Court of Appeals."

"How long will it be there?"

"Goodness knows."

"But," she broke out impatiently, "I cannot go on being indebted to you forever in this way!"

"It's no trouble to me, Aunt Clara, as I've said many times. But if it will make you feel any better you can give me a promissory note. I'll have the ranch as security, won't I?" he bantered.

A terrible misgiving went through her. Are the flowers treacherous? she asked herself. Is the grass hypocritical? For a moment she wished herself back across the river where she'd been born. But she must fight on. Somehow the ongoing flesh and spirit, the ongoing earth, must prevail, must! "Of course," she assented, seeing no other choice.

After Sedley and Victoria retired to Francisco's old room and she to hers, María Ignácia followed and gently closing the door informed her in a portentous whisper: "Señora, I have something to show!" And from under the bed she drew a short red-shafted arrow with a wooden point such as a boy might use to kill small game.

Clara exclaimed, examining it: "Where did you find this?"

"On the Wisdom Stone, at dawn." María's face was grave, her eyes wide.

But Clara broke into a smile of joy. For the arrow was crafted in the manner of her people and was exactly the kind Francisco

used as a youngster when she and Antonio insisted Tilhini teach
him the Indian Way.

"Was no one seen?"

"No one."

"Nobody heard?"

María shook her head. Clara felt proud the intruder had slipped
in and out skillfully. "It is Francisco's message," she said serenely. "His birthday present to me."

"But what does it mean, Señora?"

"It means he has a son."

María gasped. Clara lifted her finger to her lips. Hidden in the
wilderness was a little one who might someday come and be her
true heir. And the mystery and majesty and unpredictability of
life swept over her like a great blessing.

As they lay together in the darkness under the silk canopy of
Francisco's bed, Vicky urged: "Why can't we have it now? I
love it! I could bring Barbary down and ride him here!"

"What about Fair View?" he teased. The mansion he'd built
for her on their estate in the foothills down the Peninsula overlooking the Bay was like her home at Stanhope's Bend: three
magnificent stories gleaming white, a palace complete with col-
umned portico and classical Grecian pediment. But she was already tired of it.

"It's so tame! This is so wild, so exciting! When can we
have it?"

"That depends," he temporized.

"Depends? What do you really have up your sleeve?"

"Do you want me to show my cards before I play them?"

"She suspects you, I can tell."

"But she'll never guess the truth."

"Why?"

"Because it's so far fetched."

"From her viewpoint or yours?"

"Both!" he replied with an enigmatic chuckle. "Both. And
yours too!"

# Chapter Sixty-one

In October, just as Gillem's gloomy predictions about Lincoln's chances in California seemed about to come true, Ned Baker returned in triumph to San Francisco.

Since Broderick's death he'd become the city's favorite son. But he'd left it abruptly early in February for the year-old state of Oregon. "There in a matter of months," as Gillem reminded his readers, "by reason of extraordinary energy and brilliant eloquence, he became the first Republican Senator from the Pacific Coast, miraculously defeating the entrenched forces of Oregon's powerful Democratic Senator Joseph L. Lane, who is now candidate for Vice President on the Democratic pro-slavery ticket."

Baker was on his way to Washington to assume his Senate seat. When his ship, the *Brother Jonathan*, entered Golden Gate a salute of a hundred guns greeted him from Fort Point* and a huge crowd gathered at the Broadway Wharf. "Not a moment too soon," Mornay wrote David. Lincoln's campaign was going badly indeed. Mornay was doing all he could among growers, laborers, and small business people; and Mary Louise had contributed substantially to subsidizing the spiffy new uniforms of the Wide Awakes and to the electioneering pamphlets Gillem was printing. But enthusiasm for the candidate was noticeably lacking. "Many like me would have preferred Seward, our acknowledged leader," Mornay wrote. "He's more Abolitionist than Lincoln." Furthermore the Republicans had never won a major election in

*on the southern promontory of the Gate

California, were vastly outnumbered by Democrats, and The Chivalry was still in command. "They desperately want this state, and Oregon," Mornay went on. "With them in hand, they are confident that neighboring Washington, Utah, and New Mexico Territories* will follow and their long dreamed of Southern Empire extend from coast to coast."

At this crucial moment the return of the victorious Baker was a godsend. In a series of fiery speeches he began to turn the tide. These culminated in a momentous one Friday, October 26, at the huge American Theater at the corner of Sansome and Halleck, "perhaps the most important gathering ever held on the Pacific Coast," Mornay declared presciently, "for on its outcome may hinge the future of State and Union." Stores closed early. By mid-afternoon people were collecting outside the theater's doors. "When they opened the interior was instantly filled with about four thousand of us. So dense was the throng, so tightly packed, that several who fainted were passed outside over the heads of others."

Baker received a standing ovation when he appeared on stage, erect, graceful, charged with vitality. Because of his prematurely gray hair he was familiarly greeted as "the Gray Eagle!" His resonant voice, varying between baritone and tenor, was extraordinarily compelling. "Is there one land which sympathizes with the attempt to govern this country for the purpose of slavery?" he demanded. "Do you? Does England? Does Russia? Does Mexico? Why, one of the most affecting incidents I know in connection with the recent war occurred when the Mexican Commissioners met our American Commissioners to determine the treaty of peace. They said in effect: 'Sirs, we are a conquered people. You can prescribe your own terms. But we implore you, in the name of humanity and liberty, do not force slavery upon us!' " And then he began to use that eloquence so effective in defense of Hattie. "We live in a day of light. We live in an advancing generation. We live in the presence of the whole world. The prayers and tears and hopes and sighs of all good men are with us." Applause began to interrupt him. "I am not ashamed of Freedom. I know her power. I glory in her strength. I will walk beneath her banner." It was what they wanted to hear. "I have seen her on a hundred fields of battle struck down, seen her

*western Utah Territory later became Nevada; western New Mexico became Arizona

friends fly from her, seen her foes gather 'round her, have seen them bind her to the stake. But when they turned to exult, I have seen her meet them face to face, clad in complete steel, and brandishing in her strong right hand a flaming sword red with insufferable light!'' And when Baker, graceful in gesture as in speech, came to the mention of the sword, he—a veteran of two wars—appeared to draw his weapon, so that his last words were spoken with arms uplifted, ''and we excited thousands sprang to our feet,'' wrote Mornay, ''pent-up enthusiasm released.''

Cheer after cheer echoed through the theater. Even the reporters were swept up in the storm of feeling and left their tables to join in the frenzied multitude, ''and young Bret Harte, who works for Gillem, leaped upon the stage and frantically waved the American flag.''

The spontaneous demonstration lasted fifteen minutes while Baker stood motionless. When silence fell he spoke in a tone which thrilled Mornay like an electric current. ''I take courage! The genius of the American people will at last lead her sons to freedom!''

''So moved were we,'' Mornay continued, ''that after he withdrew we remained cheering, shouting, and singing for the better part of an hour, and even then were reluctant to leave, and when we did, Harte led us in a procession up Kearny Street still waving the flag.''

Overnight the speech was set in type. Next morning's newspaper headlined it and steamers and stagecoaches began carrying pamphlets containing it to all parts of the state. In many places, crowds assembled to hear it read. A few days later Lincoln received a plurality of 742 votes in California, less than 300 in Oregon. ''Baker saved the Pacific Coast, perhaps the entire Far West, for Lincoln and the Union,'' Mornay concluded, while Gillem editorialized: ''Broderick has indeed risen from his grave. The power of The Chivalry has been broken at last, as completely as it was triumphant only a year ago.''

After receiving a minority of the popular vote, as Gillem predicted, 1.8 million compared to 2.8 cast for his opponents, Lincoln won the Presidency in the Electoral College. No one had voted for him in ten Southern states. The populous Northern states made the difference. He was not only a minority but a sectional President. The news flashed west by telegraph to the end of the line being built across the plains from Saint Joseph, Missouri. From there relays of ponies, reaching speeds as high as twenty-five miles an hour, carried it in a record seven and a half days to Fort Churchill, Utah Territory,* at the foot of the newly discovered, fabulously rich silver deposit known as the Comstock Lode. From there it flashed on by wire over the Sierra Nevadas to Sacramento and San Francisco.

"This is the New American Revolution," David exulted to Mornay, "that Broderick foresaw. At last the people are taking their government into their own hands!" Mornay replied: "Baker has been in close touch with Lincoln. They are old friends, as you know. Ned is sure to have strong influence at the White House. And through him, so may we."

Stanhope declared grimly: "The die is cast. This means Secession and probably war. All thought of dividing California in two is useless since it requires approval of Congress and Congress is at loggerheads. Our best bet now is to transform her into a Pacific Republic—ostensibly neutral—and move her gradually into the Southern fold, much as independent Texas once joined the national one." Sedley agreed. So did Terry and others. But Sedley continued to hedge his bets. After the great speech he'd been among the first to congratulate Baker. "I've done business with Republicans and will continue to," he told Stanhope now. "It will give us invaluable insight into what the other side is thinking."

Many Southern states had threatened to secede from the Union if Lincoln won. On December 20, South Carolina did so and laid siege to the Government forts in Charleston Harbor. The nation seemed in process of dissolution.

*in later Nevada

# Chapter Sixty-two

David lived through these dramatic days in a strange state of unreality. His maiden sermon had been acclaimed by the press.* He was being adulated by his parishioners. Saint Matthew's was filled to overflowing every Sunday as his reputation grew. Its debt was being paid off. Stroud's handsome daughter Phyllis was obviously in love with him and her mother was encouraging the match. And offers had come from parishes as far away as Cincinnati and New York as his fame spread. In this age of great preachers, Beecher, Bushnell, Phillips Brooks, Edward Everett Hale, Starr King, he was taking his place like a rising star. His salary was increased to fifteen hundred dollars per annum. But he felt all of it unreal compared to what was happening in the nation around him. Yet if he mentioned Secession or Abolition he saw eyes glaze or frowns appear. "We don't want to break up the Union," Stroud explained, apparently not realizing it was breaking up anyway.

Impatiently David sought out the Negro leader William Still at the anti-slavery headquarters at 107 North 5th Street. Reuben had told him of Still. Still had encouraged Reuben to go West for greater opportunity. And he had helped Mary Louise and Sam to freedom. "Apathy isn't the only problem here," he declared. "This city of brotherly love is also full of hate. There was a bloody interracial riot not long ago. And no black person can ride

*which customarily reported sermons

a horse car or omnibus." Still was helping a steady stream of fugitives escape to Canada.

Fuming inwardly, David went to see the famed Abolitionist and woman's rights leader Lucretia Mott at her home in the suburbs. Mott, a devout Quaker, told him: "I have read thy sermons. Thee art gifted with the True Vision."

"I wish I'd lived a lifetime of service to that vision as you have," David responded. "What is to happen next?"

Mott was helping fugitive slaves escape to freedom. "We must continue to act as God directs."

"Even if it means taking up arms?"

"There may have to be fighting Quakers."

Moved by restlessness David went to Washington City the day after Christmas. Sermonizing suddenly seemed idle. He wanted action. Mornay's letter telling of Baker's and Lincoln's incredible triumphs in Oregon and California was burning in his mind. He wanted to hear from Baker the truth of what was happening, then decide what course to take.

"Just in time!" Baker's warm greeting was also a challenge. "I'm leaving for Illinois!" Lincoln had summoned him secretly. "Why not come along?"

David telegraphed Lippincott he would be absent on important personal matters a few days and he and Baker boarded the train for the West. "We'll stay with my stepdaughter Kit. She lives near the Lincolns in Springfield," Baker explained.

As they rolled westward David felt himself returning home. He remembered his roots in Iowa. For the first time California receded in his imagination as the mighty heartland gripped him with its endless miles of fertile earth, so solid, so enduring, carrying him back to childhood memories of a lost bliss. They were relaxing in Katherine Matheny's parlor when he happened to glance out the window and see a tall gaunt man put one leg over the garden gate, then the other. That fellow is taking giant strides, he thought. Next moment Abraham Lincoln stood unannounced in the room. "Hullo, Baker!" Lincoln's high-pitched voice contrasted to his offhand masculine manner. "It's been ten years!" They embraced, then held each other at arm's length for affectionate inspection. "I'd rather have had you elected Senator than any man alive!" Lincoln continued.

"Mr. President," Baker replied with formality, "I was about to come and call on *you!*"

"None of that 'Mr. President,' Ned!" Lincoln warned good humoredly. "Or I'll start calling you Colonel!" He greeted Kit, then turned to David. "Who have we here?"

"He was a close friend of Broderick," Baker explained. "He heard Broderick speak of the New American Revolution that was coming, bringing liberty and justice for all." And Baker told of David's work in the San Francisco Underground.

Lincoln nodded approvingly. "Yes, this is a revolution. Let's hope we can achieve it without bloodshed." Then changing to humorous tone: "Another Californian? You know, I almost became one myself. Ned, here, tempted me sorely with that clever tongue of his. Just one thing bothered me."

"What was that, sir?" David couldn't help smiling at Lincoln's droll manner.

"If it was so good, why didn't he keep it all for himself? Bless your Golden State! I may retire there some day!"

"I hope you will!"

David found himself liking the President-elect tremendously. A great humanity seemed to emanate straight from his being, forthright as his handshake and homey words. But David was surprised to find him clean shaven like The Chivalry rather than bearded like Broderick and others of The Shovelry. Lincoln was adding with sudden gravity: "Broderick, poor fellow, I followed his career closely. He was courageous, far-seeing and a martyr."

"Yes, a martyr resurrected in your California victory," Baker broke in. "He was the silent voter who never went to the polls."

Lincoln turned to Baker. "Ned, I sent for you because I wanted to hear what was happening on the Pacific Coast and knew you would tell me the truth." There and later in Lincoln's parlor, while David listened, Baker told. "They hold almost all the positions of power. We hold almost none. Federal office holders—postmasters, mail carriers, customs officials, marshals, judges, and a host of underlings—are with few exceptions sympathetic to the South. Likewise much of the Legislature. Likewise Governor Downey. Likewise—even more decidedly, as you well know—our United States Senators and Congressmen. And at this moment—with the crisis rising—the regular army with its control of fortifications, garrisons, munitions of war is being placed in the hands of General Albert Sidney Johnston, an officer of Southern origins and sympathies."

"Is Johnston taking charge with Scott's* approval?"

"We can't be sure. Old Fuss and Feathers is as bad as Buchanan. Blows this way and that from day to day. Much as I admire him, the bilious old barrel weighs nearly three hundred pounds, and his head's not always clear."

"And what about Buchanan?"

"Hopeless. The Southrons have him firmly in hand. Hammond of South Carolina and Crittenden of Kentucky, Vice-President Breckinridge, and Mississippi's Jefferson Davis and Albert Brown—plus Mason and Hunter of Virginia, and that Georgia millionaire Cobb†—run the country."

"What about Gwin?"

"Still a major influence, though a Lame Duck. He may be behind Johnston's appointment. He's on record as saying that if the Southern states go out of the Union, California will be found with the South."

"Can we hold the coast if the fur starts to fly?"

"I think so. But we must act promptly and firmly. Floyd‡ has secretly shipped California 50,000 stand of arms, besides the 135,000 he's sent to Southern states over and above regular quotas. But Captain Hancock in command at Los Angeles is a staunch Unionist. And little Phil Sheridan in Washington Territory can be counted on. But I recommend that Johnston be replaced a soon as practicable."

Lincoln turned to David. "What about Philadelphia?"

"Loyal but grievously apathetic. The only people I see display deep conviction are Abolitionists and Quakers." He told of his meetings with Still and Mott.

"I shall remember what you say," Lincoln replied thoughtfully, "when I speak in Philadelphia on my way to the capital."

"Let me interpose the gravest thing of all I've come to tell you," Baker broke in.

"What is that, Ned?"

"There are those who've sworn you'll never sleep in the White House."

"What do you mean?"

"There is a conspiracy afoot to kill you. It is widespread. At its heart is a villainous secret society called The Knights of the

---

*General Winfield Scott, Mexican War hero, now head of the U.S. Army
†Howell Cobb, Secretary of the Treasury
‡Secretary of War John B. Floyd, later a Confederate general

Golden Circle. It is well financed and committed to your destruction.''

Lincoln shook his head dubiously. "That's hard to believe. My attitudes, my pronouncements toward the South have been conciliatory. My goal is to preserve the Union, Ned, not to abolish slavery. Though I'm with you Abolitionists in spirit, I can't go along publicly yet. The country isn't ready.''

"The people I'm talking about don't believe that," replied Baker passionately. "They see you as the head of a monstrous conspiracy aimed at destroying their way of life. They are the people who did for Broderick and now wish to do for you. They are even planning to seize Washington City. You must act promptly, Mr. President, or you may have no capital to be inaugurated in!''

"What do you recommend?''

"Let me tell General Scott to strengthen the city's defenses.''

Lincoln's eyes twinkled again. "I remember you presented him with Santa Anna's wooden leg after you captured it during the battle for Mexico City.''

"Yes, Scott and I are on good terms," Baker conceded. "And he needs the right words in his ear just now. May I put them there?''

"You do whatever you think is best for the country, Ned. Tell him I said so.''

They talked for the better part of two days. "I'd like to bring Stanton into my cabinet as Secretary of War," Lincoln remarked at one point. "He's strongly Unionist. And he has brains and energy. I know. He whipped me in court once.''

"Yes," Baker agreed, "and he performed admirably for the Government in that New Almadén Mine matter—even if he didn't bring Gwin and Sedley to justice.''

"Sedley?''

"A key to California. The man behind the scenes.''

"Where do his sympathies lie?''

"Wherever they most profit him." Baker described the cabal of Sedley, Stanhope, Terry, Gwin. "And now we may add Johnston.''

But Lincoln demurred. "It's hard to believe that such a distinguished soldier as Johnston could prove a traitor.''

"Don't be surprised. Meanwhile consider the risk. If they take Oregon and California, in all probability the adjoining territories will go too. But above all they want California's gold to pay for the war they're sure is coming.''

"Wouldn't the silver of the Comstock Lode help?" Lincoln chuckled.

"It sure would!"

Later in Lincoln's parlor where the atmosphere created by the primly pretentious furnishings seemed to David incongruous, they were discussing Oregon where Southern sympathy was strong. "If you'd accepted governorship of Oregon Territory years ago, as I urged, we'd have no problem there now," Baker jested.

Lincoln nodded in mock admission. "I talked it over with my wife, Ned. She wasn't keen on it."

"Now, Father, don't you blame me!" Mary Todd Lincoln's fussily insistent voice came from the hall where she'd been passing. "It was your decision!" For a moment she stood in the doorway, a stoutish rather forbidding woman, surveying them with disapproval as if they were engaged in some nefarious activity.

Lincoln winked at the other two. "A woman has two fundamental prerogatives: to change her mind and to change the facts."

"Oh, fiddlesticks!" she retorted and swirled away. Lincoln grinned, yet seemed to defer to her. Their young son Tad burst breathlessly into the room oblivious to all but his father. "Willie's hogging the swing!" Willie followed with a similar accusation. Edward, named after Baker, had died several years before. Lincoln listened to both sides gravely. "You two work something out." He did not talk down but spoke as if they were adults. "I'll be along after a bit." David marveled at his patience and quiet wisdom. Life poured in upon him and he accepted it.

Lincoln switched back to Stanton. "He joins Buchanan's cabinet today as Attorney General. Will that make a difference?"

Baker shook his head. "Just a sop to appease the North until your inauguration, while they continue trying to steal the country out from under us."

"I was thinking about that too. But I suppose our most pressing consideration is Major Anderson."

Major Robert Anderson, commanding Federal defenses of Charleston harbor, had moved his small garrison from an exposed position at Fort Moultrie to a new brick-and-mortar stronghold, Fort Sumter, near the harbor's center. Seceded South Carolina was protesting this as a hostile act. Her militia was ready to

ire on Anderson and his men. "A misstep by either side can
mean war."

Again Baker urged the recall of General Johnston from California.

But Lincoln would not agree. "After all he has no power to
recall him," Baker replied when David asked later on their way
home. "He won't be President until March 4." Until then the
fate of the nation would be in Buchanan's vacillating hands. "Our
problem is simple," Baker concluded grimly. "How to preserve
the United States during the next two months."

Stanhope was in New Orleans in November and in Washington
in December, conferring with the fiery Yancey, Rhett and Ruffin
as he went, and finally with Davis, pushing his "Western Strategy" which Davis favored, though Davis had not publicly es-
poused Secession until now and still opposed war. Stanhope
secretly contacted leaders of the Knights of the Golden Circle and
encouraged the plot to assassinate Lincoln as the President-elect
passed through Baltimore on his way to Washington City to be
inaugurated.

# Chapter Sixty-three

Sedley said to Mary Louise: "Randolph's from Virginia. Can you give us some Virginia cooking?"

"I'll give you a Jefferson Dinner."

Since returning to San Francisco she'd established herself in a fine house on Clay Street with Sedley as silent partner. He asked no questions as to her absence; she none as to his conduct during it. It was part of their established code regarding matters outside their areas of mutual interest. Victoria, the Stanhopes, might have his name and prestigious kinship but not his heart. He might appear to live in their great mansions, but really he lived in hers, a place where he could get away in privacy and be himself. The premises were ideal for discreet suppers, luxuriously but tastefully furnished in latest fashion; and her girls, the newest weapon in her varied arsenal, were of similar elegance, carefully chosen, charming companions for a private party or gala soiree attended by prominent citizens—or, keeping to their rooms, not seen at all. She ruled them with a strict but reasonable hand. Only the evening before, her latest asset—glamorous strawberry blonde Dolly acquired on the wharf as she disembarked—had complained of being too disciplined. Mary Louise responded bluntly: "What kick you got coming? I feed you, don't I? Clothe you, don't I? You live better here than ever before in your life. And when the right time comes I'll find you a rich husband. You want to go back to the slums of Boston?" After thinking it over, Dolly decided she had no kick coming.

The house was staffed by trustworthy Negroes, headed by faith-

ul Samson. And with Hattie settled securely with Reuben and
heir young Charles, Mary Louise continued to focus her energies
on her own advancement and that of her people. To foster their
economic improvement she joined with leading black businessmen in organizing the California Savings and Loan Association,
along lines Sedley advised, to raise $100,000 for land speculation
which he helped invest; while her status as Voodoo priestess continued to give her great influence among less sophisticated elements of the black community. She also battled for the right of
blacks to give testimony in court and spoke fearlessly of a day
when they might take up arms to free their enslaved brethren as
some had wanted to do at the time of John Brown's abortive
attempt at Harper's Ferry. In these and other ways Mary Louise
assumed what would become her legendary status.

Yet her basic strategy remained unchanged: contacts with eminent persons resulting in friendships or information which could
yield her power, and thus she looked forward to the coming occasion, when Sedley's guest would be the eccentric Edmund Randolph, scion of an old Virginia family, a leading member of The
Chivalry, East and West.

When Sedley added that George Stanhope would be coming
too, she concealed her exultation. Again fate was placing him in
her hands. There was little chance of her old enemy recognizing
her by candlelight, so greatly was she changed thanks to years,
face powder, straightened hair, new surroundings. For good measure, an application of belladonna would enlarge the pupil of her
right eye to match that of her left. Therefore on the evening of
Friday, January 25, 1861, wearing her lavender taffeta with high
lace collar and two-flounce skirt, she greeted her guests with gracious confidence and could immediately tell from their expres-
sions that her charms were working and Stanhope had no idea
who she truly was, though there came an awkward moment when
he commented admiringly: "You remind me of someone but I
can't quite place you."

"Someone nice, I hope!" She passed it off as nothing, while
the others chaffed him for using an old roué's technique.

After serving juleps made with Kentucky bourbon she tactfully
withdrew. "To work her magic," Sedley explained. Later while
Samson wearing white gloves served the Virginia ham with corn
pudding and patty pan squash, cold jellied beef, damson plum
preserve, beaten biscuits and Jerusalem artichokes, white and red
wine and Dom Pérignon champagne, she overheard Randolph ex-

claiming tipsily: "General Johnston can take this state out of the Union!" A self-proclaimed Unionist, Randolph was harboring sentiments which would lead him to declare publicly Lincoln should be assassinated.

"Hush," Stanhope cautioned. He'd intended to inform them fully regarding his Eastern trip and enlist Randolph's support for his "Western Strategy," but decided Randolph was too deeply in his cups and the surroundings insufficiently private.

"Why?" ranted Randolph. "Getting cold feet?"

Glancing through a crack in the door, Mary Louise saw Stanhope's back and imagined how a pinch of arsenic in his pudding might affect it. But she did not dare interfere with that curse she'd placed on him, knowing fate must work its way in good time. Inexorably the great serpent Damballah who sits at the feet of God was at this moment entwining its coils about Stanhope. Meanwhile he might be of much use to her. Therefore she listened carefully as he muttered something inaudible, gesturing with his head in her direction.

"The cook?" Randolph raved. "By God, she's the best I ever tasted. Let's get her in here!" And when Mary Louise appeared in answer to Sedley's summons, Randolph declared: "Drat me lady, this is the best Jefferson Dinner I ever put tongue to. Come cook for me. I'll pay you any wage you ask!"

"Don't be greedy, Randolph," Sedley cautioned affably. "We all want our share of her. What about it, George?"

"I sure want mine." Stanhope eyed her lasciviously in a way that made her hot with anger but she controlled herself rigidly behind a demure smile. "I thank you, gentlemen, for your gallant courtesies. If I have served you well, I am rewarded."

Thereafter the evening changed course. As Randolph paired off with exotic dark-eyed Maud, Stanhope with gorgeous Dolly, herself with Sedley, she heard Stanhope mutter: "You're a sly dog, Eliot—always taking the cream!"

But Mary Louise was not able to extract all she wanted from her lover that night, and hearing a few days later that Randolph was sick abed she alerted his nurse Cato, a member of her Black Grapevine, and when Cato overheard Randolph whispering with Stanhope he reported it to Mary Louise who added it to what she herself had learned and passed it all to Mornay, who sent it by Pony Express* to Baker in Washington. "General Johnston will

*Mornay's records show it cost him $2 per half ounce

be asked to proclaim neutrality should war break out, and serve notice that troops under his command here would not be used against either North or South. This may receive much public backing since there are already a number of influential persons who urge neutralism. It would avoid formal Secession and leave us technically in the Union, thus placating many Unionists, until such time as we can feasibly be attached to the South. A Pacific Republic is also favorably spoken of.'' And Mornay concluded ominously: ''Though Johnston commands only a handful of troops, he controls large supplies of arms and ammunition. And he could augment his forces with members of the militia and others sympathetic to the Southern cause, of which there are many. An outright coup d'état is a real possibility. Most appalling of all: Lincoln will be assassinated before he reaches Washington City.''

Baker was inclined to agree with Mornay's views, since they confirmed his own. ''Keep me apprised,'' he replied. ''We must know precisely what they are planning and when they intend to act.''


''It was strange how I became involved in their conspiracy,'' Gillem wrote David, ''yet perfectly reasonable under the circumstances. They were impressed by my leader* urging that the Union be preserved but not by force. Since I don't like the idea of you on the end of a musket, I took the position that if states want to secede they should be allowed to go, providing they go in peace. After all, the right of states to secede has been talked about for half a century. And such is the confusion of opinion about it here—with Sedley's *Tribune* and others trumpeting for it—that our Southern brethren hailed my statement with enthusiasm and sent young Harpending† to sound me out. Harpending is a Kentuckian like me—one reason they delegated him—an infant prodigy, not yet of age but a millionaire miner-speculator—a daring young firebrand ready to risk all for the cause of his beloved bluegrass state and mine. 'California is likely to be of prime importance in coming months,' he begins as we meet for drinks at the Bank Exchange. 'With San Francisco and its forts in Southern hands, for instance, the outward flow of gold on which the Northern cause must largely depend would cease.' See-

*editorial
†Asbury Harpending

ing how the wind is blowing, I decide to blow along and nod wisely. 'As San Francisco goes, so goes the state!' I trot out my best Southern accent and carry on a bit about Northern aggression and Southern grievance, which encourages him to confide: 'And then it would be easy to open overland connection with Texas through the mountains of New Mexico, would it not? And a great new empire would extend to these shores?'

" 'And then could we not travel all the way back to Kentucky on sympathetic soil, so to speak?'

" 'Precisely!' He orders up another round of punch. Before separating we agreed to meet at an address on Rincon Hill the following evening.

"As I approach I recognize the house as none other than Stanhope's mansion, formerly occupied by our late lamented Captain and Lucinda. A slippered Chinese who looked suspiciously like our trusty Wing Sing, took my card with a bow and presently I was admitted to that parlor you will recall, more sumptuous than ever now, where a number of prominent men were seated around a table, among them Sedley and of course Harpending, as well as that supreme jackass Edmund Randolph who proclaims privately that Lincoln ought to be assassinated while professing Union sympathies. No sign of Madam Stanhope or Beau or Victoria. I could tell at a glance what was coming.

" 'Sit down, sir, and be welcome!' Stanhope receives me with regal cordiality. 'You have been chosen to join us in an enterprise of great moment. I hope we can depend on you as a man of honor not to reveal what occurs here?'

"Giving my word I was bound, had it not been for my crossed fingers under the table. The old scoundrel continued, stern as death: 'Are you ready to risk life and fortune on the outcome of what we propose?'

"I feign greatest eagerness. 'Nothing could suit me better. Justice means Force as well as Virtue,' I add, quoting Napoleon. They lapped that up. We are incredibly naive, we Southrons. Offer us a secret society and we'll join it like boys playing Indian. Tap our romantic vein—give us some Napoleonic notions like Honor and Glory—and we are yours.

" 'Then will you take the oath of allegiance which binds us all?'

" 'I will.'

"So began my career as conspirator against the United States. Our organization is simplicity itself. We are not among Stanhope's Knights who are to rise at the proper time and join us. Nor among his assassins or Randolph's who want to murder Lincoln. No, we're a special group whose single purpose is to seize San Francisco for the South! Now get this: each of us is responsible for raising a fighting force of a hundred men—a little difficult for me among my scribblers and printers so I've offered to provide my legion in the form of words—*what* words these rascals never suspect! Yet they must be taken seriously. This state abounds with reckless characters, ex-Indian fighters, ex-filibusterers, Mexican War veterans and the like, eager to undertake any venture promising excitement and profit.

"Accordingly each of us, myself exempted, will select a trusty captain of known Southern sympathy, instruct him to gather a company of chosen men for whom equipment and pay will be provided, say nothing of the service intended yet imply it may be a filibustering expedition of some profitable sort. And these bands are at this moment gathering at various points around the Bay, ostensibly engaged in fishing, wood cutting and the like. Only Stanhope knows their locations.

"At a word from him 3,000 determined men will act. Only about 200 soldiers occupy Fort Point. There are less than 100 on Alcatraz Island.* Alcatraz commands the Bay, as you know. Compared to Sumter, she is like a porcupine to a pincushion. Some of her guns are the huge new Columbiads that hurl a 120-pound shot. She is the strongest fort in the nation. If we can seize Alcatraz and turn her 175 guns on the city, what then, my boy? What a headline then, eh?

"Now all of this may strike your sophisticated Eastern mind as the sort of tomfoolery we engage in Out West. But let me remind you that a substantial percentage of the population of this state has Southern sympathies, that most of the southern part does, that Governor, United States Senators, Congressmen, a majority of the Legislature, and most State and Federal and even Municipal officeholders lean the same way. The possibility of a successful outcome to our plans is very real—so real that I am tempted to invite you to join us and thus gain a high place in the realm we shall create.

"One fell swoop and California is ours! We won't propose Secession. Oh, dear, no—nothing as blatant as that! We'll set up

*later site of a federal penitentiary, now part of the Golden Gate National Recreational Area

that blessed Pacific Republic so long talked about. And believe me it will receive a lot of support, for many people are either apathetic, or feel no close ties to Washington City, or want to stay out of the coming conflict and go their peaceful profitable way. See the beautiful logic of it all? The more I think of it the more convinced I become!

"And after we've been a Pacific Republic for a few months or years, we join the Great Southern Confederacy much as the Republic of Texas joined the United States a few years back! And there—voilà, as my French landlady says—you have it! And doesn't it make sense?"

"P.S. Later: Everything is in readiness. It only remains to strike the blow. You might tell Ned Baker about this in case nobody else has. We conspirators, you might add, want General Johnston on our side before we move. Who wouldn't want such a distinguished soldier on his side? Only one little catch remains. We haven't spoken to Johnston yet. So it might be nice if Lincoln could replace him and thus remove him far from temptation, if that's the correct word.

"Meantime if I give Honest Abe fits in my columns as a rabble rousing warmonger whose intransigence on the slavery question may plunge this nation into civil conflict, it's for a good cause. You might tell Ned or Abe. You needn't add it's also good for circulation. It pleases Southerners and enrages Northerners. Both can hardly wait for what I say next.

"P.S.S. Lovely Victoria and her mother are leaving soon for New Orleans, I learn by the grapevine, where her grandmother is very ill. Beau goes along because Louisiana has seceded and he's getting ready to fight for his state if need be. I hope you have no such idiotic notions.''

When he received Gillem's confidential report, substantiating Mornay's, Baker became more alarmed than ever about the safety of the president-elect, and the future of California and General Johnston's role in it, and resolved to act as soon as he had intimate access to Lincoln, but that might not be until after the inauguration, still three weeks distant.

# Chapter Sixty-four

While David waited in Philadelphia for Lincoln, Mornay took the early boat to Sacramento. As the little sternwheeler churned up the Bay and entered the great river, the Sierras looming ahead in the winter air—clearcut as white teeth against the sky beyond the Central Valley—made him think of his original journey into them in '49 to find gold and become rich quickly, so that he could return to his wife and daughter at New Bedford. And he remembered what had happened, in sorrow and joy, to change his plan and transform him into a pioneer settler and leader in a new land.

His right hand in his coat pocket rested on his .44 caliber Deringer, deadly at ten to twenty feet. "All of us go armed," he told David, "for we are dealing with desperate men. They've already raised the Palmetto Flag* and the Bear Flag,† symbols of their disloyalty, and even the outlandish Flag of the Pacific Republic."‡

Martha would stay with Reuben and Hattie while he was away. He worried about her a little. Since taking management of Lucinda's Rescue Mission, she'd been all work and no play, become "one of the new women" the newspapers talked about, "independent of men in their thoughts and actions." He'd been upset when she marched with Lucinda and the others on City Hall to celebrate the tenth anniversary of the Woman's Rights Movement.

*adopted by South Carolina after its secession
†of the independent California Republic of 1846
‡a grizzly bear set forth by spiky desert cactus

But he knew where her heart was fixed and his ached a little for her loneliness when he too thought of dazzling David, going off like a rocket in staid old Philadelphia, venturing to Springfield with Baker and meeting Lincoln, becoming a national figure at age twenty-six. He was enormously proud of his protégé. As he watched from the foredeck, the sun climbing above the snowy peaks ahead resembled his high hopes.

At Sacramento boom was in the air, for the burgeoning little city was now chief gateway to two of the world's richest bonanzas, the gold of the Sierras and the silver of the Comstock Lode. The secret meeting of Republican Party leaders and Union men took place in the rear of Stanford Brothers' new store on the busy river front. Present were thirty-six-year-old Leland and his brothers Josiah and Philip, also fellow dry goods merchants Charles and Edwin Crocker, neighboring hardware merchants Collis P. Huntington and Mark Hopkins, and to Mornay's dismay, Sedley. Why Sedley? He decided it must be because of his great wealth and influence and the Pacific Railroad these Sacramento merchants hoped to build with his help. He was their overlord too. And Mornay remembered that Sedley owned the roof over his head and the ground under his feet at the Great Pacific Market where he and Reuben had their stall. But instead of raising rents during recent hard times, he had lowered them in a move acclaimed even by Gillem, though Gillem pointed out it was shrewd practice to keep your tenants in business and yielding some income, rather than force them out and yield you none. "Ah, Mornay!" Sedley was amiable as usual. "You look surprised to see me!" They shook hands. Mornay was indeed surprised to sense a cool indifference instead of the hostility he expected.

Sheriff "Pug" Doane who'd come with him on the boat was asked by Leland Stanford to open the meeting with an account of the rally held by Union men in San Francisco. "We turned out fourteen thousand," Doane asserted. "If we organize and work, we can beat 'em. They may have the power. But we've got the people."

Stanford, big, heavy set, neatly bearded as Broderick had been, as Mornay was now, delivered his own views. As a youth studying philosophy in upper New York State, he'd read the widely popular *Elements of Moral Science* by Francis Wayland, president of Brown University, and been convinced by Wayland's statement that "domestic slavery is the commonest violation of personal liberty and therefore of moral law." And like Broderick he saw the coming struggle as a contest between "the democratic and aristocratic elements of our nation" and the Republican Party as the champion of the former. Though more distinguished for common sense and sound judgment than brilliance, Stanford's courage was unquestioned. At public gatherings he'd withstood the boos and catcalls—"Abolitionist!"—"Nigger lover!"—and the violent rush of the mob. With other California Republicans he strongly supported the right of black men and women to testify in court against whites, and their absolute equality under the law, a nationwide Party principle.

"Our friends from San Francisco have shown us the way," he began and Mornay was reminded what a ponderous speaker he was. "Not only must we organize Union Clubs, there must be armed Minute Men who'll keep an eye on Southerners in each locality, and we must be ready to resist forcibly any attempt on fort, arsenal or other Government property." Mornay was tempted to recall what he knew about the conspirators but held his peace while Stanford continued as if by afterthought: "And in the voting this fall we must elect Republicans to state office," meaning chiefly himself as Governor. "But before we go farther, let's take our customary oath not to reveal what transpires at this meeting."

And when they had done so, Sheriff Doane declared: "General Johnston may be hand and glove with the plotters."

Stocky Collis Huntington asked sharply: "What plotters?"

"Stanhope and that crowd. We've heard they're planning to seize Alcatraz and turn its guns on the city."

"But where does General Johnston stand?" burly Charles Crocker wanted to know.

Lean shrewd-eyed Mark Hopkins echoed him: "That's the question!"

Simon Cahn, wealthy San Francisco wholesaler who supplied the Stanfords, Santiago Ferrer and others with much of their merchandise, a prominent member of the Congregation Emanu-El, pledged support of San Francisco's Jewish community. "We know from painful experience the realities of persecution!" Cahn like other Jews saw in the anti-slavery Republican party hopes of greater liberty for all Americans. "The Catholics are with us. I've talked with Archbishop Alemany. They fear The Chivalry."

Mornay could contain himself no longer. "Can we allow a slaveowner like Johnston to command the Pacific Coast in these perilous times? Honorable or dishonorable, he's a member of the

Slaveocracy. Why, before coming here he felt obliged to free the servant who accompanies him, knowing our California law—knowing what's happened in similar cases," meaning Hattie's. "While on his Texas plantation others labor in bondage!"

Attention turned finally to Sedley as it usually did. "Eliot, you stand in with both sides. What do you say?" Stanford inquired ponderously.

"I stand for California," Sedley corrected. "It will prevail, if we do our utmost to keep things in balance." And digging slyly at Mornay: "Alarmists do their cause more harm than good. I suggest we remain neutral for the time being. Avoid publicly the extremes of Abolition or Secession. It would be better business, better politics. And should war come, we're better off out of it."

"But what about Johnston?" Mornay demanded impatiently.

"I believe Johnston incapable of such treachery as you imply." Sedley made no mention of Stanhope's plans but, to show his insider's knowledge, subtly confirmed their existence, guessing that Mornay already knew, confident that whether the conspiracy succeeded or failed, he was invulnerable. Both sides needed him. Whichever won, he won.

Amazed and infuriated at what seemed such monstrous perfidy, Mornay burst out: "Being neutral we aid the Slaveocracy. Being neutral we encourage others to be likewise. We must stand publicly for what we believe, even if it means Secession and war! You imply there is a conspiracy. What do you propose to do about it?"

"No use to call out the militia," Doane broke in. "It might not call! Governor Downey has said the Federal Government has no right to coerce the individual states. It's not likely he'll try to coerce the Federal Government's forces!"

To soothe troubled waters Stanford declared in common sense tone: "Johnston seems to be at the heart of this matter. Who will keep an eye on him?"

"I will," declared Sedley blandly. "I'm close to those close to him."

Mornay was utterly appalled. "In fact you're Stanhope's son-in-law, aren't you?"

Sedley acknowledged the relationship patiently as if speaking to one who was mentally deficient. Poor fool, don't you grasp the significance of what I've been telling you? He seemed to say. Of how far above all of you are the realms in which I dwell? Where I make my own decisions for reasons you hardly dream exist?

That night Mornay wrote urgently to Baker: "It is now certain that they are preparing to seize the San Francisco forts. This comes from an unimpeachable source: Sedley himself. The key to the plot is Johnston. Nobody knows where he stands. You must speak to Lincoln immediately."

What his role in all this might be Senator Gwin could not yet be sure. A new nation, the Confederate States of America, had just been established at Montgomery in Alabama with his old friend Jefferson Davis as president. Gwin had not publicly taken sides, still hoped for a peaceful solution. His term had nine more days to run.* Then Broderick's victory would be complete. Then Gwin would leave Washington, perhaps forever. The mansion at Nineteenth and I Streets would be closed, perhaps disposed of.

Through his mind went thoughts of an independent South as a great Caribbean Empire. It would dwarf a diminished North. California might join it—if what he knew to be developing out there should come to pass. Yet peace might still be possible. And Gwin strongly wanted peace.

Therefore when his Republican friend Senator Seward, Lincoln's Secretary of State to be, suggested he contact Davis and convey the peaceable intentions of the new administration, Gwin agreed and wrote Davis at Montgomery. And, thus, a few days later, when Seward asked for the loan of his carriage for the night of February 22, Gwin concurred, asking no questions.

*the California Legislature had not considered Gwin for reelection, so sharply had opinion turned against him

# Chapter Sixty-five

David waked keenly alert that morning of George Washington's birthday anniversary. It was bright and cool.

Without thinking of breakfast he dressed and hurried out. At six o'clock Lincoln, en route to Washington to be inaugurated, would raise a flag over Independence Hall where the founders of the nation had signed the Declaration of Independence and framed the Constitution.

As he stood looking at the ancient building, David imagined the Founding Fathers there, pondering, arguing, hammering out their differences, creating a nation. Their glory shone from the old structure with invisible radiance. But uppermost in his mind was what had happened the evening before. Returning to his room at Mrs. Wilson's shortly before supper, he found Baker's telegram: "Meet me at the Continental Hotel at ten this evening." David was waiting in the crowded lobby when a stranger with black hair and beard accosted him in a familiar voice. It was Baker. "Why the disguise?" exclaimed David.

"Hush! All of us close to the President are watched!" Baker introduced his handsome young companion. "Fred Seward, the Senator's son." Then, spotting his old Illinois friend Ward Lamon, Lincoln's bodyguard and confidant, Baker identified himself, and David heard him whisper urgently: "We must see the President at once!"

Lamon pointed to the reception room. "He's in there shaking hands. But come along, I'll take you up to his bedroom."

When Lincoln entered an hour later David was surprised to see him wearing a full beard* neatly trimmed like Broderick's, and wondered if it indicated a new public commitment to The Shovelry. Otherwise the President-elect seemed much the same as in Springfield two months earlier. "Ned, David, how glad I am to see you!" He held out both hands. "What brings you?"

Baker, who'd removed his disguise, introduced young Seward. "Fred brings a confidential message from his father of utmost importance. What I warned you of in Springfield has come to pass." And they listened while Fred told of a plot to assassinate Lincoln as his train passed through Baltimore in slavery minded Maryland the following day on its way to Washington. "Agents of the Knights of the Golden Circle have infiltrated the city and made contact with disaffected elements." The plot was being talked of openly in Baltimore. A band of rowdies would create a disturbance when Lincoln's train stopped, drawing off police and guards, while the assassins rushed the train. "Their spies are everywhere!" Baker broke in, indicating his wig and beard lying on the table and explaining the reason for them. "I strongly recommend you pass through Baltimore secretly at night, as Senator Seward suggests, by a train other than your Presidential one." Lincoln turned to Fred:

"Is that what your father suggests?"

"Yes, sir. He begs you, for your own good and that of the nation, to heed his advice."

Earlier that evening Lincoln had received similar advice from the nation's foremost detective, Allan Pinkerton, whose agents had also detected the plot. David watched him weigh matters thoughtfully, his face suddenly careworn.

"Proceed, now, tonight, to Washington!" Baker urged.

Lincoln shook his head. "I'm committed to raising the flag over Independence Hall tomorrow. After that I must run out to Harrisburg and meet with the State Legislature. Then I'm free to proceed as we may deem best." He spoke quietly, without perturbation. Turning to David as if the matter were closed he asked: "How are things on your Pacific Coast? Are they planning to assassinate me out there too?"

David told of the letter just received from Gillem. Lincoln's tone turned grim. "So they're after us from both East and West?"

Baker broke in more grimly still: "They mean business, Mr. President!" He reported Mary Louise's warning relayed through

*begun early in January, 1861

Mornay about Randolph and Stanhope. "The conspiracy has
many heads. But at heart it is one. And one of your first acts after
your inauguration must be to replace General Johnston. Or California may be lost and with it the entire coast. Meanwhile we
don't want to lose *you*. I beg you to do as Senator Seward and I
and Mr. Pinkerton advise."

"Tomorrow night, perhaps. Not tonight."

Now as he stood before Independence Hall in the early morning
light David watched with a lump in his throat as Lincoln pulled
the cord that raised the flag to the peak of its pole atop the hallowed old building. David felt he could almost touch Washington,
Jefferson, Franklin who seemed to be there in quaint stock and
square-toed shoes among the thousands gathered. Their meaning
was reincarnate in the figure of this tall frontiersman sprung from
the westering edge of the nation they created—that onward reaching edge which he himself was part of.

Then Lincoln in his incongruously high-pitched voice spoke of
the original flag which contained only thirteen stars. "More have
been added until now there are thirty-four, including the latest
representing Kansas."* David noted the four Army officers de-
tailed to guard Lincoln on his journey from Springfield to Washington and guessed that Pinkerton's men in plain clothes were
scattered through the crowd too. One officer, a grizzled, craggy-
faced Colonel, stood out memorably above the others like a
weathered monument.

Lincoln was saying: "I think we may promise ourselves that
not only this newest star shall be permitted to remain to our permanent prosperity for years to come, but additional ones shall be
placed there until we number five hundred millions of happy and
prosperous people." He'd often pondered the dangers faced by
the men who assembled here in this hall to frame Declaration of
Independence and Constitution. "What principle held them together? It was liberty as a hope for all the world for all future
time." He asked if the country could be saved by such a principle.
"But if it cannot be saved without giving up this principle, then
I would rather be assassinated on this spot," inadvertently uttering
what was at the back of his mind, "than surrender that principle."
Yet he could see no cause for war. "This government will not

---

*admitted as a free state January 29 after many Southern members withdrew
from Congress

use force, unless force is used against us.''

A deep-throated roar approved what he said. David reported it that night to Gillem and Mornay.

After his speech, Lincoln went immediately by rail seventy miles to Harrisburg and met with the Pennsylvania Legislature. No change was announced in his schedule for proceeding next day from Philadelphia to Washington via Baltimore. But at six o'clock in Harrisburg he was "called away" from a formal dinner with party leaders, went quickly upstairs to his hotel room, changed his dinner dress for a traveling suit, and slipped out the back door with only Ward Lamon as companion.

At 10:00 P.M. Baker, Fred Seward and David were waiting on the platform of the Philadelphia, Wilmington and Baltimore Railroad Station as the New York-Washington train came puffing in. Baker, again bearded and wigged, had slipped a Deringer into David's pocket. David felt it cold as death under his hand. His heart turned over. He'd never fired a gun at anyone, felt himself moving inexorably toward the cataclysm that threatened the nation. He looked warily about. But the waiting passengers seemed indifferent, harmless. And that was good because their plan depended on secrecy, not force—while racing back toward them from Harrisburg came a single car drawn by a lone locomotive.

Stubby little Allan Pinkerton, the ace detective, met the one-car special at the Pennsylvania Station a few blocks away and ushered its occupants into his carriage.

Minutes later David saw two figures emerge onto the platform in front of him. Lincoln wore a soft black hat and a shawl over his shoulders that partially muffled his face. Lamon followed like a hunting dog on the alert. Stubby, bearded Pinkerton brought up the rear like a watchful terrier. His original Chicago agency had specialized in helping fugitive slaves escape from the South. Now he was helping bigger game.

David's fingers tightened on his pistol while the three boarded the last sleeping car of the waiting New York-Washington train. With Baker and Seward he quickly followed. Pinkerton had reserved berths. Lincoln and Lamon disappeared behind the curtains of theirs. Baker and David took the one opposite. Pinkerton and Seward stood guard at either end of the car until the train began to move.

Toward midnight Baker parted the curtains of Lincoln's berth and David saw Lincoln sitting upright fully dressed, Lamon opposite him. A passenger in the next berth snored loudly. Lincoln's shawl and soft hat looked comical. He seemed embarrassed by his predicament.

"Baker," he drawled in a whimsical whisper, "I'd like to retire to that little farm overlooking your Pacific Ocean, with some fruit trees, a cow and that climate you claim is good enough to eat."

"I know just the place. It's called Carmel Valley."

Virginia-born Lamon, something of the troubadour about his dashing good looks, softly hummed one of Lincoln's favorite songs:

> "When I was young I used to wait
> At Massa's table, 'n hand de plate,
> An' pass de bottle when he was dry,
> An' brush away de blue-tailed fly.
> "Ol' Massa's dead; oh, let him rest!
> Dey say all things am for de best;
> But I can't forget until I die
> Ol' Massa an' de blue-tailed fly."

Toward 3:00 A.M. tension mounted again as the train pulled to a halt in Baltimore. Would the assassins be waiting?

"We'll be taking a leaf from your book," Stanhope was telling Sedley, three thousand miles away, "and letting others be our cat's-paw. There's a half-crazed Italian immigrant who's volunteered to do the job. Full of Garibaldi and all that shit. See's Lincoln as a tyrant."

A drunken traveler on the platform outside their car window began singing "Dixie." David heard the train crew cursing as they waited for a connecting train from the west. But was the delay anticipated? Was the drunk in fact part of the conspiracy?

Lamon offered Lincoln a revolver. Lincoln shook his head. "I'm a rotten shot, Ward. I'd likely do you more harm than them." But he seemed cool now, ready.

For long minutes of suspense they waited, hands on weapons. Then with blessed relief, David felt the train begin to move. Looking at him, Lincoln winked one large melancholy eye.

"Gwin's carriage is waiting," Baker explained. "It's well

known in Washington. No one will be surprised by it.''

"Won't it put me in debt to them?'' Lincoln questioned.

Baker told of Gwin's overture to Davis. "It may serve as token you want peace.''

At 6:00 A. M. they were relieved to see the Washington Station platform nearly deserted. Gwin's handsome landau took all but David to Willard's Hotel for breakfast. David took the morning train back to Philadelphia. As he passed through Baltimore he saw the ugly mob waiting to attack the Presidential Special.

By mid-afternoon he was speaking to his children's Bible class as prearranged. But Lincoln's parting grip was still warm in his hand.


Jefferson Davis was pruning rosebushes in the garden of his Mississippi plantation not far from Stanhope's Bend when word reached him he'd been elected President of the Confederate States of America. Davis felt reluctant to stop pruning, as reluctant as he felt about being President of the Confederacy. He hadn't sought the office, would have preferred to head the Confederate Army. But his brilliant career as civilian as well as soldier made him best fitted, in most Southern eyes, to guide the fortunes of their new nation. Yet at this critical moment he felt grave doubts as to his adequacy. "I wish Sidney were here to talk to,'' he told his young wife Varina.

His old and dear friend, Albert Sidney Johnston, was at that moment sitting in the commandant's office of the Department of the Pacific at 44 Bush Street between Pine and Sutter in downtown San Francisco. They'd been intimate since undergraduate days at Transylvania College—"the Harvard of the West" at Lexington, Kentucky, where Gillem would matriculate a generation later—and their intimacy had continued at West Point and during the Black Hawk War and the War with Mexico. Davis admired Johnston more than any other man he knew. Johnston's present position seemed fortuitous in many ways. Davis felt confident Johnston would prove loyal to the South and influence California toward the Confederacy now or in the event of war. Yet Davis wanted peace. He'd long been a moderate regarding Secession, which angered firebrands like Rhett and Ruffin. In his inaugural address a few days later he would say that only if the North tried to prevent Secession should the South resort to arms.

But by then all peace efforts had failed and Gwin's letter went unanswered.

Dreading lest he hear of his assassination, David waited for Lincoln's inauguration. But down in Washington March 4 dawned peacefully clear. The grass had greened. Redbud and lilac were about to bloom.

"He's escaped us this time," Stanhope informed Sedley sourly. "But we'll get him sooner or later."

Lincoln rode to the capitol in the Presidential carriage, its top down so the crowds could see him, Baker facing him, cavalry escorting them. And it was Baker, the phenomenon, the first Republican in either branch of Congress from the Far West—Baker "my dearest friend" as Lincoln described him—it was Baker who presented Lincoln to the multitude gathered before the unfinished capitol. "Fellow citizens, I introduce to you Abraham Lincoln, the President-elect of the United States."

Reading about it in *The Post* next day, David felt enormously proud of Baker. Looking ahead he saw him as leader of the Senate, even as President—Baker who'd defended Hattie, championed Mornay, revered Broderick, out-witted Stanhope's assassins—Baker, sprung from the people, who introduced the President-elect to the people of the United States. Baker suddenly loomed larger than Lincoln. Baker had both power and glory, whereas during that stealthy journey from Philadelphia to Washington, Lincoln had seemed diminished, even ignominious.

And now as David read the inaugural address, he found Lincoln hanging back morally, supporting the right of the states lawfully under the Constitution to maintain slavery where it existed, supporting the Fugitive Slave Law, yet felt encouraged to find him asserting the preeminence of the Union and the inadmissability of a state unilaterally withdrawing from it. "In your hands, my dissatisfied fellow countrymen, and not in mine," he said to the Secessionists, "is the momentous issue of Civil War."

In the end David felt reassured though not elated. Lincoln was aiming much of his speech at uncommitted states like Maryland and Virginia, Kentucky and California—and of course the men behind the unfired guns at Fort Sumter and nearby Charleston shore batteries where the stand-off continued. Lincoln wanted to hold the Union together. Lincoln too dreaded the firing of that first shot.

# Chapter Sixty-six

General Johnston, is it true you're here to lead California into the Southern Confederacy? The question was on the tip of my tongue," Gillem wrote David, "as Stanhope, Harpending and I dropped in at the Headquarters of the Department of the Pacific to sound out this man who, as many see it, holds the power to deliver nearly a quarter of the nation—all that portion west of the Rocky Mountains—into Southern hands. As California goes, so goes adjacent Oregon and neighboring territories, these ravens croak.

"Johnston receives us with impressive grace. Even to my cynical eyes he's a rare specimen. Over six feet. Light brown hair. Gray-blue eyes. Flowing mustaches. A natural aura of authority which inspires respect and confidence without in the least offending. As you probably know, he led our troops in a tactical and diplomatic victory in the recent Mormon War when the saints threatened to take up arms against the Government and form their own nation.* And like me and so many other great men he's Kentucky bred. And like me and Jeff Davis he attended Transylvania. Thence he proceeded to West Point and a distinguished military career which he interrupted to emigrate to Texas where, so Stanhope tells me, he enlisted as a private in the struggle for independence against Mexico, and eventually became the Lone Star Republic's Secretary of War and acquired a plantation. Stanhope has known the General since Mexican War days when they

*in Utah Territory in 1857–58

made things hot for Santa Anna, and thinks this may pay off now in the form of a confidence or two.

"At first we speak of small matters and learn that the General, who is near sixty but looks near forty, is thinking, if you please, of retiring to Los Angeles where his brother-in-law owns a farm. This mighty warrior waxes eloquent about the Southern California climate! If all who speak about retiring to this state eventually do so, we shall become an old folks home! Johnston recalled being stationed in Texas when the trouble with the saints broke out. Leaving his regiment, the 2nd Cavalry, in charge of his Lieutenant Colonel, one Robert E. Lee of whom he speaks highly, he goes to take command in Utah—and after showing old Bring-'em Young how to mind his P's and Q's instead of his wives—and not firing a shot or shedding a drop of blood in the process— here he is, our foremost soldier, ready, thinks Stanhope, to lead a quarter of the nation into the Southern camp. "Stanhope finally steers around to Secession and the present ticklish situation. 'Yes, there's been some loose talk,' Johnston replies casually, knowing perfectly well what Stanhope is driving at but never letting on, 'that I'm here to conduct a secret movement in favor of the South. Nothing is further from the truth. At the first sign of such nonsense, I shall use all the force at my disposal to correct matters.'

"I never saw a neater rebuff. Stanhope flares beet red. Harpending bites his lip. To ease matters I talk about old days at Transylvania College and the charming belles of Lexington; and after a few minutes we take our leave, with California still very much in the Union. Which is not to say it will remain so. These scoundrels mean mischief. But, then, so do I. When the time comes I shall expose them for what they are."

While Gillem, Stanhope and Harpending were talking to Johnston, a craggy-faced man in civilian clothes was putting out secretly in the pilot boat from the New York City waterfront to board the Aspinwall steamer already under way for the Isthmus of Panama. When on clearing the harbor she dropped her pilot, the belated passenger boarded.

Baker had prevailed upon Lincoln. The passenger was that same craggy Army officer David had noted as outstanding among Lincoln's guards at the hotel room in Philadelphia. And next day at Harrisburg when he learned of the plan to slip secretly into Washington, Colonel Edwin V. Sumner burst out in the presence of the President-elect: "Damned cowardice! Give me a squad of cavalry and I'll cut my way through any mob!" Lincoln had not forgotten Sumner's courageous frankness. Indeed Lincoln had grown ashamed of his sneaky entry into his capital. It seemed more and more like cowardice. It had been derided by many newspapers and much public opinion. "Men like Sumner are the kind you need now," Baker urged.

Promoted to full Brigadier General, Sumner, grizzled veteran of forty-two Army years, was traveling under an assumed name and carried secret orders to be opened when at sea. They informed him he was to proceed to San Francisco and relieve Brevet Brigadier General Johnston of command of the Department of the Pacific. And it was not difficult under the circumstances for Sumner to guess why. Donning his uniform, he prepared mentally to cut his way through a mob of Secessionists, should that prove necessary when he disembarked.

But there had been the usual leakage of information in the War Department. Confederate spies were everywhere. Word of Sumner's coming was rushed West by Pony Express. Receiving it, Stanhope hurried to Johnston and this time pleaded frankly: "This may be our last chance to win California. Give the word and my irregulars will rise and join your regulars. We'll seize Alcatraz. Turn its guns on San Francisco. And California will be ours and the South's!"

Johnston rose majestically from behind his desk and, sternly fixing Stanhope with a look he never forgot, declared: "What you propose, sir, is treason. I bid you good-day."

Stanhope went fuming to Sedley. "Shall we call out our guerillas?"

Sedley shook his head. "The game's not over. It's not even begun. There's no war yet. Why start one? Up and down the state your people are ready and waiting. If Davis eventually pushes troops into New Mexico, as you say he intends to, and on into California—then, not now, will be the time to act."

Accordingly Sumner disembarked without incident and proceeded to the headquarters of the Department of the Pacific where Johnston received him with impeccable courtesy. "Since hearing of your promotion, sir, I've been expecting you."

"General Scott sends you his compliments," Sumner replied with similar gallantry, handing over his orders, "and says that in Washington City you will be considered second only to himself."

Scott, with Lincoln's approval, was prepared to offer Johnston

supreme field command of the United States Army. But Johnston
had other plans. His resignation was on its way to Washington. Texas had finally elected to join the Confederacy and he
would go with his adopted state—and with his old friend Jefferson Davis.

That afternoon the papers carried the news of the firing on Fort
Sumter.

That evening Sumner reenforced Alcatraz with two companies
of artillery-men ferried out secretly to the island after dark.

A few days later Johnston departed for Los Angeles intending
to join his wife and children there and proceed to New York. But
before he could board ship orders were issued for his arrest and
he was obliged to change plans and proceed cross-country as a
fugitive to join Davis and become the Confederacy's senior field
officer.

"Up and down the state there is alarm and uncertainty," Mornay
reported to Baker. "Thank God for Sumner."

Gillem informed his readers in a blistering exposé of what he
termed The Great Conspiracy: "Thus our Committee of Loyalty
was disbanded, and its guerrillas dispersed and its records burned
in Colonel Stanhope's capacious fireplace." But Stanhope indignantly denied the charge as sensational journalism and demanded
that proof be produced, which was impossible under the circumstances.

Sumner began summoning loyal troops to San Francisco from
as far away as Washington Territory.

Mornay concluded to Baker: "The outcome may depend on
how the Legislature votes: North or South."

Mary Louise met with Negro leaders to pledge their support
for the Union.

David had heard the guns many times in his imagination. They
would be the final rumblings of that volcano he'd sensed under
his feet at Gwin's ball, heard years earlier in that ruthless talk at
Sedley's table, felt keenly in Mornay's account of Broderick's
death. They would signal his next step toward personal account-
ability. His mind was made up.

When the news reached Philadelphia on the afternoon of April
12, 1861, it was almost a relief. Fort Sumter had been fired on
by Confederate shore batteries at 4:27 that morning. Pulling the
lanyard of the first cannon to fire, wearing the uniform of a South

Carolina militiaman as honorary member of his battery, was
white-haired, sixty-seven-year-old Edmund Ruffin, the agricul-
tural expert and arch-conspirator, Stanhope's colleague, whom
David had met at Elinor Wright's farm and who had sworn to
Stanhope he would kill himself rather than live again under the
United States. Fort Sumter surrendered two days later.

David chose as subject for his sermon the following Sunday
that memorable passage from the Book of Ecclesiastes: "To
everything there is a season, and a time to every purpose under
heaven: A time to be born, and a time to die . . . a time to kill,
and a time to heal . . . a time of war and a time of peace." At the
end he said simply: "Dear Friends, I feel obliged to resign as
your pastor and offer my services as a soldier to help suppress
the Rebellion." He would volunteer as a private in the infantry,
not as a chaplain, though he did not say so. He wanted to submit
himself without special status. Nothing less seemed in keeping
with that inner voice he'd been listening to.

He saw by their faces he'd penetrated their apathy and captured
their undivided attention at last. Afterward when Stroud and others remonstrated that he was being too precipitous he replied
bluntly: "This is a crucial moment for all of us. Each must do as
his conscience dictates." And he was heartened when many said
they would be following his example. Nor did the imploring eyes
of sweet Phyllis and other young women deter him—rather they
strengthened his resolve. Only the brave deserve the fair, he
thought, wondering if he would live to love and be loved at some
almost unimaginably distant time beyond the war.

Next day Lincoln's call for seventy-five thousand volunteers
confirmed his decision. Had he waited a few more days until
Baker began forming his California Regiment, composed of West-
erners on the East Coast, the course of his life might have been
far different. But by then he was on his way to Iowa.

"I'm in route to my Bethlehem," he wrote metaphorically to
Mornay, referring to that passage in Saint Luke where Joseph and
Mary return to Joseph's birthplace to be taxed and censused, "following the decree not of Caesar but of Father Abraham, who asks
us to return to our native states and enlist." Lincoln had called
out the militias of the North. "I'm telling no one else where I'm
going." As an anonymous private in the ranks he would take his
chances with the rest.

And then on sudden impulse he wrote Beau Stanhope at Stanhope's Bend Plantation, Louisiana: "I hope this war never brings

us face to face. I hope we always remember that dream we shared during our walk over the hills to Golden Gate.'' But beneath this lofty sentiment he was thinking not so loftily of Victoria, Mrs. Eliot Sedley, wondering how she would look and what she would say when Beau read her the letter. Cursing himself for an egregious fool, he sent the letter nevertheless.

"I've got to go!'' Reuben told Hattie.

"No you don't. It's not your war.''

"Yes it is. If a black man won't fight at a time like this he never will.''

"But they aren't taking black soldiers!''

"They will.''

In dressing gown and peignoir, Sedley and Mary Louise were breakfasting in the alcove facing her rose garden when Samson announced: "A lady to see Mr. Sedley.''

Mary Louise looked at her partner with amusement. He returned a similar look, adding with a shrug: "It's your house!'' leaving the decision to her.

"Show the lady in.'' Mary Louise spoke calmly.

But Victoria was anything but calm as she burst into the room without further delay and announced with scathing sarcasm: "I hope I'm not disturbing anyone!''

Sedley replied imperturbably: "Not me. I can't speak for Mrs. Jackson, here.'' Nodding toward Mary Louise who'd risen while he kept his seat. She said to Victoria politely: "Won't you sit down?''

"No, thank you, I've just come to see who my husband breakfasts with when he's not at home.''

Mary Louise replied sweetly. "And I'm glad to see the kind he marries.''

The two eyed each other without flinching, each seeing an implacable adversary. Sedley sat quietly enjoying himself. Though the situation was unusual, new experience was new possession, unusual experience unusual possession, and this one was anything but usual. That added to his relish of it.

"Come on, Vicky,'' he suggested affably, "let's be mature. You're old enough to know the facts of life.''

"No, I needed a little more instruction from you.'' Her tone was acid.

"And now you have it.''

She flared out: "Am I to expect this as a rule?"

He shrugged. "Suit yourself."

"I'll tell Daddy!"

"He'll be glad, I'm sure, to know you're growing up."

"I didn't think you'd stoop to dusky flesh!"

"Following your father's example? Why not?"

"Oh, you're unspeakable!" She flung at him, stamping a foot in frustration.

Mary Louise decided to say as little as possible. She sensed this moment could be decisive, could be the moment of her triumph. Already she was having her revenge and it was sweet indeed. Vicky was demanding of Sedley: "Which is it to be? Her or me?"

"That's your decision, my dear, not mine!" matter of factly, breaking off a morsel of toast before buttering it. "Why not be mature about this whole thing and sit down and join us? Your temper is only becoming up to a point."

"You brazen bastard, you think I'll take this lying down? Two can play at this game as well as one!"

"Entirely up to you," he replied affably, munching the toast. "Come on, why not join us for a bite?"

"Oh," she lashed at him finally, "I hope you choke!" Turning her back on them with a toss of her head, she marched out of the room as proudly as she'd entered, so that he admired her courage and strength. Nor did Mary Louise fail to note these qualities in one she knew would be her lifelong enemy.

Sedley did not think Vicky's aversion would be so permanent as far as he was concerned. She would never, he felt sure, give up all she'd aspired to and acquired when she married him. And he was right. When he returned home that evening, she was there as if nothing had happened. Her tone was casual and mocking. "I hope you've enjoyed a profitable day?"

"Yes," with an amiable chuckle, "I found it very profitable, very instructive. How about you?"

"I likewise," she agreed, and there they left the matter, almost.

"I'll miss you while you're away," he added, seriously.

"Yes, I can imagine."

"No, I truly will. You are my wife, you know?"

"Yes," she said, mocking still, "I suppose I am. Even in Louisiana I'll be Mrs. Eliot Sedley!"

*       *       *

The wind whipped dust into Clara's eyes, as she sat on the verandah overlooking her valley, and brought tears of anger and despair. True, that spring had been unusually dry. Even so, she'd never noticed dust like this. It came blowing from the Jenkinses' newly plowed fields, adding to that of others down the valley and others beyond those, until it formed a huge dark cloud that was obscuring her beloved hills opposite the ranch house. The earth, her earth, was blowing away. The *A-alowow* have done it! she thought, unconsciously in her anger using the ancient native word for the white ones. The *A-alowow* were changing the face of the earth, her earth, her sacred mother beyond her actual mother. First they drive out our native grasses with their weed seeds, she thought. Now they do this. What will be next? What will be next? And as she watched, an immense weariness suddenly overtook her that seemed to emanate from the cloud itself. The cloud seemed to be enveloping her with its darkness, gradually shutting out the sight of her beloved hills, until finally it obscured that last high summit where Antonio lay buried—where someday she would lie beside him. And is this a good day to die? she wondered. She almost despaired as she saw the hills now totally obscured, those hills I have known so long, so deeply. But surely my spirit will inhabit this place, she told herself, for I have loved it so well.

She felt no weakness, no regret, only the sudden darkness, as if her eyes had closed. As if the cloud had enveloped her too.

Sally called from the house behind. "Mamá Grande! We have news!" But she did not hear.


Down at the cabins there was excited talk. "Damn Yankees has forced it on us at last!" Buck was gleeful.

Iphy warned: "Don't you go thinkin' of gettin' mixed up in it! We got all the fightin' we need right here!"

As a sensible married man, Elmer nodded agreement. Opal did likewise. But Buck was not deterred. "We'll whip their asses, eh Good?" Goodly grinned. He liked the idea of going to war.

Old Abe, as often at the start of these arguments, said nothing until they pressed him: "What about it, Grandpa?"

Then he exploded: "We gonna be that 'house divided' old Lincoln talks about? We gonna split this country like a hick'ry chunk? Pshaw, shame on you-all! Now, let's go to work! We got a crop to plant, dry as it is. Ornery as this ground is, let's put our seed into it. And shut up. First Secesh I find around here's gonna hafta deal with me!''

But Buck just laughed at him, thinking of the Knights of the Golden Circle, Stanhope's secret army, ready to rise.

When Mornay received David's letter telling of his intention to enlist he promptly replied: "My dear boy, Martha and I are deeply proud of you yet fear for your safety. Remember not to be too impetuous and fling yourself into the fray as you did in front of the saloon that day you arrived here. Our situation is touch and go. The Palmetto Flag continues to be displayed as do the Bear and Pacific Republic Flags and the infamous new Confederate banner. And there's no telling what will happen up in Sacramento where the nincum-noodle Legislature is debating whether we shall officially be Northern, Southern or neutral. Much depends on their decision. Nevertheless hundreds like you have departed to enlist with the militias of their native states. And General Sumner is taking swift steps to bolster our defenses and purge the ranks of traitors. Bless you and keep you, my son. Martha and I shall be praying for you.''

Up in Sacramento the heavily Democratic,* rather neutralist-minded, rather Southernly inclined Legislature reluctantly voted, on May 17, two days before adjournment and a full month after receiving the news of the firing on Fort Sumter, to support the Union.

Waiting on the station platform at Saint Louis, David heard a group of Union recruits, some younger than himself, singing a popular new song:

> John Brown's body lies a-mouldering in the grave,
> John Brown's body lies a-mouldering in the grave,
> John Brown's body lies a-mouldering in the grave,
> His soul goes marching on!

David thought it should be Broderick's, too. But Broderick was lying, already being forgotten, in Lone Mountain Cemetery overlooking that Golden Gate they had both passed through into a new life.

David thought of it shining in the sunlight of that June morning

---

*therefore unsympathetic to a Republican administration in Washington City

as he'd first seen it with Martha and Mary Louise and of all that had happened to them since. And now the New American Revolution Broderick had died to bring about was going to be born in blood.

In his wallet he carried Martha's self-portrait. "You can do one of Broderick," he'd challenged, "why not of yourself?" And she had done so, mischievously, in the form of one of the new ferrotypes. It astonished him. Gone was the pigtailed pesterer. A young woman of grave beauty looked out at him from the small oval photograph. Her hair, parted in the center, drew back demurely to what must be a chignon. She was wearing her best dark velvet with wide white collar but sat serenely at ease, hands together in lap, regarding him with an appraising steadiness. Don't try to fool me, she seemed to say. He felt he never would try again. He smiled at the hint of familiar impishness that lurked around the corners of the wide firm mouth, then put her in his wallet for safekeeping.

"Where you headed, Billy Yank?" one of the recruits asked him jocosely.

"Same place you are," David replied, grinning.

Francisco was standing on the summit of Iwihinmu, the sacred mountain at the heart of his mother's people's world, the center of his solitary resistance now, with young Helek beside him. For the first time he was showing the boy all the ways he might go. "It is all yours!" He gestured at the magnificent panorama of mountains, ocean, plains, desert. And after his son had gazed in awed silence, Francisco said: "Come, let us explore, stealthily, leaving no trace!" As he spoke a shadow fell upon them. Looking up they saw a giant condor, its wings spread wide, its red head cocked inquisitively as it peered down at them with its age-old eyes. Francisco pointed and cried out in triumph: "See, our dream helper is with us!"

"Will he lead us to my grandmother?" Helek asked.

"Who knows? But let us follow!" And together they slipped down the mountainside in the direction the great bird was taking.

# Acknowledgments

Since all fiction has some basis in fact I am indebted to many sources, but especially to Helen Holdredge for her two books *Mammy Pleasant* and *Mammy Pleasant's Partner;* similarly to Rudolph M. Lapp for his *Archy Lee* and *Blacks in Gold Rush California;* Lately Thomas for *Between Two Empires;* W. W. Robinson for *Land in California;* Leonard Pitt for *The Decline of the Californios;* Jeremiah Lynch for *A Senator of the Fifties;* Hudson Strode's *Jefferson Davis;* Carl Sandburg's *Abraham Lincoln;* Raymond W. Albright's *Focus on Infinity: a Life of Phillips Brooks;* Asbury Harpending's *The Great Diamond Hoax;* Travis Hudson's various writings and personal communications to me on the Chumash; Bertha Tumamait Blanco and Vincent Tumamait, survivors of the once numerous Chumash people; Roger W. Lochtin for *San Francisco: 1846–1856;* Sherburne F. Cook for *The Conflict Between the California Indian and White Civilization;* Robert F. Heizer, *The Destruction of California Indians;* William Henry Ellison for *A Self-Governing Dominion: California 1849–1860;* Milton H. Shutes for *Lincoln and California;* Elijah R. Kennedy for *The Contest for California in 1861;* Grace E. Baker, Librarian, The Society of California Pioneers; and the staffs at the San Francisco History Room, San Francisco Public Library, the Bancroft Library, Berkeley, the Huntington Library, San Marino, the Santa Barbara Public Library, and the Department of Special Collections at the University of California, Santa Barbara; also Michael A. Miller of the Alexandria Library, Alexandria, Virginia; Jack Goodwin, Librarian, Virginia Theological

Seminary; Father Virgilio Biasiol, O.F.M., Santa Barbara Mission Archives; Reverend Donald A. Stivers of Christ the King Episcopal Church; Robert J. Chandler for his work on Albert Sidney Johnston; William Preston Johnston for his *Life of General Albert Sidney Johnston;* Elizabeth A. Poulliot, director of the Presidio Army Museum, San Francisco; also Robin Adams, expert on cookery old and new, and Gilbert W. Lentz, legal historian; also George E. Frakes, professor of history at Santa Barbara City College, who generously read and criticized my manuscript and Richard E. Oglesby, professor of history at the University of California, Santa Barbara, who also encouraged it; Anne Lowenkopf and Noel Young for their enduring support. Finally I'm grateful to that remarkable woman of African and perhaps European blood known as Mary Ellen Pleasant and to my grandfather Giles Alexander Easton's friendship with her, the diary he wrote recording their intimacy and the golden chatelaine she gave him as memento.

—R.E.

**Robert Easton** was born in San Francisco, California. All of his work has been centered on the history and people of the American West. His first great critical and popular success was *The Happy Man* (1943), a portrait of California ranch life in the late 1930s. Easton went on to write *Max Brand: The Big "Westerner"* (1970), a biography of Frederick Faust, and recently edited *The Collected Stories of Max Brand* (1994) with his wife, Jane Faust Easton. After three decades of research, his epic Saga of California began with *This Promised Land* (1982), spanning the years 1769-1850, and is continued in *Power and Glory* (1989). He is currently at work on the third volume of this saga, *Blood and Money*, providing a panoramic view of California during the Civil War. Since *The Happy Man* there can be no doubt of Robert Easton's commitment to the American West as both an idea and as a definite and distinct place. Beyond this, in all of his work he has been guided by his belief in what he once described as a writer's concern for "the living word—the one that captures the essential truth of what he is trying to say—and that is what I have tried to put down."

# Incident At Sun Mountain

## TODHUNTER BALLARD

# Winner Of The Golden Spur Award
# For Best Historical Novel

The fabulous Comstock lode—the silver strike that made the California Gold Rush look like a Sunday social—grips every able-bodied man with a frenzy for wealth. The ore dug up near boomtowns like Virginia City, Gold Hill, and Silver City is enough to finance any foolhardy notion or traitorous scheme, even a civil war that will rip the young nation asunder.

Sent to Nevada to investigate reports of Rebel activities, Ken English is thrust into a region full of miners and gamblers, heroes and killers, Union supporters and Southern sympathizers. As the threat of bloody conflict looms over the country, English and scores of brave men and women will risk their fortunes, their loves, and their very lives to quell the revolt—and save the land they helped to build.

_3935-4                                    $4.99 US/$6.99 CAN

**Dorchester Publishing Co., Inc.**
**65 Commerce Road**
**Stamford, CT 06902**